THE MAN WHO HAD EVERYTHING

THE MAN WHO HAD EVERYTHING

DONALD M. MURRAY

NAL

NEW AMERICAN LIBRARY

First Printing

Library of Congress Catalog Card No.: 64-14578

Published by The New American Library of World Literature, Inc.
501 Madison Avenue, New York, New York 10022

Published simultaneously in Canada by
Nelson, Foster & Scott, Ltd.

Printed in the United States of America

THE MAN WHO HAD EVERYTHING

I

As if their words were unimportant and would not be thought back on, as if they did not know all worlds must change, the three stood on the stone steps in the shadow of the maples, which had grown tall enough this spring to intercept the late summer sun. The light was soft at this weekend's close, and the shadows gently dappled the house behind them: silent gray patterns, edges blurred as they brushed over the powdery white, everchanging yet fading so slowly there was no moment when this evening forever ended and it was night. Outside the house it was quiet, but their voices, still loud from the party, were harsh, lilting, their inflections exaggerated beyond the meaning of the words.

"You must come to see us again, real soon," said the woman.

"Don't I always?" answered the guest.

"Never too often, not for us. We do so love having you, and you know how very much the children love you."

"I only wish we'd had more of a chance to talk," the husband added. "It seems as if you talk all the time at one of these parties and say nothing."

"Of course. That's the purpose—it's perfectly designed for non-talk talking."

"You men. I get all my news at parties like this."

"Gossip. Woman-talk," her husband said, laughing.

"Aha. I hear you talking about the company with Perk. Men are much worse gossips than women. Now admit it."

"Never. Men are interested in theories, ideas, in logical discussion uninterrupted by the kangaroo hops of a woman's mind." The guest smiled as he spoke.

"Hear, hear," applauded his host.

The words came easily, without thought, and they were answered quickly, for they were lines from an empty ritual. None of the three appeared to listen to what the others said, but each spoke in turn, without prompting.

The woman stood in the doorway, her arm holding open the aluminum screen door, while her husband lounged against the iron rail. The host could not look as if he were hurrying his guest, who stood with one foot on the bottom step yet turned back toward the door, politely acting as if he were reluctant to leave.

"Are you on your way back to the hospital?"

"Yes."

"Afraid an intern may be stealing a customer away from you?"

"Of course not, and you know doctors never have customers—they're patients."

"I imagine you are really checking on the nurses," the woman said, smiling. "I understand bachelor doctors are terrors at night."

"You may not believe me, but I've never pinched a nurse in a linen closet at night."

"Your training was deficient—you should have been given the opportunity."

"Oh, I had the opportunity all right, but the nurses on night duty are all grandmothers—they have moustaches. Now in the daytime——"

"Everyone's watching," his host interrupted.

"Exactly. That's why I'm a bachelor."

"Come back in. Evelyn's sister from Omaha——"

"——Has already told me her symptoms, an obvious pelvic displacement needing therapeutic treatment of a vigorous nature."

"Really?" she asked.

"No, not really. She's a nice kid, but I do have to get back to the hospital. I have some patients to check, a paper to finish for the journal—and, of course, there are the nurses."

"Did you always know you were going to be a doctor?" his host asked, suddenly serious. "I mean really know it, always make everything else fit into the pattern?"

The man on the bottom step thought and nodded. "Yes, I guess I did."

The three were dressed informally, their manners casual. They smiled with a spontaneity that did not appear cultivated, yet behind their ease was a tension, a conflict just under control. Brad Hastings leaned indolently against the railing, but his hands gripped it so hard they were marked by the iron. His long legs were bent, but he was not relaxed. Brad was coiled; he could have sprung at an enemy in a second, shoving himself up and out with both arms and legs. His body, lean in the college clothes he would wear all his life, had only the illusion of rest. He was a man who was at ease only when he was in motion. Hastings didn't walk, he strode. He used his hands to hammer home an argument, he relaxed by sailing or by working on the lawn, he never spent an evening reading in the same chair or wasted an hour daydreaming. The dawdling on the step bored him; Brad did not need the next drink, but he was thinking of it just the same.

The short man below Brad was absolutely still, a rock around which the river of talk had to flow. No one could tell if he knew his calm was a weapon against Brad. He chatted in a gentle, ironic way with the soft voice that could be self-mocking one moment, understanding the next, and then unexpectedly as sharp as his scalpel. Dr. Irving Frank was an ugly man with the gross peasant features so typical of Russian Jewish string quartet players. His body was sturdy, his arms short, his fingers stubby. Irv's hair was thin at thirty-five, his beard dark. With thick lips, a broad nose, and brows heavy with bone, his face was Neanderthal—yet this face, when Irv talked, betrayed the man inside: his extraordinary sensitivity, his gentleness, his caring about others, his personal concern for such an abstraction as the world. He had tried all his life to protect himself, but even after the long years of training he had never quite succeeded in hiding the pity that made him vulnerable to other people's problems.

Bets Hastings stood above them both in the doorway, holding the door open in invitation—or indecision. She was not sure of what people saw in her, and she would have been surprised to discover that her illusion of unconcern was successful. Her fear did not show; not even Brad suspected the effort she had to make to appear relaxed. The hesitant second when Bets reconsidered her most casual words was accepted as a charming trait. No one knew her doubt; no one except, perhaps, Irv Frank saw a single revealing flaw. To Brad's friends and his neighbors, Bets was a lovely girl, beautiful in a startling way, with jet-black hair, a slightly olive skin, and a lithe figure unmarked by thirty-three years and two children. Not one acquaintance knew what she had lost in the battle to avoid her mother's figure, not even Brad, who she felt ought to notice that the skin on her cheek was drawn far too tightly over the bone. Perhaps he did but didn't mention it, Bets thought, for she didn't really know what her husband thought about her or their world. Bets, even after all these years, wasn't really sure if Brad was diplomatic or just unseeing. Thinking that she looked at him with something that might grow into hate, she quickly masked her face. "Will you come to dinner Friday, Irv?" she asked. "We're having just a few drinks, a bite to eat, you know, and a good chance for quiet talk—Peg and Pete will be here."

"I'm sorry, Bets. I can't get off then."

"Bets, you know Irv doesn't like Peg and Pete."

"Of course I like the Andersons. Who wouldn't? They are certainly likable, quite the likablest people I've ever met. It's just that, well, I'm busy."

"We've been friends too long, Irv. Don't lie."

"All right. Just because you have friends, it doesn't mean they'll also be my friends."

"I always hope they will be," Bets said earnestly.

"Bets, you're wonderful, but life isn't like that."

Brad explained, "Our friend the doctor doesn't like nice people."

"I like you, and you're nice," he said, smiling.

"And we like you, and you aren't nice."

"What a dreadful thing to say, Brad."

"It's true, we were opposites who were attracted, still are."

"Don't you ever feel comfortable with our friends, Irv?"

"With you alone, yes." He paused and shook his head. "With your friends, no."

Bets hesitated, "They aren't, well, I mean they aren't prejudiced."

"They are exceedingly tolerant," Brad added.

"That's a dirty word to Irv," Bets guessed.

"Yes, I suppose it is. I don't like being tolerated. Sounds different when you say it that way, doesn't it?" He smiled sadly. "So I'm a surgeon. They accept me, in spite of the fact I'm a Jew, because I'm a doctor. But it's more than that—your friends are so nice I want to do something nasty. I know that's crazy and impossible and pretty childish," he said, and laughed. "They're all so nice I could heave into the African violets or expose myself or goose Henrietta Walker. . . ."

"She'd love it."

"Exactly, and everyone would understand why I wanted to do it. They'd look the other way."

"What do you want them to do, stomp you to death?" Brad snorted.

"Of course not. It's my fault, not theirs. I had bad toilet training or something. Still, I feel uncomfortable because I know they are real people behind it all. They go to the bathroom, they screw, they hate, fear, doubt. They are growing old—they must feel all sorts of things, but they never show it. Never. They are always the same. Edson Charles must even smile in his sleep."

"What should they do? Pick a fight with everyone, make trouble, hate the world?"

Irv shrugged: "I'm illogical, and I admit it. I guess I dislike people who're likable. I can't defend how I feel—it's ridiculous, but you asked me a question."

"And no small talk for Dr. Frank. You gave me an answer." Brad smiled.

"You've got to have one friend who's on the outside looking in."

"And you, one who's in. Come on, I'll walk you to the car."

"You'll come again, soon," Bets said. "Don't even call, just come."

"I will."

"No you won't. You'll call first."

"See, Brad, I too have my social lies." He started down the walk. "You won't change your mind and let me run you in?"

"No, I'll take the morning plane."

"If you think you ought to go tonight . . ." Bets called after them. Without stopping, Brad answered, "It's settled."

"Afraid of my sports car?" Irv probed.

"Just because it's my birthday it doesn't mean I've given

up." After all, I'm only thirty-six—and only slightly gray."

"Have you in the city in forty minutes?"

"No, Irv, I'm going in the morning. I've already changed my reservation."

Bets watched them, looking like Mutt and Jeff as they walked down the drive laughing, and she felt angry that Irv would test her husband—for she had done the same thing. They were so different in height, so different in every way, and Bets marveled again at this friendship, which was Brad's only eccentricity. She liked Irv, but for reasons she didn't think Brad could understand—his alienation; his loneliness; his tenderness, which Brad must think weakness; his cynicism, which might appear as self-pity to some people but which still made her want to comfort him. Brad didn't want sensitivity in a man or a woman, she thought. Brad was everything Irv scorned: one of the chosen, a salesman, the very model of the corporation executive, conservative, almost smug, certainly complacent in his world, and yet the two of them seemed to need each other, and were, in a sense, each other's best friend.

Standing still on the step, Bets examined that temptation to test her husband, which came so frequently these days, which had possessed her and made her test Brad once again. Now she felt not victory, but shame—and the need was still unsatisfied. It had been such a simple thing: "Will you stay tonight and go to Chicago in the morning?" Yet it had grown so large a demand in the closets of her mind, so important a testing, that she was infuriated by his calm surrender: "Of course, if you want me to."

Making herself turn back to the party, Bets knew it was Brad's sureness, his confidence in himself, his easy knowledge of his world that infuriated her. She wanted to bite him. Being sure of what he was, maddeningly sure, it was no surrender for him to yield to his wife's foolish request. Of course he'd stay. It was as easy as that, no test at all. She darted into the house. "Harold, you need a drink. You too, Fran. I'll get some more of those sausage things from the kitchen."

In the driveway, Brad adjusted his long step to Irv's pace. Irv grinned up at him. "Thirty-six. I never thought I'd have middle-aged friends."

"Huh—you'll be thirty-five in November."

"That's a long time away."

"Time's passing more quickly than it used to."

"You were eighteen when I walked into that room in the freshman dorm. Now I've known you half your life."

"I wouldn't have bet on our becoming friends."

"I would, Brad. I had to have you for a friend." Brad looked shocked, and Irv went on: "Don't laugh it off, Brad. I've a confession of sorts to make: I used you."

"Used me?"

"Yes, and for some reason I realized it tonight. For all our talk on the steps, I did look at ease at the party—I appear to belong now."

"Of course you belong." Brad tried to pass it off with a laugh.

"It wasn't always 'of course,' Brad. It was not at all 'of course.' Not for the kid who won the scholarship to go to school with the *goyim.*"

"You didn't exactly live in a ghetto."

"Not exactly, but it wasn't just that. I had to move up a class."

"In our classless society?"

"Exactly." They laughed together.

"What were the strange rituals of my class?"

"Were? Are. How to mix a martini, for example." Irv stopped and turned to Brad, whose face showed his embarrassment at Irv's intensity. "What's a Gibson? How 'Drop by sometime' means 'Don't drop by.' How 'Let's have lunch someday' is 'Goodbye.' When to wear a sport jacket and when to wear a suit. What to put on a coffee table. How to say nothing entertainingly, how to stand at a cocktail party. What to do with your hands—all the very important unimportant things.

"Do you know I was twenty years old, Brad, before I gave a corsage to a girl? Then I gave her three orchids, as if I were trying to make up for something. She laughed at me and I don't blame her. But it hurt. All right—I do blame her, but I felt I should have known." Irv's voice dropped and he started walking again. "So very many things to know—when to talk and when to shut up, when to laugh and when not to pick up the check." He laughed. "When was the last time you saw a man comb his hair in public? See? Yet they do it still. They haven't learned, as I did. To me those lessons were as important as courses in anatomy later on."

"I never knew you were, well, copying me," Brad said in wonder.

"Oh yes you did." Again the sudden almost anger in Brad, the near bitterness in Irv. "You enjoyed it and you should have—imitation is fine flattery." They had reached the car and Irv climbed down into his scarlet sports car.

Brad smiled automatically, so that they would part on a pleasant note.

"You don't look the type for one of these."

"Now I can afford to be odd—I'm a doctor."

"I didn't mean . . ."

"I know, I'm sorry." Irv started the car.

"Wait," Brad shouted over the engine's roar. "Look. I don't study my navel very much and I don't like to look inside my head—I like to do things. I don't know exactly what your friendship has meant to me, Irv, but it's meant a lot. I've taken more from you than you from me. I mean it."

Irv smiled, and was gone. Brad felt both an unexplained loss and an unreasonable apprehension, but he marked them off to the plane trip. Less than an hour ago, Pete Anderson had said, laughing, "You know, I find I'm flying those planes harder than ever, helping the pilot all I can."

"I know what you mean," Brad had answered, and changed the subject, but now the nightmare he could never completely escape came back. The world tipped and Brad put out his hand to steady himself on a tree. It was an illusion that seemed to come to him just when he was enjoying himself most, when his world was right—just after he'd made a sale or made love, during the morning commute with the familiar gang, when the children climbed into his bed Sunday morning, now at this birthday party with his friends. The vision clicked on, in a moment clearer than life itself, a colored slide with every line sharp, but with more than that, each emotion, each feeling clear—all life complete in a second.

They were coming in for a landing after a successful trip from Chicago and the plane was banking over New York City when it began to slip, sliding sideways down. It was all so clear—the strange sideways skid, the way his body felt (a leather water pouch, all his organs pushed to one side in it), the sharp-edged canyons of the city, knife edges rushing up, the screaming. Was that voice his own? Everything jammed into the moment, the flame and smoke and edge of wing and seat belt and bodies and buildings growing larger and people running in the streets and the one futile lurch and the strange last thought, shameful, naked—a hatred of those, his own family, who would collect the flight insurance, for their life would go on.

Shocked again, as he always was, at that last selfish thought, too real to be denied, Brad made himself think of other things, forcing away the dream, then the memory of the dream. He stayed by the road, at the far edge of his property, comforting himself by a proud contemplation of his possessions, knowing but not caring that he was tempting the gods. Through the screen of birches, ghost white, Brad studied the lawn frosted with white lime, pleased by the way the weekend's work was recorded by the predictable pattern left by the spreader. Hastings lifted up his eyes and admired his house sitting comfortably on the wide lot. His house was warm with the sound of his friends at his birthday party, but he did not hurry back to them. Instead he yielded to an unexpected paralysis: standing unusually alone, strangely motionless, he savored his pride.

Once again Brad thought of Irv and of their friendship—so strange for a man who worked with Jews and Democrats but hardly ever knew them. He knew they had only one of the superficial ties—the same college. Otherwise they were divided—by religion, by career, by politics, by philosophy, by the fact that one was married and the other not. They were not neighbors or colleagues, and yet they were friends. Brad thought, surprised, "I have a lot of acquaintances but damned few friends." Still, he had never lost contact with Irv, even when he was in the Navy and Brad in the Army. They had met twice, once in Washington, once in London. They sought each other out, after months or even years. There would be an unexpected note or phone call and they would spend a long lunch or evening or both together, not really exchanging news of their worlds—they knew little of each other's lives—and never reliving the good old days. They talked of history, of men, of politics, of life, and these conversations, to Brad, always seemed to have a meaning beyond their words. There was anger at times, but there was always some turn of mind that stimulated him, some shared perspective, a view that gave him particular satisfaction.

It was an uncomfortable relationship, awkward yet strong, never calculated. Irv would call and then come out to visit with the children—he was the perfect uncle—praise Bets' food and walk and talk and drink and talk and eat and talk with Brad, the long discussions continuing through interruptions or overnight, the thread never lost, and then he would be gone until Brad would stop by the hospital some noon or call his office to make an appointment for lunch, when they would talk again, never bothering with the "How've you been?" and "How're the kids?" which would have been necessary for lesser, more familiar, friends.

An ugly sound rasped through the May air—the growl of Irv's sports car echoing back from a far ridge. Turning his head quickly, Brad watched for the flash of its red taillights, squinting into the sun to catch the signal of the essential braking on the rise.

The red sun, filtered blood red, splashed on Hastings' forehead, shadowed the deep crevices of his eyes, lit his cheekbones and aristocratic beak of a nose, and trailed away down the long jaw. In this unusual light it was a face from history, Celt or Pict, which under an iron helmet would have surveyed a battlefield with a conqueror's unpitying eyes. The skull was boned to be strong—driving, arrogant, possibly evil, certainly ruthless, always commanding. Yet when Hastings saw Irv's brake lights, his face was none of these things—it was vaguely anxious. Half seeing, half remembering the road, he watched Irv Frank's car, a glint of scarlet, as it seemed to halt then lifted gracefully over the far ridge and was gone the way a deer, startled in a field, will freeze, then break the suspended moment, suddenly, silently turn, arch over a rock wall and disappear forever into the black-green wood.

Feeling a strange loss, and uncomfortable with his own emotions, Hastings strode half a hundred paces up the road, checking the carefree column of cars that had been abandoned a quarter of a mile up and down Dogwood Lane. He was pleased there were no gaps, that no other guests had left his party early. He smiled and his face had no hint of the warrior in it now. It was a modern face; pleasant, pleased to be pleasing. Brad was amused at the haphazard line of cars for there were no sidewalks in West Dunston and the automobiles angled off the road, unruled by curbs. Some stood nose to nose, their headlights staring at each other with clownlike suspense while still more staggered tipsily, one wheel leaning into the warm spring mud under the gravelled shoulder of the road. Looking at the cars so gaily deserted, Hastings remembered their owners as they arrived, free of children, for the Sunday drinking hour. He could hear them hailing one another, laughing, repeating last night's punchline without the joke—"So good-bye, Amigo, and farewell as well"—shouting with laughter, reassuring themselves with the password, wishing Brad a happy birthday. He could feel their anticipation like a thirst, and his own grew as he turned, moving quickly now, and followed the route they took through the ghostly birches. Yet again a strange impulse stopped him, made him assess this stranger's house that was his own.

His father and mother would have liked this house and he liked to believe they knew he would come to this—at least it seemed to him they never lost faith in him up to the time, just before he was transferred back to New York, when a truck had spun out of control and smashed their car. They died together, too soon for pain, and the insurance had helped pay for this house, and Brad knew they would be pleased and his mother would have thought it somehow significant, God's will.

Brad smiled, remembering her unwillingness to face the family history. A Hastings, his name Bradford too, had been cast out by his family and his Connecticut village for an unrecorded crime, and he had drifted to the frontier. He became a woodsman, squatter, and hunter, his son a farmer, his a storekeeper, his a salesman in The Tilton Feed Company, and now this son, assistant vice-president for sales in the company now grown to Tilton Corporation—"Wholesome Food for the Whole Family"—had returned to Connecticut, the great-great-grandson of the banished cast-out now one of the elect.

Brad did not see his house as it was now but as it might be years from now. He had passed through the years of transfer—five cities in seven years, two apartments and then three houses—and was now established in the New York hierarchy. He would be promoted; if the timing was ripe he might even have a crack at president, but the food industry wasn't much for show. Fred Mattern himself lived in a house much the same as this. Brad said he'd do the same if he became president.

Studying the house, Brad imagined the rhododendrons full grown, the trees controlled by ruthless pruning, the house settled into the land and himself at the door, stepping out to greet his guests as he had that afternoon. His hair was white but close-cropped, he was lean still, young for his years, his face weathered by sailing on the Sound.

Happy now, Brad moved quickly toward his home, confident

and sure of his path between the death-white birches. His ear was experienced in assessing the sound of parties, and he was pleased at the pitch of the women's voices leaping in jagged peaks above the men's booming laughter. A light clicked on, then another, and still one more—Bets doing her job, he realized as he watched each light turning into a pale carpet of gold that tinted the edge of the leaves of the shrubs and then unrolled across the lawn. Released from his mood, Brad ran across the lawn, vaulting the azaleas and rhododendrons, once again young, and mounted the stone steps to the Dutch door, and said, "Happy birthday to me?"

"We figured you'd passed out, Brad," Pete Anderson answered. "I looked for you because we had—you don't have to believe this, but we did indeed have an invitation to do the routine."

"We didn't lose it, did we?"

"They can't escape. Once they make the request there's no retreat."

"Wanted or not, we'll entertain," Brad answered sternly. "But first a drink."

Pete quickly drained his full glass, then laughed. "You know, I just happened to run out myself."

"Lead on," directed Brad, and following Pete to the sun-room bar, Brad was struck again by what a comfortable person Pete was to be with. He hoped people were right when they said how much they were alike. They were neighbors and they both worked for Tilton, Pete in production. Their differences were slight. Pete was as tall as Brad but sandy haired; he was Amherst, Brad was Bowdoin; Pete was low church Episcopalian, Brad a nominal Congregationalist; Hastings drove GM cars, Anderson always drove the car his father had sold for twenty years—Fords.

As he watched Pete mix their drinks, swiftly dropping the rocks into the glass and immediately splashing in the sour mash, Brad realized a bond of their friendship was a common appreciation of doing. Pete was a good man to work with—you didn't communicate what needed to be done, you did it. He would have been a good one to have on the other end of a two-man saw in the woods—he knew when to give and when to take. He was an easy worker, lifting at the right time, holding a board steady, following your lead or taking it himself when the job demanded it. They could work silently for an hour or two walling up their playrooms, or they could talk, but they'd never talk about the work they were doing. There was no need for words there.

"Happy birthday, Brad." Pete handed him his drink, his mouth spread in a big grin.

"My God, you're generous with my booze."

"So good-bye, Amigo, and farewell as well."

They laughed at the shared joke and then Pete went on, "I hate birthdays."

Brad looked at him quickly, for Pete rarely spoke so seriously. Brad saw that his friend was immediately embarrassed at his emotions and Pete covered up the moment of revelation: "Crap. I want things to go on the way they are. You know, you're a lousy neighbor, but I've gotten used to you."

"Christ, Pete, I'm thirty-six, not ninety-six."

"But you're old, Brad, real old, and it makes me sad—you'll be talking about a little cottage in Florida, shuffleboard."

"You bastard," whooped Brad. "You're thirty-nine."

"But I think young. Now, when you're through with Bets——"

"She'd be as safe as a nun in a convent."

"Not on Saturday night."

"Even on Saturday night."

"Why is it, Brad, that the men are the romantics and the women the realists?"

Peg walked over to them and pecked Brad on his cheek, wished him a happy birthday, and traded her glass to her husband at the same time. "Filler up, Pete," she ordered.

Standing with his closest friends, Brad felt a particular warmth. Pete and Peg were good people, as good friends and neighbors as one could have. "How're the kids?"

Peg locked her fingers together in a prim gesture. "Phyl thinks she needs a bra."

"What?" said Bets, laughing as she joined them.

"She does, and don't joke about it with her. It isn't funny to her at all. Pete laughed and she hasn't spoken to him all day."

"And Roge has such a cold he can hardly talk." Pete added, "He's worried he won't be able to pitch in the championship. I told him he couldn't and he spoke all right. He's a fresh kid. 'Pete,' I tell myself, 'face it. You got a fresh kid.' "

"Little League is real serious."

"Real serious, but Jimmy has a worse condition."

"What's wrong?" Bets asked anxiously.

"He won a bugle."

"Oh God," groaned Brad.

"We're sorry," Pete said mournfully.

"You're sorry?" Brad growled. "Imagine how the neighbors feel. Us. I'll discuss this with you later. We must do something."

"I agree. Perhaps we could melt it when he's asleep."

Brad laughed. "I've got to see that everyone has a drink—we'll make plans later."

"Hey, how about our routine?"

"I'll not forget that. After all, I have an obligation to my public."

"Your public?"

"Our public."

Laughing, Brad moved into the living room, thinking what fine parents the Andersons were, each kid adopted and each one loved. The kids were proud of being "chosen" and they should be, he thought.

Content, Brad moved through his friends, each face familiar, pleased to make sure each glass was filled. The party felt right. The rooms were warm with people, but a few windows and the open doors kept the air circulating and the room clear of smoke. Everyone seemed happy, smiling or laughing, sharing the talk of people who could chat without listening, who saw one another at the supermarket or on the train, who believed in the same things.

"Hey, Brad, I heard a good one yesterday."

He turned to Percy, who was in insurance. "A true story?"

"This one is, Brad." Percy laughed. "Right in the office—I heard it myself. A girl was being interviewed as file clerk. Colored, but nice, you know—that tiger look, gr-r-r-r—and she had the job, sixty-two fifty a week to start. Now get this, I heard it myself, Brad. She said, 'How much?' And she was told again. You could see her figuring it out. Then she said, and she sounded sad, 'I can't afford it, mister. I'd like to—it would be good for my self-respect—but I can't.' "

"What was she, a hooker?"

"No, Brad. I wondered and so did Sally, who was interviewing her. She asked, right out, the way a woman can, 'Why not?' And the colored gal answered, still sounding sad, 'With the kids I get more than that on relief. Deduct carfare and lunches, not figuring in clothes, and I'd be losing money. Perhaps fifteen dollars a week. I'm sorry.' "

"What happened?"

"What could happen? She left. We couldn't match relief—not for that job. It makes you think."

"It sure does. Things are crazy today," Brad answered. "Take hospital bills. A guy in our office, in shipping, maybe he makes seven a year; well, his kid got sick, a blood something-or-other, and he had almost eight thousand in hospital and doctor bills—more than he makes in a year. 'Course our major medical takes care of a lot of it, but what are you going to do if you don't have it?"

"Make sure your company has it. If they don't, I'll sell it to them."

"A lot of people don't work for companies. What happens to them?"

"You sound like a Democrat. Watch it, Brad."

"You know better than that. I just got to wondering—maybe our team is forgetting how many people out there don't have insurance."

"Want me to give it to them, Brad? For nothing?"

"Of course not."

"All right. You work for yours—they'd better work for theirs."

"Eliminating the poor farm has made this less fun, hasn't it?"

"What?" Percy asked incredulously.

"I mean, to really enjoy this we ought to have some slaves or serfs outside the door looking in. Hungry."

Percy laughed and then turned serious. "There is a poor farm, you know."

"Here, in this county?"

"Not ten miles from here—the County Home for Incurables. I've got a great-aunt or something there. She's got the same incurable illness we'll all have—age." He turned into the crowd and Brad started to go after him, but there was nothing more to say. Instead he patted Francie Lewis' bottom, the way a quarterback might urge a lineman on, but she giggled, as he knew she would, and gave a husky, meaningless, "Come up and see me sometime," as he knew she would.

Suddenly Pete burst out of the kitchen, banging on the bottom of a cooking pot with a metal spoon. "C'mon—gather round, yo' hear," he bellowed. "C'mon—come in here and quiet. Quiet." He set up a furious banging and then yelled his commands some more and finally climbed on a sofa, balancing himself awkwardly while everyone laughed.

"We don't have a cake," he announced. "We were going to, but then we found out Brad had a cake. We were going to get him some golf clubs, but he has those too. Someone suggested a girl, but he's got Bets. That's enough girl for anyone."

There was laughter and Brad shouted, "Hallelujah, amen."

"So you see. He's got a boat and a house and car and a cigarette lighter and a traveling case and a transistor radio and one book." Again everyone laughed and Pete went on: "I always wondered who those advertisements were written for—you know, the ones that say, 'For the Man Who Has Everything.' Now I know. It's Brad Hastings. So, come up here, Birthday Boy, and get your present."

Brad pushed forward and Pete presented a box, repeating, "For the man who has everything."

Laughing, Brad opened the box. Inside was another box and he opened that, and then another and another, until he opened a small box and inside was a golf tee—solid gold. He let out a whoop. "I needed one." Everyone laughed and then Brad said, "Now I do have everything—a solid-gold golf tee and more friends than a fellow could hope for. Thanks. I really mean it."

Moving through the ocean of sound, Brad reached the hall, and glancing up the stairs, he caught sight of the children on the landing. Brad laughed out loud, delighted by their innocent delight at the sight and sound of the party. Leaping the stairs three at a time, Brad captured them both and carried them, one under each arm, downstairs through the hall and the living room back to the sun-room, where he perched them both on the top of the piano.

Then he called to Pete, who came in a mock end run, straight-arming his way through the crowd, and sat at the piano, where they started singing the summer camp songs, which everyone scorned—and enjoyed.

Oh you can't go to heaven
On roller skates
'Cause you'll skate right by
Them pearly gates.

Then Brad led the chorus, clapping out the beat with his hand.

Oh you can't go to heaven
On roller skates
'Cause you'll skate right by
Them pearly gates.
Oh I ain't gonna grieve my Lawd no more.
I ain'ta gonna grieve my Lawd no more.
I ain'ta gonna grieve my Lawd no more.
I ain'ta gonna grie-e-e-ve ma-ah La-awd no moah.

Each knowing what the other was doing, Brad and Pete led the laughing group through "I've Been Workin' on the Railroad," "Down in the Valley," "Camptown Races," and the rest of the repertoire, including the old radio commercials and the Jack Armstrong fight song, enjoying the warmth of the audience, their insults and their good humor. Between each chorus he turned from leading the crowd to wink at Eric and Pris, who sat cross-legged on the upright piano. Grinning with joy, plied with potato chips and ginger ale, they smiled and ate and nodded to the music.

Unexpectedly, in the middle of the singing, without stopping his role in the party, Brad saw his children in a way that he had never seen them before. He realized that Eric, who had just turned nine, was poised and grown-up and he felt a sadness shadow his pride, for his son's poise meant a loss of innocence. Somewhere on a playground, in a class, at home, he had discovered that if you showed too much of yourself you could be hurt, so, sitting cross-legged on the piano, Eric masked some of his delight. His long face, dark and thin, the eyes large with learning, was mock solemn, while his sister, Brad saw, was still young enough at five to react with naked joy. Pris's head bobbed with the music; her lips stumbled along after the grown-up's words; she grinned, dissolved into shyness, and then laughed out loud.

Turning from them to direct their final, corny wind-up, "Ta-ra-ra-boom-tee-ay," Brad saw Bets watching him and the children, and he couldn't understand the barren look on her face, pale, unsmiling, in the bank of ruddy singing faces packed into the sun-porch and the living room beyond. He couldn't understand that the pounding, laughing voices around her had not gathered Bets into the group but seemed to push her out. Watching her husband at his familiar party routine, her children so much a part of this world, Bets felt alien in her own home. Someone shoved up against her and she wanted to push back, angrily wondering why she felt this way, but there was no time to find the answer, for she was the hostess. She made herself smile and turn to the one who had jostled her. It was Peg, but she had to speak to her as if she were a stranger: "I hope you're having a good time."

She saw that Peg looked surprised but, being Peg, she quickly covered over any potential unpleasantness. "Of course I am, Bets. You're a marvelous hostess—and such wonderful children, so grown-up. Doesn't it make you feel old?"

"No, I wasn't thinking about that."

Again Peg was tactful. She squeezed her arm in sympathy for whatever was bothering her, but didn't guess or probe, simply tried to draw her back into the party. "Pete will kill me if I don't cue him," she said, her voice rising. "Pete says I have to request 'Abdul Abulbul Amir.' "

Brad bowed. "How'd you know?" he asked in mock wonder. "It just so happens . . ." and the crowd, groaning and laughing, joined in for the always-repeated encore. Singing along, she didn't think of the words but of her children, sitting on the piano, belonging to a world she still felt was foreign, unreal, a make-believe place to which no one could really belong, a place to come to from somewhere else and a place to leave to go elsewhere. Yet they seemed to belong. Her own children in tailored robes, in grown-up slippers, their hair cut in a style Bets found she had to calculate as they never would have to. This was their world. This was the way they thought the whole world was—one-family houses, two or three cars for one family, a second television set upstairs, good food—they even took plump shrimps, big as a man's thumb, shelled and deveined, as a matter of course, as a snack, not a sign of suburban life.

Suddenly, before the song was finished, feeling she must take them while they were still hers, Bets moved forward, declared her authority and hugged them down off the piano, nudged them to nod their good-nights, and herded them upstairs to their rooms, where she tucked them in with special hugs and pats and kisses, surprised at the bare emotion that rose in her, not love, but sheer possessiveness. "You're mine," she wanted to tell them, "mine"—and was surprised at herself. She wished she could cuddle with them in the big bed as she did sometimes when Brad was in Chicago, but she had the party claiming her, and she lingered just a few moments, patting their bedclothes and tucking them in and tracing the round mound of Pris's silken cheek before going back to Brad's party.

Bets moved quickly down the stairs, then stopped at the landing where the children had stood, holding on to the rail as she saw her husband below, not as he was now but as he had been when she had first seen him, tall in a throng of people at the sorority dance, gracefully in motion, handing a drink from the tray to someone else while he laughed at another's remark. She remembered she had already learned that the life imagined ahead was never the same, but this was as she dreamed it—a man tall and graceful, at ease. A man who was liked and admired by other men, a man who was never hesitant and fearful as her father had been, but who moved with confidence, sure of himself and his place in the world. His name, she'd learned, was Brad Hastings, and now she looked down on him fourteen, no, fifteen years later, still tall, hardly older. As she watched he reached for a passing tray, casually exchanged an empty glass in Ted Mason's hand for a full one, and magically summoned one up for himself while laughing at what Barbara Means was saying to Freddie and Gus.

Unnoticed on the stairs, she watched Brad as he moved through the hall and into the living room, turning and twisting, never spilling his drink or endangering anyone else's, moving as easily as a languorous fish idly ranging a tank.

He was indeed the man the advertisements were written for—"The Man Who Has Everything"—and looking down on him from the stairs, she was again surprised at the anger that was almost hatred. Lord, how she resented his ease, his damnable, unshakable assurance. He had everything, just everything, and she, in having him, had everything. But could you have Brad Hastings? Could you own a sea breeze or a sunny morning? Could you be needed by a man who had it made?

She could see Brad bending to listen to a story, passing on a compliment or a joke, bringing the right people together and separating others without their knowing it—Bert Massie was getting a bit high and would be getting off on stupid rebels, which made it hard on his wife, who was from Alabama. She wanted to hurt him or scratch him or break through his plastic covering. Bets watched her husband, marveling at him and trying to control her unreasonable fury.

"How does he do it?"

Bets started and turned to discover Matty, tall, ugly Matty, a horse of a woman with a bray of a laugh, who was the other person in the neighborhood who Brad thought didn't belong—even if her money and family gave her a better position than anyone else on Dogwood Lane.

"I don't know, Matty," Bets answered, her voice controlled. "He reacts to people, doesn't he? He always says the right thing, but he doesn't plan it—he just does it."

"A nice guy," Matty brayed. "Getting to be an insult to say that, but Brad is a nice guy. How do you stand it?"

"What do you mean?"

"God, it'd kill me, Bets. Frank's all faults and am I glad—it makes me feel good," she brayed again.

"Oh, Brad's not perfect, he's just good with people, lots of people. He knows their names, everything, but he isn't what you'd call a sensitive man."

"He's certainly no poet." Another bray. "He's a Jesus Christ regular guy."

"But in a way he is sensitive to people, reacting to them the way he does." Bets motioned Matty downstairs with her and she started to say what came into her head, an unexpected, vagrant thought: "Brad's business is people. He always says, 'I don't sell food, I sell people.' And he's right." He doesn't become involved with them, she thought. He just knows people; the way other men know chemicals or plastics or locomotives—Brad knows people. Uncomfortable with the thought, she rushed toward him.

As Bets hurried to her husband she was aware of the old attraction, which surprised her, for it was nothing more complicated than physical attraction. Brad was a man, still lean, still strong, who looked and moved as a male. He was instinctively aggressive, forward moving; he attacked a job and he enjoyed using his body to do what someone else couldn't do—lifting, pulling, pushing—a man's work. He was vain, proud, but his strength still attracted her; she hurried just to be near him.

"I love you."

Brad looked at his wife with surprise and smiled the smile

that was not quite the one he used on customers. "Why, I love you too." He reached toward a tray she hadn't even seen, handed her a drink, and then toasted her silently with raised eyebrows while they stood grinning at each other, somehow alone for a moment in the jostling crowd. She was pleased, but again she thought perversely: "He has not been tested. He answered my question too easily." Bets wondered what devil drove her to test his love.

"You've run a good party, Bets. Thank you."

"Oh, I don't know. I guess so. I do the same old things."

"They're the right old things."

"They are?" She was surprised at the astonishment in her own voice. "Well, I try to; you know that, Brad."

"Do you have to have me tell you?" he asked quietly, a touch of sadness in his voice.

"I'm sorry."

"There's nothing to be sorry about; it's just that sometimes I don't think you're as happy as I want you to be."

"I love you, Brad." It was no answer, but she knew she could turn the conversation away—this was not the time to talk. There never was the time to talk, and tomorrow he would be in Chicago. "Happy birthday, darling."

Brad smiled in relief and she turned quickly back to her hostess chores. She did not see the look of concern that passed over his face like a shadow of a cloud on a mountain, yet Bets felt guilty, knowing that in all their dozen years of marriage the fights had all been her fault, caused by the way she pressed obsessively against the strong points of her husband's simple niceness.

"By God, it's good to see you, Brad. I want to tell you about Sandborn. Remember him? Well, I saw him in K.C. and—" The voice was muffled in the crowd and she felt alone, realizing how many people knew her husband and strangely jealous that his public face was so much like his private one, that there were few weaknesses, no bathroom secrets, no shocking revelations about Brad she could scream to this houseful of people who knew her husband as intimately as she.

Brad talked to Bruce West, but he watched Bets moving across the room, appearing confident and poised to a stranger, but looking just a bit hesitant to his eyes, too obviously trying to be a good hostess. Nodding to West and arguing about the change in the food industry since they started after the war, he remembered Bets as he'd first met her—exotic, the Greek scholarship girl from B.U., defiant and different from any of the women he'd known. He smiled to himself, for his parents had been frightened of her effect on his life, and now she was the most proper woman in the room—the perfect suburban housewife. Her figure was still lean, fashionable. She was just exactly what he had wanted, he said to himself, and felt sad.

Damning his mood, he broke off from West and started toward Bets, but then, realizing he had nothing to say to her, he turned instead to the bar and busied his hands helping old Joseph fix a tray of drinks. "A good party, Joseph?"

"Of course, sir. Yes, sir."

"Do you think everybody's really having a good time?" He looked quickly at Joseph and saw the resentment in the eyes, realizing it was a hell of a question to ask a man you hired, the kind of a question you asked out of weakness, a need to have people love you. "Foolish question, Joseph. Of course everyone has a good time at a Hastings party. Right?"

"They do, Mister Hastings. They do."

Brad nodded and cupped one of his own drinks in his hand, not wanting to drink it, just to hold it. He looked at his friends as if he'd never seen them before. Nobody was quiet; no one was still. Hands moved, busily, desperately, clutching drinks, lighting cigarettes, gesturing, spearing bits of goodies with a toothpick, putting them quickly into the mouth, hunting another, smoking, drinking; the mouths eating, drinking, puffing, grinning, laughing, talking, drinking, smoking, laughing, smiling, talking, smoking, chewing, laughing—one expression bumping into another, a hurrying, jerking train of expressions. God, it was loud, red-faced laughter, piercing shrieks, mumble and chatter and guffaw, whine and gripe, growl and complaint, words tossing about like crazy shuttlecocks, hitting and missing, dancing, dropping, bouncing, rising, and falling without pattern.

Quickly Brad drank and stared at the sharp, brittle outlines of the women he knew so well, elbows and chins, shoulders and long fingers, and the men, pink-faced and crew-cut, rounding chin and collegiate-cut jacket. They were lean, both women and men; they were young, yet behind them he saw ghosts—the rounded lines of the people of their age in another time, another class. Soft mothers with ample breasts; hard men with sturdy corporations. These men were soft and their women hard.

Marianne laughed, the pealing and appealing laugh of a young girl, but Brad felt sick when he looked at her sharp face, jagged, a quick sketch by an artist filled with hate. She had six children and a husband who hated her and there was no humor in her laugh, just an obscenity in its youthful promise that could never now be kept. The thrusting pelvic bones, the narrow hips, the bright, smiling faces. Brad realized he was seeing his friends as Irv might see them—the revealing hammock of fat on the upper arm, the pouch of flesh under the chin, the haunted eyes, the ugly knobbed hands, the varicose veins from too many children too close together.

Brad slugged down his drink and stepped quickly away from his thoughts to the door, where he saw Bets, who was irrationally proud of always saying good-bye to every guest, chatting with the Emersons. He wanted to go to her and be near her and he did. He'd talk with her later about his vision; she'd know how he felt and they'd really talk it out, the way they used to.

Bets saw Brad striding toward her and gasped when he brushed right by Bill Heaton and then the Bolts, not seeing that they wanted to speak to him, rudely charging toward her, his face angry, no, desperate, frightened almost, and she wanted to rush to him, but of course she couldn't, not in front of the guests.

"It was a marvelous party, Bets, simply marvelous. Fun the whole time."

"I'm glad you could come, Ruth."

"What was in that dip? I had a hundred and seven scoops; won't need any supper."

"Lobster and old overshoe, Fred. I made it up."

The laughter and the farewells, the promises to meet, the compliments given and returned.

"It was a wonderful party, Bets."

"The guests make the party. All I did was open the door."

"Bring the kids by the pool tomorrow."

"That would be fun. About eleven? Grab a sandwich then?"

"And not cook lunch. Now, that's a good idea."

"Bets, if Brad ever gets tired of you . . ."

"I heard you, Barney. I'm going to tell your keeper," Brad said in mock anger.

"She's heard," Cissie said and laughed. "The playroom couch for him tonight."

The laughter and the good-byes, the things they said to their hosts Saturday night, now said to them Sunday night. Bets wondered if she looked as casual as the others, as appropriate in the doorway, a magazine advertisement, and supposed she did. "I wonder if any of the others feel as I do, a mechanical doll wound up and set down, making jagged motions, mouthing set phrases—puppet moves and parrot words."

"Jay, you shouldn't have told me that joke," Bets heard herself saying. "I'll never see a supermarket manager without laughing."

"We have had a good time." Anne's face seemed to aim each word like a thrown dart. "We always have a good time here. It's so casual. So friendly. So much fun. Nice."

"I had fun too." Bets heard herself laugh. "That's an awful thing to say, but I did."

Another hand to grab, another kiss on the cheek. "Yes, we will certainly have to do something about the school bus. We'll talk to Mr. Harris; why, Eric doesn't get home until after dark in the winter. This year we ought to be at the beginning of the run."

"We're counting on Friday night."

"Brad and I can't wait."

"It won't be a brawl; just the Grahams, Engleharts, and Morrisons."

"Sounds just right." More handshakes, more laughter.

"I wish you could stay."

"A young babysitter, only thirteen but responsible."

"Catch 'em young."

"And then try to keep them."

"Oh, George, you and Susan don't have to go."

"We do," he rumbled. "Wish we didn't, but I have a meeting at the church tonight."

"The Building Committee again?"

"Yep. All architects are crazy." He turned in play surprise. "Oh, I didn't see you, Archie."

"If you think architects are crazy, wait till you meet people. I had one couple this week who wanted a love nest with two bedrooms and five showers, for twenty-three thousand. Good night Bets, Brad, wonderful party."

"Fran, remind Mrs. Fowler she's sitting for me Wednesday night."

"I will, and don't forget dinner two weeks from tonight. About seven-thirty. We'll have the brats down by then and—no, don't bring anything, just your husband."

"I can't seem to leave him home when we have a date with you."

One couple ambled out the door and, laughing, strolled down the drive as another took their place.

"I thought you'd like the Mooneys. I can't believe you haven't met; you're both just about our favorite people."

"She's so young, five children. I'd drag if I had that many. Drag without 'em." A quick laugh. "You didn't notice, Brad? Good."

"He's in advertising, but not so anxious. You know what I mean?"

"I'll drop the trays off tomorrow afternoon."

"Then we can tear everyone apart."

"Good."

"It was fun."

"Good night."

"A marvelous time."

"Glad you could make it."

"Good night."

" 'Night."

His vision of the party had been wrong, Brad knew now. Oh, you could look at the bad side of anything, he admitted to himself, but these were good people. Grabbing their hands on the stone steps, laughing and chatting and waving to them down the drive, their jokes and farewells echoing back from the road where the cars chugged and churned away, Brad knew he was proud to be one of them, glad he wasn't like Irv, an outsider. Standing on the stone steps saying good night to his guests, Brad felt an almost overwhelming sense of well-being. The drinks were part of it, he knew, but the real intoxication came from the handshakes and the smiles, the liking of these people he knew so well, who had so obviously enjoyed his hospitality. Brad enjoyed a moment of private pride.

"You should be proud."

He jumped, startled, knowing Matty had caught him but refusing to admit it. "Who? What?"

"Bets, of course," Matty brayed. "She's an accomplishment. Remember, I knew you when—and Bets too. I never thought she'd make it. A Greek yet. Really. Oh, I like her, but she was different—and proud—but she learned. You wouldn't know her from the rest, would you?"

"That sounds awful, Matty."

"Brad, you're sweet, but it's the only way it would have worked. The other way would have been fun, but it wouldn't have lasted. You wouldn't have liked a Gypsy for a wife. Oh, I know, you were a romantic. You married her because she was oh so very different." She brayed again, "That's fine on the honeymoon but not in the company, and Frank works for the company. I know. If I didn't have my own money, I couldn't have the luxury of a failure for a husband. I'd have to be a good wife too. Matty Goodwife, and I wouldn't have made it. No, Bets is an accomplishment; you should be proud."

Brad shushed Matty and eased her down the stairs, but a moment later, catching a candid-camera glimpse of Bets through the screen of departing guests, a moment caught and transfixed, he had to agree. Her head was tossed to the side in a laughing gesture that was so appropriate, so casually proper, that he almost gasped out loud. The black, curled hair, windblown yet formal, the unapparent makeup, the single strand of pearls above the simple black dress. Brad could not understand his wife, but her voice had exactly the appropriate inflection, her hands were making the consciously unconscious gesture that exactly fitted the youthful, joyous toss of her head. Matty was right—he should be proud and he was. Bets looked as if she belonged. Later he would tell her how lucky he was to have her for a wife.

"Hey, old Brad, the birthday boy still not discouraged?"

"Not yet, Victor. Glad you could come."

"Hoss water. Plain old hoss water." His voice was ragged, raw.

Brad laughed. "You always say that." Suddenly Victor grabbed his coat and pulled Brad aside, down the steps and awkwardly through the azaleas and Brad went along, angry but trying to control himself.

"Listen. I got canned."

"So? You've gotten drunk before."

"No, not drink. That too, second. First, I got canned, fired, frigging well executed. I'm out, finished. The end—no twenty-five-year plan for me."

"God, I'm sorry, Victor. I thought you had it made."

"Oh, I did." He spoke softly and suddenly seemed almost sober. "Company loyalty. I belong here. I'll get another job. I'll make it back, Brad; you'll never see me drunk again."

"It's all right, Victor."

"No, it isn't. I'll make it back though, but it won't be the same. I was one of the self-chosen. You know what I mean—the managers, like the members of the priesthood, we join the company. Don't fight it. Never fight it, Brad, never. Respected by those above and below. Very good at committee, expert at lunch. Scored three point seven at lunch regularly. I did. I know I did. Good people we are, well liked, very well liked. We don't really know anything but the company."

"What happened, Victor?"

"Reorganization. Merger. We got it, all right—severance and thanks. The heirs get a better break that way, five of 'em. They sign the papers and the world goes smash. You know how I found out? Manager of the whole goddamned northeast division, accounts for one-third of the profits—know how I found out? Telegram this morning—it woke me up—not even a phone call. And tonight I got drunk."

"Will you have lunch with me when I get back from Chicago?"

"Of course. I'm very good at lunch. Always score three point three at least."

"Victor—" Brad's voice was slicing, angry.

"Sorry, Brad, I'd like to have lunch."

"We'll see what we can do. Got to stick together," Brad added, knowing it could never happen to him. "Who knows when it will happen to me?"

Victor nodded and Brad felt a chill. "Yes, it could happen to all of us. Say, there's Barbara. I'll go home." Brad was horrified at the fear in Barbara's face and touched by the way they fumbled for each other's hands and then walked across the lawn, almost stumbling, not talking, just holding hands. He knew it couldn't happen to him, but he was sad just the same.

"Hey, Brad, bridge on the eight forty-one tomorrow. Take a dime or two from Harry and Bill?"

"No. I'm flying to Chicago. Make it Wednesday."

"You're on."

"Happy birthday, Brad. We had a ball."

"Fun for us too, Ginny."

"Let's get together for lunch, Brad, talk about that new marketing tie-in. I think it'll work."

"So do I. Call my secretary, will you? Whenever's good for you and I'm clear." He waved over their heads. "Glad you could come, Tom."

He started up the stairs to Bets, but then heard Jim hailing him—a car was stuck in the mud.

"Come on, Pete," he called inside. "Car's stuck. Bets, send Pete out. We need his weak head and strong back."

Excited and eager at the job to be done, Brad turned and loped across the lawn, feeling just plain damned good. Tough on Victor, but he must have been a bit weak somewhere or they would have kept him on. They scouted before a merger these days and held on to the strong ones. Brad's leg muscles pushed his feet against the soft earth as he ran to where the car was stuck, his arms balancing him as he twisted and turned through the trees to the car. Here was a job to be done: the car was tipped back, globs of tossed mud decorating the rhododendrons.

The light from a headlight caught the mud, making it look like maple-walnut icing, and Brad realized that the scene had a sense of emergency. Men were milling around shouting, with no one in command. The headlight beams illuminated half a man's face, a branch of a tree, the curve of a fender—everything was unreal, half dark, half light, ominous and strange. The picture changed, shifted, as people crossed into the lights and out, a picture that broke into sharp-edged pieces, then reassembled itself.

Brad tossed his jacket on a tree limb; he'd take over. Rolling up his pants, he called out to the men, knowing they would follow him as they had in Germany when he'd finally got to the front and they had the Krauts on the run. "Come on, you bums, we'll heave her out. Get behind the wheel, Jack. Hell no we don't need a board—Pete's here. Come on, get beside me. You, Tom, and Frank. Victor, stand back. . . ."

At the back of the car Brad stood still for a moment, hands hanging loosely at his side, as relaxed as a pro quarterback standing tall, lonely, for an instant before he ordered the charge of the line.

Brad's mind sliced through all the complications—the mud, the shouted advice, the strange half-light, the people, the weight, the angle of direction—to a simple solution: Lift the car from here to there. "OK, let's heave."

He bent down at the knees, his feet digging through the muck to solid ground, his hands hooking under the sharp under edge of the bumper. "One. Two. Heave." He felt them lift together, his legs taut, pushing, his back stiff, pulling, his chin stuck out, and his neck corded from the effort of tugging. A lift, an illusion of success, and a falling back—failure.

Brad rested a minute, not speaking, the air burning deep into his lungs. Then he barked out the command again—"Hit it"—calling for an extra lift on the end. A wheel spun free for a minute, but then they all fell back. The car was still held by the mud.

Again they dug into the mud together, dirtied and bloodied, a team now, each intoxicated by the strength of his own muscles. They attacked together now. Their feet started to slip, but they dug into the mud and lifted, their hands cut by the under edge of the bumper, and Brad felt the victory and grunted his exultation, the muscles in his legs and back and arms and neck and belly all lifting. By God, they were doing it. The car moved easily, lightly almost, and they fell back while Brad alone, grunting and lifting, continued for two more steps.

On the steps Bets stood watching, Brad clear in the headlights, his commands sharp in the night. She saw him step after the car when the others fell back, seeming to lift it alone, and she was again aware of his male animal strength and awed by it, too. She heard his yell, not words, just an exultant roar, and saw, before she knew what she saw, the slow motion of the car slipping back.

It couldn't be, but it was. The car was sliding back, gathering speed, and Brad, victorious, was turned away, standing proudly, not seeing his fate. She screamed to warn him, but he stayed where he was. There wasn't time to move, and then, while standing still, he was struck down. With one great slicing blow of the car, Brad was cut down, out of the headlights—swiftly he was gone, from light to dark.

Bets couldn't see anymore, couldn't tell what she felt was sure: it was bad. An accident, something that happened to someone else, had happened to Brad. One moment he was standing clear in the headlights; the next, he was gone. The gasps and the cries, "Oh no," even her own screams, came to her as she raced across the lawn.

2

Running to her husband, stumbling, almost falling, catching herself, plunging across the limed lawn and between the ghost-white birches, Bets didn't see a thing. It was more than that. Her brain became an extraordinarily sensitive photographic plate exposed to every line, each color, all the sounds and smells and shapes around her. Even her emotions were recorded so that for the rest of her life she would be able to live again those hourlike minutes—only then seeing clearly the images now hurled against her brain: the black-shouldered huddle of men around the back of the car, the slanting-up beam of one pair of headlights spotlighting the treetops across the road, the shocking warmth of the mud over her shoe tops, a white birch right at her face sliding by as she ducked away, a single almost lilting phrase out of the cacophony of screams—"Hey, lookit his neck"—the metallic taste of fear, the confusion of orders and then Pete's voice directing the moving of the car, telling Peg to call an ambulance, the smell of her own fear—sweeter than honey—sickening to her nostrils, the moving shadow-people larger than life, their bodies shadow-bending over everything, the memory of Brad coming to her from the shower that afternoon, naked, his voice clear and his laugh echoing still; she was pushing through the mass of people, elbowing, clawing, screaming into where he lay so strangely still, his head near a rock, his legs across the tracks of the car, unmoving.

Bets fell to him in the mud, tenderly touching the blood, finding him warm, breathing; kneeling by him and not cradling him, for it might hurt his neck, just touching him with her fingertips.

"Don't move him."

"A doctor's coming."

"He's alive, alive."

"He shouldn't be moved."

"The doctor will be here soon."

She felt the hands flutter at her shoulders, saw the feet of the men who hurried to her side. Her eyes were skilled with a knowledge elemental, instinctive, a knowing she did not know she had as she studied her husband—one side of his head illuminated by a bright headlight, the other in shadow. The cuts seemed slight, skin scrapes from the ugly rock indecently stuck up, clean of mud. His shirt was torn away and a triangle of chest, fish-belly white, seemed to be breathing all right, and he did not moan. His eyes were closed; he was asleep—a frightening sleep. Most fearful of all was his neck, for his head was hunched over, off center, and he was so very still. She wanted to straighten his neck and knew she should not. She wanted to cradle him in her arms and could not, but suddenly she saw one of his shoes a foot from his head in the mud and she grabbed it, horrified by the fact that it was still tied.

Someone had brought a stadium blanket from a car and they were starting to cover him. She looked up, mute, wanting to scream, and then she realized that they were not going to cover his face.

They watched anxiously as Bets, in the ancient pose of woman grieving, knelt at Brad's side, rocking slightly, cradling that shoe as she would a child, rock-silent, unweeping, kneeling in the mud, waiting. They watched and waited with her, sharing her awful intimacy.

"The doctor's on his way."

"He shouldn't be moved."

"He's breathing."

"The blanket's what to do in case of shock."

"We've called for an ambulance too."

It was years before she could remember how she felt without

feeling guilty at the unexpected emotion. Kneeling at her husband's side, his blood warm on her fingers, her legs comfortable in the mud, she felt at peace.

The running was over, if not the fear. There was no doubt now. As a woman, Bets knew what to do: kneel by her husband and wait, ready to comfort him, to nurse him, to do what had to be done, what could be done. She felt content, as if she had been prepared by generations for the job ahead. Worried, yes, grieving, yes, frightened, of course, yet sure of what she should do.

At last the wailing of the ambulance coming over the ridges grew louder. Finally it moaned to a stop on the road and the professional hands took over, dispassionate in their examination, callously expert and routinely tender. As Brad was lifted away she stood up and turned to Peg and Pete, not bothering to wipe the mud from her legs.

"We'll take you to the hospital, Bets."

She nodded. Of course they would. "The children, I'll tell the children."

"Not now."

"I've got to tell them."

"They're asleep, Bets."

"They can't be, with the noise, everything."

"They are. I've checked. Matty's going to baby-sit. They're all right. Everything's under control. Come on, Bets, we'll go to the hospital."

"I've got to tell them."

Pete's voice was terribly calm as he said, "There's nothing to tell them yet."

Of course. She nodded and moved to the car and thought of the mud on her stockings and her dress.

Peg asked, "Do you want to change?"

Bets did not hesitate. "No. I want to be there with him." She tried to smile. "He didn't like this dress much, anyway."

Bets would always remember the ride to the hospital as a tunnel after the halting attempts at conversation—"Bets, you know they do simply marvelous things these days. Miracles."

"He may need one, Pete." Bets was surprised at the calm in her own voice. "It's his neck. I know it's his neck."

"You can't tell, Bets, it may just be something they snap in and pop, it's OK. You can't tell."

"You may be right, Peg," she said, knowing none of them believed it. There was nothing to say. All the words were thought of but not said because of special meanings they might have, and finally conversation died. Her body swaying in easy rhythm to the familiar roads, Bets saw only the dark, turning tunnel of black, pierced by the high beams, as Pete raced to the hospital. Black road, black sky, black woods and black bushes, black houses, their people away, all black and then suddenly the white glare of the emergency entrance, so bright it hurt her eyes.

Bets stopped as she stepped through the door, so quickly that Peg bumped into her, and then she stumbled forward to where a silly button of a nurse's cap sat on a granite-gray head, tight with old-lady curls, bowed over a paper. "Is Mr. Hastings . . . ?"

The head popped up, the face surprised but still hard, making a quick calculation. There was no smile and the head nodded to a shut door marked "1."

Bets stood staring at the face and it stared back, waiting.

"Is my husband . . . ?" she began.

"You'll have to ask the doctor."

"Who is the doctor?"

"You don't know?"

"I wouldn't ask if I knew. My husband was an accident case."

"Of course. Dr. Frank."

"Thank God he was here."

"Just leaving—I caught him myself upstairs. Soon as I saw Mr. Hastings come in, I knew we needed an orthopedic surgeon."

Bets touched the edge of the nurse's desk, balancing herself. "Is my husband still alive?"

"Oh yes. I thought you knew that."

"No. No. They just took him away. He was breathing, but he was so still. You know, he didn't even moan, not once. Just standing up and then he fell down. I saw it. . . ."

Peg put her arm around her, and the nurse said, "I'll get some coffee."

"Oh no, don't bother."

"Please. Black," Peg said.

"I'll be glad to," said the nurse, who rose heavily, as the submarine in a newsreel rises dripping from the sea.

"Nurse, how is he?" Now at last there was compassion in

the tired gray face, and Bets thought irrelevantly of what Irv had said—yes, the nurse had a moustache. "I don't know. He's still alive and the longer they stay alive, the better."

"Is he paralyzed or anything like that?" The nurse answered by not answering. "But I don't suppose you know that either. Will I see Dr. Frank if I stay here?"

"Yes. Sit on that bench and I'll get the coffee."

Bets sat on the long oak bench, old-fashioned and worn with time and use, appropriate somehow in the brightly lit tile corridor. Bets' fingers, still stained with Brad's blood, idly explored the wooden seat, yellow with varnish and smoothed by the waiting—the interminable nothing to do but quiet sitting—of the people who had used it during the years.

"By God, I'll find out how Brad is. I know the superintendent. He's a member of the club. I'll call him at home. We'll get things going around here."

Bets smiled up at Pete standing above her, understanding his anger and his particular need to do something. "They'll tell us—when they know, Pete." He nodded, strode up and down, sat, stood, and faced Bets again. "This Irv—I know he's a friend of yours, but is he good?"

"He's good."

"You sure?"

"I'm sure, Pete. He's very good and he's here—doing all he can. He is one of Brad's best friends." Pete nodded again—he couldn't understand that friendship, but he couldn't argue with it. He sat down again, then rose and went over to the nurse, who made him wait, not lifting her head from a chart. Bets sipped the coffee, now cold, and watched Pete. She could almost feel the adrenaline pouring into his veins. When the nurse looked up, his words exploded. "He can afford the best. Understand?"

"I understand." Her voice was a criticism.

"All right, that isn't nice to say, all right, but it's true and I don't want my best friend treated like a charity patient because I wanted to seem like a nice guy. Here's my card. Mr. Hastings is an officer of the corporation and everything will be taken care of, private room, specialists, the works."

The nurse nodded and put the card on the edge of her desk without looking at it. Bets watched Pete come back to the bench and she wanted to comfort him. She looked at Peg and saw understanding in her answering glance. Pete was the fixer.

If a car or a lawn mower didn't start, if a tree stump had to be rooted out or wallpaper laid on smoothly, Pete was the one who knew the tricks. He was the neighborhood arranger who knew the guys on the police force and where to get it wholesale, how to buy a used car or repair a bike. He saw problems as something to be done, and here was something he couldn't fix. Seeing his frustration, the futility of anything they could do, Bets realized there was nothing Pete could do—and nothing Peg could say. There were no shortcuts, no contacts, no people to be seen, no motor to be started, nothing.

The three waited together, looking up at every phone call, at each door that opened, trying to interpret the telephone phrases, the meaning of the hurrying nurses' feet. Bets sat, unmoving, forcing herself to be still, and she felt as if she were growing light, dehydrated, turned to dust, in danger of rising off the bench, floating up and away, blown by the wind.

"He's so strong, Bets." Peg touched her hand. "That must help, the fact he's in such good shape. He's healthy, not potty or anything. He's in damn good condition to heal."

"Yes, he was strong," she answered bleakly.

"Is, Bets, is." Again Peg patted her hand. "He'll fight and win."

"Damn right he will, Bets. He's a tiger."

She agreed, not at all comforted by the reminder of Brad's body, so naked and so powerful. She saw his little boy's grin, embarrassed when she watched him at his exercises. They always made her marvel, because in the world she had come from, the men got their exercise at work, most of them. Those who didn't, wore their stomachs as a mark of status; they didn't have to work, not really work, to eat—they were bosses or store owners or politicians. It would never have occurred to them to do the exercises Brad did, working up a ritual of formal squats and reachings and bendings and liftings that performed no work. She remembered him, muscular and lean, and remembered his pride. "Brad's not going to adjust easily."

"Adjust to what?" Pete asked.

"To whatever this means, in splints or casts, being lame"—she hesitated—"being paralyzed."

"He'll be an awful patient." Peg tried a reassuring laugh.

"He'll show 'em, Bets. He may have a few weeks in bed, but he'll be up."

"Invalid," Bets said, more to herself than to them. "I haven't heard that word for years. Invalid."

"You haven't heard it because there's no need for it." Pete spoke confidently. "Everyone gets well."

"Everyone?"

"All right, not everyone, but most. Most do, and listen to me, Brad's young, in good shape; he'll make it."

Bets saw the nurse turn away from watching them, and she felt a chill but made herself not explore its meaning. She just made herself wait. Pete had to do something, so he went somewhere and brought back another cup of coffee, hot and steaming, and she clutched it in both hands, enjoying the pain from the hot cardboard, aware of its texture, its weight and warmth, of the steam opening the skin of her face, of its black taste, of its cooling, the cup growing lighter, of time having passed.

Her mother would come. Bets watched the nurse rise and move down the corridor, a huge shape of stone—heavy and stolid, her feet hardly moving, a ship sailing along—and she thought of her mother, so different and so much the same. Heavy, she pushed herself out of chairs and up from tables, but she got work done, woman's work—she'd know what to do now. Knowing about fate, used to accidents, bitter and competent, experienced in grieving, remembering, nursing, and mourning. The widow, still in black after all these years, and her poor daughter. Bets shuddered. This would bring them together, connect their worlds—for a time.

The three friends sat together, in a row, waiting, Bets' hands around the empty cup, Peg's hands in her lap, Pete's hands gripping the edge of the bench. They waited, they sat, they stared ahead, waiting.

"Why don't you go home?"

"What a silly idea."

"We're staying right beside you."

The words fell back into silence. They waited.

"No, really. You have to go to work tomorrow, today, Pete. You go on; there's nothing you can do here."

"We can wait, beside you."

"Bets, it doesn't help much, I know, but we belong here."

Bets realized they had to stay; it was good form, and thinking that, she told herself how unfair it was. They were fine people and they meant well, but now she suddenly knew how far away she was from them. "It would be all right. Brad would understand."

"No, we're staying here."

She gave up and wondered why she wished they would go, for she didn't just want to be alone. It was more than that—she was alone. They could stay with her, but they couldn't wait with her. She was separated from them now, finally alone, and yet they sat together on the bench, each with his own vagrant thoughts, waiting.

She remembered how she had felt all those other days when she'd come to the hospital, wearing her pink volunteer's smock. Now she began to understand her strange discomfort. They—patient and nurse and waiting relative—all accepted her cheerful aid, but she saw their resentment and only now knew what they resented. They resented her youth, her cheerfulness, her escape at the end of the afternoon. She was an amateur, an outsider who did it as a hobby or out of a sense of obligation or to indulge her vanity—and now she had crossed over in this hour of waiting, and the Andersons, who meant so well, could not.

"I still can't believe it." As Pete spoke Bets turned to him and watched him, looking straight ahead, unsure of his words or himself, different from how she'd ever seen him. "I just can't understand it. He was right there beside me; we'd gotten the car out and then it slipped back and Brad was down, hurt, terribly hurt. It was all so quick, Bets, no sense to it at all. You'd say it couldn't have happened if it hadn't, not to Brad, anyway, because he's too quick. I can't figure it out, I just can't figure out why the car came back, how it caught him."

"There's nothing to figure out, Pete," Bets said, knowing it only when she said it.

"There has to be a reason for it. There just has to be," Pete went on. "There has to be a cause and a result."

"I know the result and I don't care about the cause."

"The cause is important, damn it. We have to know why it happened."

"Why?"

"Because we'll know what's at fault, we'll know who to blame."

"Ah, but there's no one to blame, Pete, no one at all." Bets heard her voice begin to rise and she made herself speak slowly. "It was just an accident, a silly, crazy accident. He just had an accident. There's no one at all to blame." She stopped and went on softly, "I wish there were. I'd like to hurt someone else because Brad's hurt, because I'm hurt, but I can't. There's just no one to blame."

Bets, waiting, tried not to think of them or Brad, tried not to feel or count time, but simply to sit, encouraging a trance that would take her out of this. Failing, she looked at the clock, twenty-three past, the nothingness of the glaring tile, the terrazzo floor dappled in gray-green, the awful black-rubber pad on the high-wheeled stretcher—impersonal, waiting, the whoosh of the swinging doors at the corridor's end, the closed doors with their mysteries of life and death, the time out of time, this brightness in the night, this unreal quiet, these tiles to count—eighteen up to the green border and the rows across—an infinity of similar cold tiles. She saw it all, counted, felt, waited, and looked at the clock. Twenty-seven past. Four minutes had gone by.

Bets forced herself to stay on the bench, pushed her body down on the hard slats, kept her back straight, her legs rigidly together, the knees tight, breathed evenly, and stared at nothing—the tiles blurring and her mind empty, unplanning, unremembering, unimagining, suspended, waiting for just one more minute to pass.

3

When Irv was paged, the name registered on his brain, but he gave no sign of having heard it. It had been years since he had reacted in pride, excitement, or even anger to the electronic calls, both serious and trivial, which formed the continual background music of his life. Irv continued the job at hand: examination of the dressing on a pinned hip, nodding to the repetitive complaints of the ancient patient, not listening to them, for his mind was busy balancing the merits of a new Triumph or a Mercedes. When at last he was through, he walked slowly to the nurses' station and took the call. "They want you in Accident, Dr. Frank."

Wearily he grunted, "What've they got?"

"A neck."

"Why didn't they get Dr. Collins?"

"They did. He put in the call for you."

"All right. Tell them I'll be down."

He hadn't hurried in checking the drainage on the pinned hip and he didn't race down to Accident. He moved with the even, purposeful stroll he'd developed during his first year as an intern—the doctor's walk: confident, calm, godlike. Once he'd smiled at his classmates and himself; now he didn't even know he walked that way. He didn't speculate on the call, simply cursed his luck at being caught in the hospital. "I should have stayed at the party," he told himself, and stopped by the coffee machine on 3-E to drink a cup—black with sugar. Leaning against the wall on the shadowed corridor, and sipping the warm sweetness, Irv felt no anticipation or apprehension, merely a vague discomfort, an unspoken awareness that for days or weeks or months something had been happening to him. He'd changed. Now, no matter what the case in Accident was, it would not be a surprise to him.

Pushing himself away from the wall with his shoulder, Irv moved down the corridor, carrying his half-filled cup and bending back his neck, twisting at the spot where the weariness got him. No, he told himself, he didn't know when it happened, but it had. There were no surprises—he'd seen them all and done them all—and, sadly, there were few challenges left. You knew what you could do—and what you couldn't do. He wondered again if he ought to buy the new Triumph. He would go look at the new model tomorrow. "Buy a new car and take a trip," he thought, smiling to himself. "Take a week to drive to the convention, really push the car through the mountains." He waited for the sense of excitement, and he was still waiting for it, knowing it wouldn't come, when he stepped off the elevator at the hidden backside of the Accident Ward and sauntered into the only examining room that was lit.

He hardly glanced at the patient on the table with the top of his head facing him, but turned to wash his hands while he questioned the resident, Collins, with casual efficiency.

"Auto?"

"Not exactly. Car fell on him, lifting it out of the mud or something. Hit his head on a rock."

"Skull fracture?"

"Don't think so. Mild concussion is all, I'd guess. We cleaned up the cuts and bruises. Not too many of those. His neck just snapped."

"They move him?"

"Not before our boys got there."

"Good."

"Benji and Hube were on. They did a pretty good job of bringing him in."

"He still out?"

"Yes, but he should come around any time now."

"Been drinking?"

"Of course."

"Bitter about your Sundays?" Irv smiled at Collins and the resident repeated, now grinning, "Of course."

Irv dried his hands, swung around quickly, and still using the towel, stepped around to look at the patient.

He spoke out loud. "There are surprises."

"What, Dr. Frank?"

"His name's Hastings."

"Yes," Collins said, puzzled.

"He's my best friend. I just left his birthday party. Just before——"

"Christ," Collins softly spat out the word.

For a moment Irv just stared at the unconscious man on the table, realizing he wasn't just a neck—he was a man. For the first time in years he wondered if this man, lying unconscious, stretched out, and exposed, was somehow aware of his condition. Did he resent his vulnerability and his need? Did he somehow feel the probing fingers of the doctors—and of the interns, learning on him? Did he know their cruelly intimate probings, their indecent pullings and pokings? Did he, in his subconscious, hear their brutal humor? Irv realized, looking at Brad, that he himself had never been a patient, not for anything so serious. He had never been stripped and cut, penetrated, rearranged, patched and sewn, pulled this way and that, treated with medicine's necessary impersonality.

"Doctor."

The word, spoken by Collins, carefully, softly, yet sternly, was enough to cut off the speculations, to summon up the training and the discipline, to turn his best friend—funny, he'd never used that phrase before—into a case—not so much a man but a problem, not a person but a part of a person—and back into a neck.

He started his questions again, curt, businesslike, acknowledging their answers with grunts, but it was his hands that took over. Once he touched Brad, his fingers did their job. Once Irv's fingers went to work, the man on the table could have been anybody. As his hands worked his mind realized that this was what you couldn't teach Collins or anybody—the laying on of hands. Diagnosis was a list of symptoms in a book, but it was also a look, a feeling, a feel, a hint, a touch—experience and intuition together. He touched Brad, first the shoulders, then the neck, then the skull, and he felt again a sudden pride in his skill, an awareness that he was the doctor, that he, the boy who had to learn how to open a can of beer in college, had come a long way. He felt confident in his skill, a power that just might cheat death.

"Get the portable X ray in here."

"I have it in the next room."

"Good. Bring it in." They didn't have to discuss it. They both knew what they thought had happened to the man lying still on the table. No need to talk it over, especially when the patient was the doctor's friend.

"Mrs. Hastings is here."

"Bets, oh yes. Outside?"

"In the corridor."

He saw the bench in his memory and wondered if he should go to her. "Is she alone?"

"No. She has two friends with her."

"Good. I'll wait to talk to her until I have more to tell." He leaned back, his buttocks resting on the edge of the sink, and realized again how much the practice of medicine was made up of merely waiting. Hours of preparation for a few minutes of surgery, then weeks of recovery; waiting for the lab report, waiting for a change, waiting to see, waiting for time to heal.

"I was thinking about the Kranzer kid this afternoon, Doctor."

Irv knew why Collins was talking—to keep him from thinking about Brad's prognosis—and he accepted the help. They compared notes on the boy who had needed corrective surgery, but then Collins said, "You know, he showed us how he used his left foot. We could have ruined that so easily with the tendon transplant."

"Ah, so you're just learning what not to do?"

"Well, yes, I guess."

"There's not knowing what to do and there's knowing what to do—then not doing it."

"People think doctors can do so much—they say we do more than we do. Bed rest. Aspirin," he snorted, "modern medicine."

Irv pushed away from the sink, suddenly weary of the talk that would have engaged him and delighted him only a few years before. He ended the discussion with, "Let's look at those plates," and started to walk by Brad without looking at him, but he wasn't allowed to: the moan from the table caught him and turned him around. Brad was coming to.

Irv watched Brad's naked struggle for consciousness and he realized Brad was conscious—not when he spoke, but before that, a second before his eyes were opened, when Brad, not knowing he did it, slipped on the mask. When his eyes opened, his face was guarded. His eyes looked around, and when he spoke, his mouth and eyes achieved a look of humor even though his tongue was thick.

"Corny line." The words seemed too large for his lips. "Where am I?"

"At Dunston Memorial."

"Irv?"

"Yes, Brad."

"I know you're a doctor, but I didn't expect you."

Irv laughed. "I didn't expect you."

"What happened?"

"I'd like you to tell me what you remember."

"All right." Irv knew Brad's struggle to remember, to sort out emotions and thoughts, dream and reality, but he couldn't see it —Brad's face was composed, for the years of being pleasant continued to give him control. Brad was poised, slightly amused. "First the birthday party. Hey, you were there. You left and should've stayed, I could've used you. There was a car. Car in the mud and we lifted it out. Got it out, and then, it's skidding back. That's all."

"Good," Irv said, nodding.

"What time is it?"

Irv looked up at the clock. "Ten past two."

"It's not my birthday anymore."

Irv looked quickly at Brad, but he was grinning. There was no hidden meaning yet.

Suddenly having to seek the professional tone he'd used naturally for years, Irv asked Brad, "Do you have a headache?"

"Not as bad as a hangover."

Ignoring the chance for a nonprofessional joke, Irv held up three fingers. "How many?"

"Three."

"Fuzzy at all?"

"No."

"How do you feel? Dizzy?"

"No." Brad spoke slowly. "I don't feel anything." Surprised, he added, "Not even much pain."

"Spinal shock," Irv said to Collins, ignoring the patient.

"Can you move your fingers?"

Smiling when there was nothing to smile about, Brad answered, "No."

"How about your toes?"

Collins lifted the sheet at his feet and shook his head.

"Well, Doctors," Brad asked, "did I?"

"No," he said, adding quickly, "it's normal."

"Not for me it isn't." Brad tried to make a joke of it: "I've always been a great toe wiggler."

"Normal for spinal shock," Irv said flatly.

"Well, what's it mean? How am I?"

"I don't know. We're waiting for the X rays. I was just going to look at them."

Brad smiled still. "Don't let me keep you. The suspense is killing me." For a second the smile died.

Irv hesitated, then touched his shoulder. "I'll be back," he said as he started out of the examining room.

"Bets here?"

Irv turned back again. "Outside."

"Good. I'd like to see her."

"Better wait till we clean you up, get the bandages on straight."

"Oh hell, that doesn't matter. She probably wonders if I'm alive. Bring her in, Irv."

"No," Irv said sternly.

"Why not?" Brad asked, and then realized why not. "You mean you don't know yet, can't tell her how I'll be?"

The professional tone slipped again and Irv said softly, "Yes, Brad, let me look at the plates first." Before Brad could say anything else, before he could ask the questions he would have to ask and Irv would have to answer, Irv slipped out of the room. As he moved down the back corridor, where Bets wouldn't see him and ask her questions, Irv felt irritated.

"It isn't easy when they're friends." Irv didn't have to answer Collins and he didn't, just nodded and stepped into the darkroom, widening his eyes as if he could see better in the dim, red-black light. A new technician was on and he lifted the dripping plates, handling them with a certain ritual flourish and snapping on the fluorescent viewing box in a way that made Irv smile until he read the story of the shadows.

"Christ, right between the sixth and seventh."

"Jeez, a broken neck. Will his legs and arms both be paralyzed?"

"What did you expect, a boil?" Irv snarled at the young technician, ignoring the question.

"I'm sorry, Doctor."

"Hold 'em up there so I can see closely."

Drawing near, he studied the shadow map intensely, reading each line, every shadow on a shadow, following the spine up to the fracture, over it and beyond, then back. Then over it again.

"Do an LP?" asked Collins.

"I dunno." He lectured the resident formally, knowing he was justifying himself, that he would have decided this way, but more aware of his decision than he would have been if Brad had been a stranger.

"I guess so. A lumbar puncture will tell us for sure."

"What we already know from the X rays, that it's a clean break?"

"We have to do a Quickenstedt, Collins." Irv was angry. "We have to be sure, damn sure."

Collins was silent as they started back through the hidden corridor and Irv spoke more to himself than to the resident: "But we still won't know what it means, will we? We can't tell by that test just how much movement he'll get back, not for sure."

"If it's a clean break, we can make a pretty good guess—a pretty terrible guess. He won't do much."

"But some do, some do." Irv stopped and turned to Collins. "I've seen it myself. Not many, but one in training, one here. God, that guy hit a tree in his car and snapped his neck. He had a clean break but he got almost all of it back."

Collins glanced sympathetically at Irv. "He was lucky."

Irv looked sadly at Collins and nodded, "Yes. He was lucky, very, very lucky."

"Vinke tongs?"

"Yep, and a Stryker frame. Got one available?"

"I'll check. You can wait here. I'll use the phone over there and find out." Irv wondered if Collins already knew about the frame and was just giving him time to think about what he was going to say to Brad and to Bets. He didn't argue. He could use all the help he could get. He slumped back against the wall, lit a cigarette, and wondered how he'd tell her. Irv sighed and stared at the other side of the darkened corridor. What do you tell the patient? It was always a good question, but what do you tell the patient who's a friend? Ah, a better question—and how do you tell him? The routine is upset; the moat that protects doctor from patient is bridged by familiarity. He put out the cigarette on the floor, grinding it into the floor with his heel. Not thinking, he lit another one. He felt old and incredibly tired. It was all so predictable, and that's what he'd liked about medicine, wasn't it? The limits. You knew just what you could do and you couldn't. Collins nodded—they had a frame. For the first time in years Irv asked for a miracle, and knowing there was no miracle, he walked sadly, slowly back to the examining room.

As if Brad had already developed a special ability to sense what was happening where he was no longer able to look, he knew Irv was in the room and tried to make it easy for the doctor: "Bad news?"

"Could be worse."

"What's the story—what is it, a broken back?"

"A fracture of the neck."

"Take long to heal?"

"Can't really tell, now." Irv touched his shoulder. "It'll take awhile. Like a cigarette?"

"I sure would. Thought I'd blow something up if I asked for one."

"That's an operating room, not here."

Irv lit two cigarettes and Brad laughed. "Charles Boyer, le romantique physician."

Irv smiled and grunted, holding a cigarette to Brad's lips. Brad tried to smile as he puffed on it, awkward at the strange change in the smoking ritual, both relieved at the delay in talk.

Finally Irv spoke, his voice precise, purposefully academic, "We have to do a lumbar puncture, Brad, so we can check on the X rays. We'll turn you on your side, our expert nurse will hold your head very steady, and we'll put a needle in your lower spine. It won't hurt."

"I guess not; I can't feel a damn thing." Brad smiled wryly.

Irv tried to grin back. "Nature's anesthesia. When we've got a tube in you we'll run a test called a Quickenstedt—named for a doctor who should have been in vaudeville, with a name like that."

Carefully, tenderly they turned Brad on his side and Irv inserted the needle and then the menometer, a glass tube like a thermometer. He watched the spinal fluid, spiked with blood, rise in the tube.

He knew what would happen, yet Irv felt the suspense. "Maybe, just maybe the X rays were wrong," he thought. "Maybe it wasn't a clean break."

"OK, Collins." Irv stared at the tube while Collins pressed the jugular in Brad's neck. If the fluid in the glass rose and fell, then the spinal cord wasn't severed. Irv stared at Brad's spinal fluid, which stood so terribly steady in the tube.

"Did you do it?"

"Yes," Collins answered.

"Well, do it again, press hard."

"I am."

Nothing happened.

"Perhaps it's a plugged needle. Press his abdomen." The fluid rose and fell in the tube, up and down in exact rhythm with Collins' pressure. "OK, so OK," Irv said irritably. And the tube was removed and then the needle and finally Brad was rolled on his back.

"How long will I be in bed?"

"I can't tell that."

"Bets still outside?"

"I haven't seen her yet."

"I mean, how long before I walk?"

"Brad, I said I can't tell you that." Irv's voice was impatient.

"Irv——"

"Brad," he cut him off, speaking carefully, coldly, "I just do not know. There are lots of questions that are better off not asked now. You have a broken neck. It is serious."

"Will I ever . . ." He stopped, tried a grin, missed, and said instead, "Will I have a cast up to my chin?"

"No. Tongs."

"What?"

Irv smiled at his tone, but spoke very carefully. "We have to hold you very still, so you can't hurt your neck anymore, so your neck can heal." He paused. "Now listen carefully. I want you to understand exactly what we are going to do—and why. We're going to fasten a gadget—a pair of tongs—to your head. It won't hurt. You may find that hard to believe, but it won't."

"How're you going to fasten them?"

"With screws. Yep, it sounds rough, but it isn't. Then we'll put some weight on the neck and fit you into a frame. We have to do this to hold you still." He spoke quietly, evenly. "I want you to understand this so you won't be worried. You'll be conscious. You'll see what we're doing. We have to keep your neck and your spine in position to heal. We'll put a forty-pound weight on the tongs to begin with and try to reduce the dislocation, pull the neck straight. Understand?"

"I get it, Irv."

"Any questions?"

"You said no questions, Doctor."

"So I did," Irv sighed. "OK, no questions. Now Mitch is going to shave your head." Irv started to go out to Bets but stopped. Without looking back, he felt Collins watching him. He did need sympathy, but it wouldn't help. He stepped out into the corridor alone.

"How is he, Doc?"

"Hello Pete, Peg." He nodded to them and went to Bets. "You'll be able to see him in a little while." Irv watched Bets carefully, and was struck by her control. She was worried and showed it, but she hadn't panicked, she was tough. And he thought sadly, "Her toughness will surely be tested."

"How is he, Doctor? How's Brad doing?"

Irv made himself smile at Pete. "Nice of you to bring Bets and to stay with her." He wanted to say, "She'll need you," but he couldn't.

"We'll step outside for a smoke."

"Good, Peg. I'll talk to Bets." He touched Pete's elbow. "I'll see you outside in a few minutes."

"He'll live?" Bets asked.

"He'll live." Irv smiled. "He's a healthy animal. I think he'll make it all right."

"Think?"

"Bets, sit down." He watched her slip to the bench and then he sat down sideways, trying to be casual and calm. "Brad has a broken neck. It isn't good."

"He won't die, Irv?"

"No, I think he'll pull through."

"Well, how long will it take—in that funny harness or collar or whatever it is?"

"We can't be sure just when he'll get to that." They sat for a moment, looking at each other, not saying anything.

Suddenly Bets asked, "Does he hurt?"

"Hardly at all—in fact, surprisingly little, and we can control what he does feel pretty well." Again Irv waited for her to speak, giving her time to work toward the truth at her own pace.

"Is he conscious?"

"Awake and alert, asking for you."

She stood up. "Good. I'll go right in and see him."

"Wait, whoa, slow down," he said, smiling. "Take it easy and let me talk to you a little while. Like a cigarette?"

She smiled and nodded at a no-smoking sign. "It's all right." He pulled out a pack.

"My doctor, the god," she smiled at him, trying to joke.

"No, doctors are not gods," he answered seriously. "It'll be awfully important to Brad how you react. Very important. So I want you to understand."

"Does he look awful, Irv?"

"No, he doesn't look horrible, but I'm afraid our equipment looks pretty frightening. I want you to understand exactly what we're doing. We have to hold his neck so it can't turn or stretch, twist any way. To do that we attach some tongs to his skull. It doesn't hurt, even though it's done with screws." He watched her and she watched him. "We put weights on the tongs; then we strap him into a frame—to reduce the dislocation and keep his spine in line. It doesn't hurt. He's just held in it, but it does look horrible—there are a lot of pipes. It looks like a torture machine, but it isn't." He went on hoping that a calm river of words, saying the same thing over and over again in different ways, would give her a chance to prepare herself. At last he stopped.

"When will he be able to sit up?" Bets asked tentatively.

"We'll see how he does in this for a while."

"Will it take a long time?"

"There's no miracle cure for a broken neck."

"But it will heal?"

"Yes, it'll heal, but there's probably some damage to the spinal cord." Once more there was a silence, both knowing the next question. He made himself wait for it.

"He won't be paralyzed, Irv?"

Irv stared at her and nodded. "We really don't know how much. It takes time to tell, Bets."

"His legs—he won't walk?"

"These are questions that are better not asked, not yet. I told Brad that and I think he understood."

"Not his arms." Her voice rose and she clutched at Irv's sleeve and shook at it. "Not his arms, too?"

He took her hand and held it tight. "Don't ask questions. Just be as calm as you can. It will make a lot of difference to him."

Irv watched Bets' face. She didn't speak, and there was not so much a change of expression as a drawing away from expression. The spark of vivacity that is forever kept on a fashionable woman's face was whisked away, and she was suddenly as vulnerable as if she had been caught unguarded, asleep. He studied her, and the dark eyes, sharp black, became dull, and he spoke: "You're needed, Bets—he needs you. It's a big order, but you women seem to rise to it. You'll be the balance wheel. Brad will be brave, very brave, and then someday he'll learn bravery isn't enough and he'll dip down, way down. You'll help him both times. You'll make the difference."

They sat for a long time, smoking another cigarette, and then she said, "I can't believe it's Brad—other people, but not him. Oh, it's not just that he's so tall. He's always been well." She smiled sadly. "He's always been first."

Irv rose. "I'll send Peg back in."

He watched and Bets didn't say anything. "When Brad's ready I'll come get you."

"How will I face him?" Her voice was closer to breaking than it had been. "Does he know? What can I say?"

"Bets, just be Bets. If you love him and if you understand, know what we're doing and why, you can't say anything wrong. He does want to see you, and some don't."

"Some what?" Her question was quick, and Irv answered without thinking: "Some quads."

"Quads?" she asked softly.

"Quadriplegics—quadriplegia." He had to be harsh now. He had to say it, for she had to live with it. "Paralysis of both the legs and the arms."

"Brad's a quad?"

He nodded. "Brad's a quad." He watched her steel herself. "I'll send in Peg and Pete."

Her voice was thin, robotlike: "They're good friends."

"Yes," he said vacantly as he moved through the door.

"What will I say to him? What can I say?" He didn't turn around when she spoke because she didn't seem to be talking to him—and he didn't know the answer anyway.

When he called the Andersons in and explained Brad's condition, Irv saw the familiar look in Pete Anderson's eye—a combination of awe and resentment that this doctor, who was really just another guy—you'd never pick him out at dinner as anything special—should know the secrets of life and death. Irv was almost tempted to admit that he knew no secrets, that he had no power that anyone should resent, but he knew they needed their faith in him, for they had to imagine he was an exceptional doctor and that he had a particular interest in this patient and at least they were right about that. "We're doing everything we can for Brad."

"I'm sure of that."

There was nothing else to say and yet they had to talk. Irv had to make himself available to them and they had to make an effort to make sure everything was being done. "You told them that Brad can afford the best?"

"His condition would guarantee that here."

"Private room, special nurse?"

"Yes." He almost smiled because they seemed disappointed. "He'll get the best care we can provide."

"How's he taking it?"

"Brad's a good man."

"The best, and it had to happen to him." Pete shook his head. "How much does he know, Doctor?"

"I don't know." Irv saw they were surprised and he went on. "First, we don't know a lot ourselves yet. I've told him what he needs to know." He shrugged. "Does he realize what it means? Probably not."

"And that's just as well?" Peg asked.

"It usually is."

They stood together as people stand together in crises, thinking of things to say and thinking of reasons not to say them, hoping as man always has hoped that words can do more than words can to comfort or perhaps even to change truth. "Is there a chance it isn't a break—just a severe strain or a crack or something?"

"I saw the X rays, Peg, before I came out."

"People are different, aren't they? I mean, you expect some people to die and they have a real will to live and they make it, don't they?"

"Yes, that happens." Irv hoped his voice didn't betray how seldom it happened. "Look, I know it's hard, but it will be better if you let Brad take the lead on this. Don't bring up these questions. If he brings them up, just try to get him to take one day at a time. There's a lot we don't know, and we've got to have him in the best condition possible—a lot of worry won't help."

"Paralyzed and not worry?" Pete's tone was incredulous.

"As little as possible. Worry doesn't do any good." They stared at one another, each angry at the platitudes, at the words that did so little good.

They stood silently, and then Irv turned to go, not answering the question Bets called after him. "Irv, tell me. What am I going to tell Brad? What can I say?"

4

Walking as if she were on stilts, the way she had walked down the aisle to be married, Bets moved mechanically down the corridor to where Irv stood, smiling an invitation for her to go in to see her husband. She turned her head and smiled stiffly at Pete and Peg, and they smiled back at her quickly. They couldn't go with her now—she had to go in alone. They were good friends, but Brad was her husband and her loneliness was hers alone. She moved forward stiffly, still not knowing what she would say to him.

She didn't see him at first—only white tile and bright stainless steel, clean, cold. Shiny metal boxes and steel sinks, lights and tables on wheels, bottles shining clean, basins and tall poles to hold the intravenous bottles, a room crowded yet empty, the people standing in it shapeless in white, waiting, their job done. Their faces were empty and smiling, and then she saw the long coffin of pipes with a thing slung in the middle of it, his body. At the end of his body was a skull, the shaved skin almost bone white, circled by a cruel halo and attached to wires that ran up a pulley and down to weights—sandbags that swung slowly back and forth.

"Bets."

She turned to the voice and saw his eyes, white and wildly reeling like the eyes of frightened cattle, seeking her, and she realized only then that he could not move his head. He could not even turn to look at her; he could not wave or reach out for her or sit up. She had to go to him and stare down at his face looking up through the guy wires and pipes. She made herself smile, and he, she saw, had prepared a smile for her.

"This will teach me to push stuck cars."

Bets knew he had prepared that too, and she answered with the words that sounded prepared.

"Irv's got you trussed up like a Christmas turkey."

"It's my neck."

"I know." Her voice sounded strange to herself. "Does it hurt much?"

"No, hardly at all," he said, surprised. "It's wonderful what these doctors can do."

"Yes, it certainly is."

Aware of the people watching, Bets touched her husband's hand, which lay still under her touch, and they said nothing.

At last he asked, "How are the children?"

"I haven't been home. They were asleep."

"Of course. It's still tonight. It seems like a long time's gone by."

"Just a couple of hours, but it does seem a very long time."

"I'll bet it did, waiting."

"Pete and Peg came with me."

"Good for them. Hey, can they come in?" She realized after a moment that he wasn't speaking to her but to them, the ones who knew the rules, and she was terrified because he couldn't turn to them but had to face the same spot on the ceiling while he spoke.

A voice answered, "We're not supposed to, but I think it's all right," and Bets was glad. She knew sadly that they both wanted the insulation of others, people who by being there would make them keep up the necessary pretense of bravery.

Hearing them coming, Bets stepped back and saw the Andersons at the door, hesitating. She motioned them in, smiling again, and in their faces she saw her own horror, just for a moment, before they composed themselves for Brad. She had seen it all—their distaste, revulsion, fear—and then their faces smiling, their voices loud with false cheer.

She felt like crying when Pete, unaware, used the same expression she had: "They've sure got you trussed up, fella."

"Like a Christmas turkey," Brad said and grinned back.

"Pete made sure you've got a private room, after intensive care."

"Company policy," Pete said, chuckling.

"Can't complain about the service yet."

She stood beside her husband and her friends, smiling with them, laughing when there was nothing to laugh about, being brave, saying what she was expected to say and feeling cold, apart from it all, a stranger. She moved and touched the icy metal frame and jumped away.

"Well, we aren't supposed to stay long."

"Guess they want to haul me upstairs."

"I'll be back in the morning, darling."

"If there's anything you want, you know . . ."

"I'll understand if you don't get in till late, the kids and all. . . ."

"I'll be here."

"We'll take care of her, Brad. You don't worry, just get well."

"Will do. Company policy," Brad said and grinned again.

Their words ran down and Irv stepped forward and the attendants moved in. They placed themselves around the frame, like pallbearers, Bets thought, moved him onto a high wheeled stretcher, maneuvered him out of the room, and then carefully swung it around and out, easily, casually, as if it were a load of freight. She waved and then her hand drifted down. Brad couldn't see her wave; Brad couldn't wave back. Peg touched her elbow. Irv spoke to her and she nodded, unhearing, and followed Pete out of the room down the corridor out into the parking lot, surprised at the lime-colored light that preceded dawn.

As they made the turn by the lake Bets felt a strange relief. At the hospital there had been nothing but waiting. Now, there would be things to do at home—the children to tell, meals to cook, shopping to be planned, trips to the hospital arranged. "Will you stop by the drive, please?"

"Certainly not, we're going to see you're in all right."

"No, you've been wonderful, Pete, Peg, both of you." The car slowed and she opened the door. "I'm going to have to go in alone. I've got to do this by myself, understand?"

Peg answered doubtfully, "Of course."

"Are you sure?" Pete began, but Bets cut him off with a touch on his elbow.

"You've been just wonderful. Thanks."

Bets turned and started back through the ghost-white birches, carefully not looking at the scarred place beside the road where she would always see Brad lying. She moved forward and then stopped before the house, hers and Brad's, and the lawn haunted by the breath of haze, the child of the chill air and the still-warm ground. She stood, glad to be alone, realizing she could not remember when she had last seen morning come. The dark terror of the black night had passed and light was coming. It was so quiet she could hear a single leaf rub on a lone branch, a gentle scraping, comforting and somehow peaceful.

Slowly she began to move toward the house, feeling newly strong, sure of being needed, and confident she could, now that she had to, run the home, take care of the children, and do whatever Brad had to have done. She was halfway to the door when Matty cut through the rhododendrons, hallooing at her, a half-buttoned hostess robe streaming behind her. She must have been terrifying, all hips, elbows, and righteousness, when charging the goal for the Wellesley field-hockey team. "I know all about Brad. I called," Matty said, puffing. "You poor dear. We're doing what we can, all we can." Before they got to the house Bets learned the Hastings had become a project: "We've mobilized," Matty announced.

"Everything's been taken care of. Children are fine, sleeping, cute as bugs," Matty went on, opening the door and letting Bets into her own house. "We're having them over to play in rotation, feed them supper, and then home to bed. Sitters all set until you get home."

Matty handed Bets a list and she had to smile. "I feel like an African."

"What?" Matty stopped in midflow.

"Getting all this aid."

"Time a Republican got some," Matty snorted and plunged on while Bets felt grateful and cross. She knew she must feel the way the Africans really felt, torn between pride and gratitude, independence and dependence, resenting the help and knowing they had to have it just the same.

"I ought to have supper with my own children. They'll need me now, especially."

"All right. Right you are. Sorry." Nothing fazed Matty, Bets realized wearily as her neighbor created new plans, reorganized things with a tactical brilliance that was impressive and a bit irritating. "Of course, of course, you must have dinner with the children. We'll have casseroles in. Delivered hot. Billie will make her chestnut and pork one this evening."

"She may be busy," Bets said faintly.

"All the time in the world; this is an emergency," Matty declared, pouring them each a cup of coffee. "Brewed this earlier. Knew you'd need it when you got home. How's Brad?"

"Pretty bad."

"He'll snap out of it."

"I don't think this is something you snap out of, Matty."

"Can't be defeatist. Frank is; says he's a realist. I don't believe in realism—a will makes a way."

Bets changed the subject. "Well, I appreciate all this."

"Of course you don't. Resent it," Matty brayed, and once more Bets was surprised at the slicing insight of this horse of a creature. "I'd hate it myself, want to be a pioneer woman at the bridge or something, finger in the dike. I'd want to be needed, all by myself. Naturally." She heaved herself up out of her chair. "But you need us, and we need you, and we all need something to do, a cause. Don't know how long we'll last—use us while you can." Matty wheeled and headed for the back door so awkwardly that Bets almost put up her hands to steady her. She stood up and Matty reversed her field and almost knocked her down. She expected a field-hockey slap on the shoulder, but received a warm kiss on the forehead. She never remembered Matty speaking softly, but she did now: "Let us help." Suddenly near tears, Bets answered, "I will," and watched as Matty waved and plunged out the door. She stood watching her, and then, deciding it was too late to sleep, she started to make breakfast.

"Mommy."

The cry was followed by a patter of steps down the stairs and her two children tumbled into the kitchen, hair tousled, pajamas rumpled, faces angry with some trivial upstairs battle. Her face must have betrayed her, because they stood still, their own faces suddenly serious.

"What is it, Mother?" asked Eric.

"Daddy had an accident," Bets plunged in, her words not yet ready, hoping she would, fumbling, find the right ones.

"Is Daddy dead?" Pris asked with blunt innocence.

"No, darling," Bets answered quietly, sitting down and drawing each of them to her. "He's hurt, very badly."

"Was it a plane? Did his plane crash?"

"No, a car fell on him."

"An automobile?"

"Yes, right out in front of the house."

"Here? Can we see it?" Pris asked eagerly, and Bets struggled for calm and patience.

"Later, when you are dressed, you can see the place—if you want."

"I saw the ambulance in the night," Eric said, "but I didn't even think it was Daddy."

"It is hard to believe, but it's true."

"Where is he?"

"In the hospital."

"That pretty new one near Robin's house?"

"Yes, that's the one."

"Has he had a shot?"

Bets laughed. "I suppose so. They're taking good care of him and they may have given him a shot for the pain."

"Does he hurt terribly, Mother?"

"No, not terribly. I thought he would, but he said he didn't."

She answered their questions, one at a time, growing stronger as she found a way to answer them, still not sure how much they needed to know. "Will he be home soon?"

"No, not for weeks at least."

"Whole weeks?"

"Yes, Pris-cake. Whole weeks. Now you both have to help Mommy. I have to go back to the hospital."

"Can we go?"

"No, I'm afraid not. Now don't fuss. You've got to get dressed and eat breakfast, and then I'll take you to play with"—she consulted the list, which still lay on the kitchen table—"the Harris children." They darted off, delighted at the unexpected holiday, and Bets watched them, not knowing if she were glad of their self-centered innocence, not knowing if they were cruel or sensible, or just unable to understand. She started breakfast.

After the children were fed and had gone out to play, Bets knew she had to call her mother. Still she delayed the moment—checking with the hospital, putting the dishes into the dishwasher, making the beds, somehow trying to keep her problems hers. Her mother would come and Bets wondered if she were ashamed of her. She summoned up her mother—short, with the high, rounded hips and humped shoulders of a woman who had worked hard all her life. An artist once had said her face was beautiful, but Bets couldn't see it. To Bets the face was a criticism of all she, Bets, had become—the black hair severely drawn back, the dark skin and pendulous ears pierced when she was young, the creases of years of worry, of generations of hard work, were alien to what Bets had so carefully made herself. She wore a black dress, for she was still in mourning for a husband long dead. Her manner was so sure when cooking, so unsure when she wiped her hands on her apron and came out to meet her daughter's friends, that each seemed a rebuke to Bets. Was she ashamed of Mrs. Petrakis—her name, her accent?

Pouring herself another cup of coffee and enjoying a cigarette while she perched on the high kitchen stool, Bets decided she wasn't ashamed of her mother. She had been, but she wasn't anymore. She was afraid of her, of her fierce energy—certain she would come to help, and stay, taking over her house and her children, taking away Bets' new importance. Wearily, Bets lifted the telephone off the hook and dialed her mother in Haverhill, Massachusetts, seeing the building her mother owned, the store on the first floor with the green striped awning lowered against the morning sun, the entryway and the narrow hall with the brown wood look and the brown wood smell, linoleum on the floor and steps, four flights to the top floor, where her mother lived in the same long flat in which Bets had been brought up—her front bedroom, the best, still hers although she hadn't slept in it for a dozen years.

"Hello. Who's there?"

"It's me, Mother."

"Yes." Her mother waited, the "yes" saying everything, the tone revealing she knew already. It was bad news, of course. Did Bets think she could escape the woman's lot with her house in the suburbs?

"It's Brad, Mother. There's been an accident."

"Is he dead?"

"No, he wasn't killed, Mother."

"Are the rest of you okay, the children?"

"We weren't in the car." Bets could recognize the misunderstanding and wondered why, distantly, dispassionately, they always seemed not to understand. "I mean, it wasn't a car we were in."

"What happened, then?"

"It fell on him."

"He was greasing it." There was no question—it was a conclusion.

"No, he doesn't grease his own car."

"Your father did. Saved money and he got the grease at Sears. He saved a lot."

"I know, Mother, but Brad was pushing a car out of the mud. It fell on him. He's paralyzed."

"His legs?"

"And his arms," Bets said into the black phone, suddenly feeling awfully alone. "He has a broken neck."

"There's a bus that leaves at noon."

"You can take a Pullman, Mother, or fly."

"The Greyhound is fine. We'll need the money now."

"I mean, you don't need to come, Mother. You have the building, and I can get along."

"You need me." Bets wondered if the tone were triumphant. "I'll take the noon bus and call you from Boston. I have to change there. Hug the children and tell them Grandma's on the way."

"I'll meet you."

"No, I'll take a cab."

"You don't have to." Bets was surprised at that extravagance.

"I will. Don't worry. I'll be with you tonight."

Bets was surprised by the ease with which the routine of eleven years of marriage was destroyed and a new way of life substituted for it. The house ran quite as easily on the program of hospital visits as it had on the commuter's schedule. Dunston Memorial was no worse a tyrant than the New York, New Haven and Hartford. In just three days the pattern was established: Drive to the hospital after lunch, visit Brad, do the errands, pick up the kids where they were playing, eat Mother's dinner, get the kids ready for bed, and go to the hospital for the evening visit.

She hurried through everything, keeping busy, not letting it sink in. She only half listened to the twice-daily conferences with Irv.

"Bets," he would say, "I want you to understand what I'm doing."

"I trust you, Irv. They say you're a very good doctor, very."

"I'm glad, but that isn't enough, Bets. You can't just turn it over to me, not in a case like this." Irv's voice betrayed his impatience. "They want me to do a laminectomy and I won't do it."

Bets was surprised at the "they." There must be other doctors, differing opinions, but she didn't want to know about them. "You're the doctor, our doctor, Irv. I don't want to know about what others think."

"Let me explain. A laminectomy is an operation in which we open up the neck and see how much of the spinal cord is severed."

"Do you have to do it?"

"No, Bets, that's exactly the point. The weights are reducing the dislocation and we're getting good X rays. I know all I have to know."

"Then why do 'they,' whoever they are, want an operation? Money?"

Irv smiled. "No, not money. As sort of an end to hope, in a way. If we operate and look firsthand, some patients are more willing to accept the fact that the spinal cord is cut—permanently."

"Would the operation do any good to Brad's neck?"

"No, that's the point. I don't like surgery for psychological reasons."

"Could it do any harm?"

"It's not likely."

"It could?"

"No, it's very rare."

"Then no operation. That's it."

"But do you understand what I'm saying—that Brad's a quadriplegic, for the rest of his life? We're going to have to fuse his spine. Eventually, in another operation, make it stiff enough to get him out of the frame."

"When?"

"Soon. As soon as he's out of spinal shock, when we see how much movement will return."

"Then some movement——" Bets began eagerly.

"Some. Not much."

"Some. That's what I'll think about, not the other, just the some."

"Bets"—Irv's face was very sad—"it won't be much."

She nodded as if she understood and hurried out of the office to see Brad. She was behind schedule already.

With Brad sick, Bets found that her hours all had a new purpose—the visits to him were the family's North Star. This central fact made all decisions; life had a constant simplicity. How quickly the necessary cleaning was done and how casually chores were declared unnecessary. The nightly bath became an every-other-night bath, the venetian blinds were undusted, sheets went unironed, the weeds at the back of the house were ignored. Brad had told her how quickly in combat a troopship or barracks, a row of rubbled buildings or muddy ravine home, how soon each place became a world in which it seemed you had always lived and would live forever—its shape and shadow, its smell and its feel, all familiar. Now she understood. In a week she was a veteran at the hospital, showing new visitors how to run the self-service elevator, making the turns to Brad's room without thought, casually friendly with the nurses, fat and thin, young and old, harried and serene, bitter and content, whom she already felt she knew better than the friends she used to see at the supermarket or the club.

Bets even felt a guilty excitement, for at the hospital she had a privileged status. Brad was a quad and Brad was brave and she was Brad's wife and she was brave too. Visiting Brad became a daily excursion. With the children back in school and Mother firmly in charge of her home, the trips to Dunston Memorial were an outing. She would dress up, for Brad, of course, and when she walked up to the glass-walled waiting room, she felt a part of modern medicine, a player in the great drama of our time. The vast waiting room was done in excellent taste and presided over by ladies of good manners and good humor, cheerily dressed in cherry smocks, their hair specially done for their day at the hospital. She got to know the women who were on duty and they knew her. Sometimes she ate in the Hospitality Shop, a gay lunchroom just off the lobby, which sold food and flower arrangements, the cutest gifts and cuddly animals. Peg went with her quite often. They'd drive in early and order the lobster salad, and then, after they'd seen Brad, they'd go shopping before returning home.

Only once had she seen anything unpleasant. She stepped out of the hospital and was struck by the warmth of the spring air and the fragrance of the deep flower beds when, in the early-evening shadows, she saw a black car slide gently from behind the hospital, its lights off, its motor purring ominously. She realized it was a hearse as it slithered away from the hospital like some primeval reptile.

Chilled despite the warm air, Bets realized you never saw death at Dunston. Even here, the sick were behind closed doors or hidden by flowered screens so you couldn't catch a glimpse of that reality. It almost seemed a hospital without sick people. Brad's dislocation had been reduced without an operation, with just the weight, and everyone concentrated on that, avoiding the inevitable prognosis, saying how well he had done, never how little he would be able to do. Patients strolled along the corridors in housecoats or robes and pajamas, usually new and always gay. There was no smell of sickness or even ether. Hospital sounds here were rarely groans or weeping since most people were put to sleep when they were in pain—generally there were the sounds of television or radio or friendly laughter.

Everyone was good-natured at Dunston. The Cheery Aides were indeed cheery; the nurses smiled, even on the late shift; and the nurse's aides grinned while the doctors chuckled. The clatter of plates and glasses and ice cubes had a party sound. "Our hospital is a place to get well. We're a front-line outfit, geared to fight the most dramatic battles of medicine, and we want everyone here—staff, patients, and visitors—to feel a part of what is really, well, is, a crusade," Bets was told by an assistant administrator who visited Brad when she was there. "And I just want to make sure the service is fine."

"He looks like a hotel clerk," Brad said when he left, and they laughed. The man did have a moustache and wore a flower in his lapel. Bets saw on Brad's face he was thinking the same thing as she. What about the people who aren't going to get well? Where do they go if this is a hospital for people who are going to get well? They both thought it, but neither said it—there were so many things they didn't say. Sometimes Bets thought they should say what they felt, but she never dared.

Faced with this truth, Bets felt it was better to ignore it as long as possible. Try to forget the frame with her husband, strung up, helpless in the middle of it. Try to joke despite the catheter tube that ran out of his penis, covered discreetly, until it had to make its way down to the jug from the frame where it joined the other, fatter, tube that stuck out of his rectum. Bets tried not to see them, for they were too intimate to be seen by a wife, a lover, and he didn't talk about the indignity of being flushed out, of having his rectum cleaned out afterward by the rubber-covered finger of a jolly nurse.

When Bets was with Brad she made herself cheery, full of news and smiles, and Brad played the same role. He had jokes and hospital news ready for her. They glinted on each other like bright objects that only reflected a bright light but never allowed it to penetrate. They ignored the future and tried to forget the frame. Alone they talked like strangers—protecting each other from how they really felt: their fears, their panic, their sadness.

"You are, without a single doubt," Peg said, "the bravest people I've ever seen."

"Not us," Bets said, trying to put her off.

"Yes, you," Pete boomed. "We knew you, but we still didn't realize how courageous you were. Brad's a tiger. Man, the fight he's making is really something. I tell them at the office, but you have to see it to believe it."

Brad and Bets became examples of how to take tragedy—with a certain suburban *élan,* for the hospital was aggressively suburban. The rooms were all private or semiprivate; there were no wards. Each was painted a different color—there seemed to be a hundred pastel shades—and the corridors were painted with contrasting colors on each side and a third shade at the end. The hospital was cool even on the hottest summer days, its patients and their visitors insulated from the world outside by processed, cleansed air, their minds soothed by piped-in music, all strings and harmonies, which rose mysteriously in the elevator.

The unpleasantness that had to be seen was somehow made different from what it was, camouflaged effectively. The face of the wasted, gray woman in the wheelchair was bitter, but she was rolled about with such cheeriness that her hate seemed misplaced; it was as if she did not live with the truth: she was a terminal carcinoma. They made it appear an illusion, that she would go home someday, happy and young once more. The priest beamed when he was caught coming out of a room, as if you couldn't see him tucking away the ceremonial stole he wore when administering the last rites.

Bets knew that life-and-death struggles went on, that bodies horribly mangled or wasted were fought for and lost, but she couldn't resist a bitter smile at the fact that they usually took place in the Recovery Room. Occasionally something would go wrong and relatives would be hurried off to the bright sun-rooms at the end of the corridors while doors were closed and specialists took care of the patient. They were followed by other "specialists," who cleaned up; the bedpans were always draped at Dunston Memorial and carried with ritualistic dignity—as if they were religious vessels.

There were no deathbed scenes at Memorial, at least none Bets ever saw. Whenever she glanced in a room, the visitors who caught her eye smiled back. Once a man in an oxygen tent had even grinned and winked at her. Occasionally, of course, you'd see somebody staring straight ahead—unseeing, stunned by a sudden collision with death—but everyone looked away, embarrassed, chatting even more brightly than ever to hide this public display of grief. Once in a while you'd see a woman or a man with a face torn by an ancient grief, crying. It would only be a glimpse, for the one who wept would be old and dumpy, dark like Bets' mother, and she would be hidden by the thin members of the younger generation who stood around, screening the obvious sorrow, ashamed of this public mourning.

Bets felt embarrassed too, and she hurried to Brad to kid and joke as if he were not in the frame, but sometimes she felt as if this were all insane. They chatted as if he were going to get well —and he wasn't; as if he were going to walk, run, be again what he never could be. Bets never talked about the future, not even the present, really, never daring to ask her husband how he really felt, lying so still for so long, a prisoner of himself.

5

Brad's eyes jumped awake and saw nothing. He shut them quickly, then opened them slowly. He looked down to nothing, no, to a floor, and he felt he was falling, falling, falling. But the floor didn't swim up closer. He was falling forever, he thought. Then Brad remembered that he was suspended face down, and he shut his eyes against the fear.

"Nurse."

No quiet motion, no comforting answer, no reassuring touch.

He called loud: "Nurse."

Nothing. Nothing but the space, empty under his eyes.

Brad whispered, "Nurse," knowing this time there would be no answer. He was alone.

Brad tried to hide in sleep. He shut his eyes, but now they opened against his will like the eyes of a doll held in an unnatural position.

He was suspended face down in his contraption, turned every two hours to avoid getting sores, turned on his face to void, on his back to excrete, like some monstrous amoeba. He cut off the thought and, unthinking, willed the motion that should have brought his wristwatch before his eyes so he could tell the time. There was no pain, no revolt, no struggle, just paralysis—an absence of everything. He was hung up and he heard himself chuckle bitterly at the slang.

"I'm truly hung up," he said to no one.

Brad braced his mind against the panic that was pulling him down like an undertow. He was helpless, worthless, not a man. Imprisoned. Useless. There was nothing he could do. A fire? No one would come. If he choked? He would choke to death, alone.

Immobile, not moving, Brad struggled with despair. He told himself he'd be out of this frame soon—he'd break out, by God. He promised himself, repeating it aloud, "I'll get out. I will." Then he shut his eyes once more to rest and immediately opened them to explore his world. Today he'd get them to show him, with the marvelous hand mirror, the far reaches of this world: the entire pipe frame, his feet, the door, the window, and the tree branch he had seen yesterday.

Calmly Brad began to explore his immediate horizons. He turned his eyes down until they hurt, and then he could see the ghost of his nose, too close for focus, and his shadow on the floor, for there was no bed below him. He was suspended, a carcass hung in the air, rigid over its own shadow on the floor.

He shut his eyes again. Nothing hurt, but his head felt funny from the drugs—as if it were packed with cement—and his mouth had that familiar bitter taste. His lips were parched and swollen, and he craved a piece of ice to melt in his mouth.

"Nurse." A sharp command and a silent mutiny. There was no answer. Forcing the panic into submission, once more Brad rolled his eyes up to where the mountain range of his eyebrows could be faintly seen, upside down. He saw a line of pipe, nothing more. Again he studied the monotonous topography of his floor, a calm sea of plastic tile, clear of the delightful variety of hills and valleys. He was becalmed in the air in a pipe-supported sling. Brad studied the texture of the floor. Gray on gray, his gray shadow on his gray floor. No matter how hard Brad stared, that was all he could see, all.

He looked left, straining so he could see the bedstand far away, at least four feet, its beige side hiding everything else, just a pale, natural panel of metal, and that too was all. Brad quickly shifted his eyes across the tiles, as endless as an arctic waste witnessed from a droning plane, until he came to his favorite view, the one he saved for last: the patch of speckled floor. A section had been repaired with some kind of plastic chips imbedded in it. The chips were a dozen shades of green and rising from it a single column of maple—the leg of a chair. Above the wood there was the wonderfully nubbled variousness of its upholstery, a hundred varieties of rusty red. He cataloged the colors, trying to name them all—red, purple, and purple-red; reddish brown, a thread of dark and one of tan; shadow red and blue red. Was that different from purple red? It was. Almost orange, tangerine—no, pink, deep red. What is magenta? His eyes caressed the coarse texture, delighted by its roughness. He completed the tour of this, the farthest reach of his face-down world, and then forced his eyes to shut once more.

For a moment he had peace, an acceptance of his immobility, and then, as unexpected as a line squall, came the rage.

Brad willed his legs to move, a foot, just one foot, his toes, just one toe. The sweat ran off his forehead, trickling—he couldn't even wipe his face—and dripped to the floor. A far descent. He heard it land, loud as a drum, a single drop of his own sweat. He fought for a motion, at least a tremor, a sign of life. An arm, his wrist, his right one, his left, a hand. God damn it, move—red rage now—move, move, move. A finger, a thumb, make a fist, just flutter. Oh God, please, a twitch. Was it happening? No. No. No. God damn it. Nothing.

"Nurse."

"Yes."

It was so quick he gasped. She was there; she had seen his shameful struggle.

"Did you see?"

"What?"

He didn't answer, for he realized that she hadn't seen anything, for there hadn't been anything to see. It had all been an invisible war. For all the fury of the battle, there had been nothing for anyone to see: no muscle twitched, no bicep bulged, no thigh trembled.

"Where have you been?" he asked quickly.

"To get your morning shot." She was apparently giving it to him. Brad found himself longing for pain instead of this frightening, constant anesthesia.

"Were you gone long?"

"No. I'm sorry you woke," she answered gently. "I was just down the corridor for a few minutes."

"That's all?"

"Yes. About five minutes."

He lay suspended, his sweat dripping from his brow. "Will you wipe my forehead?"

"Of course," she answered, doing with infuriating ease what a baby could do and what was impossible for him to do for himself. He thought of the routine of the day, hoping something would break the terrible monotony, the hours marked by itches he couldn't scratch and smokes he wanted but couldn't light. He hoped something, even pain, would happen and make another, yet another, goddamn day pass.

"What day is it?"

"Wednesday."

He tried to nod his head, imprisoned by the tongs. Sunday night. Monday. Tuesday. Wednesday. His third full day ahead of him and he would live this way forever. He heard the nurse start to swish out of the room.

"Nurse?"

He heard her starched movements stop.

"Am I through?"

"Yes."

Cruelly, he asked, "Did you drain the catheter?" His voice sounded strange to himself. "Did I piss well?" Then he laughed, a hoarse gasp that sounded to her like a sob.

"Yes," she answered softly, "you did well."

6

"How do you feel, Brad?"

He'd not recognized the step, but there was no doubt about the voice. "Hi, Pete. Good to see you." He could feel the embarrassment as if it were a sudden rise in temperature. Brad had been turned again and he hung face down. He couldn't see Pete, at least not much of him, just the toe of a shoe, his right one, black with a crescent-shaped scuff just off center, a touch of dullness in the shine. Finally Pete spoke again: "I know we all ask the question and it sounds stupid, but I want to know. How do you really feel?"

Brad took time to answer, realizing that silence had rarely hung between them before. "It's been a long time since I've been hung up for words, Pete." He smiled again at the *double entendre* and thought of sharing it with Pete, but then decided that Pete wouldn't think it funny. "Funny how quickly we usually answer, not thinking." The shoe moved uneasily. Weight was shifted, and finally Brad went on: "I suppose I feel as if my bluff had been called."

Still Pete waited and Brad knew he was choosing words, examining them for hidden meanings and then diplomatically putting them aside.

"I was just thinking about it, Pete. I've got less time for thinking than you'd imagine—they always seem to be sticking something up my ass." Brad laughed. "Still, I have more time for thinking than I used to, and I've decided this is sort of a moment of truth, some sort of a test."

"You'll pass it, buddy." Pete's voice was hearty, too quick, too loud. "Say, that blond nurse of yours, the one with the green eyes, she has it."

"Of course. I audition my nurses." Brad laughed with Pete, but he wouldn't be put off. "We've been taught a lot of things, you and I—Scout's honor, stiff upper lip, work hard, be brave, don't cry. It's drummed into us from birth."

"I'm damn glad it is, Brad." Pete sounded puzzled.

"So am I. So am I." Brad paused. "But don't you see, I'm called on it now. It's been pretty easy so far to obey that code of honor. Now it's different and I have to live the part, live up to what's expected of me"—he hesitated—"worse than that, what I expect of myself."

"Brad, you'll do all right." The shoe moved again, nervously. "I don't want you getting a big head, buddy, but you're the talk of the hospital, the neighborhood, the company."

"It was a pretty weird accident."

"No, not the accident." Pete's voice was excited. "The hell with that. Everyone's impressed by the way you've taken it."

"I haven't had much choice."

"The hell you haven't. Look, Brad, I'm not much good at talk—hell, Peg proposed to me—but I'm proud to know you. It's been rough, real rough, yet you haven't quit. You've fought back with everything you've got. You haven't blamed anybody. You've faced facts—hell, you even joke about it."

Brad spoke to the floor, blurred, unfocused: "I wonder where we're taught. When does it start? When do we get the words? It was as if I knew even before I came to, what to say, how to act brave, joke, smile. It wasn't real—I was playing a part."

"It was real, Brad, for you," Pete said earnestly. "We don't use words like 'our kind of people,' but we are different. You're a real man, and God damn it, being a Protestant, being white and English and Bowdoin, has something to do with it. I know, I know—we aren't supposed to talk that way, but I know it counts for something."

Brad had no answer. He felt tired, and Pete, realizing it, left soon. Right afterward, they came to clean out the catheter tube in his penis and his temperature was taken and he was turned and he looked at the ceiling knowing it was late afternoon by the light on the ceiling but he had no idea of the day of the week. He tried to figure it, admitted it made no difference now, shut his eyes, but could not sleep.

Pete might understand, but Brad could never say it to him. He felt challenged by all this, for his toughness was being sorely tried. Suddenly there seemed almost a special purpose in the accident, a reason for it. He'd always thought he was tough—well, he'd show them. He'd be the best patient they ever had. He'd concentrate on getting well the way a real pro golfer concentrates on the putt—nothing, not the sun, the clouds, a plane, the crowd, a wind in the trees, a blade of grass, the blood in his own heart, to distract him. He'd be that way, Brad promised himself. He wouldn't worry about the past or the future, just this week, this day, the task at hand, which right now was to stay still, fight it by not fighting it. Relax. Let nature do her job. . . . He dozed.

He woke up believing he was able to reach for a cigarette; then he felt the nothingness. He saw the ceiling and remembered.

"Can I get you something?" the nurse who giggled asked.

"A cigarette," he said, adding, "no, don't bother."

"It isn't a bother."

"Of course not, but I've decided I don't want one." He paused. "I want one, of course, but I want to shake it out of the pack, put it in my mouth, light it and inhale, the way they do in the cigarette commercials," he snorted. "Make it a complete sensual experience."

She giggled. "There's no reason not to smoke. I'll light it and hold it for you."

"That's the reason. No offense, but I'm going to smoke my own cigarette." The shadows grew darker on the ceiling and he had his rub and an enema and was fed, and before he was turned, Bets came to visit. She stood beside him, her hand tenderly on his cold steel frame, and he looked up past the metal bars, past the soft rise of her breasts, to her face, seen chin first, distorted the way a face is with a flashlight held below the chin.

They smiled, all out of news, spending their hour together. The day's cards had been opened and displayed on the screen inside his door, the flowers watered, the evening's television shows discussed. They would watch the same ones—he on a mirror over his head and she in their bedroom—and they would compare notes the next day. But all that had been done and the news of the children had been told—the routine questions answered routinely—and now they shared this piece of time, alone, no longer so panicked by the unavoidable silence, until it was time to leave—the corridor lights blinked. Bets smiled, touched his cheek with her fingers, and left.

Brad was turned on his face, the mirror turned to the television below him. It was at last turned off and he was flopped over for the first part of the night. Now he had no special nurses, and the door was left open by the nurses' station. "A ridiculous solution," Irv had said. "It's obviously too simple. You can't push a bell, so we leave the door open so you can call for help." Brad laughed with Irv and never told him of the morning when the floor mopper had let the wide wooden door swoosh shut and he had yelled and yelled and never been heard.

At last, long after refusing the pill that could make him sleep, he slept, and when he woke it was during the cold of the night, the dying time, he realized. He listened to the swishing movements of nurses and the occasional muffled groans and tried to imagine their meanings.

Failing to find the pattern in the nurses' steps, he felt there was no reason to that world just outside his room and he realized that he resented the other patients now that he had begun to feel as if he were the center of the universe. A grown baby, he thought, the focus of everyone: Bets, the children, the neighborhood. He saw Bets for only an hour a day, now that he had convinced her it was foolish to come both afternoon and evening, and he forgot that she spent most of her life away from him. It was as if she did not exist except when she was with him and then—reversing the coin—he thought that perhaps he did not exist for her except during her duty hour. He forced that thought from his mind.

He tried to remember the next day's program: Was this the day Irv came? Would the therapist's hands bring the necessary pains to his legs, three times a day, right on schedule? Brad felt as if all of them—the doctors, the nurses, the laboratory technicians, this room, the hospital, the whole world—were enlisted in his struggle. Drug companies and scientists all combined in a flag-carrying crusade against death, he their leader. He knew this was ridiculous, and yet he believed it, felt the exhilaration of his own importance. Brad reached for humility and achieved pride.

It was beginning to get light. Finding him awake, the attendants turned him to save a chore for the seven-o'clock shift. His face was washed, his bladder emptied, and his orange juice sucked up the straw and, once more alone, he felt it. It started in the corner of his right eye and crept ever so lightly down toward his cheek and up toward the mountain ridge of his nose, a light, almost not touching touch. It was so soft he wondered if it were not there, and then, sure that it was, he turned and twisted his eyes to see if he could catch a glimpse of what it was—a mosquito, a gnat, a fly, a something—walking upside down on him. He could see nothing and he concentrated all his anger and energy into a single eye blink, and then another and another—until the skin of his whole face was convulsed with tremors and jerks and shakes, grimaces of frustration and fury until, exhausted, he ran down.

Was it gone? No. It was there. It was no bug—it was an itch.

As carefully as a man fighting something real, Brad dueled with his itch. Stopped now, isolated on a nerve end, he tried to wiggle it clear, knowing it would remain, and it did. At first it was light, but then it seemed to dig in, grow smaller, piercing the skin. He realized that an itch was black and it was sharp and it grew hot, turned red. He had to scratch it, had to tear at it with his fingernails, dig it out, but he could not. He wanted to brush it away with a finger or the back of his hand, wonderfully rough with hair, but he could not. He wanted to call for help, to summon a nurse, but he would not give in to that tiny aggravation, a thing that could not be seen—a sensation. He could not bear it a second longer—and then it went away. When the nurse came he said, "I won."

"Won what?" she chirped.

"I beat an itch, in hand-to-hand combat."

"You do go on," she said, going about her medical housekeeping, changing his diapers, the towels that girded his loins to catch the product of the inevitable, unexpected spasms.

"The art of medical science is all reduced to the bedpan," he philosophized, and she nodded, not knowing what he meant. She left and he went on thinking. Another itch would come—and he would defeat it. Pain—he had extended his threshold, defeating the sudden pains one at a time. The vagrant pains that came from nerves that had their signals crossed. He felt cramps in limbs in which he could not feel anything, the agonies of a man who suffers pain in an amputated limb, a pain that was real because of the quirk of some nerve. Brad was sure he could also defeat the paralysis—with will power. Lying still, face down or face up, he made himself think of the motions of moving a finger, grabbing a ball, sitting up, raising a leg, twisting an ankle, rotating a hand—all the complex, ordinary, unthinking motions of an ordinary day. Nothing happened, but he was not only convinced he would forget how to command his body, Brad was also convinced that if he just tried hard enough, someday, sometime, he would move.

Fighting this lonely, unseen struggle, hour by hour, he became newly aware of his body—its weight, for example, slung in this strange hammock. You did not think of your body if you were normal, but now he did. He was aware of his skin, his muscles, flesh and fat, his bones, his shape and length—the center of everything was his mind, which he was sure could command his body once more if only he tried hard enough.

Irv always stopped before he went into Brad's room to read the chart and to steel himself for the visits he had come to dread. He woke with Brad on his mind and lay down at night thinking of Brad and the madness that had infected the hospital. "If wishes were horses, men would ride." He heard himself repeating this old saying, which he had resented as a boy because it meant the truth—his family had had no money for an electric train, a bicycle, or a week in the Catskills. Then Irv would begin to believe in wishes, for he was the only one who didn't believe in Brad's potential miracle. He moved slowly across the corridor and past the screen covered by get-well cards, hundreds of them, and around to where Brad lay, still suspended in the frame.

"Hey, Irv. How'm I doin'?"

The voice shouted down at the bed was so cheerful, so full of false hope, that Irv wanted to weep—or to beat the cruel truth into Brad. Instead he said only, "Fine. I just checked the charts." Mechanically he checked the weights.

"How are the leg spasms?"

"Some better—or I'm getting used to them."

Irv nodded.

"I asked you for the bill, Irv. I want to know how much all this is costing."

"You'll see a bill."

"I haven't yet. I have major medical, you know. It's not going to upset me; in fact, I'm not letting anything upset me."

Irv examined the neck, relieved at how easy it was to avoid Brad's eyes, for he was sure his face would reveal how fast the major medical was running out. But Brad wouldn't let it upset him. Perhaps he should; some day he'd have to accept the truth.

"Do most patients do as well as I am?"

"I can't say—professional ethics." He couldn't say that most quads do exactly the same—as much and as little—but that guts, courage, can't heal a broken neck.

"Well, everyone's been wonderful. I couldn't have better care, and the way everyone's rooting for me—it's great. And I haven't done anything yet." Irv stood looking across Brad, his hands gripping the frame, angry at this madness, hope. He hadn't done anything yet and what he would do was predictable. A few flutterings, some minor motion, enough for some rehabilitation, but he'd always be a quad and he'd have to live with it.

"What's the matter, Irv?" Brad's voice was quiet, concerned.

"Just thinking," Irv answered sadly, "about a patient."

"This isn't always such a cheery place."

"What?"

"I mean, the piped-in music, the cards and the pretty odors, the rah-rah, we'll-all-get-well spirit. It isn't always that way. Most people aren't as lucky as I am."

Irv tried to answer—was this the time for truth? Surprised at himself, he backed off. "I must be affected by the madness too," he thought.

"Did you say something?"

"No. Nothing." He stood and stared at Brad and the frame.

"That patient really has gotten to you, hasn't he? I didn't think you let that happen."

"We don't, usually." Irv's voice was harsh. "And it's always a mistake, a sign of weakness, because it doesn't help one goddamn bit. It doesn't help the patient or anyone. It makes you doubt and wonder; it blurs decisions and it slows you down; just plain tires you out. Surgeons aren't philosophers, they're doers."

"And still it gets to you, sometimes."

"You don't admit it. Not to yourself, not to others, but it gets to you every once in a while. You see it in the others. In the dark haunted eyes of a doctor with the blood all over his operating gown and his hands hanging helpless, or you see it in the bitter humor that slashes cruelly through the sickness and death. You see it then, and you feel it yourself—in a kind of tiredness." Irv paused. "I don't drink much because I think I'd find it then and my guard would be down." He suddenly laughed. "How's this for bedside manner?"

"Don't apologize, Irv. You must have some rough times. I'm glad you can let off steam with me and I'm glad I'm not the one to bug you."

"What?"

"I mean it would have been rough on you if I'd died."

Irv mumbled some words and stumbled out of the room. He walked along the crowded corridor feeling utterly alone. Sometimes he thought Brad knew and other times he was sure he felt complete faith in his recovery. He didn't know and he didn't know when to tell him. Not knowing what he was doing, he started out across the lobby to his car, taking the route he never took for a good reason—a patient's relative might catch him.

"Irv."

He stopped, knowing. "Yes, Bets."

"Is Brad all right?"

"Yes. I just left him and he was fine." He heard his own voice, flat and empty.

"You look so, well, ravaged. I was worried."

"He's the perfect patient: obedient, brave, ready to do anything to get well, just concentrating on his recovery."

"Well, is there anything wrong with that?" She was shocked at the nastiness in his voice. "You told him not to ask questions."

"So I did, so I did," Irv said, nodding wearily. "Come sit down." He led her to a sofa, suddenly aware of her anxiety, which somehow showed through the manner of casual good taste she wore like a spring hat. He went through the ritual of giving her a cigarette and lighting it, then lighting his own. Suddenly he was angry at their surroundings. The white-plastic couch, the modern drapes, low coffee tables and huge decorator lamps with grinning primitive masks, the deep rug and subdued lights—the whole lobby was in such good taste that it seemed cruelly inappropriate for those who waited for truth—death, the tumor diagnosed without a doubt as malignant, the certainty of blindness or the permanently crippled limb—the end of hope.

"If it isn't Brad, who is it? Maybe I shouldn't ask, but it might help you to talk."

"But it is Brad."

"I thought he was doing fine."

"He is," Irv said impatiently, not realizing he was bridging the moat of impersonality that protects the doctor. "He's doing just fine for a quad, and I did tell you he is a quad. Remember? He's wonderful, but there just isn't going to be a miracle." His voice grew angry. "You dance in here dressed for a shopping trip, ever cheery, ever poised. Don't you understand? There's not going to be any miracle. Brad's never going to walk, Bets, never."

"I know."

"You do? You don't act like it and neither does anyone else around here. I feel disloyal just because I know the truth, as if I had no faith in Brad. This isn't a matter of faith."

"Isn't it?" Bets looked calmly at him. "Can't faith and courage—those old home remedies—do anything? Don't they have a place in medical science?"

"Look. I should give you the same phrases I give other patients. We all do it, say nothing artfully, but Brad is my friend and I worry about him—he's getting too far from truth."

"What do you want me to do, Irv? Tell him the brutal truth, lay it on the line?"

"We shouldn't have started this."

"But we did, Irv. Now you tell me what to do," she said slowly. "I walk in there and see Brad in that thing, and then I feel—yes, feel—his incredible optimism. It's contagious. He believes he will get well, really believes it, Irv. Can I kill that? He's always been the most persuasive man I've known, but he's different, Irv. He's never cared like this before." She slumped back against the couch and then spoke again, searching out loud for meaning. "You know Brad. Everything came easy for him. There's nothing wrong in that. It wasn't his fault he had a good disposition, that he was popular, that he was always the best dancer, the swiftest runner, the hottest salesman, the fastest-rising young executive. One man once told me—he was drunk at the time—that it was a privilege to be fired by Brad Hastings."

She lit her own cigarette this time and Irv studied the planes and shadows of her face, which was changing, growing older, thinner, but was somehow more beautiful as if the skin and bones were being refined. "You know, we get Christmas cards every year from men who served under Brad in the army. Some even plan their vacations so that they can drop by and see him. And you know what his classmates think of him."

"He was all we wanted to be. And he never knew it."

"That's right. That's what made it possible to live with him—he never knew it. He wasn't conceited, for he hadn't tried hard enough. Life wasn't an accomplishment; it was just being natural, all the goals within reach."

"He was born 'in,' " Irv said and nodded.

"Yes, he was born belonging. And it's going to be harder for him, now, at thirty-six, to find out."

"That's why he's got to start, Bets. He's got to face the truth."

"Someday. You hurry it if you want—I can't. I'll let him have his hopes while he can. They don't do any harm."

"I'm not so sure. He's got to touch reality."

"He will," Bets said, smiling. "And as I say it I'm not so sure of that."

"You know the facts, Bets. I told you."

"I know lots of facts, but my facts—the Greek girl from the flat over the grocery store, which had to stay open Sundays and Saturday nights to survive—my facts were never Brad's facts. I see his courage and I'm impressed. I couldn't do it, Irv. Could you?"

"That isn't the point, Bets, and the point is simple: Brad's a quadriplegic. He is now and he always will be. Always—forever." Irv hunched up on his seat and jabbed a finger at the ceiling. "That's phony courage up there—heroics. Great stuff, but it's hiding, running away. It's fake courage and it makes me seem disloyal to speak the truth."

"Brad would answer that battles have always been won by those who wouldn't face the facts," Bets countered.

"Good theory but bad history," he said, rising. "I know the arguments, but it isn't true. We didn't win the Second World War because we had God on our side but because we had more men, guns, planes, bombs, ships, tanks. Germany didn't have a chance and neither does Brad. Not a goddamned chance."

"I hope you're wrong and that I can laugh in your face, Dr. Frank."

They stared at each other, their faces softening. "I hope you can too." He turned and started back to the elevators.

"You were leaving."

"Yes, I was, but now I'm going back to work. I had my emotional outburst for the day." Bets watched him walk away and was surprised at how old he looked from the rear. Middle-aged, heavy, solid, somehow defeated, and she rose and moved across the lobby to the elevator, smiling at those she knew without knowing she was smiling.

When she reached Brad's floor, she turned away from his room and walked to the solarium, where she could stand alone, looking out at the sea of trees, trying to calm herself with nature—the perspective of hills and sky, the feeling of a different sense of time. She stood still, trying not to remember what Irv said, trying to forget her mother's knowing look when people spoke of Brad's fight, and trying to forget, on the other side, the sure hope of the Andersons that Brad could, by sheer guts, produce a miracle. She looked at the hills and the sky, but they had no calming influence on her this day, and she turned heavily, awkwardly, and walked the long corridor to where Brad lay waiting.

That day was the first time Bets saw through the bravery to the terrors Brad felt but could not admit to himself when she told him easily, sure he would be pleased, that she had arranged for the children to visit him.

"I'm going to bring the children in with me tomorrow, darling."

"They can't visit me. No children under twelve are allowed."

"I used drag," she said, smiling down at him. "Irv got special permission."

His face was carefully expressionless. "They may bring in bugs; that's why they have the rule."

She smiled. "Rules are made to be broken."

"No they aren't." His face twisted in a way she'd never seen, as if he were having trouble getting the words out. "I won't have you breaking the rules."

"Brad, the children want to see you."

"Of course. I want to see them too, but they might catch something."

"A broken neck?" She laughed and then, seeing his face, wished she could take back the words. "Darling. Darling. It's all right—I checked with Irv."

"It isn't all right. If my kids come up here, everybody's going to want to bring their kids in."

Bets argued, realizing before she gave in to it that they weren't arguing about the real problem. The whole discussion of rule breaking hid the fact that Brad could not, would not allow his children to see him helpless, strung in the frame. They argued and then they stopped, and she sat by his head, where he could see her in the mirror, neither saying anything, both aware her visit had an hour to run.

Brad was on his back, and Bets saw his face looking for her in the mirror hung over his chest. She knew he could see her face when she sat back of the pulley, which held the weights against his neck. Bets took the strange position a yard away from the head of the frame, realizing it had become familiar, and watched his face in the mirror while she talked at the back of his head. He answered, not her but the ceiling, both of them trying to ignore their positions, neither mentioning how surprised they had been to discover it is vital to see someone's face when talking—to see in order to know the real meaning of the words.

Their conversation, trying to bridge worlds that had grown apart, halted, then started suddenly, erratically, like boxcars being switched in a railroad yard. They talked of the children, the night nurse, the church group, the joke about the lab tech, the pool accident at the club—the routine of two worlds, each alien to the other. Their pauses were not for sharing but for a hunting of topics the other would understand.

Bets saw Brad shut his eyes and understood his weariness. There was so little to do, that anyone could do; each could only cultivate patience—an illogical peace and acceptance that defied all reason. She sat and watched his face. The muscles caused his face to tighten and the veins grew dark with some black interior struggle. She gasped, then understood. She was witness to a struggle of Will with Truth. He was trying. His fingers? His toes? Nothing. His left hand? Nothing. No, a twinge.

Did he feel something or just imagine it again? His face lit and then grew dark once more. He had imagined it. Bets could not turn away from this struggle that was too private to be observed even by a wife. His jaws hardened; the mouth drew tight. He shut his eyes, and again she tried to look away, but could not; she had to share this private struggle as much as she could. If only he wouldn't quit. If only he wouldn't try the impossible. She was torn both ways, seeing her husband's silent battle, using all the resources of a once-strong man to twitch a single toe and failing.

Suddenly he spoke. "Did it?" His voice was hoarse with effort.

"What?" She stood up.

"My right hand."

"I can't tell."

"Look, damn it, look." He was laughing, and she stared at the hand lying limp on his chest, where it had been laid by the nurse after the bath. She watched, and quickly, over in a flash, the fingers jumped off the sheet and the impulse ran back under the skin to the muscles. Once, twice. Bets didn't say anything but looked at her husband, tears spilling down her face.

He looked solemn, serious, concentrated. Lightly she took her fingers and hovered them over his. They jumped and touched, and she laughed, a peal of girlish laughter, and he bellowed at her. "I did it. I can feel it. Darling, get Irv."

"You're wonderful."

"Get Irv."

Still laughing, she darted toward the door and had Irv paged. When he appeared she ran to the door and bumped into him as he came into the room. She looked up into his face and laughed at the look of apprehension he quickly masked. "Irv, he did it."

"Yes, I can do it, move my right hand," Brad bellowed from the bed.

"His right hand."

"I can move it."

"I felt him."

Irv moved to the bed, slowly, it seemed, no haste, no joy.

"Isn't it wonderful? He did it."

"I told you I could. See." They watched the doctor as he observed the hand, which once could do a thousand tasks without thinking, waiting for the message from Brad's brain, and then leaping a fraction of an inch above the sheet and falling limp.

Irv knew he had to speak, and so he did: "That's fine." His voice was dry and distant—professional.

"Fine, hell," Brad said, laughing. "That's wonderful—this is better than a right-end run. Better than being President. Damn it, it's almost as good as sex." Bets laughed with him. "I did it, I told it to move, willed it, by God, I did."

"I'm glad." Irv smiled calmly. "It's a step forward."

"Damn right."

"Do you start rehab now?" Bets asked, and was shocked by the quick look of anger that flashed across Irv's face before he answered pleasantly, "We'll wait till we get him out of the frame."

"When will that be, now?" Brad barked.

"Whoa there. Now let me examine you." Methodically, taking his time, he checked the toes and legs. "Nothing. The hand. Brad has something. Shoulders. Maybe something there too, a little bit, but let's not mention that today. Let's keep this under control," Irv thought.

"Fine," Dr. Frank said, smiling down at the man he'd known so long. "Rest, relax—hear? That's done this. Take one day at a time—no questions and no promises. Keep it up."

With a chill Irv knew Brad would say what they always said, giving him credit for nature's small healing, seeing this as the beginning, not the end. He would hear the promises he always heard at this time. "Whatever you say, Irv. Thank you. Thank you. I'm going to do just exactly what you say. I'll lick this, you'll see. Anything you want me to try, anything, I'll try." He saw the tears in Brad's eyes. "Whatever you want me to do, I'll try. This is just the beginning. I'm on the way home right now."

Irv looked at Bets, who looked straight back at him, smiling, proud, triumphant. "See, Irv, see?"

He nodded and left them alone with their tiny victory, the biggest one they might ever have.

7

"I must have been awfully scared to feel this good," Brad said exultantly when Bets came in the next afternoon.

"I was pretty worried too, darling," she admitted, knowing how little of her anxiety she was confessing to him and feeling guilty she could not share all his hope.

"Who wouldn't be, Bets, just lying here—feeling nothing? I mean, you give the orders to your hand and nothing happens, nothing at all. Even in this goddamn contraption you forget—decide to light a cigarette, blow your nose, scratch an itch, and then, nothing. Do you know how I realize I have a full bladder, something a child learns almost as soon as he walks?"

"No," she answered softly.

"I break out in a sweat. I have to go to the bathroom and I don't know it until then." His voice had a childlike wonder. "I don't know it—" he paused and his voice dragged "—I don't know it when I've gone."

"Don't think about it now, Brad, especially not now."

"Yes sir," he answered with curt, mock military tones. "Think positive, yes sir. Mission accomplished." Brad laughed. "Hey, let me show off. I've been working this morning and I think I've got a little more already." He saw the pride in Bets' face as she watched his hand flutter and rise—on command. He burst out, "That's willpower, Bets. Sounds nuts, I suppose, but that's what it is—the goddamn physical demonstration of my willpower."

He had come far enough to realize these were wonderful days—hours of reprieve in which he could sleep, without dreams, and wake to delight in the knife-edged shadows on the ceiling caused by the bright autumn light. He knew the trees were changing and could see the cooler outside air in the color of Bets' cheeks when she first came in. Food tasted better, and jokes were funnier, and he found, when the good music station had been left on the pillow receiver by accident, that Mozart never wrote a harsh note. Not tinkly melodies, but beautiful music full of darkness and strength. Brad liked the morning and the night, the afternoon and the evening, for he felt more alive than he ever had since those Saturday afternoons when he ran on the field before the game and the world was wonderful with anticipation. Now, again, he was a man—tough, hard, capable of brave deeds and amazing feats of strength. Lying in bed, Brad still felt tall. He laughed out loud at himself and his ridiculous pride, but he didn't apologize for the way he felt. He had come back from death; he had indeed. Brad showed everyone who came by his room how he could move his right hand, three inches above the bed, and then heave his whole arm from side to side, wildly erratic. When he learned to wiggle his left toe he demonstrated that too, laughing with triumph.

His feats were grotesque but he didn't realize it, and most of those who watched were deluded by his natural exuberance and felt no horror. "Step right up, step right up," he said in comical carnival spiel. "Watch the little fingers dance—they'll wiggle and twitch, do tricks that will astound and amaze you, one and all." He showed off for Bets and the nurses, doctors, and visitors, happy to have become a minor celebrity, a demonstration to be given by the hospital director before the trustees on their annual tour. One day the mayor stopped by, and a little item in the hospital paper grew into a full-length feature in the afternoon paper.

Bets laughed with Brad at the way he evangelized for medical science, as if it were a religion. "You salesmen," she said, "when you take on a product, you think it's the greatest, the absolute most. What a pitch you're making for the hospital. They ought to put you on the road."

"Maybe they should at that."

"Maybe they have. I hear the doctor brought another group in to see you last night."

"And I told 'em." He saw her face and laughed. "All right, they have to be sold. I didn't know what went on here at Dunston Memorial until I landed here. It could happen to them and they ought to know it, to realize what we need. Sure I sell 'em, tell them how many people went to work on me, how much it costs, what they can do."

Bets shook her head in wonder.

"That's a wifely look." He chuckled.

"You astonish me. Here you are like this and you don't turn inside yourself. I would. I'd get dark and deep and interior, but you turn inside out, expose yourself, and reach out to people. I bet you know a hundred people in the hospital."

"I like people."

"And they like you." She smiled. "It's wonderful, you know. You are truly an inspiration."

"Of course." He laughed at her and himself. "Now you go home. I must rest. I'm entertaining the B'nai B'rith tonight."

Brad watched the people as much as he could while they watched him. There was a student nurse who wept with pity, and a shadow touched Bets' face at times, but he felt most of the people were with him; like Peg and Pete, they cheered him on, rooting him home, as if he were a football team. Irv did seem a bit cold and distant, so Brad kidded him: "You're a poor loser, Irv. I thought you believed in the old Bowdoin spirit," he teased. "When I demonstrate willpower, you won't believe it, just because you can't bottle it and shoot it into patients."

Brad didn't let himself be irritated by anyone except Judson Ames. He'd always disliked him, although Bets thought Ames was solemn but nice. After one of Ames' visits Brad tried to set her right: "Ames is a spook, honey," Brad said, chuckling. "He started out as a hotshot, but he didn't have it. He just wasn't tough enough so he went to personnel. He's always worried about poor old Charlie or Miss Sparks."

"Somebody has to," Bets said.

"Professionally? Well, perhaps. It's good policy for the

troops, but not for me. Some companies send flowers, but we send Ames, and I'm going to give them hell when I get back for doing that to me. He's for funerals and wakes and retirement luncheons."

Brad saw the discussion made her unhappy and he was surprised once more at the unexpected loyalties women developed. To humor her he tried to be nice when Ames came, every Tuesday at 3:15, bringing Brad's monthly check every fourth week as a special service, assuring Brad the hospitalization hadn't run out—yet—and trying to bring him news of the company. Brad was amused by his idea of what would interest Brad. Ames talked of bowling teams and people in shipping as if they mattered. He didn't have any news of the company because his V.P. didn't mean anything; he didn't know the important decisions until after they were public.

Looking up at Ames, Brad speculated about him. He could remember when Ames had been on the West Coast. Brad was new with the company then and when Ames flew in—even in those days with creaking old planes and no sleep on "the red eye" midnight flight—he was bright-eyed and bushy-tailed, full of ideas. He was a driver, what they used to call a live wire.

Then Brad had wanted to be like Judson Ames, and now he looked up at him—a man now gray, fat, pudgy, and a little sloppy—and was embarrassed. Ames was good-natured to a fault, perpetually sympathetic, his clothes rumpled and just a bit out of fashion. One day Brad asked Ames, "How come?"

"How come what, Hastings?"

"You changed," Brad explained. "When I came to the company you were a driver—and then suddenly you shifted into personnel, kind of slowed down."

"My wife died."

"I'm sorry." He didn't want Ames to go on, but he couldn't stop him now.

"I didn't know her. I guess that's what happened, Brad. I'd been married to the company, the original company man, and I still am because I have to be loyal to something. Perhaps you can understand after this accident. I looked at her. She'd had a bad cold and her heart stopped and I saw her and she was dead. We'd had a home together, had children together, and I didn't know her as well as my territory. It was too late."

Brad wanted to be sympathetic, but he couldn't understand.

That was tough, but it shouldn't have broken Ames—he should have forgotten, lost himself in his work, perhaps married again. Brad wanted to tell him that, but of course he couldn't. Now it was too late for Ames.

Ames finally left, and, as Brad always did after these visits, he started to figure his income and his expenses, making a balance sheet in his mind. Then he stopped, making himself turn away from the tempting columns of figures, having learned how quickly they pushed him into confusion and then defeat. Brad tried not to let himself think of money, learning almost all there was to know about the panic of the men who slid uncontrollably into debt in a few moments of tailspinning fear. He had known men in debt, seen their eyes across his desk, their futile gestures, their hesitant voices; at lunch he had listened to the two-martini schemes of correction, the fantastic arabesques and curlicues they erected against the truth. He'd listened to their plans and, not understanding, he had always nodded, seeing his disbelief reflected in their eyes, knowing they knew he knew they knew.

Now when he tried to add up his bills in his mind, to clock the spinning numbers on the cash register at thirty-two dollars a day—just for the hospital room—to balance those ever-rising totals against the vaguely remembered benefits of the insurance program, he felt fear. Everyone was so vague, protecting him, that it increased his apprehension. How many days? How many dollars? What was covered? How much were the extras? He stopped, knowing there was no end to the figuring. He'd just scurry, a rat in a maze, until he fell exhausted, its exit still a secret to him. He made himself think of this day, this moment. He squeezed the rubber goose they had given him to exercise his puny grip, and he tried to pipe up his courage with its ridiculous squeak.

Brad knew in that part of him that was himself how comfortable, how very understandable, it would be to admit defeat. He could just slide into it, taking it a little easy here, accepting a bit more truth there, giving in, quitting. Nothing big, just the normal corruption. It would be the same as the cheery cop who first accepts the cup of coffee he can't refuse, then the back-of-the-bar shot of whiskey—no harm in that; it's bitter cold out—then the folded bill, a Christmas tip. Everyone else takes that, and then . . . It would be so easy, so natural, to feel like a cripple, to think like a cripple, to accept a cripple's world, live comfortably within the possible, never trying for more. The nearness of discouragement, the imminence of defeat, made Brad feel fragile, breakable, and he found he had to guard himself every minute, for the enemy was always there, unexpected.

The sudden wave of despair came just when he felt victory. He had the silly rubber goose, yellow and flexible, borrowed from the children's ward, placed in his right hand. Since he couldn't see his hand with his head bound by its steel halo, he could hear the squeak that meant he had commanded a squeeze and that pressure had commanded force. The order, the nerves telling the muscles, the effort, as hard as lifting a hundred-pound bag of potatoes, resulted in only the ridiculous chirp of the baby toy. This day he did it. Not once, but twice, and three times, again and again. Twelve times, thirteen cheery squeaks, fourteen. On and on, pushing himself, trying more and more. Another squeeze, twenty-three; another squeak, twenty-four. He tried, giving everything he had, remembering the first hot fall days of practice and the charges against the dummies with the rasp-throated coaches and the red dizziness of weariness and heat and effort and he tried again, with every muscle, to squeak the goose—thirty times.

He lay there, not moving, but feeling as if he'd stumbled and fallen, exhausted, to the ground. He could almost smell the grass and the black dirt and the dampness of the soil. And then, in this moment of victory—thirty-three times he had squeaked the rubber goose—Brad felt the wave, black as the ocean, heavy, crushing, beating him down, dragging him under: despair.

A grown man squeezing a silly rubber goose, that was what he had become. Brad fought as hard as he had ever fought to swim up and free himself, not to think of the past or the future, but this task, this minute, this accomplishment. He swore by the gods that he would get well, and he slept. . . .

"How do you feel, Brad?"

"Strong, Bets, strong." He was half awake. He laughed, knowing his words sounded ridiculous, puffed out against the nothing below him as he hung face down in the frame. It was the way he felt now, and she dashed on to the next subject as if his strength weren't the most important thing they could talk about. He talked with her of the children, the church, the neighbors;

relieved she didn't pursue the subject, and when she left, he did his foot exercises—lift, drop, wiggle; lift, drop, wiggle. Then he rested, making himself be patient, not resisting the cage, the invisible prison that held him—which made it impossible to resist, not fighting the nothingness and again feeling strangely strong, for part of his strength was his loneliness. He gloried in his abandonment now, in all the imagined people who lacked faith, and once, just once, he flaunted it before Irv.

"I'm the one who's paralyzed. Me. Alone. And that will make the victory all the more sweet."

"You're not alone, Brad."

"I know what you mean. You and Bets and the nurses and technicians and Pete and Peg and everyone else. No, I'm not alone, and yet I am."

"I guess we are all alone," Irv grunted. "How's that for a profound thought?"

"Pretty good, as a matter of fact, but it's all new to me." Brad paused. "I never felt alone as a kid. I've always liked people—my parents, the other kids—I was never a loner. You know, I always thought a loner was a weak man."

"Perhaps he is. I've been one and I've come to wonder."

"We cross courses." Brad laughed quickly and then went on, his words probing as they never had before. "Loneliness is strength, and to depend on yourself to find what's in you and use it is good, damn good. I'm alone, particularly alone, and I rather like it, being free of people."

When Irv left, Brad thought about it. He'd had the morning when there was no mail—not a single card—and had survived it. He'd hardly realized that the flowers had all withered and been removed. He was used to Bets' once-a-day visits, and Irv came only every other day. Pete had missed last week entirely, but since it was to be expected, Brad didn't let it get him down. "You know the kidney transplant in three West?" he asked his wife, laughing. "Well, I was jealous of him because he's getting all the attention now. I was sore, and sore as hell, then I realized why. You go kind of nuts being this long in a hospital. I sent him a note."

"If only he wouldn't be such a nice guy," Bets thought, desperately laughing with him. "If only he'd let go—cry, get mad, face the facts and be discouraged, the way he ought to be." Brad's courage wasn't an inspiration anymore, it was a nightmare. And bad as Brad's tragic charade was, making her feel torn between optimism and despair, Bets felt more of a piece since the accident than she ever had before in her life. She was the home, she, alone. Brad depended on her for love and support, and she was proud, so proud, she could give it. To the children she was the head of the family, the cement that held them all together. She had to manage. It was a challenge, an exhausting, wearing job—and it was a comfort to know the importance of her love, the importance of herself. There was no doubt in her days now. She knew what to do: manage the home, visit her husband, make sure she rested and ate so she could do both jobs evenly, cheerfully.

Matty was the one who saw it. Once she had said, "Bets, I envy you. Being a woman, not a chauffeur, tea pourer, fund raiser, but a woman." Bets knew others felt the same way, and yet there were moments when she saw a woman lean her head against her husband's shoulder, when a man made a decision, when a single touch between husband and wife was so casual, so encompassing and intimate that it was all there was to sex—then she longed with a sudden dizzy pain for the old dependence she had so resented a few months ago.

Each day followed a similar day, and she came to her husband's room, carrying her head high, proud, poised, and each day he showed off his new accomplishment. "Watch my right hand, honey." He'd strain and the hand would suffer an obscene convulsive seizure. "Hold your hand right over mine, hon. It'll jump and touch yours. See?"

Bets refused the tears, making herself smile. He was so very proud and there was so very little reason for pride.

"Hold your hand up, darling," Brad commanded. "Make me work; make me reach for you."

She never knew quite what to do at those times. Hold her hand up to make him work or down where he could really touch it—at the same level each day. She knew her face revealed her guilt, and she realized he didn't notice it, for he saw only what he wanted to see these days.

Bets walked out of the hospital, making sure she didn't hurry, moving gracefully, smiling at the nurses and the patients getting well, appearing as brave as her husband, acting as if the happy music, the bright ways, the cheerful staff, were all sane, that Brad could possibly will his miracle. And yet she now knew the truth and would never get away from its coldness, hard in the center of her like a dead baby. Her husband, her Brad, was a quad. He would never get well.

If only, if only, if only. If only truth were not truth. If only there was make-believe. If only she had not asked him to take the morning plane. If only she did not feel disloyal, the worst thing a woman can feel, because she did not have faith in her husband's power to overcome truth.

She knew and her mother knew, nodding over their cups of coffee, that each day was the same, that he wasn't going to get better, that he'd have to make do with what he had now. She wasn't surprised when Irv called her and asked her to be in Brad's room at four o'clock so that they could all have a little talk. . . .

Irv faced Bets across the frame, studying her face, trying to see just how it was different from what it had been in the spring, failing, confused by the memory of her and the fact of her new familiarity. Yet she was different, a bit finer, older, but not drawn. There was a feeling of strength, almost of pride, fighting against a half-seen shadow of anxiety. He tried to smile comfortingly and, knowing he failed, looked down at Brad. His patient's face, sunk into its unnatural position, held rigid and shaved only every other day, was broader, flatter, and yet it was harder—partly because of the rigidity of the frame, partly because of what he had seen and felt. Its expression was still gay, somehow gallant, but it was not carefree, and never again would it be merely pleasant. There were lines in it now. Irv wondered if his own face had changed in these months, if he too looked different to them. "We've got to have a talk." Irv felt as if his words were abrupt, falling to the floor like jagged pieces of metal. No one answered and he plunged on: "It's time for the fusion."

"What does that mean?" Brad asked.

"You know. We talked about it. We go in and fuse the spine, as I explained. Fix your neck to make it rigid so it can support itself, get you out of this damned frame."

"You said you'd do that after all possible movement has returned."

"I didn't think I said it quite that way." Irv even tried to smile. "Like a doctor, I hedged. I think I said when most of the immediate motion has returned."

"Doesn't it mean the same thing?"

"Brad, this isn't a question of having faith in you. You'll do all that's expected of you and more. Lots more. But it's time we fuse, get you sitting up, operate on your hand so you can turn that squeeze of yours into a pinch, making use of what we've got."

"A pinch?" Brad asked.

"Yes. We can take these tendons here"—Irv took Brad's flabby, soft-fingered hand—"and hook them up so these two fingers, your first ones, can press against the thumb."

Brad looked at him and snorted, "Big deal."

"It is, you know, it is," Irv plunged on. "It may not seem like much now, but don't forget it. We can give you a pinch, and you have enough muscle in your shoulder to make good use of it."

"A pinch," Brad snorted scornfully.

"It's one thing man has that few animals have; none that have it like we do. It's the other end of the brain. With the pinch you can turn a page, turn on a radio, choose a fork or a spoon. It makes a lot of difference, Brad."

"Not enough for me, Irv. I want more than that." He laughed. "Although I guess you have a right to be proud of it. It's a pretty tricky operation."

"No, not really." Irv's voice was sad. "I'm not selling this, you know." He felt the anger of frustration and he wanted to hit Brad for turning him down, for turning down all he had to offer. How could he make him see that the pinch was something worthwhile, the thing that could save him? He stared down at Brad, and his patient stared back, angry that his doctor had so little to offer, a pitiful little pinch. At last he spoke.

"Does this mean County?"

"Yes." Irv looked at Bets and then back at Brad.

"Oh no," Bets gasped, and Irv looked back at her in surprise. "What's the matter?"

"It's a poorhouse, sort of, isn't it?"

"Sort of. For some, but not for Brad. County is a chronic-disease hospital for him. Brad isn't an acute case anymore. When we've fused, we've done what we can here. County is the next stop before going home." They were all quiet.

"Let's have a moment of truth," Brad said softly.

"Brad."

"No, Bets, let's be honest."

"I have to be," Irv said, relieved that the time for acceptance had come for discussing the world of the quadriplegic, hoping he could say the words that would make it as easy as possible.

"Just how much is your bill?"

"Nothing."

"Don't give me that—I have insurance."

"All right. Whatever the insurance lists for this. Now forget it."

"Bets, how much have the hospital bills been?"

"You're not to worry."

"Goddamn it, Irv, make her talk to me." His voice was a snarl. "I'm her husband and I pay the bills and I'm responsible. I'm sick of being babied about this. I've let myself be because I have to get well and I have to be here. Now tell her to tell me what it is."

"I don't know, Brad. The insurance has paid for most of it."

"Did it pay for the special nurses?"

"No."

"How much were they?"

"About nineteen hundred dollars."

"Savings?"

"Yes."

"Now, Brad, this doesn't do any good."

"You said we had to be truthful."

"Yes, but not about this."

"About what?"

"Your condition. The fusion. How much motion you've gotten back."

"Irv, you may know medical facts, but I'm going to show you what I can do, fused or unfused. I've gotten back more motion than you expected."

"As much as we expected, Brad," Irv said softly.

"More than you expected. I know what you thought—I read it in your eyes."

Irv felt dizzy as he realized Brad was still going on with the illusion. He tried to speak carefully: "You've done well, Brad, but it hasn't been a miracle, goddamn it." Irv felt the anger come into his own voice and was shocked at himself.

"How much have the bills been? The whole thing—drugs, frame, therapist, lab, the whole bit." His voice spat out the questions, cold, hard.

"Nearly five thousand, perhaps six. We don't really know yet."

"Major medical paid eighty percent of the first five thousand?"

"That's right."

"We had to pay a thousand for the first eight weeks, not counting nurses."

"Yes," Bets said softly.

"It's twelve weeks. What have you been doing—printing money?"

"No. Savings, the bonds." She tried to smile. "This was the rainy day, dear."

"It sure was." Brad was silent, then he asked Irv, "Can I go to County without the fusion?"

"No."

"You think I've got to have it?"

"I know you do." He hesitated. "You have to accept the facts."

"The financial facts, Irv, that I can't afford to stay here."

"Yes you can, dear." Bets rushed out the words. "If you need to stay here, we can swing it."

"But the doctor says it won't do any good."

Irv shook his head. "You make it sound like a betrayal. Brad, you're a quadriplegic—you knew that from the beginning."

"I know I made my right hand move. I know that. My foot—I made that move. And my shoulder. They all move now."

"That's good, Brad, very good. You've got courage and there's lots you can do with those movements, but there aren't going to be new movements." He heard Bets sob and he went on: "It won't do any good to try the impossible. You've got to live within the possible."

"Well, I'm used to a lot being possible, Irv, a hell of a lot, and I'm not going to give up, to settle for the squeak of a damned rubber goose."

Angry at each other because they were angry at truth, the doctor and his patient glared at each other. "I'll operate Friday."

"Good. At these prices I'd better get out of here." Brad tried to grin and almost made it. "Look, Irv, I understand. It can't be easy for you and I know you have to do what you have to do, but I have to believe what I have to believe. Do you really want me to quit?"

Irv looked at Bets and she closed her face to him and he looked back down at Brad. "You're not a quitter—that's for sure." He left the room, wishing that goodness were good enough.

8

Brad heard the empty "drumpt" of the garbage barrels being returned to the courtyard, the rattle of dishes on carts, the chatter of the nurses changing shift, and he awakened fast, as if he could escape the frame, swing his legs—so short a time ago hard with muscle, and now white, flabby, pendulous—down to the floor so that he could stand up, stretch, go to meet the day. The sounds were familiar, even the illusion that he could arise, but there was a difference—the taste of fear, bitter as metal, on his tongue. Opening his eyes, Brad traced the acid tongue of fear back to his knotted stomach, enjoying the sensations that proved he wasn't yet tranquilized, a drugged thing on which they would operate this morning. They couldn't understand why he had not accepted the pill last night, why he never wanted to take drugs, even when he had leg cramps or the pains shooting through his back, the man-breaking grabbing of a giant hand. . . .

"You always wanted Novocain to get your teeth filled," Bets said, laughing. "I can't understand why you won't take something now."

"You tell her, Irv."

"He's stubborn."

"Hell, you make it sound childish. It isn't." Not able to look at them to see if they understood, Brad had tried to explain. "Pain's one of the few things I've got that's mine. I mean, it's something I can fight. I can't do much fighting, but when I don't have the happy pills, I can at least feel and resist what I feel."

"All right, Brad, I understand," Irv had answered quickly, and Brad wondered if he were being humored. Bets didn't understand it at all; he knew that. To her feminine mind his resistance to pain-killers was a stupid male gesture—gallant, perhaps, but foolish. She knew, with woman's eye constantly on the practical, just how much of a gesture it was—and she had little hunger for symbols.

Brad stared at the familiar ceiling, longed for a cigarette, and defeated the longing. Another victory. This morning he was especially grateful for the lonely moments in the gray light he usually hated. Most days he was anxious for the comfort of routine, the sweeping on of events, each an insulation from thought. Today he felt like hoarding time, using it to prepare himself, mobilizing the will, which had to make a difference during the operation, had to.

He gathered his blanket of time about him, a warm comforter of solitude, but it was torn from him.

"A very good good morning to you, Mr. Hastings."

"Never mind breakfast this morning, Millie."

"Aha. Of course; in fact, you can't even have water. Not even gin. The operation, you know."

"I know."

She laughed, but Brad didn't joke as he usually did. "I'd like a few minutes longer by myself."

"Yes, but it can't be." Her voice was understanding. "We're late now and you've got to be fixed up for a busy morning."

He tried to pull within himself but couldn't find a private place as his rectal temperature was taken by the nurse, who efficiently emptied his bladder at the front at the same time. His blood was sampled by a chirping laboratory technician—"My, you're a cheery one, Mr. Hastings." He was prepped and shaved—he even met the anesthesiologist, who introduced himself as if they were going to a cocktail party.

"This is the most socialist hospital I've ever been in."

"Don't let the trustees hear that, Mr. Hastings. They're conservative businessmen. Republicans all."

When Irv dropped by a few minutes later, already in surgical greens, Brad asked him, "Doesn't anyone ever look sad, even serious, around here?"

"Yes, but it is against hospital policy, Brad."

"Lord, everyone who comes in here jokes. Even with this damned frame, everything."

"It's your salesman's personality."

"I play it big, huh?"

"Yes, Brad." Irv smiled down at him. "It's good, and that helps, on the whole."

"As long as I face facts, huh?"

"Yes, Brad. We'll do a good job today, but you know there won't be any miracles."

"You mean I won't take up my bed and walk."

"I'm afraid not."

"Well, Irv, I may just surprise you some."

"If you do I won't be mad," Irv answered tolerantly.

Brad's voice rose: "There is a thing called the will to live. You'll admit that, Irv?"

"I'll admit that—every surgeon will. It does make a difference."

"Well, I've got the will to live, and I don't call this living. I want more and I'm going to get it."

"You'll go as far as you can, Brad," he said softly, "further than anyone else in the same spot. This operation today is the beginning."

"OK, Irv." He hesitated, then said, "Good luck, roomie." He saw Irv start at the antique word they had never used in college and was surprised that he had used it. Irv didn't say anything, just balled up a fist and tapped him on the chin in a manly gesture of companionship, and left.

Things speeded up. Brad became a piece of timber torn from a riverbank by a spring flood, carried away, resisting and turning, out of control, hurried along to a destination he didn't know, unable to stop, even to pause, to contemplate what was happening. He was given the needle, removed from the frame, handed onto another table before he could even taste his freedom, strapped down, covered and bound, rolled under a dozen strange ceilings and the unfamiliar arches of doors he could not see, until he lay beneath huge, mirrored lights, a bright giant eye, still trying to remain himself, to will a victory, and then drifting away, drug bound, becoming a thing, thoughtless, will-less—without senses, without consciousness, without pain, a thing. Brad fought back in the operating room, consciously, secretly, trying not to become a thing. At first he used cunning, joking with them: "Tell me, Senior Resident, does Dr. Frank really do his own operations? I know he sends out his own bills."

"I wish he didn't, sir. We just stand around, never get a chance to practice."

"That's too bad." Brad laughed with mock sympathy. "Too bad." Seeing their expressions, he knew he was keeping up the pose and he was proud of that. Still a person, not a thing. And then somehow they were all busy and he was lying there under a great eye of light, bound as if he could move, then turned dispassionately, a thing flipped over by a dozen hands, suspended face down. He still felt the eye on his neck, exposing his vulnerability. He refused to go under. Brad kept his eyes open and had the satisfaction of hearing Irv Frank say, far away, "Is he out yet?" and the distant answer, "Not yet." He waited for them to be angry—or worried, but they were neither. They sounded so damned sure he would go under, that it was inevitable.

Finally it seemed logical to Brad, proper—and a relief—to relax. To be just a thing and to forget the foolish pose. Slide under, relax, deliver yourself to them. There was no public face to prepare now, no damned rubber goose to squeak. Now he could allow himself to become a thing, a body to be worked on. His will was no longer important. He was not important. He was it, a thing on which they would work.

Brad slept. . . .

Bets sat, alone, in the cheery sun-room. She could not stop thinking, could not succeed in shutting out either her apprehension or her hope. The operation could not be routine for her, for all surgery was a brutal knifing that broke the laws of nature. She rose, tearing at the handkerchief in her hand, and paced to the window, then back to the sofa. A necessary brutality to cut Brad, perhaps, but it must be a gamble: if there were no danger—of a mistake, of infection, of something going wrong—why all the ritual, the years of surgical training, the special team, the careful precautions? This slicing of flesh might be a casual morning's employment to Irv Frank, but to her it was obscene. She rose again and sat once more, less prepared for this morning of waiting than she had expected. The sun was too warm and the odor too sweet—the flowers reminded her of funerals, not of health, dead flowers cut down to die and stuck into vases. Bets stared out the glass wall three floors above the ground, at first seeing nothing, then noticing the treetops, an ocean of green leaves moving, light and shadow, blue-green and black, yellow and brown. The day was so full of life going by, outside, and an emotion overcame her that was stronger than logic. "If life was so good," she thought, frightened, "bad must inevitably come to balance it, the beautiful and the ugly, the victory and the defeat."

A man shuffled in, not old, but gray. She watched him shamelessly. His weight loss had come too fast and his neck skin hung turkey loose. His hair, thin and gray, was uncombed, and he shuffled, aware of her but not caring, to the television set, which he clicked on without noticing the station, sitting dutifully before the toothpaste grin of the MC and his portion of cued laughter.

Bets shuddered and had a treacherous thought: "Would it be better if Brad died on the table upstairs?"

"Hey, honey, you look as if you lost your best friend."

Bets looked up in horror at the old man she saw in the corridor each night she visited Brad. She always passed him, guiltily looking away from the shape of the stumps of legs casually covered by a sort of apron and the grotesque right hand with all the fingers gone. Now he was rolling over to her in his chair with a jumble of wheel squeaks and an old man's cheery cackle. He skidded up in front of her, laughing. "I can really handle her, can't I? A regular Barney Oldfield. Can't keep me in bed, they tell me. Get up by myself." He laughed again and she tried to smile with him, trying not to see his nose, swollen by age—and too many drinks, she'd bet—the pendulous ears, the straggly, white moustache, the cock-eyed halo of white hair.

"How are you today?" she asked prissily.

"Today I'm just fine, fine," he bellowed. "And how are you? How's he doing?" He nodded back down the corridor.

"He's being operated on."

"Neck?"

"Yes, they're fusing it."

"Good," the old man said, nodding his approval. "Get him out of that damned contraption, on the road back. He's got a rough time, a quad, but I'll bet he'll make it OK." He cackled again.

"Look at me: sawbones gave up a dozen times—so'd the family—but I'm too tough." He thumped his chest and Bets thought his virility nasty. He ought to go hide, she thought, for he was a freak. There were no fingers on the hand he waved in her face; he needed a new upper plate; his body was a battered, bloated casing for organs that were surely swollen and misshapen—except for a sturdy heart, which must thump like a dynamo. "He must have that," she thought bitterly, and was ashamed of herself for resenting his healthy heart.

"Feel my muscle." He whirled around and presented his right arm. "Go ahead—a girl can trust me these days," he said, chuckling and looking at her with bright eyes. "Touch it—you gotta get used to us cripples, a queer lot and proud. Feel that muscle."

Carefully she touched the iron-hard bicep.

"Guess my age."

"I couldn't," she lied. "Sixty-two?"

"Eighty-three," he answered, and she was indeed surprised. "Yep, last May—gonna make ninety." The humid warmth of the sun-room almost made her sick. "He going out to County?"

"I don't know."

"Sure he is," the old fellow said and leaned his torso forward confidentially. "Better than it used to be, much better—perhaps more young fellows do it. Bet that man of yours has got pull."

"Oh no, I don't know." Bets felt as if they were talking about a world she'd never heard of."

"He a lawyer?" he asked slyly, and when she shook her head he sat back. "Too bad. We could use a lawyer." With terrible certainty the old man added, "We'll get one yet. Gotta go. Be seein' you at County." He whirled about and rolled off, leaving Bets the memory of a spirit that would not be defeated—and the slight odor of urine.

She was sure she would be sick, but she won control of herself and made herself sit tall, still, in the lovely sun-room, not seeing the lovely flowers, waiting, envying her husband his anesthesia, the pain-killer he had probably resisted until the end.

Upstairs, the neck—not Brad's neck now, just another neck—was exposed and vulnerable. Shaved and draped, the white skin was forlornly nude. A line was drawn down it—quickly, apparently carelessly, by Irv Frank. The line became a cut only when the blood stood up above it, a brilliant red. Blood and banter between professionals who joked because they had to protect themselves against their own arrogance. Efficiently they stripped back the flesh, peeled the layers back like a drawing in a textbook, clamped off and anchored out of the way so there was a long trough filling with black blood, which was sopped up and the sponges counted when they were tossed on the sheet in the corner.

"There it is."

No surprise, for it was just as it had been on the X-ray plate: between the sixth and seventh, the neck unnaturally set off, a child's tower of building blocks ready to topple. Man could not set it right without further damage to the nerves, the message paths that made muscles useful and the brain an obeyed command post.

Brutally, intentionally working like a sloppy whittler, Irv Frank cut slivers of bone from the neck and let them fall across the joints that once had allowed his roommate, without thinking about it, to stand or sit, roll over or reach, twist and turn in a hundred ways, yawn, stretch, toss back his head with laughter, duck under a low tree limb—movements thought of only when they were forever impossible. Careful only that he did not jar the neck, Irv Frank operated. His movements were not delicate, as if they were unsure; he worked with familiarity and ease, his fingers stubby and dexterous, creating the stew of bone chips and blood that would fuse the neck into a solid column, which would protect the few nerve lines still running from brain to body.

Irv Frank did not force himself to think that this was not Brad, for it wasn't Brad to him. It was an operation on a neck, a job to be done. He worked with confidence and pride, knowing exactly what to do. He taught the resident across from him with words, but more by deeds, by example. Irv was in command, sure of the respect of the nurses and the anesthesiologist, who knew the secrets of the operating room, who gave their respect only to the few within the club which was his profession.

At last Irv finished his job: he had chipped and slivered Brad's neck, destroying it forever, making solid what was meant by God to be supple, finishing the damage that had started when Brad stepped back, proud of having lifted the car, and had been knocked back, his head against the rock. Now the event was complete and there could now be no false hopes, no illusions. Brad would be able to leave the frame, but he would be a quadriplegic for the rest of his life, hardly able to move his arms or his legs. There never could be hope for or any repair of his fused spine. For a moment Irv saw the neck as part of a man, of Brad, his "roomie," who was sentenced to imprisonment within his body.

The suety flesh was drawn together, the incision gutted, the cast slapped on—the job was done. There had been no miracle cure, no moment of high drama, no godlike hand on the knife—just a piece of work that had to be done, had to. Without that brutal breaking of the spine, Brad would inevitably die of a slight wrench, a tremor, a twitch. Now at least he would survive.

Irv Frank followed his patient into the recovery room, saw that he was set up, left his instructions, washed, dressed, and now, feeling the weariness, flexed his shoulders as a batter might after sliding into third on a close play after a triple to the right. Slowly he walked to Bets, plodding through the corridors and then across the sun-room, not seeing the other people, only Bets, who looked up at him, not rising, sitting still, her hands in her lap, the way she had sat on the Accident Ward bench so long ago.

"He's fine."

"You're all done?" she asked stupidly.

"Yes," Irv answered, smiling.

"It wasn't long. You weren't able to"—she took a breath—"fix anything?"

"We fused the neck," he said quietly. "That was what we went in to do."

Bets was struck by the intimacy of the phrase, how sexual it was to say "went in." This man had violated her Brad's body.

"Bets. You knew there wasn't any chance that we'd perform any miracles."

"Who gets your great medical miracles?" She stood too fast and almost fell. "Who do you dole them out to?"

"Oh, Brad got one," Irv Frank answered seriously. "Understand that and remember it. The medical books still say that a man with a neck broken like his is doomed. It is indeed a miracle he's alive. The result of good luck at the scene and getting to the hospital without more damage . . ."

"Did they make it worse, taking him? Would he have walked if—?"

"Stop it," Irv interrupted, cutting across her questions. "Brad has had good care. He didn't die and he won't until it's his time.

He'll survive for years. In fact, he'll be watched over far more carefully than you or I and he may live longer than both of us. And he can have a pinch."

"You say he can live?"

"Yes, live."

"Live?" Bets' face twisted into a travesty of a smile. "Live?" She leaned toward Irv Frank's face. "You saved him; now you tell me, Irv Frank, you tell me. He'll live, for what?" She sobbed and stepped past him. "For what?"

9

Bets drove halfway home, then off the highway and out by the river. Not crying, not thinking, just driving, concentrating on keeping the car in control as it curved along the road. At last she stopped at a lonely phone booth and, feeling strangely exposed in the glass box, called home to her mother, who seemed disappointed in the good news that the operation had gone so well. She had obviously prepared for the worst. Bets explained that she was going back to the hospital to wait for Brad to wake up. She knew it was silly, but she was going to do it, and her mother, making herself very clear with pauses, resigned herself to her daughter's eccentricity. Bets swung the car out of the turnoff and drove thoughtfully back to West Dunston, again aware of all the life around her—the cars going somewhere, the trucks with destinations, the river craft with ports, and as she neared the hospital, the pedestrians who walked with purpose, busy men and women.

Brad had returned to his room without his frame. Instead he wore a huge plaster collar, and the crib sides on his bed were up as if he could rise, even in delirium. It was hospital routine; it was done. He was asleep. Bets motioned for the special nurse to stay in her chair by the window, where the light was good for her knitting. Bets took the straight chair, sliding it gently on its padded feet to where she could sit and watch Brad's face. She felt she had to see his face when he woke, the moment when he knew there had been no miracle. She belonged with him then.

Bets studied her husband's face, noticing the small bandages where the tongs had been removed, the different aspect of his jowls now that his neck, which had been stretched for so many weeks, was now packed in plaster as white as new snow. His bed was high, and she could see only one eye and the familiar profile —nose like a beak and the chin thrust up, a harder face than she remembered it before the accident, and she wondered if it were because of something that had happened to him the man, or just the body, or a bit of both.

She waited, watching, her hands folded in her lap, her ankles crossed, as the room grew dark. The nurse, making signs that she was going to eat, tiptoed out. Bets didn't put on the light, but then changed her mind when she realized that she had to if she was to see Brad's face that first naked minute. She twisted the hospital floor lamp so that the light hit the ceiling and bathed the room in reflected light, an artificial twilight not unlike the melancholy gloaming she had both loved and feared as a girl. Bets stared for a moment out at the town clicking on its lights, and then, feeling he had wakened, she turned back quickly to Brad. He had not. Only the shadow of pain had crossed his face, a grimace, a frown, a fear, chased away by a drug, swept from the face, which was left heavy and stunned. Not peaceful, not in sleep—unconscious. Bets sat again and waited, gratefully accepting the cardboard cup of tea brought by the nurse, warming her hands on its sides, waiting and sipping, making it last while she watched the familiar face, which could not toss or turn but stared up at the ceiling like an old churchman covered in stone on the top of his vault, his face forever heavenward, his hands forever crossed.

She tried to conjure up what she expected from him so that she could play out in her mind the coming scene and the ones that must follow and therefore learn her role as trusting, understanding wife. She imagined what she could: Brad, angry, raging at the world, cursing his fate, and she at his side, fiercely supporting him; Brad, his defenses destroyed at last, waking to weep, a strong man crying, needing her strength, depending on it; Brad, cynical and bitter, twisted by hatred, able to trust only her; Brad, hopeful still, against all logic, confident there would be a miracle, needing her faith and the sureness of her love against the day when he would face the truth.

Bets shook her head, ashamed of her fantasies, seeing herself before Brad as the heroine. Looking at his body, which could never wrinkle a sheet, she felt despair, for there was no way to imagine herself in his position. She could not comprehend what it must be like; she could not even feel a hint of it when she woke early and lay alone in her bed, making herself rigid, staring at the ceiling, trying so hard in this way to be with him. Feeling cold, she knew there was no way of predicting how he would wake, no way to be sure she would have the particular brand of love he would need.

She sat so still, staring at the face, gray as stone, still hardly moving, and she missed the moment, for she realized he was awake.

"Brad, I'm here."

"Where?"

She rose and reached him before the nurse did, strangely pleased at the short race won. "Right here beside you. I've been waiting." She looked down at him and he grinned at her, a mask as casual as he would have worn to meet a roommate's sister up for a football weekend a thousand years ago.

"Irv said it went well, very well."

A pause and then a flat, "All right." Pleasant enough.

"Haven't seen you, Nurse."

"I'm Miss Dexter, Sarah Dexter."

"New England?" Brad smiled, a salesman again.

"Newburyport."

"Related to Lord Timothy Dexter?"

"Old Frozen Face actually giggled," Bets thought angrily.

" 'Fraid not, sir, just clam diggers in my family." Brad laughed with her, and when he turned to Bets his tone was just the same, as if nothing had happened.

"How do you feel?" she asked solemnly.

"Oh fine, for a guy with a pain in the neck." He grinned that same covering grin. "You eaten dinner?"

"No, not yet."

"You'd better. Had a long day, I bet."

She looked at him, wanting to cry and not wanting to let him see her crying, wanting to joke with him and wanting to scream at him. Why was he so nothing? Didn't he know? Didn't he realize? She swallowed and spoke: "You look different without the frame. I'll bet it feels better."

"I'll miss that like a hole in the head," he said easily, too easily.

"I think he'd better rest, Mrs. Hastings." Bets stared at the nurse, resenting her dismissal, and looked down at Brad. She knew he had to struggle against the drug, which was dragging him down again, back to unconsciousness, but he still wore the mask, the casual smile, the eye cocked in amusement, the expression of constant pleasantness, and she hated it, the pose of the nice guy. Bets was suddenly fearful of her own violence, her momentary hatred of Brad. She wanted to rip the mask from his face, reveal him to her, to himself. She opened her mouth and said, "Good night, darling." Brad winked and went to sleep, almost smiling.

Bets drove home stunned, went through the ritual of having coffee with her mother, telling her the things that had to be told, answering the questions her mother had the right to ask and she didn't want to answer. Then she slept. That morning she drove again to the hospital, sure that Brad would now be changed, but he was the same, clearly as friendly to her as he was to the day nurse, the aide, the doctors, giving not one hint of how he felt. For days Bets waited for the reaction, which had to come sometime, and each visit became a test. How long could he suspend his reaction? How long could he make believe there was no truth to face? She would stand by his bed and he would be the same —smiling, casual. Only his cast changed, grew gray from the dirt that was carried even in the cleansed hospital air.

Not once did Brad allow her to say anything that meant anything. They chatted and they smiled and they said nothing. He kept a door shut between them.

When a visit from the children was suggested again, Brad agreed as if it were unimportant. He didn't seem to care and permitted the visit as if it weren't worth arguing about.

The children weren't casual about the decision. They received the news that they could visit their father as if it were an excursion. Pris danced and darted around, planning the dress she'd wear, and Eric, laughing, let the questions tumble out of him: he was going to be a doctor—could he see the operating room, an X-ray machine, the frame Daddy had been in? When they turned down the corridor to their father's room, they grew solemn, moving together and back against their mother, almost tripping her.

Bets felt guilt and anxiety. She was, she knew, using the children as weapons to batter down Brad's defenses. He'd have to face them honestly. They moved closer, passing by the admiring gaze of the nurses, and then the three marched softly into Brad's room, silent until he called out, "Hi, kids." They ran to him and then stopped, unable to comprehend that he could not turn to them, fearful of hurting him, needing so desperately to touch him, to have him hold them. Tears ran down Bets' cheeks as she got chairs and perched the two on them so they could look down into their father's face—and so he could look at them.

"My, you're tall," Brad said and chuckled.

"On chairs we are," Eric said, smiling.

"Does the collar hurt?" asked Pris.

"No, not much."

Bets' hands gripped hard at the bottom of the bed, bracing herself for the moment her husband, faced with his children, would surely break.

"Do your legs hurt, Dad?"

"Only sometimes. Cramps."

"Can't you move them at all?"

"Just a few toes," Brad answered calmly, as if the legs belonged to someone else, as if this weren't his son but a tourist passing through.

"I'm going to be a doctor."

"And I'll be a nurse."

"Fine. Fine. How's school?"

"I love Miss Pilo," chirped Pris.

"Girls," Eric snorted. "It's a drag."

"I'll bet you like it secretly," Brad smiled.

"Recess. I like that."

Bets realized that they accepted him, a cripple, as easily as they accepted the fact that he used to shave, drive the car, go to the office, take showers instead of baths, stay up late at night, drink coffee, and do all sorts of other mysterious grown-up things. It was wonderful and it was horrible because they began to talk of camping trips and hikes and projects, which she knew would never happen but which they apparently, Brad included, still had faith in. Suddenly Bets realized that the visit was over and that nothing had been changed. She started to herd the children out and then she went back to stare into her husband's face, to see if it had been marked by the visit. He merely said, "Great kids. See you tomorrow, hon." There was not a hint, in the look of his eyes, in the tone of his voice, that he had been touched. She wanted to slap him awake, make him come out of it, but all she did was to touch his cheek gently and try to cope with the children's chatter as they left the hospital and drove home.

Even Irv found Brad's bland neutrality a challenge. It almost seemed as if Brad, by simply ignoring his condition, was scorning the hospital and its staff's pride in healing. Most of all, this attitude kept Irv at arm's length. At a time when they should be planning a rehabilitation program, perhaps even working with a psychiatrist, they chatted about the news, their friends, the affairs of the hospital, the way commuters might discuss Wall Street, the President's press conference, or the World Series. Brad had been lucky: owing to the fusion, he could turn his head; he even had some movement of his shoulders. There was a harness that would help him feed himself, but Brad would not hear of it—he was going to recover. If Irv didn't have faith in him, that was all right, but there was no need to talk of it. Brad changed the subject every time.

Irv went to the staff psychiatrist, who had made routine visits to Brad. "What do you want, Irv? Your friend doesn't want help."

"I know that, but he needs help."

"Yes." The psychiatrist's glasses glinted as he nodded, bobbing his head up and down quickly. "He needs help, but he isn't ready."

"He isn't a loaf of bread. He's a man. The fact that he won't admit his future, won't accept his need, is proof that he's all the sicker."

"Of course, of course." The glasses bobbed again.

Irv glared in exasperation and stood up. "You mean he's got to come to you before you can do anything?"

"That's exactly what I mean. I can't fight him."

"Humpf. Then you treat only those who are half cured."

"Don't you ever have a patient who knows, really knows, about a carcinoma? There's no doubt of it. An intelligent, ordinarily sensible person, who won't do anything at all?"

"Yes, an uncle."

"What did you do? Knock him down? Cut him open against his will?"

"Of course not." Irv nodded and spoke softly: "I'm sorry. I don't know what I was thinking."

"You know, Irv, it frustrates me too."

Irv knew he had to make Brad just another patient, one who little needed him now. He had to accept the truth: there was no cure for Brad. Yet his years of training and discipline deserted him. He found his mind searching out alternatives, some prognosis that carried hope—and he was ashamed of his weakness. He who told others to face the truth, who counseled the inevitability of facts, should, he told himself, be able to stomach his own medicine.

Irv attempted to comfort himself with work. His schedule was an advantage, bringing new patients with conditions he could correct to replace those who were discharged or beyond further care. His rounds, his office hours, his clinics, his consultations, his papers—all left him with no time to worry about Brad; yet this concern caught him unexpectedly, at odd moments—when he was immersed in the ritual of scrubbing; when he was driving to his apartment late at night, his mind ordinarily absorbed in the satisfaction of controlling the car; when he attended one of the interminable staff conferences that had to be sat through. Thoughts of Brad struck home. And, of course, he had to visit him, for Brad was still his patient.

"How's the doctor today? Making a buck?"

Irv resented Brad's familiarity, feared it, for he could not use the constant defenses of the professional manner—the glances that cut off unwanted questions, the lies that brought false comfort; the polite dismissals could not be used against a former roommate, a present friend.

Irv tried to respond with a smile, nodding hello to Bets, taking Brad's pulse to be doing something. "I have an uncle in the Bronx," he heard himself saying to make conversation. "When I was down on a visit during the holidays, he asked me, 'How's business?' That's a funny thing to say to a doctor, you know. He caught me off base and I mumbled something that he took to mean I was doing OK. Gleefully, he poked me in the ribs. He'd never approved of my going into practice in the suburbs before, but now he chuckled and said, 'Good, good, plenty of gentiles to be sick.' "

They both laughed and then Brad asked, "Why did you come up here to practice? I would have thought you would have stayed in the city."

"I do spend some time at Center."

"I know, but why did you come up here?" Irv studied the chart, not seeing it, somehow angry at the personal question. No patient should know him well enough to ask it, he thought. He had tried to reestablish the proper gulf with rudeness, he told himself, with subtle hints, distance, but Brad was so damned nice—he understood Irv was tired; he made allowances—that you couldn't be rude. After all, Brad had been a friend longer than he'd been a patient; he had the right to ask a personal question and he deserved an answer.

"There was a man here who could teach me something I wanted to know. It was part of my secret program." Irv laughed. "That was why I went to McGill for a year, why I fought to get on at Polyclinic. You know, student surgeons are like barnacles. They attach themselves to the bottoms of good men." He chuckled. "We have a more indelicate way of describing the process of the struggle upward in our profession."

Brad laughed and then spoke with a trace of wonder: "You've carefully calculated each move."

"There's a lot of luck."

"But you planned, figured out where you wanted to be lucky."

"I tried to," Irv admitted. "I was a finagling, ambitious bastard." He hunched over and imitated a diabolical Iago, hoping he could at least entertain Brad. "Not on talent alone do I succeed," he whispered hoarsely. "I'm a graduate schemer."

"You know, I never made a plan about my life, not once, consciously." Brad spoke with wonder, and Irv wondered if this was the time, if he was now going to break the pose. "I never realized it until now. I always knew where I was going. My father and mother may have made plans. I can't ask them now—they're dead—but I'd like to. I guess I was an extension of my father's plan to have a son who went to college, who went into Mother's family business. They never said anything to me—I just went along. It was so easy," he added defensively, "that I guess something was left out of me."

"No," Irv said thoughtfully, "you didn't have to scheme. I did. That doesn't make you worse than I—or better, I suppose."

Bets came in for their visit and suddenly Brad suggested, "Hey, why don't you take my wife out to dinner tonight?"

"With the children?" Irv pushed the question aside with a laugh, realizing Brad wasn't going to be serious. This wasn't the break, not yet.

"No, you know her mother's there. Bets was going down to the tuna-fish club—the coffee shop—tonight. I'd like to buy you both a dinner at the Fireside, on my card."

"I've got my own card," Irv said.

"I don't think we ought to, Brad," said Bets.

"I want you to. It was my idea."

Irv said quickly, "I have a paper to do."

"A couple of drinks and a good steak will do your paper good."

"That's the kind of reasoning I like," he said sarcastically, "no reasoning."

"He's scared of me, Brad," Bets said and laughed. "Alone with me by candlelight, he'd give up his bachelor existence and marry the first nurse he saw."

"Miss Ingrams."

"Yes, Miss Ingrams, moustache and all," Brad said, chuckling.

"I'll never go to dinner now." Irv laughed.

"Yes you will," Brad said. "It would make me happy and we must have happy patients at Dunston Memorial. Look, I appreciate how much you've——"

"Oh God, not that." Irv put his hands up. "Gratitude makes me sick. I'll take your wife to dinner."

"On my card."

"On your card, big shot. Pick you up here at six, Mrs. Hastings?"

"Yes, Doctor, you can supervise my diet."

"Nutrition," Brad cut in. "Let's see—an onion in the martini, lobster, Roquefort, éclair. A good, solid, balanced diet to offset the tuna fish."

Irv waved as he went out the door. "I'll tear up the paper and see you at five fifty-five." He walked along the corridor, head down, wondering where he'd made his mistake, why it was so easy to be professional with everyone else, when he was trapped by Mr. Buchanan in the hall. The administrator, a tall man who had the grace of a giraffe and the personality of a bill collector, had his plastic robin's-egg-blue notebook under his arm. "Well, Dr. Frank," Buchanan said in the tone he used when he tried to sound like one of the boys, "I've been wanting to share a cup of java with you."

Irv Frank conquered the impulse to bark, "Coffee, damn it. Java went out with the Ink Spots." Instead he said, "I have an appointment, but thanks."

"It will only take a minute."

"I'm really busy today, Mr. Buchanan."

The administrator pushed on: "You know that we in administration never interfere in medical matters."

"Never," Irv said wearily, knowing the sarcasm was wasted.

"Of course. But we do need beds. Dr. Follensbee has——"

"Seventeen itchy hysterectomies."

"A joke, but a joke in bad taste." Buchanan continued. "He has operations to schedule and he's on the staff and it's my job to find room."

"Well?"

"M.S. thirty-three."

"Hastings is my patient."

"Well, I mean when there's nothing else that can be done . . ."

"Should I send him home?"

"Oh, now, he needs care, but he's not really an acute case. I mean, Dunston Memorial is aware of its responsibility to the patient who needs immediate care."

"And the chronic patient?"

"Doctor Frank, you've always been on my side on this one: special facilities for special situations." The S's hissed out between his teeth. "I'm surprised to hear you sound like old Dr. Knapp."

"Old Dr. Knapp's got some damned good ideas." Irv marched off, aware of the astonishment in Buchanan's face and pleased at that, but well aware of the fact that the pressure would not be decreased. This was the beginning. And he, who'd always been on the other side of this argument, was in a hell of a position now. He had always argued about wasting beds in an acute hospital on incurables. Brad's days here were numbered. . . .

Irv was still in a black mood when he drove Bets to the Fireside. Bets was amused at how Irv's emotions betrayed his illusion he was a cold man of science. She knew now that Irv Frank cared. Bets suddenly felt that she knew him well, was certain his silence would break in a flood of talk, that she would help by listening.

When they were seated by the window overlooking the pool, when she had pulled off her gloves, accepted his ordering a Gibson—"Dry, very dry"—and waved away the menu for the moment, saying with a smile the doctor's orders would come later, and sipped the crisp, cold bite of the Gibson, she felt a companionship and a quiet that was like the eye of a storm. They would have to talk about Brad, but later. Now was the time to recover their friendship, to rest for a moment and gather their forces for the struggle ahead. She would encourage him by revealing herself. She smiled at her escort and said, "It seems so natural, eating in a place like this. So easy, knowing what a Gibson is, when to eat your salad, if you should guess at the French on the menu. I have to laugh now at how much I had to learn."

"Oh, you weren't born to the purple?"

"Irv, I never in my life thought I'd eat in a place like this."

"And when did you learn how to do all these things?" he asked, raising his glass to her.

"Before I learned what was more important."

"That it doesn't really matter?"

"Yes, that, and that everyone else is looking—or at least a lot of them are. If you act at ease and do something wrong, whumpf, they'll copy you. I know that." She smiled. "I wish I could practice it, wish I still didn't care."

"I know, I know, we haven't grown up—our society, that is." He sipped again. "I'm talking about society—this must be potent."

Bets sipped her drink and they looked around the restaurant at the people, working so hard to enjoy themselves, seeing together the restrained tension in the parents with the three girls, the too-hearty businessman entertaining a customer, the retired couple—her chatter and his alcohol-sullen nods.

"We must have another drink," Irv said. "They all look fat, frustrated, ugly, hateful. God, I wish I didn't have to look at the world."

"And try to figure it out?"

"But how much fun I'd miss, not feeling superior." He smiled and spoke to the red-coated waiter: "Two more—and the menu." They ate and talked and were quiet, sharing good food and a split of wine. Time slowed down. In the soft, uneven light of the sputtering candle, squat in a copper pot, they saw each other differently than they had before.

Irv looked at Bets and saw how young she still was, able to appear beautiful with only soap, water, and a quick line of lipstick. She still had a face that sparkled with delight and she was capable of quick enthusiasm. He responded to her joy in this evening away from care by entertaining her with stories of his family, his tour in the Navy, the times he had waited on table summers at a Catskill resort, and his ambition to spend two weeks driving a trailer truck across the country and back. "Someday I'm going to get a truck-fleet owner as a patient and that'll be my fee." He sat back and spun a great imaginary wheel. "A cigar in my mouth, a cap on my head. That'll be it."

She laughed with him and found herself seeing him as a gentle man. Sweet, that's what he was, surprised she'd never seen this before peeking out of his professionalism. She understood his manner better. He was sad and funny. He could laugh at himself because he knew he was ridiculous—that indeed all men were ridiculous and she felt his compassion when, over the second cup of coffee, he spoke of Brad.

"Bets?" She looked up at him and knew. She nodded. "I'm going to have to discharge Brad and send him to—" he hesitated and then forced himself to say it "—County Home for Incurables."

"I understand. It's what he wants anyway, I guess."

"He'll have to accept the truth there." He paused. "It's a very truthful sort of place." They both traced squares and circles with their spoon handles on the tablecloth. "It has to be," Irv said intensely, "but it isn't the end, damn it. He can start on the road to a good life if he accepts what he has. Just the pinch. That simple ability to push two fingers against the thumb can save him, Bets. It can make him a man again."

"A man?"

"A man," Irv said simply.

"Irv."

He looked up.

"Are you on the staff at County?"

"No." He paused and knew he was not free as he agreed to the masked request. "I'll visit him. They'll let me. I'll still be his doctor and supervise his care."

"Thanks, Irv. That helps."

They stood up together, and when he came over and stood next to her, she touched his hand in thanks. He smiled sadly and nodded with an ancient knowledge, accepting the trap. "So, we'll schedule him, tomorrow, for the end of the week."

"Maybe that will make him face the truth."

"I hope so," Irv said as they walked out of the restaurant and back to their responsibilities. "I hope so. And yet I wonder. Of course it has to be; we know he has to accept it, but can we really resent his having a few days of illusion?" There was nothing else to say, but when they were settled in the intimacy of his sports car, isolated by the dark of night and lulled by the sound of the road, he tried to say more, to justify himself to Brad's wife—and to himself. "You understand, Bets, don't you? We can't get close to patients—it isn't fair to them or to us; it obscures our judgments."

"I understand." And she added, "You have other patients you can help."

"Yes." He drove on. "I wonder why I care so much about Brad."

"Why, he's your friend."

"Of course, of course," Irv said impatiently, "but it's more than that. I've had friends for patients before, but Brad's gotten to me in a different way. I don't know, perhaps I wanted to be God to him, wanted a miracle to prove something to him; he was always so much I wanted to be. I lie awake and wonder, something the surgical personality rarely does, if I resented him or hated him for what he had and I didn't have and so now perhaps I feel guilty that I have so much more."

"I can't believe that."

"Maybe it's just that he's hit the right time," Irv went on without acknowledging her. "I guess I had a pretty fine opinion of myself. I was able to pride myself on my success and forget my failures." He gave a bitter snort. "Bury them." He knew Bets wanted to speak and couldn't and he plunged in, "But Brad isn't dead and you aren't going to let me forget him. He's going to County."

"Is it bad there? Tell me honestly, Irv."

"It's better than it was."

"Oh fine, fine."

"You want honesty." His voice was savage. "All right. I don't know much about County, about the care there. It's a miserable place. I send people there and I go to a clinic there at times, but that's where we send our living failures."

"Irv!" She was shocked.

"You wanted honesty. I'm ashamed, but it's true. I'm so damn busy—we all are. I'm not only at Memorial, you know. I have private patients, go to Center one day a week, teach, do research, am on the staff at the Crippled Children's Hospital and at Community and St. Ignatius and Beth Israel over in Blanford. If there's a broken hip at the Daughters of Miriam Home, they bring it to me."

"I don't know how you do it."

"Ah, that's what I want to hear. Well, I know how we do it: we run, go like mad—sure of our skill, our virtue."

"But there isn't anything you can do for Brad?"

"No simple operation to make everything all right. But I have fused his neck and later, maybe, I'll do some tendon transplants so that he can use his hand, help him with rehabilitation so that he can be more than . . ." He hesitated.

"A vegetable?"

"Yes, a vegetable. You see, Bets, I don't know what I can do because I've been so busy doing other things."

"Helping lots of people."

He snorted, "That's what I thought, but now I have to take another look at my wonderful success. You were the one, Bets, who asked the question. 'Alive? For what?' "

"I was upset."

Irv nodded. "And you should have been. Why do we apologize for good questions? It is a good question. For what? Where do I put him on my scorecard—as a life saved? Saved for what? Do I have a responsibility—remember that word 'responsibility'—for his brain? For his soul? God had him killed. When he hit the rock he was dead according to God and the medical books."

"Irv, don't. You'll only hurt yourself."

"I hurt Brad by saving his life. He knows he'd be better off dead and you know it and I know it and I want you all to be grateful to me." His voice was scornful: "A successful neck fusion."

"It's all you could do, Irv."

"It's all I could do." His voice fell. "But does the responsibility end there? Do I walk away from this one, the way I did from all the others? Do I plant another vegetable and never, not once, have a nightmare or a regret, a wondering or a thought for the living dead for whom I am responsible?"

"You can't kill people, not here, not in our society."

"There are sins of commission and omission, Bets." His voice rasped. "Doing and not doing. Going to extraordinary means to prolong life—for what? Brad's got a marvelous future, unlimited compared to some. You'll see at County. You'll see the 'for whats.' "

"Irv, Irv, I wish I could comfort you."

"I wish you could too, but it isn't that easy. I'm no little boy. I'm a surgeon who saves lives. People think we are haunted by our failures." He grinned bitterly. "It's our successes that ought to haunt us—the Brads who are alive because of 'the miracle of modern medicine.' "

They drove into the hospital parking lot and when he had backed into place, he turned to her angrily, "I shouldn't have talked to you this way. We have a professional relationship with professional fences kept mended for good reason. Doctor-patient. Doctor-nurse. Doctor-patient's family. I should not have talked to you this way."

"But you have."

"I have."

"Irv, don't be angry. There are relationships that are different, needs that are different. We are each of us, well, involved with Brad. If we are to help him we have to know each other; we have to face the truth."

"Easier for us than for him."

"Irv, do you think he'll ever face, recognize, what his real future is and adjust to it?"

"Oh, he knows what his future is, Bets, and he's adjusting."

"He's not—he's running away."

Irv got out of the car and his voice was harsh, bitter: "Brad won't run very far."

10

The nurse was there, busy at him, when Brad woke. Half asleep, he didn't understand what she was doing at first, for the cast held his face rigid and he couldn't see anything but her white shoes and he felt nothing at all. Then he heard the sound of his urine in the stainless-steel duck and he knew then that this nurse, a woman under the starched uniform, had come to his bed, flopped his limp penis into the urinal and, bored, had stroked his thighs in a mock lover's caress to stimulate the nerves that would initiate the flow.

Brad heard the sound of his urine, as a stranger's, feeling nothing, and the rage grew in him, that he, who had once been a man—erect, strong—could have a woman handle him without effect, and gently, with butterfly touches, stroke his inner thighs—so softly, up and down—with the only result a pale stream of piss. He wanted to hit her or scream, and once more he choked down the anger, once again swallowed his bitter frustration, and said, almost lightly, "Nicely done, Nurse."

"You a critic? Like in the newspapers?"

He recognized the voice. It was the pretty one, Miss Bruskin.

"Yes, that's it, a critic of the drama of medicine," Brad answered.

"My, my. I hope I get rave reviews."

"You always do, Miss Bruskin."

The banter was easy and he liked their thinking that he was brave, but it didn't mean anything now, and that's what they didn't know. He said what he ought to say, for the years of training, the hiding yourself in what others thought you ought to be had paid off. But it didn't mean anything. He was pleased, in a vague way, that the masquerade was going so well, even with the children. You said the things you were supposed to say and everyone else did the same. He did everything Irv wanted, not as if he were himself, but as if he were delivering a side of beef to him and saying, "Here, it's yours."

This day, this hour. That was the way he seized control of his life. He discovered that he could not carry the weight of the past or the future on his back, but he could handle a visit, an hour of treatment, one night, one meal pushed into his mouth by a yawning feeder. He became a thing to himself and began studying himself as one would a stranger. He was suspended in time and space, a floating body. It was levitation, a trick, that allowed him to escape from himself.

The doctors who had given him his life controlled his day, his will. He had abdicated his responsibilities as a person. He was free—free of decisions and choices, free to drift within the dimensions of this strange life. Let them move him and turn him, strap him on the tilt board and stand him up—a laboratory specimen pinned to a board; let them poke him and stretch him, open his mouth to their food, and make their pleasant visits.

He had fought them, but not anymore. They had it now, the body, and he, alone, had his—what? His spirit? His mind? His soul? Something, he had something private, something the bastards couldn't touch. Be a good patient, a prison trustee; take their medicines; joke with them; be agreeable, good-natured—but don't let them know you, how much you care or how much you hate.

Nothing bothered him now, Brad told himself, because it wasn't him; he was somewhere else, private, apart, in limbo, invisible to them all. Even this day, this special day, had to be lived through as that other day when he was drugged and the frame taken away, the frame he hated and loved, which had become a part of him until they made his spine—they had broken it against his will—into his own frame, placing him in his own prison, his body. And now they would take off the cast and put on the harness, and he would watch them as if it were happening to someone else—because it was. They couldn't reach him where he was.

Strong. He thought of that as they wheeled him down to the plaster room. He smiled and joked, for he was strong, invulnerable. Ambition made you weak. Fear made you weak. Fear of what? Failure, pain, death. But he felt no fear now. Fear had been experienced in the past by that thing on the table. Now they couldn't touch him, not him.

He laughed at Irv. Dr. Frank in his plaster room, uncomfortable before the good nature of the patient on the table. And later, when the nurses oohed and aahed over the obscene harness designed to take the place of the cast, he laughed with them (and his other self, at them).

Peg and Pete came by to cheer him up and he found their banter as easy as ever. He could turn them off and still hear himself talking with them, smiling, no effort at all. Others came from the church and the office, not as many as before, but enough to rib him about his collar and to praise his guts, awkwardly. Brad knew that the man in the bed was ahead of them. He was casually amused to see the way the patient made it a point to greet his company, put them at ease, lead the conversation along easy channels, and dismiss them by thanking them for coming. Brad wanted, a few times, to tell Bets how he felt suspended, outside of himself, and once he almost said it to Irv, but he stopped in time. It might upset the balance. It was like having just the right amount of drinks. You were out of touch but still in control, just breezin' along, taking it real easy, nice, everything cool and smooth. The morning after would come soon enough and he'd have himself back, he knew that. They'd get through tinkering and ship him off to County, and he'd be his own thing then; he could try again or quit. "Don't worry about that yet," Brad told the thing on the bed. "Just ree-lax, lie back, and take it nice and easy for now." He managed to keep floating along until the morning he was sent to County. Even then, when he woke, he felt real cool, still in control. . . .

"Do some people hate to leave the hospital?" he quickly asked the nurse who leaned over him, before she harpooned him with her thermometer. She didn't answer, first taking his pulse, and he was amused at the theological air all nurses adopt as they participate in the sacred ritual of pulse-taking.

"More used to," she answered at last, and Brad had trouble r membering the question. "I've been a nurse thirty years."

"No," he interrupted politely, thinking she'd probably been nurse forever.

"I don't look it, do I? Taken care of myself, haven't let myse go." She smiled grimly. "People used to stay in hospitals a lo longer, but now we get 'em up and out, most of them." She gav him a horrible grimace of sympathy. "When I first came here remember lots who wanted to stay; some cried, grown men even when they went home; they liked being taken care of. Maybe would too if I was on the other end," she added as she attende to his functions.

"Yep, they'd cry, not wanting to take care of themselves," th nurse grumped as she carried out the container of his wastes "Cry they would," she repeated as she turned into the corrido and Brad laughed, bitterly, and napped. . . .

At home Bets wakened quickly, almost angrily, on the da they were taking Brad to County. Before the accident she ha always been the one who lay abed, stretching, enjoying a mo ment of sensual relaxation, edging up on the day. Brad was th one who attacked the morning, instantly awake. His eyes opene the way a window shade rolled up; the covers heaved and wer tossed back in one motion; his feet hit the floor and he charge toward the bathroom, full of energy, ready to do his best work She was different, more female than ever in the morning, hal asleep, feline, and when she was able to lure Brad back to bed on a weekend morning she was especially good for him. Wanto and alluring, enjoying the warmth in the sheets, the light patter on ceiling and wall, her husband, the anticipation of coffee an a leisurely beginning to the day.

Not anymore. This morning, like the others now, Bets stum bled out of bed, almost falling, not feeling female, not feelin much of anything. Glue-eyed and brown-mouthed, grabbin clothes, fixing coffee, herding the children out of bed, shovin them off to school, muttering through a breakfast with he mother, forcing herself to do the morning chores, the house keeping, which once kept her busy all day but were now com pressed into a hurried morning divided by one period of peac —ten minutes and the second cup of coffee at ten. And now Bet remembered, as the flame under the coffee was turned up, a she splashed cold water on her face, that she would not even

ave this today, the day Brad would be transferred to the County
Iome for Incurables.

When Irv Frank woke, his day seemed no different from another, for he had slept deeply and woke with the slate wiped
lean. He shaved and bathed while running down the day's cases
bjectively, the jobs that could be done, just those. No time to
hink about those that couldn't be done. He had to take life one
ay at a time. He complained about his schedule but he knew it
vas a comfort as well as a curse. No one case, even Brad's,
ould long dominate the others, no single failure obscure the
uccessful ones, and yet he found himself, as he prepared his
achelor breakfast of coffee, orange juice, an egg, toast, thinkng of Brad, who was going to County this day.

Irv slipped quickly into the hallway outside his apartment to
ick up the *Times,* but it had not yet come. Not believing that
his part of his morning ritual could have failed him, he searched
he hall and then, disappointed, went back to his apartment and
hut the door. He put his breakfast on the plate, poured the
offee, and sat down with a rare sense of loneliness. He debated
etting a book as a companion but there was no time for a book.
nevitably he thought of Brad's being transferred to County.
irst the technical aspects, the ambulance, the time, the papers
o be signed. He had decided to go along, to help Bets. He began
o wonder about his patient's prognosis. When Brad was ready
hey could take the tendons in his wrist, tie them to his fingers,
nd give him a pinch. That could be important, make the differnce, when Brad was ready. Munching on his toast, bittersweet
vith marmalade, Irv tried to estimate the course of his friend's
llness. Medically, everything was routine. His neck had fused;
e'd have the regular quadriplegic complaints—contractions,
pasms, irritations from the catheter—and they would respond
o the normal treatments. Brad would have twenty years of life,
naybe forty. No one could tell how long because those who had
uffered the same accident a generation ago had all died—every
ne of them.

Irv Frank turned away from the subject of Brad—no use in
vooling that—and clattered through the dishes. He went down
o his MG, concentrating on the driving, the best relaxation he
new, until he was suddenly frozen in a parkway traffic jam.
rustrated and angry, Dr. Frank stood up on the seat of the
onvertible and tried to see over the long line of unmoving cars

that climbed the hill ahead. Nothing. Just parallel lines of car
all stopped. He stepped out on the grass to look for a telephon
or a police car that could radio the hospital. Finally he gave u
and sat helplessly. Pitying his own paralysis, Irv suddenl
thought of Brad's and felt, for the first time, old.

At the hospital, a nurse asked Brad, "Are we ready for ou
little trip today?"

Brad forced a smile and answered, "A-okay," as if he were no
irritated at the childish cheeriness of the nurse, the one who al
ways had a light BO through the overdose of cheap toilet water
Brad thought of the foulest Anglo-Saxon expletives he could us
on her and was amused at the meaningless smile of the thing o
the bed, which tolerated her imperious, unfeeling charade o
sympathy. She bustled about the thing he was, doing the chore
of bedpan and wash with bouncy goodness, chirping at him i
a first-person-plural baby talk he refused to listen to but hear
just the same. When at last Bets and Irv arrived, within a minut
of each other, he, the one on the bed, entertained them. "I'm th
maddest man in North America," he growled, and laughingl
mimicked the cheery nurse, exaggerating her baby talk, gettin
them laughing with him so that the expedition—his being lifte
to the stretcher lying almost on the floor and wheeled out th
door while he looked up at the world from a new vantage point
all feet and legs and tall walls skidding by—started as a holida
excursion.

People had been coming in all morning to wish him good-bye
and the man on the bed had handled them all quite well, he
thought. Elvena, the lab tech, Bob and Smitty, the OT's, the
nurses going off duty and the ones coming on, the volunteers,
residents, interns, the cleaning women, and the orderlies who
had shifted his frame around. Brad responded as he had at a
sales convention, remembering every name, hailing each individual as they moved into his range of vision, not able to pump a
hand or beat a shoulder, but carrying in the enthusiasm of his
voice, in the ritual of male banter, a genuine pleasure at meeting everyone.

The Brad on the bed made his departure a party. He had a
joke and a promise for everyone—"I'll be back on my feet"—
and the hospital, so used to cheeriness, responded with delight
at his courage, not admitting its falseness. Even Mr. Buchanan
beamed as they praised him and told him to keep up the good

work, and even those who knew best the sure prognosis seemed, the other Brad thought, to share the moment's illusion of hope.

Bets felt shoved aside, in the way, as the parade behind the stretcher moved out of the room and down the corridor. She felt as if she were always standing in the wrong place these days. There was nothing she could do and nothing she could say to further the carnival air of the departure, for she could not avoid the truth. "He isn't going home," she wanted to scream. "My husband's going to the County Home for Incurables," and as she thought this everyone laughed at something Brad had said.

She glared down at him, hating him and guilty at the thought. But his courage was a shame, she told herself; his heroics were cowardly now. She looked at Irv's face, the jaw clenched, the eyes hard, and knew he too felt the joyful spirit of the departure obscene. They all stopped at the nurses' station for jokes, rode down in the elevator with laughter, and she wondered if they were right, if it were important to keep up the illusion, and at the same moment knew it was not, that truth could not be denied, that saying the unhappy were happy did not make them so. There were people who were hopeless, she wanted to screech; death was a visitor, she wanted to weep, as much as the Red Cross gray ladies who were issued cheery pink smocks at Dunston Memorial.

With laughter and shouted mock insults and hearty rejoinders the small crowd around the stretcher spilled out of the hospital and shoved Brad into the ambulance like an artillery shell. Bets and Irv, bending over, duck-walked in and squatted on the little bench beside him, and the rear door, hearselike, swung shut and the ambulance, no hurry, no siren, eased out of the parking lot.

Irv was irritated at the time this was taking in a day scheduled to the minute, and Bets was still infuriated at the false cheeriness of the hospital. The Brad who was a thing on the stretcher just smiled. The other Brad, the real Brad, felt further away from himself than ever, as if he might spin out of control, panicked by the touch of fall air on his cheeks. Only his face had been exposed to the outside air above the buntinglike blankets, and that only for a moment, while he was rolled down the ramp into the heated ambulance; yet that breath of autumn caught him unawares and overwhelmed him. The evening air had been summer soft when he had been hit by the car so long ago, and now the air was a season different—it had October’ bite. He’d lost a season, for always.

Brad, inside the body on the stretcher, felt the ambulanc twist and turn and tried to figure out the route it was taking, bu could not. He smiled helplessly and knew that Bets smiled bac at him, but he didn’t speak. He tried to figure out why the ai had bothered him so much, to beat back the despair with logic Why had that touch of outside air gotten to him? Was it the sea son, the time lost forever? Or was it the simple fact that it wa outside air? He had not felt outside air for so long, and woul not now at County.

The three sat silently as Brad watched the trees, now turne yellow and red, or the branches left stark black, slide by abov the ambulance as it stopped, started, turned and spun on th route to County. Brad heard Bets gasp and knew that Irv ha silenced her before he saw the black iron gate roll over the ambu lance. He knew he was there and without reading the words h knew what had been wrought in black: *The County Home fo the Crippled and Incurable.*

Brad’s eye caught a corner of brick, and his memory com pleted the buildings seen casually years before when he drove b on the way to the train—three stories high, dark red, and slate roofed. A New England charity building of one hundred year ago, built by factory builders. High ceilings and tall, narrow windows, black trimmed. Silent, cold buildings.

Brad lay alone while they went to find someone to unload him, and he learned in those long moments of waiting that time was different here at County. The acid smell of disinfectant told him all he wanted to know. When they rolled him by the green walls and the corridors lined with people doing nothing, he was not surprised. Wheelchaired or platformed, benched or hunched over crutches, waiting in line, they glanced at him with eyes that couldn’t care less; even the young, he realized, looked old. Up another elevator and they were at the ward, and this simple thing surprised him. He would no longer be alone, no longer be the center of a universe. He would be only one in an army of sick. He had been the only quad at Memorial. Surprised at the bite of jealousy, he wondered how many quads there were here.

“Don’t worry, Bets,” he heard himself say. “I won’t be here long.” He felt a chill as his helpless body was lifted and lumped down onto a bed. He waited for her answer but it didn’t come.

She chatted cheery, manufactured words that were only sounds, yet communicated her terror and her futile love. They, the doctor and the wife, did things they had to do and talked to the people they had to talk to and made the promises to come back they had to make and they left. He forgot he was not alone in a private room and was startled when a voice floated over to him.

"My name's Carey. Welcome to County, the arse hole of the world." The voice didn't seem bitter, despite the words, and he wished he could see the face so that he would see its meaning in grimace or glare, punctuating the words with a glance, a raised eyebrow, a shrug.

Brad hesitated, then answered at the ceiling, "Glad to meet you. My name's Brad Hastings." He knew he shouldn't speak but the words ran on, out of control: "I'm only going to be here for a while, just until I get well. It won't be long and I'll be going home." He knew as he said the words that they wouldn't believe him; he might even have hurt them or made them angry because they weren't as lucky. They were condemned. Brad braced himself for their anger and when the voice—Was it young or old?—answered only, "You're lucky," Brad thought he'd cry. He fought back the tears. If he wept they'd see him and then a stranger would have to wipe away his tears.

II

Brad's dreams began at County.

He was running, his legs reaching forward, finding the ground, gripping it and then pushing away from it, each step a leap. The ground sped past and the sapling-edged wood was blurred by his speed. He was running along a dirt road that curved to the side of the hills and he followed the right rut, the grasses high in the center and only slightly grease-tinged from the bottoms of occasional cars. It was morning—dew held down the dust, and the air, moist and thin, was cold and cutting in his lungs. The light fell gently on the brown road and it was spring—there was yellow in the green of the uncurling leaves.

Brad was gloriously aware of himself in the concentration of running, his head held up and the breeze self-made against his face, his chest large, his heart pumping, his lungs full, his arms following the hypnotic rhythm of his legs. He had his second wind and he felt he could go on forever as long as nothing broke the rhythm of his long legs, bare, his feet sockless in the ankle-high moccasins that were soaked to the shape of his feet. They were quick to feel the contours of the earth, to seek a firm purchase, and then to spring his legs' power against the ground. He thrilled at the strength of his own legs—the muscles coiling and uncoiling, the strength of the matched thighs and calves, each doing its job of propelling him forward, up to the bend where the huge rock, lightning-cracked, stood, whirling by it and down the slope to the stream white-foamed with melted snow, almost falling pellmell down the slope, and then pulling up against the rise, reaching up and achieving the top, swinging right along the birch grove, following the road, enjoying the pain in his legs, their strength, the joy of running, until he woke, no longer a boy of fifteen but a man lying in a dark ward, immediately aware of where he was and hungering instantly for the freedom of the dream, which had been, for its few moments of eternity, so very real.

With this dream began another day. Summer had become autumn at Memorial and now autumn had turned into winter at County. Brad could feed himself slowly and sloppily; he could sit up and turn his head, for the collar was gone, but there had been no miracle. Brad shut out the shadowed ward, the sounds of breathing, lay like a turtle imprisoned in his own shell, shut his eyes, and forced the regular breathing that might bring the oblivion of sleep and, possibly, if he were fortunate, the false comfort of a dream.

He heard the kitchen sounds and knew he had cheated the worst hours before dawn. Too often he had lived through their particular emptiness—no wonder so many people seemed to die in those chill hours, when the body and the world was at its lowest ebb. He had to learn how to survive those hours. Sleep was the best escape, of course, but it was not easily found. The bedridden napped often and could rarely win a full night of peace; pills were not allowed him just for sleep, now, when he would welcome them; Brad had early learned that the hours in the shadowed ward were no time for thought: logic could not combat the apparitions that populated the stark hours, when depression caught at your legs, dragging you down to oblivion. Brad could not yet lose himself in it but had to struggle, and he found no pleasure in this primeval, hopeless war.

Daydreams, the boy's secret stretching of the imagination, were the best escape. Soon, calculated imaginings eased Brad through those hours when he was not blessed by sleep. They were the intimate dreams never revealed to anyone in the daylight hours. In them all was possible—Brad did not walk, he ran.

Those daydreams were his friends, but their cousins, the unexpected illusions that struck traitorously from within during the day, were his enemies. The sudden knowing that he could get up and walk; the certainty that at 5:00 P.M. that very day, the test would be over and he would walk into the administrator's office, have a cigarette, and joke, man to man, about those ridiculous fears that his condition had been permanent; the sudden pumping sensation made him think he was making love, more vigorously, more perfectly, than he ever had. Those moments, insane, inexplicable, came when he was talking to someone, his mind apparently intent on the subject. They struck swiftly, cruelly, and they never carried the comfort, false but still warming, of the purposely dreamed worlds of the early morning.

The calming dreams he so carefully constructed were myth and legend, woven to delude, the battle picture painted with the soldiers in parade dress, the dying general dignified, the blood a delicate decoration. He made himself a defensive linesman, a pro: battered, tough, experienced, renowned. He was strong in his athletic armor, dug in for the goal-line stand; and his magnificent weariness felt real, the ache of bruises, the burn of cuts and scrapes, the heaving chest, the pain of a body pushed beyond its usual limits. He rested on the earth, hands and knees, then rose on his toes, both hands resting on the ground, shifted into position and, with the movement of the ball, braced himself to absorb the crush of the enemy. Parrying them, he could follow the play; it was coming his way, and with a grunt he shifted his body aside, hurled the blockers out of his way, and threw himself at the ball carrier, feeling the satisfaction of contact, head and shoulders, the arms not necessary, for his force alone, pure and direct, had stopped the play.

Catlike, waiting and wary, coiled and ready to spring, Brad led the defense, always successful in this man-to-man combat, the personal conflict of head and shoulder, forearm and elbow, cleat and knee, that was line play—the crosses and circles on the coach's blackboard turned into the snarling conflict of quick, cruel instincts and brute, bone force. He dreamed and then, exhausted, he slept, satisfied.

Other mornings Brad became an Indian scout moving into the Appalachians before the Revolution. Forgetting the breathing and muttering of the others in the ward, he reveled in his lonely responsibility to probe the frontier, explore the wilderness, eat off the land. He observed the enemy Indian and slept without a fire. He saw the lost beauty of the virgin country, hill upon hill, range after range, uncut, falling away from green to purple to blue, and he walked with the sponge of the ancient forest under his feet. He felt hunger, weariness, and fear—even the swarms of gnats, which were tests of Job for any man. He also felt the freedom and the satisfaction of loneliness—and the need for violence, the primitive satisfaction of the kill, justified for him by his mission.

Other times Brad dreamed he had captured control of the corporation. He appeared one day at the board meeting and exercised control, receiving the reluctant tribute of the directors, earned by his ruthless operations. He made policy and became, immediately, a power in the industry. Brad saw himself with steel-gray hair wearing a brown tailormade suit, moving from conference to meeting to convention speech, walking, in this dream, with casual dignity—joking, directing his affairs with gentle power, giving counsel and advice, even to the President of the United States.

Brad considered the dreams a harmless narcotic, addictive possibly, but certainly not dangerous, a way to get from the cold darkness of the ward at 3:00 or 4:00 A.M. until the kitchen sounds announced the dawn. After the night, the day was anticipated. Bets, he knew, imagined long hours of emptiness, but they were few. He discovered that life in a chronic-disease ward had a pace and a ritual that filled the hours. For a quad, anyway, the process of living filled hours instead of minutes. A healthy man did the day's necessary tasks in minutes—rising, bathing, dressing, eating, and excreting—up at seven-fifteen, out of the house at eight, the paper read, the day's family decisions discussed and made.

To Brad breakfast was a morning's work. He had to be hoisted into position, hitched into a sling hung from a high pulley, which allowed his weak right arm to stab at the food, already cold, and propel it in the direction of his mouth. One piece of egg required a strong man's entire concentration, his whole hoard of energy, to make the repeated pursuit across the plate to the bumper, an aluminum pie-plate clipped to the other plate. Success. The food was impaled. Now Brad lifted the egg awkwardly, unnaturally, toward his face. It hit his cheek; his mouth, held foolishly open, was still empty, and he shut it, ashamed. The fork swung back, out of reach until he made it move toward him again. At last it hit his teeth. He bit. The fork was empty: the egg had fallen into his bed.

His day was divided by mountain ranges of effort. First the plan and the anticipation—the getting up or merely the turning over. The realization that the time to be turned was coming, the impotent waiting for the nurse and the aide, the struggle, and at last the success. Then the resting—and the struggle between a sense of achievement, the exhilarating feeling of victory, and the frustration that eroded his spirit with bitterness. To Brad the world of the ward became a strange place, detached from all other worlds. New friendships were formed and new hatreds. Brad discovered that he felt an animal anger at the healthy doctors who seemed, quite naturally, he supposed, to resent their failures, row on row in this ward. He found the ward had its own life, and all the doctors, nurses, and orderlies were almost as much outsiders as were the visitors, the relatives, neighbors, and employers.

Brad learned that the ward was seen differently from each bed. In a wheelchair he had explored the hospital, but all of it, the confusing corridors and look-alike rooms, remained unreal to him. His world was Ward F, seen from his bed. Brad memorized the ceiling, soot-gray and cracked, a map of nowhere, his only view when he was on his back. Lying on his right side, Brad saw the edge of pillow and mattress, the crevasse between his bed and the next one. Rarely did they leave him near the edge, where he could see the floor beside his bed. There was a vast space between his and Carey's bed. Brad didn't know if Carey was tall or short, for he never got out of bed. He was a profile, the chin sunk into his neck, the reddish stubble of beard—for they were shaved only twice a week—the sign of youth in his voice denied by the tousled hair, white and red-brown, on the pillow. Brad studied what he could see, trying to understand it: the hospital bed, paint-chipped; the army blanket, surplus and cheap; the wall beyond Carey, sick green, puke green. Green had been his favorite color, but now he hated it for its obscene use to cover all the walls. The wall beyond Carey was decorated by only two long cracks and three pustulated areas of bubbles and peeling boils, revealing underneath a layer of earlier paint—crap green, sick green—the same as above.

Left lying belly down, his face hanging free between the pillows piled under his chest and forehead, Brad had only the sheet for a view, and its grayness was decorated with only the shadow of his arm and the blurred half vision of his nose. It was all too close to focus, a cross-eyed view of the world. On his left side he had infinite vision, a vista of beds, two rows of them. The row near him was a sequence of lying or sitting bodies, mounded and mummied, the other side of the room a parade of feet. In the bed next to him there was an ancient man whose name he didn't know. He was called "the Smiler," for he wore a beatific smile that, from the first day, seemed to warm the room. Brad learned it was Death's grin. The smile reflected no mind behind it. The face, so peaceful, so happy, looked as if it were pleased with its lot: condemned to a bed in an institution, afflicted with pain and sores, and unable not to wet its pants. Old beyond belief, he had become a thing who had outlived his children and his grandchildren, his generation, his time, his usefulness. And so he smiled. He was an it. It did not talk or think; it enjoyed no superior wisdom; it was just a biological creature that took matter in at one end, absorbed the goodness from it, and expelled it from the other end, the human being reduced to a device, and it smiled at the joy of it.

On this side Brad could see more, but he often shut his eyes, unable to contemplate what he saw. Yet even with his eyes closed Brad inevitably explored the ward. Smell, the most intimate of the senses, constantly reminded him of where he was. There was the institutional smell that was always there—a staleness in the air that became more unpleasant than the dank odor of incontinence, the decaying odor of illness, or the acrid odor of unguents and salves. Brad found he could accept those, but not the smell of the soups and the steamed vegetables, the nose-burning sharpness of the disinfectant, the constant sweat odor of his own bed. There was no window he could see from his bed even when he twisted his head, but his hearing ranged far beyond the ward. He heard the early-morning sounds of the kitchen, the clatter when the trash trucks rolled in, the traveling drone of the power mower, back and forth, back and forth, the seductive moaning of the planes on their regular course overhead, the Sunday-morning clangor of bells.

At first, sounds meant a great deal to Brad, and he would listen to them intently, clinging to the contact with another world. He was not aware when he changed, when the distant sounds lost their magic and the nearer ones of the ward became the outer edges of his world, the smaller sounds becoming louder. The squeak of a wheelchair; the turning in bed; the low moans or sleep-talk of his wardmates; the squinch of the corridor doors; the sound of the rising elevator, which might bring something worth noting but usually didn't; the feet of the stretcher pushers; and the particular dirge of the castors on the cart that rolled a body away.

As familiar as the ward became, Brad still felt alien among society's rejects—the 4-F's of life, the failures (no fault of their own, to be sure) who were the unaccomplished, the unsuccessful, just the same. Brad liked people who paid their own way, who didn't think society owed them a living. He was astonished that his wardmates didn't express shame instead of anger that they didn't get more. To them charity was a right, and Brad, staring at the ceiling, listened to their bitter complaints with wonder, waiting for the tone of apology, the sound of embarrassment, which must, he believed, be hidden beneath their complaints.

He even held himself separate from Carey's causes. That morning Carey presented his latest case to the administrator and Brad followed the argument shamelessly as it bounced off the ceiling over his head.

"It's right," Carey's voice roared. "That's why I want it to be done. It's just right that it should be, and you know it and I know it and I expect you to do something about it."

"Now, I realize it would be pleasant." The administrator's voice fell in globs like jam from a spoon. "But you must also realize, Carey, that, of course, we have certain other priorities that must be achieved——"

"Mush. Mush. That's all it is," said the bed-bound voice, shaking with justified rage. "It's not as if anything had to be done. Just put 'em on the pipes. Tell the nurses to put 'em on the pipes. Rest 'em there all night. That'll do it."

Brad could see nothing but the ceiling with the gray covering of soot revealed when the ward maintenance man touched it to steady himself while replacing the unfrosted light bulb. Teetering on the tall step ladder, he left white fingerprints, three fingers, not four, and one thumb. Did he daintily hold his little finger apart or had it been sacrificed to another chore ineptly done? Looking only at the ceiling, Brad could imagine the combatants as clearly as if he could turn his head and look at them.

The administrator seemed eyeless, for the light always seemed to glint off his glasses; his hair would be slicked down and his round, dough-colored face was, as always, feigning patience. He treated life as if it were a serving of mashed potatoes which didn't need to be cut but could be softly shaped, pushed back, mashed down, patted and formed. "I can understand how you feel, Mr. Carey."

"That'll do it," Brad thought. He could see Carey, lusting in his anger, his voice lashing out with righteous indignation. "Understand? You? You can tell me you know what it feels like to have a cold bedpan stuck under you the first thing in the morning. It's hateful and improper. It isn't right."

"You tell him, Carey." Boraski laughed from across the aisle. "It won't do any good, but you tell 'em."

"See, see?" Carey's voice rose. "They've lost faith, they don't think they have any rights. It's easy to get to thinking you're a charity case here, but we aren't. We're taxpayers—or were. This is our right and it's proper we be treated as citizens and not as castoffs."

The administrator reacted as he always did, with a soothing concoction of half promises, and Brad turned off the voices. Looking at the ceiling, he could conjure up Carey as he saw him when he was turned on his right side. Then Brad could see Carey, his profile hawk-lean, his hair tousled. After a day or two you realized he was not an old man waiting to die but almost a young one, an angry man, young enough to have a vision of justice. Brad discovered that Carey had no sense of perspective, and was delighted at the passion and energy that could be unleashed on international affairs, on melted ice cream, on Washington, on the bedpans—would they be cold or warm? There was no issue too trivial for Carey to debate.

Brad had held himself aloof, amused by the argument but not involved in it, astonished at the fury displayed by Carey and surprised at the hatred of the administrator, which flowed from bed to bed, for Brad knew it was all out of proportion and was proud of his outsider's perspective. He clung to it as a drowning man might cling to a rock until one noon, when he was served chocolate pudding. He didn't push the button for the nurse, for there were no buttons at County. He bellowed, "Nurse. Comear."

It seemed like hours before one stood before him, lumpy and aggravated. "Whatja want, Hastings?"

He just pointed at his tray.

"Yeah. Lunch. I see it."

"Chocolate pudding."

"What do you think it is, a puppy dog?" she cackled. "Everyone got it."

"Not me."

"Yeah, you got it too." She smiled at her logic.

"That's just exactly it; I shouldn't have it."

"Why? Yah special?" She still smiled.

"I'm allergic. It's on the chart; I get hives from chocolate."

"So don't eat it." She was plainly puzzled and started to turn away.

"Wait right here," he barked, the rage making his voice tremble. "Get me my dessert. No chocolate."

"Now listen here, I'm no servant of yours or anyone else's. You're no different than anyone else here, quad or not. Get off that high horse."

"I'm allergic to chocolate."

"Am I making you eat it?"

"I ought to have a dessert I can eat. It's my right."

"Oh, rights, is it? All right, I agree," she said with a sigh, "but we can't run special service, special desserts. Don't eat it and you won't have no hives."

She started to leave again, but with a cold fury he growled, "Stop," and with concentration swung his arm up to his face and then let it fall in the swivel, its weight making it a giant hammer. It swung down, hit the dish just right, and swept it to the floor, where it skidded across the ward and slapped up against the wall. He glared at the nurse, who, infuriatingly, looked at him with understanding. "You won't have no desserts for the rest of the week."

It was Carey who seized the cause as his own: "I'd like to speak to the administrator."

"He'll be on his rounds Friday," the nurse grumped, picking up the dish of chocolate pudding and absentmindedly licking her fingers where they had poked the trembling mess.

Carey argued Brad's cause well, taking it up with oratorical delight, but Brad knew, listening to him, how ridiculous it all was. He shut his eyes, tried to stop his ears, all his senses, tried to flee the ward to escape in a daydream, but he did not succeed. This time he could not lose himself in the shadow action at a phantom goal line. He had joined the ward. Brad opened his eyes wearily. The nurse was gone but the tray was there. He tried for a piece of meat that had been cut up for him. He thought bitterly, he had special service, after all, didn't he? He got it to his mouth and chewed it, a piece of gray cardboard essential to life. He stopped chewing at the thought and then continued, slowly.

"Thanks, Carey."

"They're bastards, all of 'em. Outsiders."

Brad smiled and agreed. "They're all bastards." The truth was there, finally accepted—he was a cripple and he always would be. Brad spat out the gristly piece of meat and let it dribble down his chin and then his chest.

12

The empty rocking chairs on the deserted porches rocked. Bets sat in her car, waiting for visiting hours to begin, and tried not to watch the haunted chairs. She studied the main building with its slate roof, black, sharp, cutting into the sky. She tried to follow the vines of ivy, withering there, flourishing here, and could not understand the reason for its success or failure. She made herself map the maze of wings and outhouses—wood paint-peeled, stucco plaster cracked—and could not understand the pattern of the wooden-covered walks, above-ground tunnels, which connected them. She ended up, as she always did, watching the rocking chairs—dark green wood with brown wicker arms bent and twisted and cracked—which were left out on the porches for the winter. Each rocked to its own rhythm, fast or slow, touched by the wind or ghosts. Suddenly one would start rocking madly while the one next to it slowed down. Another kept up a regular motion while others stopped or never rocked. There was no reason in it, no order, no purpose when they rocked, no meaning when they stopped.

Bets got out of the car and stumbled wearily up the curving stone walk to the front door. Entering those great black doors, bubbled with years of paint slapped over other layers of unsanded bubbled paint, Bets was always unsure of herself. At Memorial she had known how to act—poised, fashionable, optimistic, brave, cheery; here she was never even certain if she should look at the faces of the patients who forever lined the corridors or sat sullenly in the dayrooms. If you looked away too quickly from their bodies, their misshapen limbs and swollen-to-bursting growths, there always seemed to be a knowing smile, as if you had betrayed a weakness. Yet how could she look at them normally? The simple fact of her health always made her feel guilty before the twisted and the abandoned. It was more than the humped backs, bodies that looked as if they'd been placed in huge vises and twisted by a fiend, more than the stubby protuberances that might have grown to legs, the huge heads and the mumbling mouths. Bets could almost get used to those who had to lie face down on sort of a go-cart or the legless, who scooted along on special chairs, the great lumped bodies, age all slumped to belly, the skeleton's drawn, taut skin, the things who shook. Bets could get used to it, even the smell of urine, hating it and wanting to clean the place, but not fearing it as she had. She no longer fled the black-armored cockroaches that scurried around the edges of the floors, busy and familiar.

It was the eyes that haunted her nights. Watery, old; bright, shining, cynical; young, all-knowing, bitter; angry or hateful; frustrated or despairing. The eyes were windows into dark and dreadful places, more horrible than the most monstrous body she had seen.

Each day she looked to see what was happening to Brad's eyes, but she saw nothing, for they no longer looked into hers. He had ordered her not to bring the children, told her not to come herself, and she didn't argue; she just came, not yet wondering why she did.

Bets had learned to be careful to take the most direct route to Ward F. Step inside the front door, first corridor on your right, and go to the end, left up the ramp, another left, right at the second door down to the end, then three flights of stairs and back to the end of that corridor. Each hall shellacked oak, green paint on the plaster, and all the same brown linoleum floors. There were no signs, no arrows, for few strangers ever walked the halls. They were used by inhabitants, long-term patients and long-term staff, condemned together.

Bets knew the way, and knew better how important it was to stick to the familiar route, but she grew careless this day, hurrying by the rows of mocking eyes, aware of the strange noise of her high heels, quickly clicking along the halls, and took the wrong turn. Suddenly she was through a door and into a vast hall, lined with old pews that looked as though they had been collected from a hundred different churches. The pews were filled with the lumpen, clay figures of old ladies, feet flat on the floor, ankles swollen, knees unashamedly apart, hands fitfully plucking at what was in their laps—a bit of busywork, a handbag, nothing. The hands twitched and trembled in front of the swollen bellies, uncorseted, and fallen breasts, unsupported. The wild gray-white hair, uncombed, crowned the faces, each empty in its own way, talking to itself, staring at another world, another time, not one visiting with her neighbor, all sitting in the pews, which faced a blank wall.

Bets fled, turning right instead of left, not seeing the bars on the windows until a man crossed her path, pacing back and forth like an angry lion caged in an imaginary cage. She rushed past him and down a ramp into a newer building, where middle-aged men wet their pants and played happily with children's toys. She turned and ran, back up the ramp and then some stairs, until she came to a quiet corridor, which she walked along carefully, not thinking of what she had seen, shutting it out of her mind, erasing it for the moment, searching for a landmark. . . .

"Watch out."

A boy careened past, knee-high. A blond head, beautiful, laughing. A blond head and a torso—that was all—pursued by a girl who was pushing him, thin, intense, absorbed in the game, marvelously dexterous on the roller-skate wheels attached to her stumps. Bets wheeled and darted up to another floor, to a corridor lined with cubicles, each door revealing a single room, each room a bed, each bed a body and a face with deep sockets for eyes, black holes at the end of the nose, and a great gaping mouth. Few sounds, a moan, a few groans, a curse, or a word: "Mother, Mother, Mother." Each one waiting for death long overdue. Bets, hearing her heels on the floor, knew she was staggering, but she moved on, almost running, hoping she would find Ward F or the way out, escape. She ran past long rows of benched derelicts, alcoves with wheelchair huddles, turning this way and that until, at last, coming at it from the wrong side, she found Ward F. She started in, then stopped. She couldn't run to Brad this way. He couldn't comfort her or hold her anymore. She had to go to him strong. She slumped against the wall and shut her eyes.

At last Bets forced herself to walk the gauntlet of beds until she came to Brad's. Even when he was sitting in his wheelchair, he'd never watch her coming. She had to put herself before his eyes and only then did they speak—without intimacy, practicing a carefully planned program of meeting. She hated their casualness but could not pierce it. They were never alone even when she wheeled him to the dayroom and they were forced to perform their marriage before an audience of the bored and casually curious. Now that Brad had faced the truth—and surrendered to it—sinking into a bleak depression, there were no longer even private glances or special tones of voice, just a protective correctness. Bets learned to wish for anger, rage, bitterness, instead of his politeness, which shut her out, divorced her from him.

"How are the children?"

"Fine. Eric passed his test."

"His test?"

"Yes, Cubs. Wolf badge."

"Oh, of course."

He didn't know, Bets realized, that she'd had to get a substitute father to sign his card. Their worlds, hers and Brad's, were now East and West.

"The cook got caught," Brad told her, almost smiling, like an old man happy to see a lifelong companion dead before him.

"Caught doing what?"

"The same thing. Serves him right."

Her visits could not be a bridge between them. Their conversation, always conscious of its audience, was hesitant and incomplete. They meant too much to each other to chat, and there was nothing important they could say. She stood beside the bed, looking down at him, her husband, and he looked up at the ceiling. Both had been careful since that day when Bets had wept. Bets, that afternoon, had broken down, forgetting the audience, forgetting to be cheerful, aware only that she was losing Brad when he must need her the most.

"I need you."

"Like this?"

"Yes, like this. I need you. A woman has to be needed." He had been silent and then she'd gone on: "I'd do anything for you."

"I know, but they do everything for me. Feed me, shave me, get me up, put me down, feed me, change my diapers." He'd hesitated. "You can't be my wife and, by God, I won't let you be my mother."

She wept and he sank deeper away from her and had not even spoken the next day when she'd come. Now they were cautious—and the visits seemed interminable.

"How are the children?" He had asked it before—and forgotten it.

"They're fine." She hesitated. "They miss you."

"They'll stop."

"They won't, and you should let them visit you."

"Nope."

"Why?"

"You know why. They've got to forget about me."

"They won't."

"They will." His voice had a certainty to it, and as she stood there she remembered the last picnic of the year, on a Saturday, warm even for Indian summer. She had dreaded taking the children for that day's outing, but they deserved something. Even her mother had said, "They ought to have a day alone with their mother." It had become one of those rare, unexpected days when the world was wonderful.

The mother and her children rode along the highway with a sense of companionship and ease, no hurry. There was free time to talk and laugh. It was a silly day, without plans or purpose, a day of whims. They followed the river north, seeing the winter hills, each turn in the road revealing a new view. "Can we see the bridge that's being built, Mommy?" They could. Bets parked and they explored the construction site. "Can we eat out?" They did, cheeseburgers and ice cream and Coca-Cola. "No milk, Mother?" "No milk." "Yippee!" There was time to ask questions and to talk; to feed the deer Cracker Jacks at the state park and ride a pony around a roadside ring. When the time came to turn toward home, they grew silent, still driving slowly, enjoying the long shadows and the companionship. Suddenly Eric began to sing: "A friend on the left and a friend on the right, vive la compagnie." They shouted and sang "I've Been Workin' on the Railroad," "The Bells Are Ringing," "Ta-ra-ra-boom-tee-ay"—a dozen songs they half remembered and didn't care about, inventing new verses as they went along. When they reached the end of their street they all grew silent, and as they turned into the drive Pris asked quietly and with no concern, "Is Daddy dead?"

The wheel spun into the curb and Bets stalled the car. "No," she said, weeping, "no, he's just sick, terribly sick."

"I'm sorry, Mommy."

"Pris, you know you shouldn't say that," her brother lectured. "You're terrible."

"No, no, darling, it's all right." She drove carefully up beside the house. "Daddy isn't dead," she repeated. "He's just sick, very, very sick."

"We just wondered, Mother." Eric's voice was very grown up. "Is Daddy ever coming home?"

"I don't know," she answered softly. "I just do not know."

Now Bets stood looking down at her husband. Finally she patted his hand and said her good-byes, promising to be back tomorrow, terribly aware that he didn't care if she came or not.

When Bets left, Brad didn't even listen to her heels tapping along the ward, out the door, and down the hall. He didn't even have to let go anymore, turn it off. It was only a small part of him that was surprised at how easy it was to give up. He didn't sleep or lie awake; he didn't think or dream; he just was. Outside of time and place, suspended. He no longer even realized it was odd he knew only one man's name in the ward. The nurses weren't people—they were just nurses. He'd always been proud of the names he'd known, but now he just couldn't care less. His world was the ceiling, Carey, the Smiler, and his toes. Brad wasn't even curious about the boy who came with the tray, another high-school kid. He supposed they meant well, that it was part of some damned project.

"Mr. Hastings." That marked the boy as new. Regulars always called the patients by their last name, male or female, young or old. Brad didn't answer.

"Mr. Hastings," he said hesitantly, "you have to eat your supper."

Brad refused to answer and the boy picked up a fork, speared a piece of shoe-colored steak, and, uncertainly bending over a bit, aimed it at Brad's mouth. When Brad felt it touch his lips, so gently, trembling, he opened his mouth and accepted the food. Before the long meal was finished, the boy said, "Thank you, Mr. Hastings."

Brad looked at him then, saw the tears in his eyes, and wanted to hit the boy for his pity. He couldn't, so he spat the food out of his mouth at the boy and saw the horror on his face and laughed at it.

Later, Brad felt sad, not for the boy, but for himself, knowing he didn't really feel that mad, that he didn't really care that much anymore. Once he began his surrender, his welcoming the paralysis, his exit visa, his excuse not to fight, Brad found that nothing became a way of life. He felt a little bitterness, a little self-pity, but mostly a comfortable numbness. It was as if a tent had collapsed on him and, after struggling for hours in the enveloping blackness, pushing at it in wild motions, shoving it, he'd given up, exhausted, accepting the darkness and the suffocation. He found it was easy not to resist. Anger was naked and so was effort; caring revealed yourself, but not caring, not doing anything, made a strange privacy possible.

Nothing became the solution to everything; not doing, not caring, not acting or reacting. People came and fed him and bathed him. Brad felt as if he'd burrowed into mud, a warm, blessed ooze from which he did not want to be extricated. He was dead. Living, but dead. If they wanted to save him, to give him the gift of life he didn't want, that was their concern. They could save him and try to figure out what to use him for. He was no longer his own concern. He saw Bets when she came and stood for an hour or forever beside the bed. He felt her touch, saw her tears, her twisted face, but he found he could rarely hear her words or remember them. She spoke sounds, not meaning, and he waited for the day when she would not come, for they had nothing to say. He was dead; she was widowed.

Irv Frank came to see him every other day, not at the same time—his schedule was too full for that—but he came, early or late, to ask him how he felt, check his neck or his catheter, look at his chart, go through the ceremony of examination.

"Has Bets made you promise to see me?"

Irv hesitated, his face sad, and he nodded. "But I'd come anyway."

"As a friend?"

"Yes."

"You don't have to."

"Well, as a matter of fact, I do have to. Yes, I do. Because I promised Bets and myself. Because you're my friend."

"But not as a patient."

"That, too."

"Crap, Irv. I'm another vegetable you planted."

"You're not. You can't have that miracle you wanted, but you can use what you've got—and I can give you more."

"That pinch you talk about."

"Yes, that pinch." He could see Irv's face harden, almost feel him get angry and then guilty because he was angry at a cripple. He spoke slowly, carefully, the way he would to a child. "We can attach the tendons in your hand to the muscles you still have left so that you can bring your thumb against your two forefingers." He stopped and then went on: "The pinch makes a lot of difference."

"Not difference enough."

"A lot of difference. With a pinch you can choose between a fork or a spoon, not just have to use the utensil the nurse has stuck on your hand. You can pick up a stick and use it to dial the phone, poke at a typewriter or an adding machine. You can pick up a single piece of paper or turn a page. It's one of those small but important abilities that make us more than an animal—or a vegetable. I had a patient who could pick up a razor blade, edgewise, his pinch was so sensitive. With a pinch you can pick up a cigarette and a cigarette lighter. You can decide to eat a piece of candy. Play cards or chess, turn on a light or turn it off, pull up the blanket. Damn it, Brad, you have to make use of what you have."

"Why?" Brad barked back, surprised at his anger, and then he saw Irv try to use it.

"Because you're a man."

He felt tricked, babied, used. "Shit."

"Brad." Irv's voice was kind, and that made him even angrier.

"Pity." He spat the word out. "You can give me that. And a pinch. Can I write my name? Probably not. Can I butter a piece of bread that isn't anchored to the plate? No. Can I go to the office, do a man's work, support my family, shake hands, pour a drink, drive a car?" His voice fell, the anger draining away. "Make love to my wife, wipe my ass, scratch the itch behind my ear?"

"You can't just give up, Brad, not you."

"Why not me? Look, Irv, you did what you could and it kept me alive. Well, that isn't good enough for me. You wanted me to face facts. Well, I have. I'm a quad. I can move my right arm a little bit. I can twitch my toes and shrug my shoulders. I can breathe. I can take food in and let it out. I can sleep and wake and think and dream and what do you want, Irv Frank? Me off your conscience? I wish it were so easy because I don't want to be on your conscience. I don't want to be a spook in your closet and I don't want your goddamned pity." They glared at each other and Brad went on, his voice hard: "I was a proud man, a competitive man. I wanted to be first, to be best. That may be square but that's the way I lived my life. I didn't want to understand the girl with problems. I wanted to date the prettiest girl I could find. I was a man and I liked being a man." He made a sound like a laugh. "You know, I was content. I liked what I was, what I had. The man who had everything. Remember the gold golf tee? I had it, Irv, and I liked it. I couldn't understand those novels that criticized the suburbs, because it looked like a pretty fine life to me. And then this happened and I did what I was supposed to do. I was brave; I fought back; I didn't give up. Wasn't I a good patient? Wasn't I?"

"Yes, Brad, you were a good patient."

"You did what you could?"

"Yes, all I could."

"The knife didn't slip or anything?"

"No." His face was twisted. "I did a good job."

"Then be proud of it. You saved my life. You saved me. Now it's my life and I don't want to be seventh best, a cripple, a parasite. I don't want pity or sympathy or understanding. I want success and respect—as a man. Not respect for doing a baby's work, for feeding myself. I don't want some nurse chirping over me because I haven't wet my pants. Irv, Irv, Irv—can't you understand? I've been an all-out guy, all the way. I didn't hold back when I played ball or when I was in the army. When I took a job I gave it everything I had. When I married Bets I was faithful to her. All or nothing. Go for broke."

"Brad, there are a hundred kinds of success, more than one way of being a man."

"Not for me there isn't. Not for me. I don't want to be a successful guy with a tin cup and I don't want to get any favors from anyone. I want to be what I can't. You face it; I have. I don't want this lousy life you gave me. I don't blame you, but now that I've got it, I don't want it."

"Brad, you still care."

"Yep. I care, and you've broken through to the caring. Does that make you proud? You've made me mad and if there's a spark—aw shit. I know the arguments. Well, I'm tuning you out, Irv, and you ought to be glad. You didn't really expect Pollyanna on this channel, did you? Just what did you want? Hope and happiness, gratitude, absolution? I wish I had 'em but I don't. I've got hate and bitterness and self-pity and just enough pride to shut the door and keep it all private."

Irv tried to talk but there was nothing else to say. Brad looked right into his eyes and then, without shutting them, just unfocused them as if there were nothing worth seeing here, as if they were looking at another world where Irv couldn't go. He turned and left the ward.

It was quiet in the ward and finally Carey said with a snort, "The men in white," and Brad knew he was asking, "Are you all right?" and he answered, "I'll bet he does a paper on me." And they knew he was all right.

Carey watched over him as if he'd been appointed a committee of one. Brad appreciated his concern because he never pitied him or even understood him. He talked to him as a man should be talked to, half joking, half insulting, giving him no special tribute because he'd lost the use of both legs and arms. Yet Brad realized that the others did just that. He ranked high in some invisible aristocracy that he could not understand and was not even curious about. A man who had had his legs cut off by a train joined the ward and he was bullied into position, made to shape up, fit in. Brad was left alone and he was grateful. He wanted no friendships, no confidences exchanged, nobody else's problems on his shoulders. He wanted to be isolated, left alone with the unusable gray-white extension of his still-usable head, his body, which lay heavy under the covers to the end of the bed. He wanted to be by himself and he was, as he had never been in his life.

For days he didn't speak, doing only what he had to do, eating when the food touched his lips, letting them empty the bags of urine, the pans of crap, allowing them to bathe him, raise him, lower him, put him in the wheelchair, exercise him, air him, return him. And when people came to visit him, Brad found it easy to keep them at a proper distance. After Irv's visit Brad didn't let any of them get close to him.

The Reverend Jordan Robertson, "Jordie" to just about everyone in Brad's neighborhood, was a big, bluff type who would have been called a man's man a generation ago. Jordie was more comfortable providing the ministry of the cocktail hour or dinner party than the pulpit, but he'd managed his quick professional visits at Memorial quite well. He'd bounded in, reminding Brad of a big, floppy dog, with a cheerful quip or two, and was gone. There was never a suggestion of saying a prayer or a discussion of the hereafter, just the comfortable assurance that all was being taken care of by Jordie and by the fact that you were a "right guy." And Brad had to give him credit. Even when he'd thought there was a miracle and that Methodist preacher had made so much of it, Jordie had played it cool; he hadn't acted as if the miracle had been his doing.

He still came to County on Tuesday and Thursday mornings, making a joke about this not being on his regular route. He didn't have to tell Brad that. He acted like a stranger at County, made uncomfortable by the hopelessness, aware of the audience in the ward. Brad was almost amused at his lack of poise. Carey mimicked him and laughed out loud. Brad just didn't talk to him and watched Jordie's discomfort behind the insulating glass of his depression, waiting for him to preach at him, but Jordie didn't mention God or Christ or the Bible, and soon Brad realized he had nothing to offer but good humor. And then one day, after weeks of visiting a man who never spoke, who never reacted as if he heard, Jordie stood silently by the bed, finally speaking softly, almost to himself: "I know, Brad, what I should bring you. Something to help you understand why God did this, something to give you hope, something to grab on to. And I don't have it, Brad. I'm sorry. I don't have it. I don't have anything to say."

Brad watched Jordie stare down at him, a look of utter desolation on his heavy, ruddy face, and he wished he could say something to comfort him but didn't have anything to say either. That night he felt peculiarly alone as he was sat up, then fed, then laid down for an evening filled only with the distant drone of the voices from a television set at the other end of the ward. The lights were turned down by those who looked at the sets—"Hey, mind if we dim the lights?" No one ever did, and so Brad's ceiling was lit by the flickering lights and shadows from the television set. The light was eerie from that distance, not so much a light but a memory of a light, and there was no reason to the movements, merely a flickering shifting of brightness and grayness. Brad, each night, watched the lights on the ceiling, half hypnotized, never pondering about the reflection of an illusion, light and shadow three times removed from reality.

Bill Barnes wasn't as easy as Jordie. He was the chaplain for all the county homes and he wasn't put off by unpleasantness. He didn't have much of a sense of humor and couldn't chat easily, but he had a pity in his eyes that Brad couldn't resent. He didn't offer sympathy or cheeriness. He asked about the food and the bed and the draft, making it clear he was ready to attend to the needs of the body—and the needs of the spirit too. He knew most of the patients and he always seemed to have time for everyone. He didn't bound in; in fact, he almost sauntered in, and Brad wondered how much he had to give of himself, if he didn't have to pay a price to be so concerned about so many people who had been forgotten by everyone else.

"You can't make it up, you know," Brad told him once.

Understanding right away, Bill Barnes answered, "But I have to try"—not as if he were proud of it, but as if it were an eccentricity.

Another time Brad asked when he was going to finish his tour of duty and move to a fashionable church. He'd answered, smiling, "Oh, this is my work."

Brad felt his quiet faith and wished he could reach out to it, but he couldn't. He felt a nostalgia for the religion he had never had, for all the years of Sunday School and churchgoing. Brad knew that he had to seek faith, and Bill seemed to know that he was not yet ready for seeking. Brad realized Bill Barnes was the only one except for Carey and the rest of the ward who accepted him as he was, who didn't want him to act according to the codes of a world he had left, a world of men who had a lot to lose—property, pride, face—who had almost unlimited horizons.

Day by day, hour by hour, County became Brad's world. Without realizing it and just by accepting it, Brad drew in his horizons, shrunk his entire globe until it was Ward F, then just his end of Ward F, then just his bed, and finally just that part of his bed—his brain, spirit, soul—that was still alive, still capable of thinking, feeling, caring, and even it drew in, atrophied, shrank with disuse, as he spent mornings and afternoons and nights in mere existence, nothing more.

Ames came and Brad could see in the horror in his face at what he, Brad, must appear to the world: the Brad Hastings who was once tall, vigorous, on the go, the guy who had it made, the envied, not the envious. Ames brought him news of the company, knowing how little Brad cared about bowling leagues and the girl in the treasurer's office who had triplets. Still he made his appearance, stood the allotted time beside Brad's bed, looking down at him or, if Brad was on his face, crouching awkwardly on the chair and leaning over to look across at him, head turned, even though Brad hardly spoke. It was when their heads were twisted close, like some strange birds mating, that Brad received the formal word he was on one-third pay. He tried to make it easy for Ames and then told him, surprised at his bitter rage, "Tell them to stick it, sideways," knowing that Ames wouldn't tell them. Ames had to say it all and he did. "The company had to do it, Hastings. Policy. But it doesn't mean we're forgetting you, counting you out." He knew what it meant and so did Brad. He closed his eyes and when he opened them Ames was gone. That night he was fed a hot meat sandwich—lamb—that was cold with the gravy turned white and hard. The faithful feeder didn't force him to finish his portion that night.

Brad tried to tune them all out—Peg and Pete, Bets, Irv, Bill Barnes, the world. When the psychiatrist came—"I'm Doctor Dunlop, staff psychiatrist"—Brad ignored him and discovered that you couldn't ignore Dr. Dunlop. He was young, scientific, and imperious because he "understood." No matter what you said or did, he nodded and he smiled. He knew and he knew why. "Hastings, quadriplegia is a way of life," he began, and Brad made his ears go dead. Dunlop's face still moved, his mouth obscenely shaping words, his head nodding, his face smiling. He'd been through it all, the great things that were possible. "We can even talk about sex when the time comes," he imagined Dunlop saying as if he had a strawberry lollipop to offer.

"No," Brad told himself, shutting his eyes as well as his ears, "I don't want to buy understanding or hope. I tried hope and I didn't like it." He found he could drift, forget it. He let himself go, no longer felt shame when he discovered by his visitor's expression that his bladder had let go, ahead of schedule, no longer worried if he didn't have his pillow between his legs to keep them from mysteriously crossing when he sat in the wheelchair. He suffered the terrible, always-unexpected spasms of the crazy messages sent directly to the muscles by a draft or by bad news. He'd cut out, quit making an effort to survive. They said because he needed dilute urine he had to drink three quarts of water a day. Let them keep count. They said he'd only know if his flesh was burning by the smell. Let them keep his legs from the radiators. He couldn't cough, but he'd choke before he begged for the corset that would help his diaphragm. His body thermostat didn't work and he was cold and hot on an eccentric, individual schedule of his own. Let them figure it out and take care of him. Pneumonia? Was he to be scared of the old man's friend?

He saw Bets' face as he lay, not talking to her, ignoring her, rudely refusing her sympathy, her pity, her love, and he didn't even rationalize it. It wasn't for her good; it was just the way things were and the way things had to be.

"Pride? A man has pride," he snarled at Pete while Peg looked on, hurt and frightened. "Are you a Boy Scout? You know what I am, how I eat, how I crap? Can I have the luxury of pride?" Yet he knew he had a strange sort of residual pride, a pride in his separateness from all of them, a pride in the extremeness of his paralysis. In a perverse way he was proud of doing nothing, of seeing how far he could sink into despair, allowing the blackness to close over him, to reject all but breathing, loving, caring, hoping, God—going so far into despair that it was an adventure beyond despair into a state unknown to man.

When Pete came he was a stranger, no longer able to joke, the old ease between them gone. There was nothing they had in common now and they both felt sad at the distance between them. Brad could not be disturbed by Pete's discomfort. It was too bad, perhaps, but not very important, and he urged without much regret that Pete not come to see him. Not understanding that it wasn't self-pity, Pete swore he'd come regularly, but he came irregularly, with more and more days between visits. And while Brad drifted, apart from it, all that was still alive within him, call it soul or mind, would betray him at times with a mutiny of memory. Brad was haunted by the things done and not done—liming the lawn, seeing so many people but knowing so few, the imperative flying trips to Cincinnati, Akron, or Roanoke, the sales won or lost—all so important once, but which seemed futile now.

Brad remembered what was important: the Saturday breakfast alone with Pris; so rare and wonderful it had been to be father and daughter. She so loving and proud, sharing their solitude and their relationship—why had they so often been strangers? He remembered the times he had been too busy for Eric, the time that was lost and could never be taken now.

One day when Brad was slumped in a canvas sling hung in an antique tub, abandoned in a room of tile while water swirled automatically around his stranger's floating limbs, he remembered the camping trip with Eric. It was so real, man and son, driving to New Hampshire and, each with his pack, climbing the hill that was to the boy a mountain. They passed, just barely, the timberline, and now he could again smell the low birches, the cold of the pine groves left behind and the heat of the sun on the rocks above, as they cut through the fields; no need for a trail now, for the peak was ever in sight. They stopped to look back at the view and hurried on to the next view. "Lookit, Daddy, over there—the lake's so small from here."

They were companions to the clouds. They stood on the peak, a rounded one but still the highest place around, and saw valleys, mill towns cleansed by distance, and the multiple, purple horizons of other hills. They watched, alone together, shadows black, blue, and purple cross the hills.

There was time for everything on that trip—hours and minutes in which to examine and touch the moss and pale-green lichen. They gathered firewood, found a crevice for a fireplace, and cooked their meal by the sunset's orange light. They talked, feeding the fire, and then sat quietly, silence filling with unspoken companionship. At last father and son crawled into their sleeping bags and stared, silent with awe, at the endless roof of a sky filled with stars, planets of a universe of worlds, and, so small, so tiny in wonder, they fell asleep not knowing when.

Brad woke first and saw his son's face, serene, open to him and to the world. The sun was reflected in the light from a hundred surfaces of a universe jeweled with infinite drops of moisture. Eric jumped out of his sleeping bag, and then was hushed by their magnificent aloneness. The clouds were low in the valley, only the peaks poking through, and the sun painted castles on the clouds.

Brad remembered the fire and the breakfast, the pancakes filled with blueberries—low-bush ones, small, and sharp-flavored, reached out for and picked an arm's length away, it seemed, and flung into the white batter in the black iron frypan. They watched the world revealed as the sun burned the valley clouds away while they ate their breakfast. Brad remembered it all, and now, behind his slack face, impassive, stupid in the warm steam, he suffered, for that wonderful camping trip had not yet been taken. He had never found time to take his son to the mountaintop and he would never have it now. They came and hoisted him out of the water and he didn't even look to see who "they" were. When they got back to Ward F Bets was waiting, but he had nothing to say to her and they sat. He felt abandoned in his wheelchair and she felt deserted, a wife with a husband who didn't want her. Yet she stayed and she came back the next day and the next, hoping this nothing was a crisis that would pass.

One of those days in the endless chain of days when Bets went shopping as an escape, she realized she couldn't forget Brad and decided to go to the hospital early. The unexpected impulse reminded her of when they were just married and she would lunch with him in the city. She felt a hint of excitement. She would surprise him—perhaps that would reach him. She would take him some jelly doughnuts—fresh, warm, the way he loved them—and later, carrying the white paper bag, she hurried to his ward and his bed. It was empty.

"Where's Brad?" she asked.

"I don't know," Carey answered. "They took him away."

"For good?" she blurted in panic.

"Oh, no such luck." His voice underlined that what would have been a tragedy for her would have been a comfort to him. "Not for good. He'll be back for supper." Bets wanted to hunt for Brad, but Carey had her trapped. "Isn't that an evil hour for supper, four o'clock in the afternoon? Just so they can go home. We don't eat from then until eight the next morning. That's sixteen hours, two-thirds of a day, Mrs. Hastings. No food, not even a snack. They shave us and then, quick as begetting a bastard—beg your pardon—three meals. Breakfast at eight, lunch at eleven, and supper at four—swoosh. Now, you know, I just bet the county commissioners don't realize that."

"I don't suppose they do."

"Would if they visited," he whispered. "Do you know any of their wives socially?"

"I don't believe so."

"Find out," he ordered hoarsely. "Find out. Get 'em to come in and see us."

"I will," Bets promised, seizing the moment of escape, "I will," knowing she wouldn't. The nurse in charge didn't know where Brad was, and Bets was made to realize she didn't care. The nurse's mouth was filled with a cheese Danish and Bets shivered as the creature sloshed in some coffee, tan with cream, and slogged out the words, "Burgie took 'im." But no one knew where Burgie, the half-wit orderly, had gone. Bets hunted through the corridors, ignoring the resentment of patients and staff, looking into wards and offices, examination rooms, day-rooms, and down every corridor, realizing that Brad had no control over where he'd been taken—and that she, his wife, had no right to know where he was. She was not wife or nurse, merely a visitor. Running, Bets turned a corner, opened a door, and there he was.

Brad sat in his wheelchair in the center of a vast hall, utterly alone. The room was unlighted, unshadowed, but dark with the gray light of winter, oozing through a few long windows on one side of an unused assembly hall, the windows that were barred and then caged with wire and finally frosted with grime, dark to the sun. Her husband sat unmoving, his body slumped in the canvas wheelchair. His hands lay, palms up, in his lap, useless, the way they had been placed there by some stranger. His face was toward her, but he gave no sign of recognition as she ran, then slowed down and walked across the bare wooden floor, her footsteps the only sound, each step hitting on the echo of her past step. "Jelly doughnuts," she said, her voice too loud in the echoing hall as she lay the white bag on his lap, an offering.

He gave no sign, and she took one out. Obediently her husband opened his mouth, and she broke off a bite and placed it in his mouth and her husband chewed it, slowly, and she broke off another piece and he ate that, dutifully, no pleasure or pain. She was beyond weeping as she bent over, the two of them in the vast hall, and fed her husband a sloppy red jelly doughnut, bite by bite, as she once had fed their children. When she was through, Bets took out a Kleenex and neatly cleaned her husband's chin.

13

Outside, her fingers still sticky from the jelly doughnuts, Bets sat in her car and stared at County.

The stern buildings, so empty of hope, rose high above her, sharp-edged lines reaching up, unforgiving. A red-brick prison and a cement sky. Jet-black trees, stark limbs, acid-etched; the terrible iron fence; the hilltop-huddled buildings, sharp, neat, ominous. A black wash of hills graying to purple off to the right and the bright black of the town trees in the distance and the black blocks, square, squat, of houses and factories. The cheerless rain puddled the walks and the roads, sheened trees and slate roofs, reflected the white light of the unseen sun from a thousand unexpected mirrors—from the wet bricks, crystalled grass, tree trunks, and hearse hood alike. Each surface seemed hard, each limb brittle, each line sharp, each color no color, barren in a bleak landscape.

Bets watched a black, huddled shape slowly lumber down the steps, each step planted heavily; watched it walking, hatless in the rain, down the long walk. It bowed its head, its shoulders slumped, its feet plodding their course, moving steadily through the puddles the same as on the dry pavement; a sad, lonely shape. Surprised, she realized it was Irv. He looked so alone that Bets opened the car door and called to him. "Irv, Irv, over here." She waved and called again. "The station wagon."

He looked at her and she was troubled by his hesitation, for that was unlike him. Slowly, even slower than he had come down the long walk, he moved toward the station wagon, got in, and closed the door. Startled, for she'd merely expected him to chat with her at the window and then drive off in his own car, Bets looked at him closely. When she saw his face she knew his need and asked only one question: "Are you free? No hours?"

"I'm free"—he nodded and hesitated—"of hours."

Unexpectedly sure of herself, of her being needed, Bets backed the car out of the drive and swung it almost joyously onto the highway. No need to tell him she would have to stop by the house to check on the children, no need to say they were going out for dinner. She knew what she had to do and she knew she could do it.

They didn't talk as she drove home, and he waited in the car while she dashed into the house and, with the executive ability of the suburban housewife, arranged for her mother's dinner, half explaining where she was going, and then, not changing her dress, she hurried back to the car. Bets glanced quickly at Irv and then backed down the drive and took them across town again to the low-beamed country tavern with the high, dark-wood booths, the great roaring fireplace, and the waiters who knew how to give service without rushing those who came to talk as well as to eat and drink. Knowing that she was in charge, that Irv needed her, Bets ordered for them both, good, dark, sour-mash bourbon on the rocks, and then, no time to be coy, she spoke: "There's absolutely no reason for you to destroy yourself, too." Irv shrugged and cupped his drink. "Are you quitting too, Irv? Are you trying to balance things by just giving up?"

"You know, he's said it's up to me, that since I saved him, it's now my job to make life worth something."

"I know."

He drank deeply. "I don't know. It just isn't me to become involved. It's against everything in my training, in my personality, to let this get to me. It's a weakness."

"It's a weakness, it seems to me, not to care. And I think it is you to care." Bets spoke softly, moved by the sadness of this face, so familiar these days, the features gross and yet sensitive. In one light his face—the nose and lips large, the eyes hooded, dark—could seem brutish, and then his features were, in a second, transformed, and every promontory and valley of his face softened. "Irv, you look like the saddest man in the whole world." She touched his hand and smiled.

"I am the saddest man in the whole world," he said, smiling at her and at himself, "the absolutely guaranteed saddest man in the whole world. What's more, by myself I've created an entirely new emotion—instant self-pity."

"No, Irv, you pity others." Now Bets turned serious. "Our language is unequal to emotion. It's corny but it's right. You feel. You care."

"Doctors can't feel and care." He looked at her sharply and nodded to the waiter to fill their glasses again.

"You've told me that before, Irv, and I believed you when I didn't know you so well. I don't believe you now."

He studied her face, flattered by the light of the sputtering candle, and said, "You've aged."

"Thank you, kind sir," she said coldly.

"No. Don't, I won't play." He drank again. "It's a compliment, for aging is as good in a person as it is in a cheese, perhaps even better." They sat quietly and then he added, "We've all changed."

"What can we do about Brad?"

He turned his hands up. "You ask me. He asks me. I ask myself and I don't know. I just don't know."

"You're seeing yourself, Irv, and not too many people see themselves once they've grown up. It takes a death or a business failure or a fire to make them look at themselves, really look."

"If you really look, you'd kill yourself."

"Perhaps. I have a confession to make."

"Not to me," he said quickly. "I'm not your priest."

"You're my doctor."

"Not yours, Brad's."

"I've got to tell someone, someone who knows, can understand."

His mouth twitched to a smile. "I cry on your shoulder. You cry on mine."

Bets started to speak but couldn't. She moved her glass through the ringed patterns of moisture left by the other glasses, lit a cigarette, ground it out, and then spoke, crying, "I hate him, Irv. Isn't that horrible? I hate him!" She saw the surprise and the horror on his face. "I tell myself I love him, I tell myself I feel sorry for him, and I walk in there and he shuts me out and I hate him for it."

She took a drink and he said nothing and she stumbled on. "It's wrong. I feel guilty, God knows, but that's how I feel. I understand why he's quit but it doesn't help. He has quit. He's given up. He just lies there feeling sorry for himself, a lump. And I look down on that thing that used to be my husband, the strong one, my man, and I resent him—oh, how I resent him. Am I going crazy?"

Irv shook his head, still not saying anything.

"I've heard of people being mad at their husbands or their parents for dying," Bets went on, "but I never believed it. I do now. I do now. I go and visit him because I have to, and I have to not because I love him but because I hate him. Do you understand? I hate because he had everything and this happened to him, and if it happened to him it could happen to anyone. He was what I held on to, Irv. Women don't need philosophies, they need a man, and he was my man, but he isn't manly anymore. He's just a glob."

"Bets, Bets."

"Aren't you surprised that wonderful, brave, sweet Bets feels this way?"

"Yes," he answered simply, "but I shouldn't be. It's real. It's life. He has failed you. That doesn't excuse you, but it may explain you. We all have to live with the darkness in our souls. We don't grow up until we see the bear."

"See the bear?"

"Yes, the things that can happen to us, the failures, the weaknesses, the terrors that lurk just beyond our doors and just below our consciousness."

They sat for a moment, finished their drinks, and ordered, nothing solved but something soothed by the talk. The sharing helped, and they went on to talk of politics and fashions and cooking and the vitamin fads until finally, while they were having coffee and cheese, Irv twisted sideways in the booth. "Bets, your mother staying with you?"

"It seems so," she said, and smiled ironically.

"That's good." He nodded. "I have a job for you at the office. No, wait, hear me out. It's not charity and it's not made-work. You deserve better than that. You need a job. You can use the money—and the activity—but most of all, we need your help. There are five of us in the Center, you know, and our records are a mess. What a bunch of dumb broads we've had—medical secretaries," he snorted. "They come, they start to learn—some of them—they get engaged, they stop thinking, they get married, they get pregnant—thank God—and they leave. Perhaps the next one? No, the next one's as bad. We've had four girls in three years at our files; they're a mess. I'd like you to put them in order."

"But I don't know anything about medicine."

"Good. Doctors we have plenty, intelligent file clerks, none. How about it?"

"I don't know," she said, looking frankly at him, "if it's a good idea."

"I think it is. I've made my pitch and I won't pressure you." He accepted another cup of coffee from the waiter and began to talk of himself. "What's happened to me and Brad isn't only Brad." With a finger, he traced a design of boxes made into imaginary cubes on the dark wood table. "It's something that happens to everyone, I suppose, but I didn't expect it to happen to me—not so soon, anyway." He paused and she was pleased that she knew not to interrupt his silences. "It's running all your life and then winning all the races there are. What do you do? You've been trained to run, not to be a victorious runner. I wanted to become a doctor, a surgeon, but I'm not trained to be a surgeon—I was really trained to be a man working hard to become a surgeon. Does that make any sense?" Bets nodded and he went on. "I've spent all my life becoming a doctor. Now that I'm a doctor I don't have to run anymore and I don't know what to do." He stood up. "I need to talk and drive. Will you listen?"

"Of course." She rose with him, content with being needed. "I'd love to listen." She handed him the keys. "You drive." Irv Frank took the same river highway she had driven along with the children, but Bets was struck by the difference—the forgotten intimacy of being in an automobile at night, alone with a man: encapsulated, cut off from time and space, the road leading anywhere, following its own lights; the seductive motion of the automobile, the comfort of the seats and the mysterious soft light from the dash; the trees rolling by, row on row, picked up by the headlights and tossed back beside the car; the sound of water and wind; the illusion of escape. Bets sat sideways, one foot under her, leaning against the door, watching Irv's hands as he drove. They gentled the wheel, his fingers stubby but delicate, easy with an experienced competency. "I like to watch hands," she told him.

He answered by not answering directly: "I like to drive and I always have. I've driven dozens of nights right through, just driving. It's not the speed anymore." As Irv spoke, his words were an exploration as much as a conclusion; he spoke as one free to talk, knowing he would not be held accountable for each revelation. "It used to be the speed. I was always in a hurry, the kid who wanted to get there. Where? I always knew, always, and I didn't even realize that was strange. You know when I decided to be a doctor? When I was six years old. My grandmother was sick and she was the most wonderful person in the world, and I saw how much she needed the doctor, how they all waited for his coming and how they respected him and how he moved, a bear of a man—rough and competent. He made her well, and they thought of him as a god, and I decided to be a doctor." He laughed. "When she died and the doctor could do nothing, I was older. I didn't decide not to be a doctor because of that." He gave a quick laugh. "You see, I was already thinking like a surgeon—I knew I'd be a better doctor. I was twelve years old, smart in school, and I knew.

"You know, I never once doubted it, never." Irv swung the car around the lazy horseshoe, climbing turns with ease, and drove away from the river up the ridge parkway. "I see the look in my father's eyes now, in my memory, but I didn't see it then when I told him, so sure, so many times I'd be a good doctor. Not a doctor, a good doctor. It wasn't fear or envy of the son who was going to be a doctor, but he looked at me in wonder—sheer wonder—that his boy could be so sure, that he could look out of the same flat, work after school behind the same candy counter, and be sure he'd go to Bowdoin, a real *goyish* school, and become a doctor. Since I never had any doubt about being a doctor, I didn't doubt anything else. All would be solved when I was the doctor. We were poor? We'd be rich when I was a doctor—Mother would have a one-family home. I was lonely? Wait until I was a doctor and I'd have a thousand friends. Pimples? No dates? Wait for the nurses. I was a shrimp? I'd be a giant with an M.D. after my name. It was all I had, no friends, no temple—I stopped that nonscientific nonsense as soon as I was *bar mitzvahed.* Everything I studied, each penny I earned, all had one purpose: medical school. Did Brad tell you the night of the party that I told him I had used him?"

"No. What do you mean?"

"Of course he wouldn't have mentioned it. It would have embarrassed him—if he believed it. It was the kind of revealing thing a gentleman doesn't say." Irv stopped as they both realized they were talking about Brad in the past tense, as if he were dead. Then Irv made himself go on, without apology. "He knew so much he didn't know he knew, how to walk or stand, casually, what to wear, when to wear gray flannels and loafers, when to wear a sweater without a shirt. Brad knew. He knew how to light a cigarette, how to mix a martini, when to laugh. And you know something? Humor is a very secret language."

"Yes, I know." Bets spoke softly and Irv looked quickly at her. "I know," she repeated, "I know very well."

"I didn't understand the jokes and I thought they were laughing at me," Irv said, shaking his head, "but I didn't care. So I was serious, a grind—I was going to be a doctor. They didn't like me for it, but they understood. This was what you did to be a doctor if you were Jewish and poor. How important was it that I was Jewish? I don't know. It was lonely, but I would have been lonely anyway. Perhaps even it was good, for it gave me an enemy; I had something to prove and someone to blame." They broke out along the river's edge and he drove more slowly, seeing the moonlight, specially bright after the rain, metal-bright on the black water, and the distant procession of the car lights on the other shore, going the other way.

"I've always wondered," Bets asked, "how do doctors make themselves work in school? How did you keep going during medical school and the training afterward, the hours, and all that?"

"You know, it comes easy. I guess it's like asking a drunk how he can drink so much. Work becomes everything, an obsession, a drug. Part of it's because you are motivated. As much as I hate the word, it's what we're talking about, isn't it? I was motivated; boy, was I motivated. That's part of it. Another part is that you're busy. Not with introspective things, because there's little time to think or to wonder about what you're doing; you just do it. Every minute you have jobs to do, places to be, problems to solve, things to learn; you're moving and learning, and people are always checking up on you. The carrot—perhaps it should be the

Cadillac—on the stick. But it's more than that. It's like eating too much or doing anything to excess. People respect you for the years of struggle, but it's no more virtuous than sitting drugged before a TV set. Work becomes a thing in itself: work, work, work. It keeps you from thinking or worrying or even being tired. It's a glorious, virtuous oblivion."

They shared another silence as Irv swung across the bridge, which arched gracefully over the river, and then they started back along the bluff. "It wasn't Brad, his accident, you see. If it weren't him, it would be something else, someone else, because now I'm the doctor and it isn't enough. I have no God, no family, no purpose, I suppose. Make people well? All right, but I know how much I can do and how little I can do. There are damned few miracles. Medicine is a pretty predictable thing. You know" —he turned to her with wonder in his face—"it was just yesterday, it seems, that I was fascinated at putting a pin in an old lady's hip. Now even a clubfoot is routine and even the gratitude is routine."

"Irv, this is growing up."

"Is it? I suppose so. When everything is possible, we have to make choices and then wonder about them. Would Brad have ever doubted like this?"

"I don't know, Irv," Bets sighed. "I used to wonder and then I decided he wouldn't but I don't know now. I'm not so sure about Brad, about anything. Yet I see this sickness around me, in the people who live around me. They wouldn't understand the dissatisfaction in someone else; yet it's happening to them. They've all got the same sickness. I think it's something men used to feel in their forties; now they've gone ahead so fast, they get it in their thirties."

"What do they say about it, those who have it?"

"Oh, they don't know they have it. At least they don't talk about it, but I think I see it in their eyes, in their third drinks, in their voices, in the importance of unimportant things, in the anxiety—no, not anxiety, a desperateness. Oh, I'm not making any sense."

"Perhaps you are."

"Well, I know how I feel," Bets said and laughed. "All right, how a woman feels. I don't think in theories, but I felt lost and guilty because I felt lost when I had everything." She leaped ahead with woman-logic: "And when I didn't feel lost after Brad was hurt—it was almost as if I welcomed his injury because it gave me a place—I felt guilty again."

"Why were you lost?"

"I had everything, like you, I guess. Nice Greek girl, be clean, neat; learn how to walk and talk and dress and if everything goes well you'll marry an American and live in a white house behind a green lawn and I did and I had everything and for a while I ran along on momentum and then I sort of ran down. I began to feel as if my life was all over, that all my dreams had come true and I was dead."

"It's a luxury, to have all our dreams come true."

"I suppose, but it's awfully cold, too."

"Cold?" Irv snorted, then nodded. "Yes, perhaps. Cold and lonely. Did I want to doctor or to be a doctor?" He smiled and shrugged and they drove on, not talking, until Irv, not asking her, swung into the eye-blinding brightness of a diner's parking lot, weaving her car between the haphazardly parked, elephant-sized trucks. They had coffee, two cups each, both black. They cradled them, elbows on the booth's table, talking less, ill at ease with each other, face to face in the fluorescent light. At last they drove on, both noting the hour, neither mentioning it, wanting to let the spell spin on. Irv turned inland, away from the river, into the hills, driving slowly on the curving roads, and Bets, back in the intimacy of the car, felt a need to sit primly front, to look straight down the road, not at Irv's now-familiar profile or at his hands, but to stare straight ahead at the tiny, twisting line that ran down the road ahead. They broke out on a village common, dark and silent, a hundred years old, and then drove up in the farther hills, talking slowly, as if they had forever. They drove on and talked on, knowing they were going farther than they intended and still unable, unwilling, to stop.

Suddenly Irv banked the car, picking up the ridge road, and their bodies swayed right and left as he let it down the serpentine descent onto the highway back of the city. They didn't speak on the way back to the hospital, not mentioning that the sky had lightened and their capsule was exposed in the light, destroying their privacy. The ride, the night of talk, were ending. The car rolled across the gravel in the parking lot beside Irv's low MG. He turned to her and they sat facing each other, his voice hoarse when he spoke. "We didn't do anything."

"No"—she smiled, feeling warm—"I guess not."

"But it helped me a lot, your listening."

"It helped me too," Bets said. "I wish he'd let me help him. Perhaps, then, I'd learn to love him again, better."

"He will."

"Oh, I don't know. I just don't know anymore, Irv. We're back and it's all there and I feel lost. Useless."

"Let me make you help me some more." He touched her hand on the seat and she turned it over, touching him.

"I'll take the job at your office, Irv." There was no need to say anything more, and he quickly got out of her car and into his own. Jackknifed behind the wheel, he waved and was gone. Feeling like a woman again, Bets watched him and then drove out through the gate under which Brad had passed coming in, aware that she had made her decision to take the job without asking Brad.

14

The next morning Bets called Irv Frank and told him she couldn't take the job unless she had her husband's permission. Even before they had children, Brad had refused to allow Bets to work, and when she had been offered a job two afternoons a week while the children were in school, he wouldn't even talk it over with her. Angrily she had said, "Your wife doesn't work." And he had answered, his own voice harsh, "That's right, my wife does not work."

She had to ask him about Irv's offer, even though they needed the money so desperately. She hadn't wanted to worry him, but it was a fact: she would have to work if they were to keep their home. And Bets thought that Brad had to have their home. It might be a goal someday. If their home went, so would their marriage. Each day she promised herself she would ask him and each day there was a reason not to bring it up. Monday he was in his bed in the ward, and there was no privacy. Tuesday the ball game was on at top volume in the dayroom where he'd been carried and left. She would have had to scream to make herself heard. Wednesday the young man who had been a ball player was dying, with his family around him, in full view of the whole ward. It was not the time for a talk. Thursday Brad had contractions and his face, racked by pain, stopped all conversation. She stared at him, her face giving him the pity he resented while he fought the battle he had decided was his alone. Then on Friday there came the time. Carey had been taken away for X rays and Bets could talk softly with her husband, trying for the illusion that they were alone.

They talked of the children and of the fact that Pete had put up the storm windows and her mother's habit of falling asleep with the radio on, loud, and Carey's treatments, which weren't working, and then, saying too much, knowing it but being unable to stop, Bets began to tell her husband about the job.

"Irv's offered me a job at their offices. It isn't charity, although I guess we could use the money. With Mother there I could take it, adjust the hours for the children if I had to." She realized she was twisting her wedding ring around and around and made herself stop, but the words tumbled on. "They've had girls who keep leaving to have babies and they need someone to keep the records. I guess they're a mess. You know the records on each patient; you'd think they'd have been coordinated, but they haven't—they're not even up-to-date. Irv said it would be my job to set up a system and take hold. I wondered if you think I should take it. I know how you felt, but things are different now." Her voice fell and she stopped. Brad was silent. "I mean, do you think I ought to take the job?"

"Of course."

She'd been prepared for anger, so his indifference confused her. Bets brought out the arguments she'd prepared: "I wouldn't let it interfere with the children. I'd be home when they're home. You see, I wouldn't really be working a full week and I could take work home." She talked of the challenge, of the fact that she'd like to keep their home and that they'd have to have more money coming in to do that, and then, still talking, she realized he wasn't listening. "You don't mind if I take the job?"

"Why should I?"

She analyzed his tone, the look in his eyes, to find bitterness, anger, sadness, but she found only the same indifference. It wasn't his affair anymore. She tried to talk of other things, but each subject, the church program, the bond issue for the school, the Perrys' trip to Europe, Grant's promotion, was stopped before it was mentioned, by his lethargy, his sunken acceptance of his world. Trying to think of the things that would interest him, she realized he was a man drugged, doped into a world smaller than she had realized. His world wasn't bounded by the high iron fence and the grounds, not by the brick walls of County, not even by the limits of Ward F. His world was his own bed with Carey's bed a Europe away. He was putting in time, and where she had to rush—shop, drive home, see the children and listen to them, help with supper, bathe and dress so she could go to the Hodgkins' dinner party, they had insisted she come—Brad was in no hurry, had nowhere to go and nothing to do but let his long hours pass by.

Bets said good-bye and then, as she was leaving, she asked again, "Are you sure you don't mind? About the job?" He shrugged and she left, thinking that her husband didn't even know—or care—that she had gone.

She told her mother that she was taking the job, and her mother, busy over the stove, only nodded, imitating her daughter. "So you knew, Mother?"

"I knew."

"You know everything?" Bets' voice was sharp.

"No, but some things. You act as if this was you alone, that it never happened to anyone else."

"I know, I know," Bets said wearily, tucking her gloves under her hat and placing them on the newel. "It's happened to a dozen wives in your neighborhood that you know. A hundred."

"They have had to go to work."

"It doesn't happen here, in this suburb."

"They move away?"

"It doesn't happen."

"It does. They're people."

"I suppose. Oh, Mother, they don't seem like people sometimes. I should have stayed home, been like you."

"You couldn't and I didn't want you to. I'm in between. The old world and the new, the old ways and the new. No longer Greek, not yet American, like you."

"Like me? I'm nothing. At least I don't know what I am."

Her mother smiled, surprisingly tender. "You? A pretty, good girl. Call the children in, see them, and then get ready for your party." Her mother reached up and patted her shoulder. "You'll do good on the job."

Bets dressed and drove to the party alone, dreading it and excited by it, feeling exceptionally alone, eagerly hoping the evening would bring something different, a break, a relief, new people and new talk. The Hodgkins were good friends, the first people to have them to dinner when they'd moved in; yet Bets felt an alien, walking up to the house alone, imagining that the warm greetings at the door were the exception, specially put on for her because of what had happened to Brad. They were his friends anyway, she thought during a quiet moment during cocktails. People fussed over her, for him, because of what had happened. They were nice, honestly, decently nice, but they didn't know her.

"What can we do for Brad?"

"Nothing. Nothing at all," she said, turning to Hal Johnson. "Sounds terrible doesn't it?"

"Yes." He nodded with sympathy. "I'm ashamed of myself, of all of us—for not visiting."

"It doesn't make any difference."

"Oh, Bets, it must. I mean your visiting—golly, you've been faithful—it must mean everything to him. I've heard that few wives remain, well, true. It's pretty awful, I guess."

"Hal, I was shocked too, but now, although I couldn't do it myself, I can understand." She tried to explain it, not really hoping he'd understand, but somehow anxious to make him try, knowing that others, now they were at the table, were listening. "Brad's left this world. I'm beginning to understand what that means. You see, he's in another world. My visiting him at first helped and it may help sometime in the future, but it doesn't now. I go to see him because of me—to salve my conscience—and because of other people, to prove I'm the good wife, but not because of him." Bets half laughed. "If anything, my visits upset him. They must. I'm healthy."

"He's not so alone," Hal said tentatively.

Bets sipped her drink, aware of the laughing in the room, of the smell and sound and feel of all the people together. Friends and neighbors, sellers and buyers, advice taken and advice given, patients, clients, golf partners, club members and church members, and then she answered, "He's just as alone."

He didn't speak and she continued, talking down into her drink. "He's alone. He's incurable. Those are facts." Hal looked at her, touched her shoulder awkwardly, and left for the bar. Bets turned to the people on her right and entered into the conversation quickly. It was about the new high school principal and it was the usual conversation. She could handle it easily while her thoughts drifted from Brad to herself and from herself to Helen, Hal's wife, who thought she was watching Bets unobserved. Bets saw her face speculating, worrying, before she saw Bets looking, and then Helen smiled. Bets went to her, feeling she had to explain. "Hal was talking about Brad. He's so understanding."

"Yes, he is." Helen couldn't help it—her voice was cool.

"Helen, don't feel guilty," Bets spoke quickly, impulsively.

"I don't know what you mean."

"No, perhaps you don't. But you were looking at me as if I were a threat. I'm not," she said and smiled.

"Bets, I'm ashamed. We had a fight before we came—you know, a silly thing and, well, he said he's going to leave me."

"Oh no."

Helen smiled. "He won't. We'll patch it up, but I guess it showed. You two were talking and it's been a long time since we talked. With six kids you don't talk." Bets listened to her troubles and made her peace, but she knew, before she had to sit at the corner of the table, what she had known at every party, what she saw in the yard and at the store and in church and at the club: the suburbs are like Noah's ark—everything goes two by two.

Driving home, the time of special loneliness, and coming up to the dark house, Bets faced the fact she had only felt alien before but was really alien now, a widow, in fact, an outcast, and she realized the good sense of the wife who hurled herself on her husband's funeral pyre. She brushed aside the bitterness, stepped out of the car, and walked wearily, so very alone, to her house.

She took a warm bath to soothe her and it betrayed her. Lying in the warm water, she became aware of her body, thinner now, better than it had been. Half floating, half asleep, she felt a need for Brad, cruder, more physical, more direct than she had ever had when he was well. It shocked and surprised her. Bets could not put her thoughts, intimate and passionate, away, and so she rose out of the tub and scrubbed herself red, and then ran to the bed, where she was so especially aware of its size and awful emptiness. Haunted by memories, breathing hard, almost laughing at herself, and crying, she got up and took one of the tiny white sleeping pills that the doctor had given her after the accident and that she had never used.

In the morning, afraid of what she had felt and aware that

she could no longer live the married life of the suburbs, she called Irv and accepted the job. Then she spent the day going through her dresser, mending and sewing and ironing, working with a compulsive speed with her mother, now understanding in a way she never had before why her mother worked doing the dishes the dishwasher could have washed, wringing out the laundry the drier could have dried, scrubbing the floor that was already clean. They worked hard together, not talking much, losing themselves in the chores of fixing a working wardrobe, and that night she took no bath and needed no pill. She slept.

Bets enjoyed the job. The first day Irv said, "Remember, this isn't charity. We need you" and it took Bets only three days to realize he was right. In a week she was obsessed with creating a system that would work. She visited other doctors' offices, wrote to the AMA, went to the library, talked to salesmen of medical systems and office supplies, was endlessly fascinated by the intricacies of the talk, forever challenged to bring order out of the confusion of doctors' scribbles and half a dozen girls' eccentric ideas of filing.

Bets enjoyed going to work as she had when she first left school, stimulated by her independence and excited by the comradeship of the workers—doctors, nurses, and secretaries who shared a crisis, a cup of coffee, or a joke. Each evening on the way home she stopped by for her visit with Brad, steeling herself against the depression that could draw her under at the sight of his face, which had always been so pleasant, now lined with bitterness. He wore a mask of sad weariness that treated her, the ward, the entire world, with cynical contempt. And she felt guilty that her resentment showed. He spoke when spoken to, fed himself, bathed and sat, accepting what rehabilitation was initiated by others with amused tolerance. He made Bets a stranger, and was invulnerable to her visits in this new pose. Still she visited him once a day, and they talked as strangers talk. Spring came and he allowed his wife to wheel him along the walks, silent trips, for the most part, for how can you talk over the back of someone's head and he answer when he has to speak to the far hills? They ranged from one end of the grounds to the other, and she no longer asked him to allow the children to visit—he would have none of it. She feared his wanting it now, for their father was a bitter, broken hulk, and their lives were full of things more real. It was a cruel fact that it was better they didn't visit this father who had been dead to them three seasons of a year.

Bets brought him things—food, which he partially ate; magazines and books, which he left unread—pitiful offerings to a shared past that was dead. She knew she was fulfilling an obligation, for love thrives on need, and Brad, if he needed her, would not admit it. There were fewer and fewer moments of despair or aching pity; there were memories, but they were rare now, and she was surprised, although she had been told it would happen.

"At first they ask, 'When can he come home?' " Irv had told her in one of his cynical moods. "Then it changes to, 'He can't come home, can he?' " Bets couldn't believe him then, at least could not believe she would ever feel that way. Now she understood, for this was no crisis, this was forever, a word she'd never understood before. Nothing before had been forever—life was marked off in easy steps: until you graduate, when the children are in school, after you've been promoted. A house was bought to be sold. Only Brad thought that life went on, that things were permanent, that you could have roots—and he never believed life could be without hope, not if you really tried, not if you really wanted something badly enough.

Her friends kept wanting to make it easier, saying that perhaps a special drug, a miracle injection, an extraordinary operation, something could be done—as if false hope were better than no hope. Only those who knew, who had a child who would never learn to read; only those who lived without hope, not for a few hours outside an operating room but forever, day after day, week after week, year upon year, could understand, and their sympathy was mute—a look, a glance, a quick pat on the hand. They knew, and they knew the special horror of what they all were—not saints, but people who resented what had happened to them, who could hate as well as love, get mad as well as be understanding, who lived constantly with guilt. When she first learned at County how many men abandoned wives who were sick, how many wives deserted their crippled husbands, how few children or parents visited, Bets was angry. After one winter, just one, she was sad for them and for herself.

She made herself care for the children and keep the house and be pleasant to her mother, and lived for the hours in her cubicle at the medical building, where she could work with the files.

"I'd like the names, weights, and blood-pressure readings of all patients with inverted belly buttons."

"Certainly, Doctor," Bets answered quickly, not looking up at Irv. "Adams, Elmer; Adams, Elvira; Adams, Eva; Adams, Rebecca; Adams, Sam; Adams. . . . It's congenital," she said in mock seriousness, "and besides, all our patients have the same condition."

"Inverted navels?" Irv asked, shocked.

"Yes, I'm sure of it," she answered proudly.

"How can you tell?"

"Have you looked at a belly button recently?"

"Fairly recently."

"See?"

"See what?"

"The navel, the belly button, *dummkopf*."

"Not inverted."

"Of course they are, all of them," Bets said airily.

"How do you know this new medical truth?"

"They've got to be," Bets said with certainty. "They're so silly looking. They must be inside out." Shaking his head, Irv smiled and started out the door. "I'm counting on the zoo—I need a day away from broken hips."

"We'll give you the sweet odor of the elephant house."

Holding his nose, he left the office, and watching him, his step now familiar, his smile still warming her, Bets suffered a sudden recognition—too clear, too sure to be denied or even argued—she was happy. It had been so long since she had thought in those terms that it surprised her; yet she knew it was true. It did not deny the sadness in her life, the nostalgia for the times that could not come back, the pity for Brad, the hopelessness of the future; yet this was sure: her life was full, the hours were busy, she was needed as she never had been when Brad was—she almost said to herself "alive"—when Brad was well. Bets forced herself back to the job at hand, thankful she had a job to do that could protect her from her thoughts, but that evening, driving home, rushing so that she could help with dinner, planning what she would say at the PTA meeting, Bets again realized she was content. More than that, she was sure of herself. "You've been tested, Bets," Irv Frank had told her, "and you've passed with a hell of a good grade. You should be proud of yourself." Bets found that she was. Her mother helped, but Bets made the decisions. She was clearly in charge. Her children were healthy and doing well in school; in fact, they seemed to have adjusted to a home without a father surprisingly well. She went to sleep tired and slept hard, and when she woke she hardly ever looked back at the wide, barren bed, for she had a day's work to do.

Then, late one afternoon as she was comfortably absorbed in the work at hand, a pencil stuck in her hair, her desk piled with papers, Bets reached for the next folder and was flipping through the papers before she saw the name: HASTINGS, BRADFORD.

Bets stared at the folder and felt the tears well up in her eyes and flow down her cheeks. She had not yet thought of him that day; it was as if he were dead. She had ordered the dishwasher fixed that morning without wondering what Brad would have done; she had made plans to take the children to the zoo on Saturday without a regret that Brad would not be there; she had lunch with Ruth, a nurse at the group and her best friend there, a warm, wise woman who had been such a good friend, but whom Brad, incredibly, had never even met.

Staring at the folder, she remembered Brad not walking, not coming in from work, not at parties, tall and sure of himself, graceful, belonging, his face forever pleasant. She saw him slumped in his canvas wheelchair, his skin an unhealthy gray, his flesh unmuscled and smooth, his hands lying palms up and useless in his lap.

She made herself finish the file as if it were a stranger's, and then she went on to Headley, Hendricks, Hendrickson, Hopgood, and Hopson. By the time she reached Hulme, it was all right. She had found again the comfort of her work and had forgotten, for those few hours, her husband's gray, sullen face.

15

Dr. Frank was even busier than Bets, but his work no longer comforted him. Making his rounds, answering the calls of emergency, keeping hours, visiting his clinics, even working on his paper, he was a priest who continues the ritual of his vocation after he has lost his faith.

He felt a lethargy that he thought he hid from everyone, but it became a topic of conversation in the small world of the hospital. A colleague noticed that his gait was different in the corridors; he seemed almost aimless on rounds. An intern was shocked by his unusual cynicism: "Do you think it makes that much difference what you do?" A scrub nurse saw that his skill was not affected, but noticed that he took longer to scrub, that he seemed to have to make an effort to rise to the moment of surgery.

He was surprised when he was named Chief of Orthopedics, but he felt no joy. He became obsessed with himself, spending hours in unusual self-examination, as if he were unique, no relative of the minister who doubts, the physicist who reaches the horizon of reason and sees the black abyss, the businessman who finds that profits have become meaningless, the actor who comes to despise the cheering audience, the athlete who recognizes that he, a grown man, is master of a boy's game. Irv's vision, which had always been outward—on the goal, on the case at hand—now turned inward. Patients found him distracted;

friends felt that his attention was turned inward, tuned to an internal radio station they could not hear. Ignored by him, they ignored him, and he was more alone than ever.

The trick he learned as a intern, to fall asleep in a moment, cutting everything off—his brain, what happened yesterday, what could happen tomorrow—was lost. He turned in his bed, thinking of himself, of his life, which now seemed so barren. He cursed himself for what he had once been so proud of. He called himself a technician with a knife, and saw his own loneliness. What had been a defense now became a prison. He remembered all the patients he had forgotten, the failures who were buried, the failures who were crippled, the successes of which he had been so proud, who had, like Brad, been given life without meaning. Irv rose from his bed and went to eat sweet rolls and coffee in an all-night restaurant, and then he returned to his apartment and tried to read. When he slept, he woke unrested. One morning he had the illusion, a half dream that pinned him to his bed, that he was Brad, unable to move, no longer a man, useless.

Most of the time, however, he didn't think of Brad, he thought of himself, short and dark, gross, felt he was a caricature of a man. He imagined his race was etched on his sleeve as it would have been in Nazi Germany. He felt abandoned and looked into himself to rediscover his pride, his faith, his purpose, his self-respect, and he saw only a stumpy little man growing old, looking forty-five when he was almost thirty-six, a technical virgin, uncommitted, a surgeon not a man, a thing growing fat and losing its hair, aging before it had ever been young. He cursed all the years of study, of application, for he could not recapture the motivation or restart the engine that had once powered it all.

His furious rages at the interns, at the nurses, no longer burst over them, and they were strangely disturbed. His face became sadder, his voice softer, his step heavier. Irv Frank saw people at their worst, something that is easier for a doctor to do. He saw parents ashamed of their crippled daughter and he saw others who lied about the beatings they had given to their own infant. He saw a perverted mother who selfishly kept a son from treatment, cheating him of a normal life. He saw the patients who arrogantly bought a new car with the hospital insurance money that was paid to them and refuse to pay their legitimate bills. He saw fear and cowardice in the eyes of his patients. He saw the sick hate the healthy, and he saw a family's relief when Grandfather died before he'd used up all the money that would now be theirs. He saw the fakers, the malingerers with the phony backaches and put-on trick knees, the insurance collectors, and the chronic complainers. And he saw none of the others—the brave and the good—who usually sustained him. It seemed to him as if the good ones had died and the worthless survived.

Stubbornly, only because of the promise made to Bets, Irv Frank visited Brad. Twice a week he made the time to drive over to County, park in the lot, walk the corridors lined with the human ruins who stared at him with resentful eyes, their bodies bowed or swollen, twisted, shrunken, gross, shriveled, only their eyes the same to him—bitter, lost.

Visiting Brad, Irv felt he understood what Bets must feel. Brad in a bed or in his chair, on his side or on his back, no longer showed he was aware of the steps in the ward that were coming toward him. Irv had to speak directly to him—and then Brad might not admit he was there. Irv would say what he had to say: "How are you, Brad?" "How's everything today?" "Feel any pain?" "Everything just the same?" Anything he said had a double meaning, every question was cruel, every comment on the world outside an insult, and still they had to chat. He had to read the chart, to take the unresisting pulse, to touch the shoulder of his patient, to say something. At times Brad looked right at him and then his eyes would insolently unfocus as if he could make Irv disappear.

Aware of his public humiliation, for he felt that the whole ward was watching, Irv grew angry and then ashamed of himself. He felt pity and suppressed it, felt hopeless despair and put it aside. Visit after visit he came to Brad, and was always frustrated. Once he confessed to Bets, "If only he was bitter or mad. If he only hated—" And then Brad would speak and Irv was not sure it was better.

"I can give you a pinch in your right hand, Brad."

"Gee, thanks," Brad mumbled sarcastically.

"It would help."

"A miracle?"

"No, no miracle." Irv tried to keep his voice from being too patient, condescending. "With a pinch you could, however, feed yourself better, pick up a cigarette, turn a page in a book, turn the dial on a television set," he said once more.

Brad didn't answer him.

Once, when Brad was in a wheelchair, Irv lost his temper for no reason and told him off: "You're nothing. Nothing. You've quit. God damn it, Brad, you have a head and a soul. Your brain's fine and you could use it to do something, with Bets' help. You can't go all the way, Brad, not even fifty percent of the way, but you can use what you have, not quit, not make yourself a vegetable."

Brad answered, "Would you?" And they glared at each other in silence, for how could anyone answer that? Each time Irv left County he felt older, more alone, and yet this desperate loneliness came at a time when, in a way, he was more aware of people than he had been for years and, at times, less alone than he had ever been. He talked to Bets about Brad a good deal. He saw her at the office, ran into her at County, and told himself he ought to keep an eye on Eric and Pris. He even enjoyed a cup of coffee with Bets' mother, sitting in the kitchen and visiting the way he had at home. With them he felt more natural and at ease than he ever had away from work. And now, when his work was barren of pleasure, he felt as if he lived for those brief visits. When Bets suggested he share a formal, old-fashioned Sunday dinner, he could not refuse.

After that dinner with her mother and the children, Irv and Bets drove alone to the park at the Point and walked in the early-spring woods. Turning off the bridle path up the cliff trail, he took Bets' hand to help her, and then when they reached the top and saw the ocean, black-green, a winter ocean still, each clung to the other's hand as if they needed strength. Not looking at each other, not speaking, they moved together to the parapet, where they could follow for miles the hills that ran down to the shore. The purpled slopes were textured by saplings bare of leaves. The greenness of spring—of fern and leaf—was something more remembered than seen from here. Sky and land and sea were stirred together in a meringue haze, and a lone boat, white, small, rising and falling, moved steadily along the coast. Together they turned and followed the walk, slowly, still not speaking, taking in the scene right through their skin, so that it would always be a part of them. Then, suddenly, the mood changed, and they talked, words tumbling out as if the sentences had been waiting right in their throats for a release.

"Think of the settlers who first came here."

"It must have been cold."

"You can understand why they didn't move inland."

"Except at the rivers."

"I've always wanted to take a canoe trip up one of the rivers, Irv."

"You have? So have I." He laughed. "Henry Hudsonstein."

"Don't, Irv."

"All right, I won't. Today everything is possible," he said, laughing, and immediately he began to use "we" without, at first, realizing it. "We'd read everything we could find about that country."

"Old maps."

"Of course, and faded journals in libraries."

"Find out how they ate and slept and worked and dressed."

"I'd like to know, Bets, what they really thought of the country and the Indians. We'd have to know where they came from and why, what they expected to find. Then when we started up the river in our canoe we could see the river as they saw it."

"Wouldn't it be fun?" The question wasn't answered, for it couldn't be. Silent once more, they turned their backs on the sea blackening in the dark and walked to the car, sharing a nostalgia and in some strange way a contentment, as if they had really made that impossible trip up the river.

When Irv returned to his apartment the contentment fled and it was the same as it had recently become, a place to escape from, no longer the place to flee to, not a haven but a group of rooms, lonely, barren, filled with possessions that had no meaning to him. Each night when he let himself in, there was no joy of possession, no delight in the hoarded opportunities for sensual or intellectual pleasure. He'd always delighted in the freedom that now frightened him. He'd always treasured his opportunity of choice—to eat now or later, in or out, read a journal or a book of history saved for this moment, walk through the apartment naked, stay up late or go to bed early. See someone if he wanted to or no one if he wished. He had interests enough—his collection of all the recordings of Bach cantatas he'd been able to find; his military maps from the Middle Ages; his own sketches, ink and wash, raced off without planning or thought for the one happy accident that might be saved from an evening's furious activity. He told himself that he did not need people for entertainment, and in the past he had never felt so alone in his apartment as he felt with others, not knowing what to say, not sharing their delight, drunk or sober, in just doing things together.

Now, standing alone in his apartment, the door not yet shut behind him, just one light to chase the first shadows, he thought of Brad and of himself. At college he had never understood why Brad wouldn't go down to the diner alone, visit the library or go for a walk by himself. Everything became an expedition with Brad. "Who's going to the Libe?" "How about some coffee?" "I'm taking a walk." That was enough, and Irv remembered his wonder at how Brad could be so sure they'd come. They did, all right, just to walk with him. He saw Brad, in his memory, so young and so sophisticated, terribly appropriate in the letter sweater worn next to the skin, the wash pants, the moccasins, no socks. Laughing, Brad had stood waiting for those who would join him, one hand in his pocket, the other on a pillar of the House. He, Brad Hastings, belonged. He'd ask Irv to go along, but Irv would nod "no" usually, wondering what hidden cause, never mentioned, never hinted at, must have stood behind their sharing a room. On the room-selection card he had put Hastings' name down, cynically, the way another man might write on a form that he wanted to be President. He didn't know Brad, just heard the name, Bradford Hastings, a fine, Ivy League name. Irv knew he'd be placed somewhere else or in a room alone—which would be just fine. You couldn't ask for a single, for the administration believed that part of a college education was getting to know different people, and apparently they were unaware that the Jew, the foreign student, the lone Chinese, almost always seemed to end up in a single room by their junior year "because they wanted to." Brad had accepted Irv tolerantly, and they were roommates; strangely enough, they'd forged an unusual bond that leaped understanding or even much communication.

Irv tossed his coat on the couch, nudged the door shut, and nursed a Scotch splashed on ice. Still not turning on the lights, he sipped his drink and tried to understand why he resented this tie to Brad that he still could not break. He had it licked, he told himself. He had built his salvation not on people, but on skill. His was no phony solution; he was no backslapper. He had his purpose for being in his fingers, and that should give him all he needed, and it had been enough until now. Irv kicked off his shoes, unbuttoned his shirt, and hung up his pants. If he were in shorts, he would be less tempted to go out. He poured himself a second drink, which he rarely did, and turned on the Mozart G-minor quintet. He had the whole evening ahead of him, and quickly he got out the drawing board, his ink, the manuscripts on loan, which were pertinent to the moat he was working on. He stared at the drawing with pleasure—a crazy, useless hobby, but fun. He was designing a medieval fort, using only the materials of that time and the medieval soldier's knowledge of engineering. Irv even forced himself to share the medieval vision of war. He, Irv Frank, a thousand years too late, was creating the best fort of the times—invulnerable against siege.

He played fair at his game of intellectual solitaire; to build his fort he had to know all he could find out about the armor and weapons of the time, the tactics, the way people ate and lived, how they thought. He had no deadline; he took his time; this would be a monument to hundreds of evenings, an intellectual accomplishment he would share with no one. He had been asked to join historians' clubs and other organizations by the men he had met at libraries and in the bookstores where he collected his materials, but he felt no need of their company. It was enough to create this for himself—he needed no one else's approval, and he would not risk their ridicule. His fingers neatly sketched in the moat, its measurements, the drainage ditches, the location of the drawbridges, but his mind would not travel back into history this night. He thought of Brad, who never wanted to be alone, discovering loneliness in Ward F, and then irrationally he wanted to spread out his fort, like a little boy, for Bets' approval, show her each detail, his library, the maps and manuscripts he had collected, filed and indexed.

Irv reached for the telephone, spun the dial eagerly, and then hung up before it rang. Moving as if he were chilled, he stiffly put the drawing board away and walked to the kitchen, where he heated a can of chicken soup, watched the grease puddle on the surface, stared at it until bubbles formed at the edge, then poured it down the sink. He dressed and went out to walk the streets with strangers until he was tired enough to sleep.

16

Peg and Pete came to see Brad out of guilt—it had been six weeks or perhaps seven. They told him it was spring.

"Your dogwood's out. It's lovely," Peg said.

"You were right about pruning it back," Pete added, too eagerly. "Remember I agreed with you? Well, you were right."

"The shape's just right," bubbled Peg.

He had to look at them. They stood right in front of his face and he couldn't turn away. He felt the anger, the way they could walk in on him in the ward. He had no privacy; they just came in, dropping by from their other world, to remind him it was spring.

They talked on, these good friends, ignoring his ignoring them, hesitant and awkward, their sentences rushing out, becoming jammed in double meanings, breaking free again. The paragraphs broken by awkward pauses—these people with whom he once had been always at ease; now it was awkward, and he had nothing to say.

"Permister's been made VP in Chicago. And Blagden retired, five years ahead of time, told Mac to stick the Washington office. Sales are holding up, but we miss you, of course, really do. Tilden's not the same. A good boy, but still a bit inexperienced. He'll catch on, hold the fort till you get back. . . ."

"Bets looks fine, just fine," Peg broke in to rescue Pete, "and those kids. Eric's the little man. The Johnsons have separated—and with six kids! Cub Scouts have a jamboree this week. Pete's taking Eric. Two nights out—bet neither one of them sleep."

Peg and Pete laughed until they heard the echo of their own voices and then they stopped suddenly and said, "We'll be back, old buddy."

"Yes, not so long this time."

"Next week."

"What can we bring you?"

He didn't answer, and at last they left.

Brad didn't care if it were spring or if the company went broke or if the cubs jamboreed or if the Yankees won again or if the Johnsons performed cohabitation on the church steeple at high noon or if the dogwood bloomed. He didn't care about anything. He was an alien in the ward. He didn't understand them and they didn't understand him, not even Carey.

They had tried, the two of them, imprisoned in their corner together, to understand each other. Politics and pro football, sex and hospital management; they had even talked about cars for an entire afternoon, but they didn't communicate and Brad couldn't understand why. Carey thought him odd for all the things he had always considered ordinary: college and having a pediatrician for his kids, voting Republican and living in a one-family house.

"Did you belong to a country club?"

"Yes," Brad grunted defensively.

"What's it like?"

"Come on. Let me up."

"No, I'd like to know." Brad had been placed on his right side and he could see Carey and that he was serious. "I've always wanted to know what a country club is like, inside. How you get in, have a membership. I mean, what's it cost? When do you go there? Does your wife go? What do you do?"

"I specialized in the nineteenth hole."

"What's that?"

"Oh, come on," Brad snorted, then saw that Carey was hurt. "It's the bar," Brad said evenly, carefully. "There are eighteen holes on the course, and when you come in, you go to the nineteenth."

For an afternoon he lectured on the country club, stopping

to think about the things he'd never had to think about—how members were chosen, how you got up a foursome, if you cut in during a dance, how some members "decided" to resign, why he liked his club and didn't like the other clubs in town, what was different about them. But Carey was the only one who could get him to talk. With all the others he was on guard, wary of their pity or of their ridicule, ill at ease, unsure of himself.

One day, while he sat, inarticulate, in the dayroom, Brad remembered a conversation with Bets just after they were married. She'd heckled him about what she called his "charm," his "twenty-four-hour-a-day-nice-guy-likableness," which allowed him to slip into the manner, the jokes, the outlook of his customer. It was always a compliment and a comfort to the customer that Brad could understand; he knew it was his greatest business asset. Bets kidded him that night about the fact that he seemed to drawl when they entertained L. C. Simcoe from Columbia, South Carolina, and Brad laughed with her before he realized that she wasn't laughing. Then she'd asked tensely, "Do you ever feel you're losing yourself, like an actor who really is the part he plays and, well, nobody off the stage?"

"Well, I'm not nobody off the stage," he remembered answering.

"Of course not," Bets had said, "but I'm serious. You react to people. They seem to like it and it's an extraordinary talent, but frightening to me. Why, I'd feel I was just, well, slipping through my own fingers. I've just never seen anyone you react to in the wrong way."

"I never think about it," he answered, as serious now as she was. He thought a moment, and then, "And I'm not just a yes-man." Brad smiled. "But I guess I realize that men like Jim Botts prefer a no-man—if he's a tame no-man." Bets had looked at him and waited, and he felt he had to go on. "I've never thought about it, Bets, never. I guess I want people to like me, and I like them. Is it so wrong that I want to get along?" he asked, a bit angry. "You know, I don't think that's so bad. If more people could talk the other guy's language, we'd get along better."

Bets had studied her coffee and said unsurely, "It seems to me that a lot of people we know speak only the other guy's language. I wonder what a crude, direct, outspoken character who said just what he thought would do to the corporation."

"He'd bounce off the front door and never get in." Then Brad laughed and went around to kiss her and ended the argument: "Or he'd be chairman of the board."

When Brad first arrived at County he hadn't realized that his perpetual good manners, his flip, sophisticated answers, didn't go over at all. For the first time in his life he was on the outside—he didn't belong. His good manners, his charm, the thing that had always opened doors, now made him suspect.

"You see, Hastings," Carey had once lectured him, "you have an illusion of a classless society. Everyone's in. The bus driver has hi-fi and an encyclopedia for his kids; the messenger boy wears Ivy League pants; the vice-president's wife shops at the A&P. Both political parties are the same; we're all the great, wonderful, middle class. But there's a residual aristocracy—people who really have it—and a residual proletariat, and more levels in your middle class than there ever were in a feudal society. I read up—I know. Tell me the difference between an Episcopalian, a Methodist, a Presbyterian, a Unitarian, a Baptist. It's money, job, education: class. You're suspect here because you belong in a private hospital. You were a have. Most of us have always been the have-nots. Maybe it's luck or maybe we failed or maybe we're the unfit who didn't survive or who quit. We may be bums, but we resent the things you hold dear." Carey laughed. "Not having them, it's easy. Most of us could be bought for a TV set and a private room. Relax. This is for life. It's no Boy Scout adventure and you'll find out, you'll find out, you'll learn to belong, but when you belong with us, you won't belong with them."

"You mean I might even vote Democratic?" Brad laughed.

"You might at that." Carey laughed. "And once you're in, the things they suspect you for now will become a matter of pride—they'll say, 'See Hastings? Bowdoin man, real Ivy League, money. You shoulda seen his wife, real class. He's a helluva guy. You know it? He's a helluva guy.' "

Carey got to Brad. Carey was everything he didn't like—a griper, a troublemaker, a pro-union liberal, a cranky, irascible irritant. "Look, Brad," Carey once said, "understand this. I don't hate businessmen. Some of my best friends are businessmen, but there's nothing sacred about the profit motive. So you do it for money. There are worse things, but there are also better things. This country wasn't built on the profit motive."

"What was it built on, apple pie with ice cream?"
"Dreams, damn it. Dreams and hunger."
"Hunger for money."
"A part of it, perhaps, but hunger for freedom even more."
Brad didn't know how to argue with Carey. His reasoning was fuzzy, but his arguments could be razor-sharp, and sometimes Brad felt as if the ground had been cut out from under him. Once Brad argued that the men didn't want to join the union. "I know, Carey. I talked with them."
"Do you think they told you the truth?"
"Yes, I do, goddammit."
"Crap. You were conned; you are the enemy. I never saw a strike but what management said, 'The workers didn't want it—it was those Commie organizers.' " Carey laughed. "It's the same way with the tame niggers in Mississippi who make the Massa think they don't want no integration—'Boss, nawh, suh, we don't want none of that down here.' But who are the ones who are fighting for their rights? Their children. The ones they raised and taught how to fight. Who's that Clara you quote about how the colored people feel? Your cleaning woman?"
"Yes, it happens that she is, but——" His answer was cut off by Carey's laughter.
He got mad at Carey all out of proportion to the subject, and, realizing it, he got madder still. He would not speak for days; he lay on his side, staring at him, ignoring him. Then Carey would needle him until they would go at it. Why, they would hear the same story on the news piped into the ward and get opposite reactions. "You assume that an American company investing in South America is going to do the wrong thing, don't you?" Brad would hear himself saying.
"Not the wrong thing, exactly," Carey barked back. "It may be the right thing, but it isn't going to be done for the humanitarian reason they say. They don't want to raise the standard of living all over the world—they want to make a buck."
"Of course. Anything wrong with it?"
"Not if they don't prance about like hypocrites."
Back and forth they would argue, and Brad discovered that he had a begrudging respect for Carey. The man was a bleeding-heart liberal, an idealist, but he did believe in his ideas. Here he was dying of cancer and he was fighting a hundred causes, from warm bedpans to Africa for the Africans. And he was in

pain, pain as Brad had never seen and hoped never to feel; pain that had become Carey's condition of life, worse sometimes, better at others, but pain that never left him alone, awake or asleep, when his face would grimace and his teeth grind at the pain, the constant, consistent, bleeding, paralyzing pain. In his sleep Carey would moan—once he even whimpered like a puppy—but awake he'd never make a sound. He'd not complain when his face would twist and tear apart; tears might tumble out of his eyes, but awake he'd never sob. Each day he'd get up, at least once, forcing himself; never able to go farther from his bed than the hoses to the obscene drainage jars would let him.

Carey, dragging his plastic umbilicals, seeking a scrap, a cause, was a born troublemaker who couldn't be ignored. The others disappeared into shadows; they meant nothing to Brad, and when he realized this, suddenly one afternoon when he didn't think his head was working—"I don't give a damn about any of them with the exception of Carey, perhaps"—he was surprised, for he had always been interested in people: his parents, his teachers, his first employers. Everyone knew that Brad was interested in people, that he could make contact with anyone. Everyone liked him because he liked everyone. Liking people had been the condition of his life. He didn't love people, of course; he wasn't a do-gooder. He didn't think there was good in everyone—and he couldn't care less. There were a lot of bastards in the world, he used to say, but most of them were amusing bastards. Brad Hastings didn't so much avoid arguments; they just never seemed to occur. Things were always pleasant when he was around because he went along with the rest. Brad was proud that he took people as they were—saint and sinner alike. He asked the people he met about themselves, and he seemed interested in their kids, their jobs, where they came from, where they were going. Nothing profound, a handshake, a grin, and a joke, but it was good, he had always said, "to find out that the other guy isn't so bad after all."

Now, in Ward F, he just didn't care about people. He was insulated from them all by a massive indifference. He didn't really know much about Carey, and the men in the beds at the other end of the ward could be in California for all it meant to him. He had known a thousand names, maybe five thousand in the industry; hell, he had sent out seventeen hundred and fifty-three Christmas cards, but he didn't know the first or last names of guys he was living with, and was surprised when he found that just fine. Some of them forced themselves into his consciousness. The Smiler in the next bed, waiting to die. Foster, the old fool who kept rolling up in his wheelchair, the self-appointed joy boy who told him every time he came by how worried Bets had been in that waiting room at Memorial. Lambert, who screamed and cried and roared until he got his drugs. Wallace Wallace, the big Negro whose dignity was even larger than his shoulders; Brad knew him because the rehab man came to Hastings when he was through with the great colored man. Imbertini he knew because Irv was operating on him, and the dark Italian thought Dr. Irv Frank was God. "What will he be when Irv gets through?" Brad asked himself. "Still a cripple, a man who will always have to live at County," he thought. Francis Dougherty, who had found his personal savior and came to each bedside to make converts, praying over you whether or not you wanted to be prayed over. Where did they come from? It made no difference—they were all equal now. Where were they going? Nowhere. He dismissed them from his mind whenever he could.

Brad had been proud of being a regular guy who didn't go in for couch stuff, but for a man who never had thought much about himself, he realized he spent a lot of time examining his navel. When was he going to get fed? Why had this happened to him? What could he do to earn a living now? What kind of a world had he lived in before the accident? The questions attacked him and he tried to fight them off, to turn his mind off, to ignore them all. Then would come an unexpected nostalgia, a pain, a dream, a memory, or Carey would start them off.

"I'll bet you own an Andy Hardy house."

"I do," Brad answered. "I never realized it, but I suppose I do."

Carey was unexpectedly quiet until he said softly, "I'm a bastard. That's nothing to laugh about. I guess I'm jealous of all the people who think they can lick the system, have one themselves."

"They can," Brad answered. "Corny or not, our neighborhood is full of self-made men."

"Is it?" Carey came back. "Sure, men who've moved up from the lower-middle class to the upper-middle class. Father managed a five-and-ten; son is a district sales manager. Father a draftsman; son an engineer. But there's rarely a step across class lines. Did you save the down payment for that house?"

"No, my father's insurance——"

"Fine. My father didn't have the money to bury him."

"Well, maybe not a great step in a generation, Carey, but how about grandparents?"

"A few, a few, Hastings," Carey admitted. "But it makes me mad to think of all the guys whose wives think them failures because they didn't make it into an Andy Hardy house right away. Zoom. Boom. And those guys themselves in this land of freedom and opportunity who never had a chance, never had the contentment of knowing their place, of being a good workman."

"Two points for me," Brad said, grinning at the ceiling. "If you believe that, you'll want the nigger to know his place, the workman to stay happily by his machine, the serf at his plow."

Carey was silent, then he laughed. "You win—this time—but I'll be back."

He would be back, Brad knew, with another argument, another cause, facing each day as if he weren't dying, as if it mattered what the hell he thought, what he said, what he did. "Damn Carey," Brad said to himself, "you just can't ignore the dying bastard."

This became his world—this corner of the ward inhabited by Carey, Brad, and the old man, all waiting in their fashion for death. Brad no longer received flowers. Ames stopped coming. There had been a day without a card, then a week without any mail at all. County was a fifteen-minute drive from home, yet Brad was on another planet, a dark world of people waiting, waiting, waiting, spinning through the darkness. Until Carey asked his questions, Brad realized that they rarely spoke of death, and euthanasia was a word used outside.

Still death was there, always, the best thing that could happen to them, and Brad found himself hating hope and faith, and welcoming death, the great painless nothing. Francoer, the old man five beds down who sobbed about death, terrified at the thought of dying, ate at Brad. The old man sobbed and cried, "I don't want to die," endlessly until they gave him his needle. And one night Brad yelled at him, "Welcome it—death."

"No, no. I'll be nothing."

"You are nothing," Brad answered back, and then Henderson from his iron lung had said, "Shut up, Hastings. Don't infect us with your goddamned self-pity." And Brad had lashed back, "You, too, you're alone. You ought to have the plug pulled."

"Oh, shut up, Hastings," Henderson answered, his respirator rasping, puffing. "You're a snob, sorry for yourself because you have to be in here with us common cattle."

Brad felt the fury rise in him, red, burning, out of control, "Well now, Pollyanna," Brad said scornfully, "when was the last time your wife waltzed in to see you? What do you think she's doing? Enjoying some mystical togetherness with you or humping that TV repairman, Schneider, that you keep talking about in your sleep?"

"Stop it, Hastings."

"Not until you admit it. We're alone, each of us," he shouted, and his voice echoed out of the corridor, empty of visitors on Sunday afternoon. "You're alone. Say it. Alone. Alone. Alone."

And the voice did come back, a sob, a surrender, "I'm alone," and Brad was frightened as he lay there, a stranger to himself.

It seemed hours later when Carey whispered in the dark, "Maybe you understand."

"What?"

"Understand how I feel. Maybe you'll help me."

"How can I help you?"

"You can."

"To do what?"

"Kill myself."

Brad knew at that moment that Carey was serious, that it was possible, that Carey had a plan, and all the idle discussions of mercy killing were past, that this was a moment of truth.

"Don't answer now," Carey whispered. "Think about it. Just promise me that," he begged desperately.

"I'll think about it," Brad answered, shocked by Carey's begging, by this revealing weakness. Brad knew he'd think about it now that the question had been asked. "Will you help me kill myself?" Carey had made no self-pitying threat but a proposal that demanded action. There was no sleep for him that night, and as he tried to apply logic to the problem he realized that it wasn't a problem of logic, even here at County, where they waited in this enormous death house. Even here suicide was strange. He knew it happened: sometimes a patient did it alone; sometimes he was helped part way by a friend or relative, perhaps even by a staff member. Brad knew that. There were rumors about those deaths that had a particular certitude about them and a peculiar fascination. On Ward F they didn't talk about the theoretical principles of mercy killing, but they gossiped endlessly about patients who had died.

"Mrs. Reilly finally made it."

"Last night. Right after visiting hours."

"Her daughter?"

"Yep."

"Whose daughter?"

"Mrs. Reilly's."

"The one married to the plumber?"

"He there?"

"Don't think so."

"She always said she was going home."

"Yep, that's what she called it."

"Investigation?"

"Just wrote heart failure, Dr. Snyder did."

"He know?"

"Of course. He wouldn't do it, but it'd be OK with him if the daughter did."

"A good child, her."

"Was the best thing, considering."

"Of course, but few know it."

"How could they?"

"It" was never named, but the question, reports, rumors, speculations, ran up and down the beds like fingers racing up and down a keyboard.

Brad didn't sleep, he just lay there listening to Carey's low, sedated moans, which meant that Carey'd had his second capsule, and then Brad remembered a day two or three years ago. He was driving along the river on one of those clear, crystal days, in December probably, when you could see the city a dozen miles away, black points against the rose-purple sky. They'd just come from Joe Boynton's funeral, and it seemed to Brad that he could still feel the heaving shoulders of the weeping widow under his hands. He could see her ravaged eyes and he remembered his last visits with Joe, his skin taut on his skull, his religious ravings and false hopes and the one wild, animal scream. "Bets, I want you to promise——"

She interrupted him as they rode along the side of the river. "No, Brad. Don't talk about it, we don't know, we can't promise anything."

He remembered how fiercely sure he was, his hands on the wheel, how strong and certain. "Don't keep any secrets from me, Bets, ever. Don't let the doctors try to play games. I want to know the truth. I don't want any false hopes."

Now he laughed out loud, bitterly, in the dark, and heard the patients shifting at his braying laughter, and he thought how they had tried to tell him the truth at Memorial and how he'd clung like a child to his warm, comforting false hope. Then he forced his memory to take him back to the car and what he'd thought then, when he could think dispassionately about the subject, which he believed at that time would never affect him. "I know what that awful newspaper phrase means now," he'd said. "Mercy killing. Well, it is a mercy—and I want that mercy. Let's make a pact."

"Brad, you can't be serious."

"I am. I've seen Joe and Mary and those kids. I know."

"You can't be sure, Brad. I mean, how do we know now how we'll feel if——?"

"I know, for sure." Brad remembered his voice had been so confident. "When I'm like that I want out. I want to die like a man, and if I have to have help I want you to promise to help me."

"I can't, Brad. I couldn't do it."

They argued and, of course, he won, by bullying her into agreement. Now it seemed he'd been a child, enjoying his courage in the face of an enemy he knew could never be real, impressing Bets and himself. How brave he had been and how little he understood. Carey awakened. Brad sensed it and knew, before it was asked, the hoarse question: "For God's sake, will you, Brad, will you?"

He pretended to be asleep, knowing he couldn't fool Carey, but knowing he had to run from that question, and this was the only way he could run, pretending to be asleep. When he woke in the morning the question—Should he help Carey kill himself?—was there, brutally clear, waiting to be answered before he opened his eyes. When at last he was up and lifted over the side and slid on the wood bridge to his wheelchair, he asked the nurse to push him near Carey, who looked at Brad without speaking while Brad looked at him, studying his face, not answering. In this one winter of knowing Carey, Brad had seen him being eroded, eaten away by pain, by the destruction of his body, and at the same time had seen his marvelous, perverse, mean cussedness grow stronger as everything was cut away but this core of a man, until he had the craggy glory of a granite cliff in the White Mountains—stark, stern, irascible, perpetual.

"Think I'm a coward, Brad?"

"No," he answered quickly.

"I would have once." Carey's tone was softer than Brad had ever heard, the words made gentle by a rare trace of brogue. "I was religious once and headed for the seminary. Taking one's own life then, I knew for certain, was a sin, an awful sin—worse than dancing and such things," he added with a quick grin. "Oh, I was so sure in those days. Don't tell the administrator, but I'm never quite so sure of things now, and I guess I want you to do more than help me. I want you to tell me it isn't a sin" —he barely hesitated—"and you can't do that."

"No, I can't do that." Brad joined his silence, then broke it. "I was always so sure it was not a sin—the opposite of you. I was a churchgoing pagan. Going to church was something you did, like eating steak raw or floating a twist of lemon peel in a martini."

"Oh, wouldn't you like a drink now, Brad?"

"I'd walk a mile for a bourbon on the rocks." Brad laughed. "That's what they ought to try. A jug over on the table—and a glass—so I could drink if I could make it."

"Now, that would be rehabilitation." They grinned at each other, two men still, friends, bound by their disabilities. Brad looked tenderly at the sharp peaks of sheet that betrayed the skeleton body with the obscene watermelon pot, the wasted claws that lay idle, and he realized that Carey's spirit was far larger than his body. Brad wanted to weep. Instead he said, "If I do, I'll miss you, you old bastard."

"You'll do it?" Carey whispered eagerly.

"I'll think about it, goddammit, I'll think about it. It's no abstract thing when it's you lying there, you, whom I know."

"I understand, and it's no abstract thing for me either, though I don't fear it at all. I think dying's a pretty fine thing, and that in a better time it would have been allowed me before this—before we had the bountiful blessings of modern medicine."

The conversation was over, but Brad had nowhere to go and neither did Carey. So the man on the bed shut his eyes and the man in the wheelchair sat in the slouch in which he had been abandoned, staring for an hour at the friend who wanted him to help him die, just watching him, not thinking, just hoping time would make his decision, that Carey would die naturally, in his own time; staring at the tubes running out from under the covers to the horrifying jugs with their foul liquids below, Brad knew it would be a close race.

They didn't come for him and Brad sat, hating the fact that Carey had broken into his loneliness, had involved him in his suffering, had made him care. He wanted none of this. Brad stared at the sheet, so irregularly, so faintly rising and falling. He shut his eyes and heard the slight moans, unconscious now, a pitiful revelation of which Carey would be ashamed. Brad heard even the nasty seeping from the tube into the jug. He wanted to put his hands over his ears and he could not. He sat, abandoned by the nurse. Brad started to call her and realized that even if she came she couldn't take him far enough away. He sat. He wanted to talk over this unexpected problem of ethics with Irv or Bets or the chaplain, someone, but there was no privacy. Anyway, how could they understand? Should he help Carey? Carey had asked him. He alone had to answer Carey. With the question, they'd have an answer, each of them—an abstract answer to a question that to them had to be theoretical. Each would react as he should, with no doubts, and if Brad did speak, he'd betray this man who had no one else to ask, Carey, who had on the other side of his bed a wall, and of visitors, none.

Brad seized the only escape he could find. When Carey woke the question was immediately in his eyes, and Brad answered that he would if he could, but that it was impossible, and he reminded Carey that he was a quad.

Carey closed his eyes, his lips trembling as if he were praying. Then he opened his eyes and said, "Thank God, Brad, thank God."

"But I can't do anything."

"I'll tell you what you can do." Carey slyly looked down the ward. "I'll tell you later, not now. They'll be coming on rounds later; it's a good plan. I've been working on it for a long time." Three times Carey started to tell it to him and three times he stopped, but the next morning Carey had the nurse wheel Brad close to his bed, and Carey, who was only forty-three years old, used the hoarse cackle of a man of eighty to speak with the joy of conspiracy appropriate to a boy of nine. "Now, this is what you'll do." Brad was engulfed by a wave of faintness, of unbelief; yet he knew this was real, that this was happening to him, that he was plotting to help his friend kill himself, that this nasty ruin of a man was his friend, that he was here, a hopeless cripple, that they were both at County, that this world of pus and green walls and hopelessness was his world, and that death was real. "You promised, goddammit, you promised."

He stared at the emaciated man, who glared fiercely at him. "I promised, Carey. I'll do it, but first answer some questions."

"Yes?"

"I'm surprised I don't know, but I don't, and I want to."

"All right."

"Are you married?"

"I was."

"Divorced?"

"No." He smiled serenely. "She doesn't know I know, but there's always a bearer of bad news—I was told. She's a Mrs. Sweeney, living in sin, and a force in the woman's Sodality—has three little bastards."

"No."

"Yep. I didn't always see the humor of it, but I delight in my private little scenes now. He comes here—the husband comes here."

"To see you?"

"Yes, but he never speaks. He just walks slowly by in the corridor every month or so to see if I'm still around, although I'm not sure I know why. They'll have to live the lie anyway. Maybe it'll be easier on them when I'm dead." Brad was silent, and finally Carey asked, "The other questions—what were they?"

"Oh, never mind. It was crazy to ask."

"No, go ahead. I understand. It's all right."

Brad spoke quickly. "How tall are you?"

"Six feet one." Brad was astonished, for he had thought of this man he knew so well as a short, little man.

"I weighed in here at two forty-three." He was proud and Brad whistled.

"Another question."
"What's your first name?"
Carey hesitated, then smiled and said, "You'll be the first in the ward to know. Even the chart's C. Michael Carey." The smile broadened to a grin as he said, "It's Cecil."
"Cecil?" Brad's voice was unbelieving.
"You'll not tell anyone?"
"Never," he promised solemnly, and suddenly they laughed, out of control, desperately, until they stopped together.
"And now, Brad, for my plan." It had the awful simplicity of a plan that would work. As Carey talked, his voice hushed, hoarse, Brad realized how long he must have worked over his strategy, devising its neatness—each problem foreseen and solved. "I want you to get a sleeping capsule, the Sodium Amytal. They'll give it to you. Save every one."
"Sure. I'll just stick 'em in my pocket," he answered bitterly.
"You'll hold the capsule between your teeth with your lips shut. It won't get wet enough to deteriorate. I've tested it. I'll come get it."
"You?"
"Yes, me," Carey said angrily. "I'm giving up my afternoon stroll. I'll be able to make it for ten nights."
"Ten nights?" Brad said, the horror of the scene, inevitably, night after night, filling him.
"Yes, I saved four," he said and laughed, "before they cut me off. Now I get my shot. I've got to have ten more."
"Will that do it?" Brad asked, seeking the protection of pronouns. "Will the ten take care of it?"
"With a second shot. That's another way you'll help me," he said triumphantly. "I'll fight the first shot, stay awake—I can, I've tried—and then you'll help me convince the nurse I need another. When she gives it to me, I'll take all the capsules—fourteen I'll take. That'll do it good."
"What about the others?" Brad asked, knowing there would be an answer.
"They won't know or they won't care."
"Why me?" Brad asked. "Why not one of them?"
Carey answered simply, "You're nearest."

17

Bets woke gently, aware of the air already warmed by the sun on her skin and then conscious of the light itself, filtered and shadowed by the pines outside her bedroom window and the ghost shapes of the curtains blowing in. The house was empty and there was nothing to do. She shut her eyes to sleep and was aware of sounds that were not there. There was not the whispered Saturday-morning plotting of the children, their tiptoed passage downstairs, the muffled clatter of the cereal bowls, the faraway background music, insanely repetitious, of the TV cartoon show. They were at camp, sent by the church to a place where there were substitute fathers. Bets turned on her side, realizing she could not hear her mother banging her way through her toilet, the opening and shutting of drawers, the creaking of her rocker, the flushing and the turning on and off of water so that she could race the children to the kitchen, and with a fine clatter fix them the breakfast they would rather get themselves. Her mother was visiting back home, awake and up, no doubt, but not here. Bets lay on her back, stretching and reaching out across the emptiness of the bed, hearing no breathing, no half-waking grunts from her husband. He was—— She turned off her mind, shut her eyes, and flung herself over on her face to try to make this Saturday morning disappear in sleep.

She could not. She felt the warm, nostalgic air, the emptiness of the whole house, the rooms that had no purpose this day—the living room in which this Saturday there would be no living, the dining room in which no one would dine, the family room without a family.

Bets rose and showered herself awake, drank her juice and coffee standing up in an immaculate kitchen, and made herself walk along Dogwood Lane. Pete and Peg were at Nantucket, Fred and Bertha at Lake George, Matty up at Bar Harbor, Dick and Sandy at Shelter Island, the Martins at the Jersey shore; the Rossos waved to her as the whole family jammed into the station wagon for a day on their boat, and she went back to her house, alone.

She had things to do. She cut the lawn and then looked at the roses. There were plenty to cut and she chose them carefully, then arranged them on the tables, knowing that they would not be seen and that some evening next week she'd waste an hour tossing them out, clearing up the fallen petals. She bathed again, hot from the mowing, and in a negligee that mocked her half-widowed state, she sat down to write, dutifully filling four pages with words to be sent to her mother, four more pages to Eric, and four to Pris. Walking into the kitchen again, she took out a hard-boiled egg, the last of a dozen that had been cooked on Sunday, peeled and ate it, scraped a raw carrot and crunched it down, heated the breakfast coffee and drank it, still standing. Then she washed the one dish she'd used: Brad's favorite breakfast mug.

The Roberts had asked her out to the lake, but she wouldn't go—they always played bridge on Saturday nights and a fifth hand, no matter how gracious they were, ruined the game. She did yearn, however, for the oblivion of any game that would kidnap her attention for an hour or an evening. She found the weekly paper in the trash, studied the movies at all the towns around, and found only one she cared to see. It was at a drive-in and she tossed the paper aside, remembering that all she could see when she last went to the drive-in were the shadowed, close-together heads of the youngsters coupled in each car.

She'd visit Brad, buy a book—that took time—eat out, and then come home and read. Bets went upstairs and dressed for Brad, the aqua shantung he'd liked so much, in defiance of the fact that her clothes would again be out of place at

County, where the women who visited in their Sunday best wore clothes that were drab or overflowered as they sat, their pocketbooks in their laps, holding them with two hands, out of place and out of fashion.

She drove to County, fast, fleeing the emptiness of her house, the summer-deserted neighborhood, running to Brad, and when he saw her, he smiled. She could hardly believe it—he smiled. Frightened, and aware right then that this moment was different, she sat close to him, refusing to notice the line of beds, each with its tortured body naked in the heat; she ignored the smell of disease, the Coney Island lack of privacy. She spoke softly and they talked as they had not in a year. Words came easily, as if they were no longer afraid of what meanings the words might have hidden in them, just talking naturally, man and wife, the pauses companionable, not silences that had to be filled. Brad even ventured humor. When Bets asked him how he slept, Brad answered, "You know I used to hate to dream. Now I love it—I really get around." It wasn't much of a joke, but it was a start, and Bets thought he seemed pleased when, instead of calculating his reaction, she laughed coyly and said, "Am I in your dreams?"

Calmly, Brad started to croon, "I see you in my dreams."

And she cut him off with: "Your singing hasn't improved."

He laughed gently and then went on talking, suddenly anxious to share his feelings with his wife. "The dreams are so real now, more real, I guess, by comparison with what's real. You know, Bets, I'm never crippled when I dream. The nightmares are never about the accident or the operation or here. They don't seem even to have anything symbolic in them; I mean, I'm not tied down or anything. I may run, but I always dreamed of running."

"I didn't know that."

"Oh, I wouldn't have talked to anyone about my dreams," he said as if he were referring to a third person.

"I never even knew you dreamed. Ever." She laughed, as if she were embarrassed or ashamed. "I would have bet anything you'd never had a dream."

"I remember one. We were only married a year, I guess, and I had an awful dream. Remember we went to the convention—at Montreal?"

"Yes, and we stayed in that hotel with the large room and the twin beds you hated."

"Those damn twin beds," he said, laughing. "Well, I had this dream that everybody got laughing at the convention, everybody—from all the companies, their wives, the waiters, bartenders, thousands of people laughing—and there was nothing funny at all. Not at all. I was laughing too, and I couldn't stop. I laughed so hard it hurt, but more than that, it was frightening. I mean, everybody laughing and it didn't mean a thing. They sounded happy, but they hated each other and they hated laughing. I can remember that whole dream, the laughing grimaces and the unlaughing eyes, the waves of laughter. It was awful, and I wanted to come over to you and have you cuddle me." He stopped and looked around with his eyes. "Can anyone hear me?"

"No," Bets answered. "You should have, you know, let me cuddle you."

"Oh no, I couldn't. No"—Brad laughed—"I couldn't even have told you about it then."

"Why not, darling?"

"Well, it was ridiculous." He gave an embarrassed grin. "You know, unmanly, I guess. Lord, I wanted you so much." He was silent, again aware of the others, who might be an audience.

"A woman wants to be needed," Bets said and tossed her head. "It's more than that—that's why it's been so hard for me. A woman has to be needed, Brad. It's not so bad in a way for me that you've been hurt, but that you won't let me comfort you—I have to have someone." She was crying. "I want you, Brad, you, I need you, you, you're my husband. I need a man, you."

At that terrible instant she saw his face, so dear, so open to her at last, close, and the darkness and the bitterness come back into his eyes. "You wonder why I don't want to talk, to chat, to visit? Do you really wonder why?" He still whispered, but his words were spat out in hoarse, harsh-breathed volleys. Snarling words, swirling with self-contempt.

"You need a man and I am no man."

"You are."

"I'm not. God, you're a woman, a young woman, able to make love, to have more babies. You're right—you need something more than a barren house, kids off to school, a cranky old mother, a make-do job, a crippled husband. Get a divorce."

"No."

"Well, get a man, then."

"Brad."

"Are you different? You need. Get someone who can give you what you need."

"You can, Brad," she said hoarsely, trying to remember to whisper, trying to maintain their privacy but determined to get through. "I need to be needed. I need to give, not to take. I don't want sex, I want love."

"Sex isn't love but love is sex." His mouth was twisted.

"I can give you care and comfort. Love and companionship and sharing—all that's love. I can give you a home, Brad, home. Please don't shut me out, please. I don't want anyone else. I want you, my husband."

His voice was quieter, but his words were terrible to her. "I don't want you, Bets, not on those terms. I don't want your pity, sympathy, and your strange mother-love. Oh, it might be fine for you. Women like to dominate, I guess, to be in charge, but inside this ruin I'm still a man, I'm still proud. I want to make love on top. I want to take you. I want to give. I want to be the strong one and I can't. It's simple, I'm not a man." He paused, but when she started to say something he spoke again: "I can't make love, not like a grown man, anyway. All right, I'll live with that. But I can't support you, either; I can't drive the car; I can't open the olive jar that's too tight for your hand; I can't bring in the fireplace wood and light the fire; I can't get up in the cold and close the window for you; I can't go downstairs to see if there's really a prowler. I can't put up the kitchen shelf; I can't wipe myself; I can't, I can't, I can't, I can't. I can't see my life with you—a neighborhood spectacle, a thing to be resented by you, a chore, an obscene body that will make my son and daughter ashamed." He breathed deeply. "You want to talk? To share dreams? To make plans? I don't have any. Memories. You want to share memories? I don't want any because I'm here to die, to die. And I want to wait the time quietly, without hope, without memories, with nothing." His hand rose and dropped wildly on the bed, fluttering and flopping like a fish on a boat bottom, struggling without hope to return to what had been. "Can you understand? Can you leave me alone? Can you give me that? Can you drop the phony pose of loyal wife you love so much and let me be?"

She touched his forehead, and he could not brush her hand

away, could not turn his head far enough to escape her touch, and she felt she was violating him, inflicting herself on his defenselessness. Helpless, unwanted, understanding how he felt but not knowing what else she could do, she left and came back the next day and the next and the next and the next and the next, but they did not talk.

18

Brad no longer had to withdraw from life when he woke in the morning, for he had discovered a third condition of life. He was neither conscious nor unconscious; it was like being on automatic pilot. He drifted, knowing that time was passing—slowly—and things did happen to him: he experienced dark and light and a sort of dozing sleep, a form of drowsy wakefulness; he had enough hunger to allow him to accept food and enough pain to be relieved when it went away. He knew it was summer, for it was warm, and he was aware when they fed him and drained him and shaved him and sat him up or turned him over or exercised him. Even when he did not speak, he knew they were there—the nurses, the therapists, the feeders, the doctors, Irv, Bets. Yet none but Carey disturbed him, and he enjoyed the unexpected insulation he had achieved. Brad no longer fretted. Time would pass, and with it hunger, pain, limitations, life. Staring at his ceiling, he achieved an enormous patience. Nothing was important, nothing. No one really counted except Carey, not even himself. He had gone beyond the invalid's self-centeredness, he thought, to something Oriental, a suppression of caring, a trance that was humorless and, being purposeless, was therefore godless, but it wasn't death, for that was black oblivion and he hadn't reached that yet.

He was tempted, less each week, but he was still tempted to reach across the barrier. Most times he was able to resist the temptation. The feeder shoved spoonful after spoonful of cold canned peas or beans into his mouth, feeding him by rote—all the gray meat, then all the gray potatoes, all the green-gray vegetables, the lukewarm drink, the crusty slice of bread, the yellow Jello—each portion served all at one time—and he wanted to spit or yell or ask her to vary the method, but he did not. It didn't really matter if he ate or, therefore, how he ate. She was retarded and she probably ate that way herself. It wasn't important. Irv talked about his goddamned pinch, and Brad felt no curiosity, only an obligation, as if he ought to comfort Irv, to inquire about the pitiful hope he offered, but he didn't. When Pete came by, Brad wanted to talk to him because Pete was so doggoned good-hearted, a real friendly guy, and he could see how much it hurt him that Brad refused to talk—but what was there to say?

There was nothing to say—nothing to say to Bets about the children, who were hardly his anymore; nothing to say to Bill about God and a faith Brad couldn't feel and no longer even craved; nothing to say to the administrator when he made his rounds. What could be said that would change the fact that County was a death house, a place to wait? There was nothing that the administrator, anyone, could do.

But Brad knew he could take it and he felt a residual pride in that. Not all of it at one time, the years of waiting until Bets found someone else—she would have to, she had such a need to be needed—the years of waiting while the children grew up and people forgot about him, the years while he existed and slowly died, deteriorating, growing old the way people did on the outside. He couldn't take that—no one could—but he could take this morning, this afternoon, this particularly long night. He could get through Bets' visit, not responding at all, not once letting down the barriers. He could do it for one day, one visit, one meal at a time. And Brad found that he liked his drifting, cocoon world, for in it he was invulnerable. He did not expose himself to pain or to caring. He had no hope and therefore no disappointment; he had no involvement; he was detached. But not entirely: one single responsibility tied him to this world, one strand of obligation. Once each twenty-four hours he had a commitment to Carey. He could not escape that tie to this man who had no one else, who wanted to die with dignity. Brad hated this responsibility, this necessary return to life when Carey would come for his capsule, but he could not fail it.

Carey was cheerful, busy, occupied, planning for his death. Brad thought that the pain seemed to bother him less, for an end was in sight. Carey now had what Brad had lost: a purpose in his life. Even if this purpose were perverted, even if it were the ultimate nothing of death, it gave focus to each day and to his life. Carey could judge everything else by that single standard: did it advance or halt his progress toward his goal?

All day Brad was aware of Carey's efforts—not seeing them so much as feeling them across the moat between their beds—Carey hoarding his strength, deciding not to argue with the administrator because he needed his energy, forcing himself to eat so that he'd have the strength to make that yard-long trip down the side of his bed and over to Brad's. And Carey's purpose became Brad's. He lived for Carey's moment of death, wondering if the nurse would find his cache of pills, planning his role in the charade of that final evening when they'd play on the sympathy of the nurse and get the necessary extra injection, perverting her sympathetic instincts, which had driven her as a girl to care for the sick. Her wanting to give comfort would betray her into killing, giving the ultimate comfort, the one not allowed.

Brad asked for the sleeping capsule each night and captured it in his teeth, pretending to gulp down the water before the eyes of the bored, unobservant nurse. Then he kept it dry by neatly holding it between his teeth. At last the nurse left, and Brad heard Carey's rasping breathing and the slow, oh-so-quiet movements of his covers being folded back. When Brad heard the noises, he saw Carey in his mind, his jaw veins pulsing over the bone, covered by little flesh now, his eyes bright with purpose, the sweat rising right out of his skull-like forehead. Brad could almost feel Carey's pain as he rose—using the distended belly muscles that had been pushed aside by the growth and weakened by the bed prison. Carey had to line up his tubes, sit up, and force himself to dangle on the edge of his bed. He rested then, having achieved an Alp. Then there were the other sounds, which became familiar to Brad. The deeper breathing, a naked foot reaching shakily for the floor, skin sliding on tile, the sound of a body moving against its clothes, and then the depression of

Brad's mattress as one claw hand reached out and rested the weight that remained while Carey's other hand, seen only for a second, swept up and over Brad's face and plucked the capsule out of the teeth.

Brad followed the sounds of the return, himself involved, caring so much as they reversed, the slow, uneven movement, weak but triumphant. At last the gasp, Carey's single admission of pain. One more trip had been made. Brad marked an invisible calendar—three done, seven to go.

Brad escaped Carey, life, in sleep—until he dreamed. These were not nice, neat story dreams with a beginning, a middle, and an end; they were raw images hurled against his brain: sex as he'd never felt it, sex worse and better and more poignant, dreams that woke him and then caught him as he dozed and pulled him under and woke him again during a night that never seemed to end. The violent, pounding moment of sex, isolated, no preparation, no relief, just the pound, pound, pound and awakening. A savage moment, imprinted on his memory. The silhouette of one of Bets' breasts as she stood a moment before the light, preparing for bed. Not the feel of the breast, just that vision, and the remembered desire, stronger now that he remembered it. Her wanton, loving touch, surprising in her, a private gift. The wonder in her fingers and then the gripping, sharp hurting, wanting—wanting him. That single minute alone. Then a blurred montage of a thousand motions, odors, whispers, the years apart were now shuffled together—a special kiss, a caress, a giving and a taking, a laugh, tears, a discovered position or rediscovered pleasure, a cry heard and enjoyed, a thrust, an aching in the loins, a bite, a long, gentle, feather-light caress, her clutching legs, a shoulder suddenly most exciting of all. Cool skin and hot, tangled covers and laughter, mornings and nights, an afternoon, sun on the bed. The wonderful shared making of a baby, and the completion of it. Quick hunger, demands, haste and no haste, play, need given and need answered. The quick and the slow, the crude and the subtle, the unusual and the familiar, love blended and alive in a dream, not one moment, but the accumulation of years, stored up and then flung back in his torturing dreams.

Brad woke at the screaming, his own, realizing that the animal, throat-hurting yell was his. They came and touched him and tried to comfort him with words, and failing, quickly used the needle that made the night go away. When Brad woke again, it was light, and his mouth was bitter and dry from the drug. He remembered the dreams and forgot them, turning them off, lying still within his permanent stillness. Unable to rise, he did not allow himself to think or feel or care.

Breakfast happened to him: the one fig, stewed and slimy (the cook made a cut on figs, manufacturer's overstock, Carey thought); the usual piece of brown cold toast, burned at the edges, with the icy pat of margarine that he couldn't spread sitting arrogantly in the middle of it; the round, cold glob of scrapple with its halo of grease on the plate rouged by the pink memory of last night's spaghetti sauce, half washed off. The coffee cold. He wouldn't feed himself and the feeder fed him, a new one, who whistled through her teeth, looked at the wall over Brad's head, and missed his mouth three times. He took his time swallowing, and at last, bored to impatience, she took his food away half finished. It was ten after ten and almost time for lunch.

Things happened to him. They cleaned him in their fashion and pulled his legs straight as casually as if they were straightening a bed, dealing with things. He rather liked their impersonality. These things they dealt with, the unfeeling legs, were things to them as well. The handlers putting in their time didn't expect anything of Brad and he could tune them out, too. Tune out time. They, all the theys who controlled his existence, forgot his lunch and he didn't know it. They came to get him up and he didn't object as they heaved and hauled him around, a bag of skin with a body inside. He let them handle him, for he had no choice, and when they had him tied in the new wheelchair, chrome and canvas, they showed him what it was. "It's electric, Hastings. Second one we've had and you've won it."

Brad didn't let his eyes turn to the voices. He hadn't even noticed it was Chaplain Bill, and he supposed he ought to speak—but where would that lead? "Look at those buttons—feel them?" Bill pressed on and Brad felt his right hand being plopped on a cold, metallic panel. "You can push this one to go, raise your hand against the bar to stop. Nudge to the right or left and you go that way. You can use this, Brad. It's safe—I've checked—and you can go anywhere you want"—he laughed—"in the hospital. No trips outside yet. Not till you've got a license." Bill went on with his sales pitch, but Brad turned him off. Where would he go, up and down the corridor, to Nineveh or Tyre? After a while the talking stopped, and he was pushed out of Ward F down to a dayroom and placed before a black TV set.

"I'll leave you alone." Bill was tuned in again. "Try it by yourself if you want. I know how it must feel in the ward. Practice here if you want. It's quite a gadget—it really works." The voice faded away and a while passed—an hour, a minute, three-quarters of an hour, more than an hour—time went by. Someone came and turned on the television set and a man laughed and waved his arms at some rather bewildered people on a stage somewhere and they all made noises. More time ran on. A woman, old though young, came in, looked at him quickly, then, ignoring him, cried. A man shuffled in, sat down, and stared straight ahead, and Brad didn't know when he left. A group of men were herded into the room by an attendant, who said, "I'll be right back. You stay heah—heah? Heah me now. You all stay an' watch the TV and play cards. Heah's some cards. Set, relax, and stay heah—heah?"

Brad was surrounded by them. They walked about, bumped into his chair, and paid no attention to him. He saw one man, his back still straight, his white hair still neat, walking through the group with a camel's look of disdain. He looked like a statesman or general. Then that same man pulled a candy bar out of another man's pocket and started to open it. The other man, cherry-cheeked with a bishop's jolly face, screamed the cry of a beast and swung his crutch at the tall man, ex-statesman or ex-general. Brad was caught in the middle of the fight. The tall one fell into his lap and the crutch once hit Brad's shoulder, but he found he could tune them out, all of them, the old men with their grunts and curses, their wild swings and clawing grabs, their slipping, stumbling, falling-down battle. Brad saw the candy bar, which had been forgotten on the floor, and some time later he realized they all were gone and he was alone.

The sun was hot, the shadows long. Sweat ran off his forehead, unwiped, off his brow onto his cheeks, down his nose, over his lips, down his chin. He could follow the single, tickling touch of a drop and he could ignore it. The smell was different. Burning. That smell drilled into him as a boy or perhaps bred into the race, that instinct still active after thousands of years, alerted him. Something was on fire.

Now there was no doubt about the smell: it was acid, hot, the smell of smoke and of rubber burning. The elemental fear in him was so strong that Brad heard himself gasp, but he did not scream. He did not call "Fire." Silent, frozen in fear, Brad looked as far as his eyes would turn, along the walls, back and forth, the floor, the radiators, the ceiling. Nothing. No flames, no smoke there, but still there was a haze near him and the smell, stronger. His fear grew to panic, then stopped, suddenly, with the realization that there was nothing to do but to yell, and that if he did, how could he be sure someone would hear? He could not move—and then he remembered the electric wheelchair and his nose told him where the fire was. He was sitting on it and, of course, could not feel the heat. His marvelous electric motor was on fire, and he could be broiled to death without pain. He started a laugh that sounded like a sob, and then a strange listlessness came over him that was almost a relief. He felt no fear of dying, and as the last, desperate desire for life had drained away he sat, forgetting about the fire, forgetting everything.

When they came, shouting and hurrying, tugging him out of the chair, hurling him aside on a sofa, splashing water around, he felt nothing and showed nothing. He did not answer when they asked him how he was and he did not thank them. They were not surprised and they pushed him back to bed in an old-fashioned wheelchair and fed him supper while it was still hot, as if it mattered to them if not to him, and then he drifted through the evening, not there at all in his bed in Ward F but nowhere, apart from it all, until the nurse asked him if he wanted his sleeping pill, which really was Carey's, and he had to speak —for Carey if not for himself—and had to come back to life, pretending to drink the potion and holding it all the time in his teeth until Carey began his interminable journey across the three feet between their beds.

The clawed hand came and went and Brad could not tune Carey out, could not dismiss him. He was concerned as Carey made his long trip back, not allowing himself to admit publicly his pain with a single groan. Brad cared if Carey made it to his death in his own time, in his own way. Brad couldn't ignore that. "Are you OK, Carey?"

The pause and then the grunt and then the answering question: "And you, Hastings? How are you? Are you still with us?"
Brad didn't want to speak but he couldn't refuse Carey. "Yes," he said bleakly, "I'm still here."

19

Irv would remember it at odd times—stepping out of a patient's room and catching a glimpse of a young woman in summer green getting on the elevator, going to bed tired and then lying awake, when he was reading a medical journal, driving across the high bridge over the river, eating the chicken-rice soup right out of the can late at night in the apartment. Then he'd remember that Bets was alone, her mother back home, the children at camp, her husband. . . . But he would not call her. He avoided the office when she was there now, tried not to go by her desk, and if he did, was always in a hurry, didn't stop. He saw the look on her face and he wanted to tell her why—that she had become all the things he'd never had; that she had become more important to him than his work, than anything; that Brad was his patient and his friend and still her husband. There was nothing to say, and everything, and he did not trust himself.

Dr. Irv Frank promised himself that he would not see her alone; besides, he felt foolish, like a small boy, for he was not sure how she felt. Looking into the mirror, he saw his ugliness, and he became unsure, aware of his ridiculousness, his Jewishness, his guilt.

To make up for it somehow, he visited Brad more often, obsessed with the idea that there was something he could do, and when Brad refused to acknowledge him, he suffered more guilt. He would look at Brad and see the man who had it made, who had the perfect life and knew it—before. He remembered how he had envied Brad Hastings and admired his poise, his grace, and his energy. He just could not be still. When Hastings was playing football he couldn't take Sunday off; he ran cross-country. Not to keep in condition—that wasn't a problem—but simply to burn off the energy. Now he lay where they put him, utterly quiet except for an occasional unexpected spasm, which made his usual stillness more terrible. A hand would flutter uselessly or a foot take one silly dancing step. And now for months the man who had been always outgoing, friendly, reaching out to everyone, had drawn into himself, retreated into a state of complete absorption in himself and beyond that into a passive interior world where Irv could not follow.

Irv came and stood by the bed. He went through the movements of an examination, and he tried to find in Brad a spark to fan. He tried persuasion, friendliness, argument, even tried to goad him with hate. He comforted him and lectured him. He tried logic, appealed to every mood and sense, but failed. He could not get through. Once he stopped to speak to the head nurse, knowing that she scorned his useless visits but still hoping that she, with her experience, might have the key. "What can we do for him, Nurse?"

"Hastings?"

"Yes."

"Care for him. Pay our taxes and care for him."

"He doesn't want to live. I just can't reach him at all."

"No one can except, perhaps, Carey, and I'm not sure about him. Anyway, he's terminal CA."

"But can't anything be done for such a man as Hastings? I knew him before. He was vigorous, strong, alive—no quitter."

The nurse looked at him impatiently. "I've been here twenty-two years and I don't know what to tell them or you, Doctor. There are a few heroes, mighty few, but I can't figure them out either. What are they trying to prove and to who?" She snorted, "If I were Hastings, I'd give up too. Might as well let us feed him. Facts are facts. He is not a man; he is another vegetable."

Irv started to say something about Brad's good mind, his soul, but he realized that it would sound sophomoric in the face of County's reality. He nodded and left, passing the huddled bodies, the twisted and the abandoned of the human junk heap. "The very essence of reality is here," he thought. "No room for illusions or hopes or dreams—just the truth that this is the end."

He drove back through the summer evening and, thinking of Bets, decided to go to the hospital and work on that paper, now a half year overdue. When he walked in he heard his name over the public-address system, debated leaving, and grabbed a phone at the nearest station. "Dr. Frank here."

"They want you in Accident."

"A bad one?"

"A beaut, Doctor."

"Tell them I'm on my way." He hung up and picked up a container of black coffee at the Hospitality Shop. It would be one of those nights.

"What happened?"

"Head on . . ." the resident on duty at Accident said in the tone of wonder everyone always adopts after a terrible accident, as though it were unbelievable, forgetting how close every driver came to it every day. "That kid over there hopped the dividing section—out on Route 43 by the river. Trooper said he hit the other car head on. It seemed as if he were driving right down the other lane. They never had a chance."

"That girl with him?"

"Yes."

"Lord. I see you're using the other room. How many in the car that was hit?"

"Five."

"Five." He nodded professionally, saying cynically, "Good score," but unexpectedly he felt like screaming.

"Mother, father, and three kids."

"What have you got for me first?" He was weary before he began.

"Two kids and the mother haven't much chance. Better look at the father. Roach and Hene are working on him."

"Both?"

"Yes, and there's some left over for you. Whole rib cage, pelvis, neck, maybe." Irv washed and joined the other doctors at the Accident Ward table, quickly fitting into the teamwork of their trade. This job absorbed him for the moment and he forgot about himself as he attempted the repairs. Then the father died, and, unmourning, no time for tears or even surprise or regret, they moved together to his daughter, to help Whalley. Soon he nodded, indicating that there was nothing to do there either, and the resident said that the rest of the family was gone. Irv nodded and moved to the hot rodder's girl friend. She was breathing, but her head was pushed out of shape like a rotted pumpkin a month after Halloween. Irv set her broken legs—a simple job—while Franklin tried to do something with the skull. When he was finished, Irv asked the neurosurgeon, "Planting another vegetable?"

He nodded, his face bitter. "A good night's work, a beauty; she'll be at County for years." Irv turned away from the blond, who would be little more than a human worm, a breathing, wiggling digestive tract for tens of years, for a lifetime, and worked coldly on the driver, so young, so young. Clavicle, left shoulder, forearm, thigh, ankle. He'll limp, nothing more. Not a cut on his pasty, sensual face. Irv ordered X rays, and when he turned back, the kid opened an eye, winked, and before he spoke, the face was transformed from that of a boy to that of a man—an evil man; one of those soft-skinned, puffy men, weak and selfish, who seem evil at birth. "Hey? I'm gonna make it, Doc?"

"Yep."

"Hey, that's good, man."

"How about the others?" Irv prompted the question angrily.

"Yeah, yeah. Hey, how about them? Man, that was some tah-ra-ra-boom."

"Your girl?"

"She's not my girl, man—I just met her."

"Your companion will be a vegetable for the rest of her life." Irv's voice started ice cold, but there was a tremor in it now. "And, man, you know what else you did, man? You killed a whole family." He whirled around to an astonished orderly. "Take him to X ray before I kill him." Then Irv walked through the examining room turned morgue, making his way quickly among the five bodies, each face covered by a sheet. He rushed through the door to the parking lot, fought back the sudden attack of nausea, and slumped on a bench, staring at the comfortless pattern of the lighted windows, hearing the visitors coming and going, cheerily. He ignored the doctors and nurses who spoke to him. "A whole family," he heard himself saying out loud, and he forced his mouth shut. Somebody at the hospital knew them; he remembered overhearing something an hour ago, or two, yes, that there was nobody to notify, nobody at all. This was the end of the line. The fact pushed aside when he was busy sprang back like a whiplash. Sometimes he wondered why people wanted babies so badly, medical students who couldn't afford them, the blind or deaf or ill who might pass on a congenital ailment, the educated and ignorant alike. Why? Now he knew. It was the only kind of immortality you could buy, the only insurance against death: some of me will survive in my children. I'll be a father, I'll be a mother, then a grandparent—I'll be that anyway. When I'm gone, there will be children—they'll remember me. Unsaid but felt by all, the most powerful instinct of the human animal, and it worked, for it did cheat death, Irv thought. Then he remembered the five white, shrouded forms: a family wiped off the face of the earth by a punk, a stupid, pasty-faced punk.

Irv Frank stood up by forcing his feet against the ground, making his muscles push up, consciously balancing and stepping forward, all the way back across the parking lot, into the Accident Ward, around the silent, sleeping family, back to the kid. Irv did not speak to his patient again, but coldly, competently healed him with all the skill he had, feeling at the same time how useless, hopeless, aimless his training was, how he was somehow being used, perverted, and dirtied by the healing of this animal, and when he was done, Irv walked quickly, almost running, through the corridors to his office, where he dialed the number, and before she spoke he said the words he always knew he would use, and knowing he would hate himself for using them, he said them just the same, appealing to her weakness, to Bets' desperate, womanly need to be needed: "I need you."

"Where are you?" Irv paused, breathing deeply, grateful and aware that it was not "Who are you?" but simply "Where are you?"

"At Memorial, in my office."

"I'll come."

"Yes."

"Wait."

"I will. I will. I need you." He put down the phone and repeated the words at the dark corner of the room as if he were practicing some foreign phrase he had to memorize. "I need you. I need you. I need you."

20

Brad was on his right side, having been left with his backside exposed when the therapist was called away an hour ago, and he stared at Carey, unable to forget that this was the man he was helping to kill. He didn't want to look at him—the basketball growth visible under the covers, the teeth clenched in silent suffering. Who would want to be forced to stare at a brave man dying before his eyes, a man who managed a grin or a wink when he thought of Brad staring at him, a man determined to maintain his dignity despite the growth, despite the charity ward and the peeling paint on the wall, despite the lack of privacy on Ward F, despite the public tube traveling out of his entrails to the bottles under his bed.

Brad could ignore the doctors who came to poke him, but he was enraged when he heard the voice of the tall one coming on the ward, saying in his aristocratic drawl, "I have one I want you to see here, gentlemen. Name's Carey."

"One what?" Brad wanted to yell. "One man, god damn it." They strolled down the ward, teacher and admiring students, ignoring all the other cases. Their steps were successful, their voices cheery and proud, their manner arrogant. First the chart rack came into his view, then the obeisant nurse, admiring and grinning, then the cluster of white-coated physicians led by the tall one, who lifted Carey's chart from its place and flicked through it idly. "Terminal carcinoma," he drawled. "An interesting case, very." And although he discovered Carey was awake, and was surprised, he did not apologize. "Been here how long, Carey?"

"Sixty-seven months."

"More than five years—and some people do not think of cancer as a chronic disease." The doctor began his insulting examination, exposing Carey's wasted form, inviting each of the students to poke a finger at the offensive pumpkin in his abdomen and to see how it could be shifted from side to side. "Remarkable how a man can survive so long with this. Astonishing." He turned to Carey and added patronizingly, "You're quite a man," then launched into a technical lecture.

Brad studied the doctor, impeccable in his long white coat, gray hair flecking his temples, and decided that his face was not so bad as his words. He had a sort of residual sympathy, but he had protected himself by his casual manner. He had to, Brad supposed, and that made it worse, that he was not a quack or a butcher, but a feeling man, trapped the way they were all trapped, able to offer so little despite his honors and his titles and his skills and his caring. His voice even had a compassion when he asked Carey, "Ready for that nerve block?"

"When?"

"Day after tomorrow, when I'm back here."

"All right, Doc." Not knowing why Carey gave in, that he would be dead and gone by then, the doctor was surprised. "You've been a stubborn man." There was respect and perhaps disappointment in his voice, although he said, "I'm glad. It makes good sense." Expertly he flipped Carey on his side and showed the craning students how he would cut, what he would do. One of Carey's tubes flopped out of the jug and into the side of one of the student's shoes. Fascinated, Brad watched until the red, draining pus warmed through the sock, and the student reached down, irritated, and removed the hose, placed it in the pot, and wiped his sock. He seemed only angry, but when he'd wiped his fingers on the tissue and thrown it away and turned back to study Carey's bare back, the bones almost piercing the yellowed skin, Brad saw that the face that had been so young, so eager, so pleased with itself, was still unlined and chubby, but it was older than it had been before he'd been contaminated by the pus of a laboratory object that had been a man.

All the rest of the day and the evening Brad expected Carey to speak. It was a time to sum up, to explain to Brad what it all meant. At the very least, he could say how he felt, he could say good-bye. He was turned away from Carey, but they could talk. Instead, all he heard was Carey's breathing, ragged, close to sobbing, but still breathing. Brad realized that he should speak himself, comfort Carey or amuse him, help the time to pass, and he wanted to, but he couldn't find the words. He wanted to talk about anything: his first football game—he'd told that story before; or his first date; the army; the time the general . . . ; the corporation. He looked for topics: politics—an argument would make the time go; baseball—Carey was a Dodger fan still; anything—but there wasn't any topic that wasn't part of life, and he felt an overwhelming sadness. How could he remind Carey of what he was losing? Brad wanted to talk of God and Heaven, but how could he talk about what he didn't know? He left Carey his privacy. Every animal wants to go off by himself to die, to face it alone, unobserved. Carey couldn't do that, but Brad was quiet. Still, he expected some word from Carey and he waited. There was none until the lights were off, and he wondered if Carey would make it this last night, keep his appointment with his own end.

The nurse came in at last with Brad's capsule and he automatically tongued it between his teeth as if this were not the last time he'd do it. Then, when she had gone, Carey started: first, a silent gathering of his forces, more slowly than ever before. Brad couldn't see or hear it, but he could feel it, a careful summoning of his strength to push back the covers, swing his legs under the hoses, lift them over his belly pregnant with death, ignoring the pain, the dizzy, light-headed weakness, until he sat up and rested again. Carey's breathing was just a gasping flutter, but Brad heard the bare foot pat the floor, seeking a secure footing, and then the other foot and the steps, and suddenly Brad knew that Carey had fallen. There was no crash, just a hushed crumbling as if clothes were falling to the floor, rags, and then an astonished curse in a tone that seemed surprised that all the planning, all the effort, could be destroyed so quickly. Forgetting his own paralysis, Brad started to go to him, but, of course, he went nowhere. Brad willed his body to move, and only an arm futilely spasmed, a pitiful, erratic waving. Then he heard Carey moving and felt a hand clutch his bed and then the other,

and he felt a waving, shuddering effort that rattled his bed. Noth
ing seemed to be happening, but then, suddenly, right over him
was Carey's skull grinning horribly and triumphantly, too wea
for words, the claw hand able only to snatch the capsule an
push it right into the gaping, black-holed mouth so that it couldn
be dropped on the way back. Brad realized, now, that Carey ha
the cunning of the animal, the weak cleverness of the thing tha
lives entirely in a world of enemies. In his imagination Bra
traveled with Carey the entire three feet back to his bed, feelin
his weariness, his weakness, not seeing but knowing how h
rested, hanging against the edge of the bed the way a ship
wrecked survivor might cling to debris. At last the hushed strug
gle, the starting and the halting, the stopping and the beginnin
again, the failing and at last the succeeding as Carey climbe
back into bed. The covers nestled up, Carey gave his gasped com
mand—"Now"—his first word of the day.

"Hey, Nurse. Hey, Nurse," Brad shouted, and the ward stirred
"Hey, Nurse. Hey, Nurse," he repeated.

"OK, OK," he heard her answer, and knew she smiled. Th
best of the lot, she was, not too bright and certainly no beauty
she had a maternal instinct as warm and sloppy as her figure
but still powerful enough that it could not be denied by the lif
of failure and frustration that led her to this unrewarding nigh
tour, the effort it took to support her family and her parents an
her incompetent husband.

"Yeah, Hastings. What is it?"

"Carey. Can't you give him a capsule? Like mine?"

"Is he bad?"

"The old bastard won't admit it, but he hurts. He's keepin
me awake."

"That's tough."

"So OK, but think of him, ask him. He's in pain."

"He's not supposed to have any capsules."

Carey spoke: "A shot. This is the first time I've asked, isn't it
Give me a shot."

"You had the shot." She repeated it by rote: "Sodium Amytal
three and three-quarters grains."

"It didn't work," Brad plunged in. "He's awake, isn't he?"

"There's nothing I can do."

"A booster?" Carey asked desperately.

"No. Nothing. I just can't do it."

She started to leave, and then Brad called to her. "Wait, just a econd." He knew he'd made her wait and he knew he'd have to ell as he'd sold before, speaking her language, picking the right rguments. She came closer and he began in a stage whisper, rawing her closer. "Look, you know the kinda nurses we have n Ward F. Most of them aren't nurses at all."

"Not even capped, some of them."

"Right. You're different, you've had training, and I'll even bet ou worked OR."

"How'd you know? It was at St. Vincent's, and I was one of the est, all the doctors said, before I got married. You're certainly ight—I had the training."

"It's a vocation, a real vocation."

"That's what the monsignor told me when I took care of him ven."

"I'll bet he asked for you."

"He did. How'd you know? Yep, he said I had a vocation, was ust as good as a sister, almost, anyway."

"It must be wonderful what you can do, even here for a guy ke Carey, who's dying. He hurts and you give him relief for a ew hours from that pain. He's a brave one."

"He's one of the best. Some of the whiners I can't stand. I houldn't say it, but I can't. Carey's different."

"But tonight he's in pain. He's not crying out the way some of hem do and he's not begging either. He won't beg, but I know e needs a shot."

"Well, I don't have the order."

"You can take care of that—you know the ropes."

"Well . . ."

"Look, there's no worry he's gonna be an addict," Brad whis-ered and she bent over to hear him. "He's not going to be here hat long, not with that pain. Just a few hours of relief—you an do it."

"All right, but I won't tomorrow night." She turned to Carey. You promise, Carey? Just tonight. Not tomorrow."

"I promise, I promise for sure." She left, and in a moment, it eemed, she was back. Brad realized that time was racing now. he didn't speak and he could imagine her flipping Carey over, ght as a bag of air, and placing the shot in the only lumps of esh left, his buttocks.

"Got the pills, Carey?"

"Just took the last one."

There was no defiant hurling of a body into space, no gashin of wrists, no wild blood gushing, no mouth-swallowed shotgu roar. Just the ordinary night noise. Quiet.

"Thank you, Hastings."

There really was nothing to say, but something had to be said "I won't forget you, Carey."

"You know, that is important, not being forgotten. It helps I guess."

Brad waited. For what, he didn't know, for death would com unseen, as it always did, and yet he stood vigil with Carey, hop ing that he knew Brad did not sleep and that he was no mor alone than any man dying. Brad stared at the ceiling, wishing h could watch Carey's face, to see if peace came to it. He had t wait for other signs. For minutes or hours he heard the sleep the open-mouthed gasping sleep. Carey was still alive, and the sometime before the light on the ceiling changed to dawn, h smelled the odor and knew that Carey had been dead for quite while.

Brad prepared to mourn, but shamefully found himself exult ant—he was free. He had no ties to anyone, now that Carey wa gone. He could, like some great sea turtle in the black of th ocean, draw back and into himself, where no one could eve reach him again.

21

When Bets reached Irv's office, the door was half open and the only light came from a closet. She had to search the shadowed room to find Irv, a crumpled heap of surgical greens, humpbacked in his chair, slumped over his desk. Not knowing what she ought to do, Bets did what she had to do, before thinking, knowing only that she was needed and knowing the wonder of that knowing. She walked to him and laid her fingers on Irv's exposed neck. He leaned back and clutched her, holding her hands with his shoulders, and she felt she knew him as she had never known any man before. Irv allowed her the intimacy of his weakness, allowed her to comfort him.

She stood relaxed, letting her hands carry strength, calm, comfort—whatever he needed—faster, surer than words ever could. At last he stood and turned with a rueful smile, but she did not return it. There was no need to apologize. She willed her message to him and he was still. Seeing his face when he moved into the naked light from the closet, she had the illusion that she could see through his present face—heavy-bearded, heavy, infinitely sad—back to the face of the boy, a thin face, sensitive, eager, a face that made you hurt, for it reminded you of the innocence you always believed you once had. Bets touched his hand, and he put things together on the desk, opened and shut drawers, phoned the operator to tell her he was leaving but would call back. He stood still, and Bets, seeing him distracted, his face puzzled, could see his need and thought how much we idealize doctors. They are always gods in our minds, man-made gods—or devils. "Who needs a doctor who doubts?" she thought. Bets laughed silently. "I do," she admitted, "I do."

Irv put the cap on his fountain pen—and he fumbled. Those sure, stubby fingers fumbled; an unimportant slip in another man became a startling sign of weakness in this one, a surgeon. He piled papers on the left on the desk, then restacked them on the typewriter table, finally put them in a drawer, and then knocked an ashtray to the floor. Bets turned out the light and led him to the door. He followed her out to the parking lot, where she spoke for the first time: "My car's over here." Irv didn't argue. He went with her and she started the car, driving before she knew where she was going.

"Dinner?" he asked formally.

"Whatever you want," and as she said the words she realized the simple beauty of the language. She repeated it, unafraid of any meaning, hearing not only her words but also the timbre of her voice, saying the words so easily because they did not need to be said: "Whatever you want, Irv."

"A drive, dinner, I don't know, I just thought we might get together. I don't know." They drove on, and she thought for just a moment that he was backing off or that he was being clever or hesitant, but immediately she knew it wasn't true. Irv Frank, who had never cried out, had now cried; but, being a man, he needed to know why, to analyze, figure things out, rationalize everything in advance; being a man, he had to complicate life. Driving to his apartment, Bets smiled and knew it was one of those smug smiles called women's smiles, because that's just what they were. She smiled because she had the superiority of simplicity. He wondered, while she knew. "We'll go to your apartment so you can change."

He looked surprised. "I forgot I was in these. Did I leave the hospital in them? Of course I did."

"One doesn't do that, does one, if one is professional?" She smiled.

"No," he answered, "one doesn't," almost laughing.

Bets realized she had the same selective awareness that she had had the night Brad was hit. Everything was different; the proportions changed; the small became important and the ordinarily significant faded away. Time slowed and sped out of pace with any clock. Light and dark changed and she felt the shadings of shadows and of sound. She felt sound and motion right through her skin and knew none of this night would ever be forgotten.

To all the others, the people they were passing on the street, it might be an ordinary summer night, and it seemed incredible to her, for the very light—had she ever realized before that night was light?—had a particular texture, a quality that was seen only in reflection: off a pavement, from a storefront, the bright light of a parked car; in a face suddenly revealed on a sidewalk —a quality unique because of this night's light. On a corner she saw a policeman laughing, a wide-mouthed joyous laugh, and she laughed with him. A sign, THE ARABIAN TENT, in blue neon and the flashing light below, an uproarious obbligato, ITALIAN SPECIALTIES. A car cut in front of her and she slowed, unresentful, and pitied the other driver's haste. They went through the underpass and heard the crossing train, a clatter and a clunk and a clatter and a clunk overhead, and it seemed significant, as if it had a destination as did they, they did, they did. She followed Irv's directions and the unfamiliar streets seemed familiar, and the delicatessen, where she stopped without asking Irv, was more wonderful this night than any she had ever seen. Cheese, meats, breads, in infinite variety—yet she felt no indecision this night. Bets invented a sandwich right on the spot: a creation of salami, black Russian bread, thick spread of cream cheese and chives. It would be good, she was sure. "I'll take those pickles over there," she said, laughing, "and some cold German beer. No, no potato salad, but potato chips, of course. And a ball of provolone and that liverwurst, the smeary kind. Never mind the cost tonight. Yes, and that plump loaf of bread, the dark brown one with the crisp, cracked crust. No, don't slice it." She paid and laughed and cradled the large brown paper bag in her arms.

There was a place to park right in front of the apartment house, and before he got out of the car, Irv turned to her and said, "I don't know what it was, why this happened tonight."

"It doesn't matter," Bets said, and it really didn't matter to her.

"But I have to figure it out—it doesn't make sense."

Bets watched his face as he spoke, and understood again, putting this thing into words for the first time: "You're a man, Irv—

you have to know why," she said casually. "You have to have reasons. Relax. You will. Come on, let's go up and have some beer and a sandwich. You change, and we'll talk if you want to then."

Bets walked into the apartment as if she'd been there before. She knew it all as it jumped to sight in the single flash of the light. He laughed oddly. "I had it done last week. One switch and all the lights go on."

Bets understood that revelation too, that it was a confession of a weakness he'd had to admit to himself and now had to admit to her. She also knew it was a recent thing, the dark apartment bothering him. Quickly she moved to the kitchen, telling him to change while she arranged the plates, feeling at ease, looking for things, but sure she would find them. Her hands were busy and therefore her mind was, she thought. She laughed at herself, telling herself it was shameful to be so happy at Irv's unhappiness, and then not feeling guilty at all, knowing she was only happy at his need, as any woman would be. She began to cut the bread in thick slices, the crisp crust and the soft inside; arrange the salami; pile up the cream cheese and chives; peel the provolone; line up the pickles—performing the ancient ritual of preparing food. She felt as old as time, sister to all the women who had prepared food at times of crisis, funerals and births, wars, illness, filling the waiting. When she was done and the beer was opened for Irv to pour, she called to him and laughed out loud when he came out in sweatshirt and slacks, slippered and his hair tousled. He looked so much the contented, middle-aged man—sloppy, at ease, content—that she was caught off balance by the surge of tenderness she felt. They sat down to eat, their silence awkward for the first time.

But even that didn't matter and that made the difference. Neither felt the need to fill the silence with words. They ate and they enjoyed the food and the not eating alone. He, by her being there, was saved from his usual silence; she, by escaping the incessant chatter of the children, reveled in the adult quiet. Afterward, he put a Mozart quintet on the hi-fi, and when he poured their third beer he tried to explain to her how he felt, what got to him. Bets, who didn't care what it was, understood how much he needed to explain things to himself, and listened to an hour of talk. "Maybe some doctors let it get to them, but I never did. I don't mean this to be a confession, Bets, because I won't make apology. Weeping for patients, well, it just wouldn't do any good. You do all you can—everything—and then you forget the look of appeal on his face when he asked you if he was going to be all right and his gratitude at your lie. It does no good to second-guess, to wonder what would have happened—and didn't. Live with it. Look, it may be bad for a television series, but you're no good if you care about people too much. That's one reason I'm so good. That's been my strength—I don't care about people. I don't care how many kids they've got, if they worked their way through college, why her husband loved her, if the boy's an only child—none of that matters."

He turned the record over, and Bets smiled at his lies—which he believed, which he had to believe. He would have to learn now, if this was happening—learn to live with it. "You care too much, Irv."

"I don't give a shit about people." His answer was vicious, quick, too quick. "Look at me here, with you—and Brad there." His words were harsh. "I called you—his wife." He walked the floor and fought her, trying to believe what he said. He spoke again, quietly: "I just haven't felt for people, Bets. I'm sorry. To me, people are, well, pretty mechanical. Bones and joints. A contraption that can sometimes be repaired—or can't." He sat down. "If you think too much or feel too much, you can't be ruthless, and if you can't be ruthless, you're no good." He sat looking at her, and she looked back at him. "Bach, that new recording of the Shostakovich Fifth, Heifetz, Rubinstein, jazz—I've got it, you pick it."

"Whatever you want, Irv."

"No, I want to play what you want."

"The Mozart was nice."

"He's always nice." Irv picked up another record. "But he isn't just pretty. He's so melodious that people don't hear what he has to say. Listen to this piano concerto written after the death of his mother—it's pretty but it's also desolate." They listened and she felt what he felt. She realized she didn't know what time it was. Ten? Midnight? One? And it made no difference at all. They turned the record over and then suddenly, while pouring some coffee he had made, Irv jumped back to the reason he had called her. "It's been getting me." He paused. "Brad, his loneliness, my loneliness, being a successful doctor, getting there, being there, and wondering what it means. Damn it, I've wanted people, just to talk to, to be near." His voice was full of wonder. "I've even wanted to go to parties."

"That's no weakness." Bets didn't laugh.

"It is, it is for me." He was angry. "For me it is. Why I feel this way doesn't matter—I mean, how it started. Blame my toilet training—that's ancient history, but it's also wisdom. I've always known that when you care too much about people, when you dance to everyone's tune, that's weakness, madness."

"Anything is, when you go too far," Bets answered, "but needing people, a few people—that's proper, Irv. Respecting people who deserve respect, caring for those worth caring for—that's different."

"Scotch?"

"All right." He poured it, straight, then floated a couple of ice cubes in it. She sipped the strong, burning potion, and then he went on: "Now listen, caring doesn't do any good—it doesn't change anything. We're all alone in this world, you and I, everybody. I can't hurt for Brad or die for him or walk for him, and although you love him, you can't either. He's alone and so are you. Everyone's alone. God, what if that punk's right?"

"What punk?" Bets asked, and the story poured out about the hot rodder, his girl friend, now a vegetable, and the family, the family that could never be. Bets felt for him, helping by absorbing some of his hurt, his so desperate caring, the caring he'd always felt and always denied. She watched Irv's face with its unusual nakedness, believing she could comfort him, hoping she could, hoping that this strange evening—cold cuts and listening—would be enough, that it would answer his telephoned cry. And Bets was amused that this man, who was so good and so very smart, could believe that he was above being human, that he could stand apart from hurting and caring and failing.

"You should go home."

"I should go home." She smiled.

He spoke quickly: "But can you stay for a while, just listen to me?" He laughed. "It makes no sense, but I'd like you to." He hesitated and she waited, every sense alerted for his question. "I'd like to show you my fort."

Relieved and off balance and disappointed and confused, all in the same moment, she laughed too. "Your fort?"

"Nobody's ever seen it." The man became a boy before her eyes. He opened a closet and pulled out a drawing board, and she got down on her knees on the floor beside him, fascinated by the intricate drawing and at the maps and books he pulled out to answer her questions—good questions, she knew—about this secret project of his. Sharing this with him, Bets forgot how ridiculous it was. Womanlike, she was curious about the people who lived in the fort, how they cooked and slept, where the children played. She realized that she had populated his fort, not just with soldiers but with the families that were there. "You know, all I heard was the clank of armor," he said, surprised and pleased. "Now my fort's filled with the sound of kids and dogs. There probably were hundreds of dogs." He laughed and spoke quickly, showing her everything, how his fort worked, revealing how he worked on it, how he didn't need to show it to anyone, not hearing his own delusion now that he was caught up in the showing of it—explaining how much he had learned about the people of that time long gone. Not only how they fought but also why they fought, for that could be as important as the way they quarried stone and hauled it to the site, lifted it into place, and made it secure. Reaching for a drawing he had made of a lift he had invented, not using modern knowledge but limiting himself to what they knew a thousand years ago, his arm reached behind her, and she felt it before he did, and compulsively he clutched her, almost automatically, and he looked at her and she knew that not once had this brilliant man, usually perceptive, perceived what she had known all along: how much he had needed and how this one kind of human need, symbolic of all need, could be part of it.

She could feel his surprise and his rejection of his own humanness and they went back to the fort, awkwardly, the magic of that distant, unreal project gone in the face of their immediate needs. Bets waited for Irv to stop fussing about another drink, picking out a record, talking about forts and armor and siege tactics until she knew with that same marvelous sureness what she had to do. She could not construct an elaborate structure of explanations and excuses—if that were needed, it could be built later. Now this man needed her. That was her purpose—his need created her need.

"Irv." He stopped fumbling with papers, still on his knees, and she leaned back against the couch, feeling so good, so sure of herself. "I need you too, Irv." She wanted to laugh all the way through. He was so clumsy, and they were in such a silly place, on a medieval fort, and she wanted to cry, for his need was so great. No words could communicate this hunger; she felt as if she were the first person in the world for him—mother, sister, friend, lover, wife, all women for him. Each baring of herself, each loving of him, excited him so much. He was so naïve, this doctor. Bets was surprised, amused, and then, at last herself surprised, carried beyond any amusement, her need matching his, lost, beyond control, no stopping now, one with this other one, and at the final moment one surprising, shocking thought hurled up from the black of her mind: "This will show you, Brad Hastings."

22

It was morning when the new nurse found Carey. Brad heard her stop, then move quickly to the quiet bed and hurry away. Four men Brad had never seen before blurred past the foot of his bed and, ominously experienced, did their job without speaking. In a moment they were gone and Carey's odor was gone and when they turned him on his side Brad saw that Carey's mattress—stripped to the impersonal blue-striped ticking—had risen: there wasn't even the impression of his disease-lightened body left behind.

Unable to turn away, Brad lay there and remembered the time when they'd all gone down to a football game and were driving back to Cambridge across the Massachusetts Avenue Bridge just before dawn. A railing was missing halfway across, and they stopped the car, still laughing, and ran to the side, where they looked down at the black, rippling Charles and the dancing glints from the light before dawn, and they stopped laughing.

"I'll wait," Brad remembered saying, knowing then that it was foolish. He grabbed a life preserver hung on the bridge and, feeling helpless, waited. He'd never forgotten that waiting, for there was a quiet on the bridge he had never heard before. He hadn't realized until then that his life was filled with voices, talking and laughing, and with the radio quickly turned on when he was alone. The water idly slapped the pilings and there was no cry for help, no scream, no floating wreckage, just the black river more terrible and more beautiful than he had ever seen it.

At last his friends returned with policemen, firemen, even a police boat, and they all waited until noon, when the car was grappled up with its white-faced, floating cargo, and Brad was sick—not because of the dead bodies, although they were the first he'd ever seen, but because of the beautiful river and of the fact that these human beings, young like themselves, had left the world without a trace. It was like that with Carey. They found him and were unsurprised. They hadn't even called a doctor to pronounce him dead. Some other day a doctor on duty would scrawl the cause of death on the certificate, in Carey's case carcinoma, in cases when they didn't know, heart failure, for all hearts failed at death. Brad had thought that there would be an investigation, and he had steeled himself for it, but he found this more terrifying. There would be no investigation, for no one cared. Not even Brad. He couldn't feel sorry for a man who had lived with so much pain as Carey, now that he was free of pain. Who could feel sad for him? He couldn't feel guilty for helping Carey kill himself. Was it a sin to pass away with dignity at the moment of his own choosing, by his own hand, in his own hour, in his own way? Brad sought guilt, but couldn't find it. There was no sorrow and there was no guilt, but there was loss, and Brad couldn't or wouldn't see that, for he was free. All he felt was freedom. Without Carey and that obligation to get his capsule and save it for him, Brad had, he thought, no reason to live. None. No purpose, no point. He could cut out now and he tried to—Lord, how he tried to.

He let them bathe him and feed him and sit him up and lay him down and he never gave them a look. He spoke to no one. It was easy because he had prepared the way. They didn't try very hard, he thought bitterly. Irv came by, hasty and awkward, hurrying through his examination, his futile attempts at conversation, and rushed off. Bets missed a day, then two, and finally came to stand by the bed, her face stiff, standing there as if she were following some necessary ritual. She didn't look into his face and she didn't speak, she just stood until what she apparently thought was a proper time had passed and then she left.

He'd made it. Only he hadn't. He drifted, detached but not out of sight of land. At night he still dreamt, during the day he was still aware of the ward, of morning and of evening, of Carey's not being there. The strand wasn't broken. He still heard Carey arguing his causes—he couldn't forget that. He remembered Carey, worse off than he, raising hell, and the ward seemed a barren place without him.

He slept, he woke, he turned off his thoughts, but he couldn't forget Carey. The kids, yes, they had their life to lead. Bets? She was gone. He knew that now. Irv, Pete and Peg, Ames? Good-bye—they didn't even visit anymore. But Carey, somehow, was still there, and he wondered one afternoon how much his drifting out into the nothing, his letting go, had been a stunt of self-pity made possible because Carey was there to drag him back. Had he been putting on a show? Had he really wanted his freedom to be a vegetable?

Of course he had, Brad told himself. He had wanted to go. It had been wonderful out there, dark and warm and aimless—drifting. No struggles, no hopes, no hurts. Now he could cast off again. He tried and he failed.

For days Brad lay idle, but he couldn't let go of life. He caught sight of Bets standing above his bed looking across from him, or he heard Nickerson singing that old folk song softly to himself or saw a shadow on the ceiling or felt a twinge in his right hand, which still could have a pinch, or tasted the coolness of lemon sherbet or dreamed of running or remembered Carey, raising hell, irascible, indomitable, cussing mean, squeezing all the juice from his little bit of living that had been left. Each thing for a moment snagged him and held him, kept him from drifting out, away.

None of them were strong enough to hold him for long—an image half seen, a feeling half remembered—and yet he couldn't quite escape now that Carey was gone. And gradually, not admitting it, he began to turn toward shore, not quite swimming onto the beach but not still seeking the current that would carry him away altogether. He floated—aware of the world still, not a part of it but aware that it was there and caring about it—until suddenly, surprising even himself, his voice broke out of him, crackling with disuse, breaking and scraping: "Nurse. Nurse." He could hear the stirrings of surprise along Ward F. "Hey, let's open the windows. It's August." She didn't come, and he yelled louder, feeling his hand leap erratically with the excitement and not caring. "Damn it, it's hot. Let's open some windows. Nurse. Nurse. Come he-a-ah. Open the windows, damn it. We're men in here and we need some cool air. We deserve cool air, by God. It's cheap and available, and let it in. Nurse. Nurse. Open the windows."

Suddenly the nurse was there above him, surprise on her face too. "Why, Hastings, you've been a quiet one."

"Not anymore, by God. Let's open the windows."

"They are open," she said quietly.

"Then turn on the fans."

"There aren't any fans and you know it."

"No fans? There'd better be fans—it must be a hundred degrees in here, two hundred." He laughed out loud. "Get me the administrator. I want to see him now, today. We'll get some fans. This is no way to treat human beings. The place ought to be air-conditioned."

"You sound like Mr. Carey."

Brad's voice rose even louder: "God damn it, I want some fans in here today. You hear? Get me the administrator."

23

Bets had stepped out for coffee at the office and when she came back she got the message: "County called and said you'd better come over."

"Why? What's wrong?"

"They didn't say."

"Who was it that called?"

"I'm sorry, I didn't get that either." Exasperated, Bets started to dial the hospital and then slammed down the receiver. She could drive there faster than she could get through the red tape on the phone. She swung the car out of the parking lot, not thinking, concentrating on getting there, until the traffic trapped her and she saw the drawbridge up and she had to sit in the car.

Brad was dead? She waited, prepared for the fear, and there was none. How could there be? Her husband was a vegetable. He wanted to escape, and if he made it she would have to go to the funeral dry-eyed, just have to, that's all. The day was hot and muggy, but Bets felt a sudden chill. "Someone's walking over my grave," she said out loud, before thinking, and then added, "Brad's grave." He was dead or dying. Those could be the only reasons they would call. He doesn't want me, he wouldn't call, and they would call only if they had to notify, according to routine, the nearest relative. Therefore it was over, the life that had begun—or ended—when Brad slipped and changed—in one decisive second—from the man who had everything, the solid-gold golf tee still in his pocket, to the man who had so little, and had lost most of that because he couldn't settle for less than everything. Bets had never seen it so clearly, and seeing the drawbridge start down, she started the car, but concentrated on her feelings now: was she rationalizing what she had done? Justifying Irv? Driving slowly in the still-clogged-up traffic, she knew she couldn't know that.

She felt none of the guilt she told Irv she felt. It was worse than that, she had to live with this awful memory, the ugly fact she almost enjoyed doing it to Brad, who had thought he had everything, thought he deserved everything and would always be one of the deserving. Was it that or did she enjoy doing it with Irv because he needed her so much, so very much? Had she really had that vagrant thought? Had she hated Brad that much?

This, she thought, the car moving swiftly now, was her only salvation—being as honest as she could be. Not rationalizing it all, not blaming others, not being the victim. It was her own choice. And yet, and yet. Would she have gone to Irv if Brad had not rejected her? Bets pulled into the parking lot at County—small but always empty—and walked slowly up the path to the main building. If Brad were dead he had really died a long time ago and she had mourned a long time ago and now there was nothing more to do but sign the papers. Again she felt the chill and she walked a bit faster to the receptionist, bookkeeper, telephone operator, who didn't know why she had been called. Bets hurried to Ward F and before she found the nurse she saw Brad propped up in bed, more alive than he'd been for months. He was even talking.

Bets ran down the ward, angry and hopeful and pleased and furious, asking, "Brad, Brad, did you call for me?"

He stopped, right in the middle of a word, and looked at her. "No."

"Someone did, at the office. I was out for coffee and I came as soon as I got the message; the drawbridge was up but I came and I thought——"

"I didn't call."

Her husband's voice was distant, as if he were guarding himself, and she just didn't know what to say and felt foolish at the way she'd been babbling, so she matched his tone, saying, "You've been talking."

"I can talk."

"I know, Brad"—she tried to smile—"but you haven't."

He took a breath as if he were going to try to explain it to her and then shook his head and was silent, but when she didn't speak, he spoke: "They shouldn't have called you. It had nothing to do with you. I got mad and that rattled the bastards." His voice rose. "Well, I've been mad for some time. Now I'm going to yell." He lay his head back and howled and Bets stepped back in horror.

He looked at her, not smiling, just interested, and she tried to say something and couldn't. "Go back to your world, Bets. This is mine. Ward F. Don't try to make too much of this." He almost smiled. "We've had our share of false hopes—don't let them make too much of this. I'm staying here. I've got nowhere to go." Suddenly he laughed a laugh she had never heard before and he howled again, "Nurse. Nurse."

Bets stood looking at her husband, his right hand jumping in a meaningless dance of anger, the damp puddle between his legs, his gray body flesh, his hair long and slovenly, his red, unshaven face, his mouth open, the sound of animal fury pouring from it, and she ran, she didn't walk, she ran, and heard Brad's laughter as she did.

Brad stopped before she reached the stairs and he didn't make a sound again until lunch the next day, when he ordered his feeder, "Get the harness. I'll feed myself." He had to start all over again and he made a mess of the food and himself, but he made his feeder keep her hands away. His arm swung wildly in the sling and his few remaining muscles, virtually unused for weeks, cramped and ached. There was food on his cheeks, in his left eye, on the bed and even on the floor, and although he had to let them wipe him off, he would not let them feed him. "I'm no goddamned baby anymore. I'll feed myself or I won't eat."

For a week, feeding himself took all of Brad's strength. He had to drive himself to make the Herculean, frustrating attacks on the food, infuriated by his inability to do what his little girl could now do without thought or effort. Brad fought the food in angry, grunting battles before the eyes of the ward, refusing anyone's sympathy or encouragement, wishing for a private room and still struggling to get his food, always cold, from plate to mouth. After he was finished he lolled against his pillows, exhausted, more tired than he had ever been. Brad wasn't hoping for a miracle now, he wanted only to be a man—angry, perhaps; bitter, of course; a freak, inevitably; a cartoon of a man but still a man. He began the course of toilet training that he had always refused, trying as much as possible to regularize his lack of control. He insisted on the therapist's exercises, which he had only tolerated before, and he raised holy hell if he wasn't lifted into his wheelchair twice a day.

Totally involved in his own struggle to feed himself, control his bowels, sit in a chair, he felt an angry contempt for those who didn't try to do what they could for themselves. There weren't many of this sort in Ward F, but Terhune Paxton, who was famous for his previous visits to the hospital, had to land in Carey's bed, which irritated Brad beyond all reason. Paxton had suffered heart trouble, back trouble, blood-pressure trouble, all difficult to diagnose, and now he suffered dizzy spells. He thought he had a brain tumor for sure. Brad thought it a sacrilege and a personal insult to Carey's memory to put him in that bed, and Brad tried, right in front of the lumpen's face, to have him transferred. No one paid any attention to Brad's complaints, including Paxton, who smiled with infuriating understanding.

"Don't you tolerate me, you crud," yelled Hastings, astonished at himself and at the strange anger that controlled him; surprised at how deeply he hated that plump baby of a man, soft and pink, surrounded by a train of women: one wife, one sister, three married daughters. Brad realized that in his whole life he had never really hated before, but now he hated Paxton, as his women—all overweight and overmaternal—comforted him and patted him and talked at the same time, no one listening, while Terhune Paxton himself, self-pity hanging on his face like wet snow on a pine tree, proudly suffered in the middle. Getting into bed, he groaned and moaned while the hands fluttered over him. Propped on his right side, Brad was forced to witness the whole production. Terhune pouted and he puffed—oh, how he suffered—wheezes and grunts and groans. He had a whole symphony of sighs, each one practiced and perfected, each used with infinite variety. His words were a complaint, but his tone revealed his delight in his lot. He introduced himself to everyone in the same way: "Name's Terhune Paxton, salesman before I had my troubles, religious articles, to all faiths, of course. Terrible thing to end up here. I don't like taking charity, but I had no choice." A little trio of sighs and then a happy coda: "I had no choice."

"Oh, Carey," thought Brad, "you are missed, indeed you are." When Paxton spoke to him, Brad pretended to be asleep.

Terhune Paxton made time, which, at County, had moved as imperceptibly as a glacier, slow down until Brad was sure it would stop. An hour washed in Paxton's warm prose seemed like a day; a day's concert of his groans and grunts seemed like a week. Brad knew that outside, summer had changed slowly to fall, but it seemed inside that the afternoon would never turn to evening. Lying on his right side, he was forced to observe Paxton's contented complaints. He hauled and eased his doughy body around in bed with constant lowings and increasing satisfaction, mentioning his heart, his dizzy spells, his weariness, to every doctor and nurse. He experimented with new ways of supporting the small of his back or a shoulder or an arm. He plumped up pillows under his knees, sat up like a gigantic infant playing with his toes to adjust the covers, and, that chore done, reclined, looking like an obscene Cleopatra.

When Brad was forced to lie there watching him and had forgotten to close his eyes, Paxton took it as an invitation to conversation. Brad learned all about him, his parents, his grandparents, his wife, her sisters, her brothers, her parents, her grandparents, their daughters, their husbands, their parents, his grandchildren. No disclosure was too intimate, for he lacked any sense of privacy. He was endlessly fascinated by himself and, therefore, thought the world must share his hobby. Paxton fired off machine-gun generalizations in all directions and defended his arrogance with the peroration that all people had the right to free speech. He was for preventive war, other people paying their bills on time; against farm subsidies, young marriages, foreigners, spiced food, and doctors who didn't listen to you. He never seemed to listen to anyone, but Brad admitted that in a week Paxton knew more about the people who lived or worked in Ward F than he did. He sucked up other people's private affairs like some great, bottom-dwelling fish that gobbles up everything without discrimination. Brad tried to understand why he was so disgusted by Paxton's appetite for gossip, and he finally understood it when he watched this blob of a man sitting cross-legged in his bed, mouth open, eyes sparkling, unashamedly eavesdropping on Madison's conversation with his daughter, who said she wanted him home—and perhaps she did—but whose husband decidedly did not. Paxton gulped in their private words, nodding agreement and disagreement, eagerly enjoying the suffering of these two people pulled together as they were pulled apart, feeling guilt and sorrow, forced to lie to each other, hating and loving at the same time. Then Brad realized why Paxton was worthy of his hate: he was without compassion.

Paxton was full of such phrases as, "I've always tried to do the right thing," "No one can ever say my children didn't come first," "I may not be rich, but at least I can go to my grave knowing I've never intentionally hurt another fella." Brad, sighing, realized that Paxton believed this—all of it. He reveled in the downfall of others, in their weakness, their suffering, their dying, for each failing of another seemed to prove his own virtue to himself. Brad was glad when they left him to stare at his patch of ceiling or even when they turned him on his left side. Still, in a quieter way, the other, the compleat institutionalized man, was as depressing as Paxton. The "waiter" who went on forever, aged but not aging, imbecilic and therefore happy, his sweet smile a mockery of all reason, tranquilized years before by a stoppage of oxygen to the brain, not enough to kill, too much to let the brain function normally. His smile was a grin painted on a skeleton, a breathing nightmare; his head was haloed with white hair. His features were sensitive with an expression which seemed ready to give birth to an important Supreme Court decision, but when he spoke, his mouth drooled the saliva-laden babbling of an infant.

Instead of returning to his bed, Brad fought to stay up in the wheelchair and escape Paxton. He would have them roll him to the other end of the ward, where he could kibitz Flanders and Yount's daily gin game, or he would sit and listen to Perry's stories, which, at least, always changed. Joshua Perry, his eyes sewn shut, would lean back in his chair, in his imagination see the battlefields of France, and talk on. He had long since forgotten what was fact and what was fiction, but Brad didn't worry about that. He realized that a man who had spent thirty-nine years at County had to at least have a past, real or not. He got to know Fraggio—a man torn in half by a stroke. He had been a pretty fair fighter, but wished he had become a priest; his faith grew stronger than ever now that he was in County, which was something Brad could respect but not understand. He would sit by Johnson so that when he woke, he wouldn't be alone but could talk about other times and other places. In the evenings Brad would have his bed pushed around so he, too, could watch television.

As winter came Brad felt he would last out his life with these strange companions, the leftovers from life, and was not displeased. It was where he belonged. They seemed to respect him, even need him.

One day Brad heard Cavanaugh talking to a friend from the Legion post. "See that guy over there, the quad? Well, he's a Bowdoin man. Yeah, rich man's college up in Maine. Had a hell of a job in New York. A hell of a guy, speaks right out. Me and him get along just fine. He's regular, y'know?"

Carey had been right. Without effort he'd been accepted, and knowing he was doing it, he took over. He sent a message to the chaplain, Bill. "Hey, how about that electric wheelchair?" And when it came he made rounds every day. He'd stop by Pete's bed and talk, knowing how Pete wanted to be left alone, yet sensing that he needed a visitor who could look at him—his pustulating, bursting skin, the sores that ruined the features of his face, swelling the skin and tearing it apart—and talk calmly, without horror; so Brad made the one-way conversations with Pete a part of his day. He visited with Gabe, who hadn't known who he was for years and didn't care where he was. He even made himself chat with the fakers who filled the ward, and he began to understand them. He didn't like them, but he could see a man like Herbert Charles, unschooled and black but caring, oh so caring, who had been hurt and didn't want to be hurt anymore. He was hiding. Listening to his gentle, self-deprecating jokes one afternoon, Brad recognized that he understood for the first time the nature of the battle that had made Herbert Charles run, and later, going back to his bed, he realized how lucky he had been before, how arrogant he had been in his innocence.

He thought about his life before the accident and spilled it out on the bed, spilling it out in front of him, the way a child might spread tiny play buildings on the floor. He remembered his pride and felt it again as he saw the Bowdoin buildings, the one-family homes, his parents' and his own, the corporation skyscraper, the commuter train, his new car, the green lawns and trees of the neighborhood. He examined it all that day and the next and enjoyed playing with the idea of his past, surprised that there was so little regret. He could hardly believe, as familiar as it was, that it had been his, for that world was so far away.

He wanted to talk about that world to Bets, who'd come to it from outside and had always been a bit discomforted in it, but when she came, there wasn't much of anything to say. There never was, now. Brad realized he had no right to take down the wall he had erected himself to give her hope where he could see no hope.

When she came to see him, once or twice a week now, they would talk as strangers. She was always ill at ease these days, picking at her gloves or her handbag or the cover of the bed, smoking with abrupt movements, not talking or talking too fast, looking away, then back. He blamed one thing or another, depending on his mood, calling her in his mind a snob or a weakling who didn't have the guts to look him in the face. One day he had been convinced she was just bored with him and the next day he would feel with rage that she had a lover and was waiting for him to die. That day she had been called and rushed in, her face when she first saw him . . . He choked back the thought. It wouldn't do any good.

Usually they would stick it out, each tolerating the other until the time of a proper visit ran out and they could escape. Some days it seemed appropriate for her to wheel him on "walks" around the grounds and he would let her. He supposed she had to do something. When they returned he always made sure he was busy—so that she would leave right away. And, in fact, there usually was someone needing him.

Back in the ward, Brad was hailed by Hopkins after the trip with Bets. "Hey, Hastings, they haven't given me my rub yet."

"You haven't forgotten?" Brad queried sharply. "They didn't give it to you?"

"No, Hastings, I'd remember, really I would. Besides, I have the itch—I know they haven't touched me today."

"Goddammit," Brad snapped at Bets. "Push me over to the nurses' station, will you?" When they arrived there he snarled at the nurse, "Give my wife the telephone. I'm going to call the newspaper and tell them about old Hopkins. He was a minister, down at Union Methodist on South Maple, a good man, and he needs that rub on his skin."

"I forgot."

"Forgot? Forgot?" Brad snarled at her. "Well, remember." The nurse got up angrily and walked off. "She'll come back and take care of him. Quite a world, isn't it?"

"It's funny, I know I shouldn't laugh, but it's funny, you yelling. Brad, you never yelled at me."

"Well, maybe I shoulda."

"Oh, Brad."

"Well, yelling's what gets things done around here," he grumbled.

"And you're the doer."

"Yeah, I guess so, now that Carey's gone." After Bets had left, Brad thought about the way he had acted with the nurse, and seeing himself through her eyes, was as surprised as Bets. He called a nurse: "I'd like a shaving mirror."

"What for?"

"I want to look at myself all night," he snarled. "I'm in love with me. Is it against the rules to have a mirror?" When she propped it up before him he studied himself, realizing it had been a long time since he had seen himself in a mirror, a year, perhaps. He was shaved by someone else and at County he never had to straighten a tie. In his memory his face was clean-shaven, as smooth and pleasant as it had been under a thin-brimmed hat. The face he remembered was a salesman's face—smooth, untelling, agreeable—and his tie was always neat and his collar fresh each morning.

Now Brad saw a stranger, a man who needed a shave and whose eyes were dark, angry, and marked at the corners with sharply etched lines. There was nothing pleasant about this face. It was a face of corners and edges, hard. His hair stood up in a ragged rooster's comb and there was gray in it. His neck looked terribly naked above the hospital johnny. Brad thought that he looked like a bricklayer or a sailor on a tramp steamer. To cover up his embarrassment, he laughed and winked and mugged at this face he could not now avoid, but he studied the face just the same: the pores of his skin seemed open, the texture rougher, and there was a snarl lurking in the twist of the lips. He wondered at the bitter, down-drawn lines at his mouth's edge. His face was thinner, sharper, than he remembered, and his teeth were dirty—they kept forgetting to brush them. Tomorrow he would get a toothbrush on a stick—he had seen an arthritic use one—and a comb as well. He called for the nurse, and when she came she wasn't angry. Instead she asked, "What are we going to do about Foster?" He noticed the "we" and wasn't surprised. Somehow his anger, added to his extraordinary paralysis, had given him authority. He had become the king of the ward without realizing each ward had one.

"Is he gone over the line again?"

"I think so; he's getting up at night, raising Cain. You know that. Last night he got over to Ward H and fought with Miss Hempster. She must be seventy. His wife is smuggling him in the booze, you know."

"Speak to her."

"Humpf, we've tried." The nurse didn't like Mrs. Foster. "The social worker has too, and the priest. She smiles that smile of hers and then we have him."

He realized he was some sort of Uncle Tom, a go-between, being appealed to so that he wouldn't rouse the natives if Foster was railroaded. "Can he go home?"

"No."

"Psycho?"

"That's where he belongs."

"Hate to see that. Sit me down beside him tonight, during TV. There's a ball game. I'll talk to him." He laughed at himself, but he couldn't resist the power and the responsibility. He liked it. He laughed with Carey in his imagination and he could hear the old bastard say, "Thought you'd escaped that old middle-class sense of responsibility, huh? You got it, Hastings. You're middle class for sure." Brad laughed with Carey, knowing he had had it, too; for all his talk, he had had it, too.

Brad laughed at himself and talked to Foster that night and dealt with the administrator about the Sunday-night suppers, made sure Bates got his shots, fought for clean sheets, got Costigan to snap to and shut up at night, and comforted Wilson's widow as best he could. "How could I have comforted her when her husband died of syphilis he got from some whore?" he thought bitterly. "How should a woman feel who is sixty-three and broke and has heart trouble too? Should I tell her to be happy?"

Slowly Brad's pride returned, and it was as strong as ever, although its possessions were far smaller. Instead of a thousand friends, he had the proud self-respect of a man who could sit alone in a wheelchair for an afternoon without hollering for help. He could not win his set in easy matches and vault the net, but he could now feed himself. He could not stare at his acre and its comfortable home, but he could be proud of his self-possession, the fact he was in control of his world, that he was independent and, within his limitations, a man.

On the days Bets didn't come, Irv did, and their banter, now that Brad talked, had a bite he couldn't understand. It was the joking of men who are familiar with each other, but it was always just wrong, an inch off target, a quarter note out of tune.

"Hey, Dr. Frank, over here, by the window."

"You get around these days, Brad."

"Yeah, I sure do. Hey, you've got something I want, you old bastard." Irv looked wary, worried. "Don't look as if I think you stole it." Brad laughed. "I may want that pinch one of these days."

Irv was wary. "Well, that's fine."

"I thought you were selling that pinch real hard. What's the matter—worried I'm not good for your bill?"

"Of course not; there's no bill for you."

"Crap, I'll pay the going rate."

"I'll never give you a bill," Irv said loudly, then changed the subject. "When do you want me to operate?"

"I haven't made up my mind yet," Brad snorted. "Don't know if it's worth the trouble. Just wondered if it was too late for the tendon transplant. Guess part of me's still a Boy Scout—want to do the best I can. Duty, honor, all that crap."

"You won't be a second-best guy, you once said," Irv said, a peculiar look on his face.

"Yes, that's it," he snorted bitterly. "I can't escape my good, middle-class upbringing. I want to do the very best I can."

"There's nothing wrong with that."

"No, perhaps. But nothing very great either. The best I can do isn't very much, is it?"

They stared at each other as if they were angry, and Brad laughed.

"I'll check the hand," Irv said finally.

For the first time in months of ritualistic examinations Irv studied Brad's hand with absorption and care, for this was a purposeful examination. Looking at Irv's head bent over his hand, vulnerable, the birth of a bald spot visible, Brad spoke softly. "Funny how hard it is for me, proud bastard that I am, to even consider asking this favor from you."

"It isn't a favor, Brad. I'm a doctor."

"I feel that it's a favor and, frankly, I hate asking anybody for anything." He laughed awkwardly. "Especially you—I wonder why."

Irv looked deeply at him. "I don't know, I don't know, and I especially want to help you, to do anything for you I can." He tried to joke: "As if you were the only patient I had."

"Funny, isn't it, how people get involved?" Brad said lightly. "The accident, operating on a friend, this, the whole doctor-patient relationship screwed up with friendship, involvements. Funny, isn't it?"

Irv was quiet, then he answered, "I'll schedule surgery whenever you decide. Couple of days' notice and we'll do it." He straightened up for the last time. "No, our involvement isn't funny. It's human and we're all human."

"Hey, I thought I was the one who learned that. Don't tell me the men in white are human, too?" His tone was mean.

Irv choked back his answering anger, thinking that he had no right to be angry at this man, as he spoke softly, "You know something? We are human, very, very human."

24

"I don't know whether I'm lost or found," Bets said to Irv as they met in the park on her way home.

"I'm found," Irv answered, reaching through the window of her car, touching her cheek ever so gently, and then, one finger finding and tracing her ear hidden under her hair, he said, "Come, let's walk." She put her hand in his jacket pocket and he surrounded her hand with his, holding it tightly as they walked, slowly, their steps carefully in rhythm along the trail, aware of finger touching finger, of thigh matching thigh. There was no need to talk, for they had no plans to make, only these moments to live as they could. Each in his own way rejected the inevitable tomorrow by clutching the familiar illusion that time had stopped, at least for them. The air would be forever soft and truly warm, the evenings would always be light, long-shadowed, and this walk, which would be barren in the winter, would always be autumn orange as it was now, their secret, winding walk through the woods. Pacing beside each other, they shared views, looks, slight pressures pocket-hidden, secret knowledge, and a handful of memories worn smooth by almost constant caressing. "Lunchtime tomorrow, Bets?"

"I'll be there, darling."

They reached the cars and left quickly, each disciplining himself, each beginning the rationed anticipation. They had spontaneity now, and each was old enough to know that it might pass under the burden of time, the draining deception, the return of conscience. Now they wanted just to be as they were these weeks, resting as if they had been on a long journey, not yet far enough removed from the traveling to want to examine and re-create the trials of the past or even to try to figure out how they got here; and they could not consider the future. This was a time out of time, a stopping of clocks.

Proudly, without shame, and surprised at her wantonness, Bets went next noon to his apartment, having covered her trail with lies at the office and at home, lying now from habit. He was not yet there and realizing she was not what she had always thought herself—the girl on the block who had kept herself pure, separate, better than the others—Bets now knew that she was no different from a million women and she was proud of it. She undressed, slowly, sensually, spinning out the anticipation of his need, knowing in advance his delight and wonder, feeling a satisfaction that she was, for him, particularly wonderful, proud of her body and of her experience with Brad alone, which now made her a healing gift for another man.

She heard the key before it probed the keyhole, saw the door open before the key turned, enjoyed his face before he saw her and was not disappointed when anticipation became reality and the door opened and she went to him. His booming laugh was all things, exultant, proud, surprised, amused, delighted. They rushed, trembling, tearing at each other, she undressing him. They both felt as if the minutes became hours as they caressed, rising too quickly—but who could stop now?—to an unthinking giving and receiving. Even now, lying back, breathing deeply, sweating, the time for shame, despair, the thoughts of death and hopelessness, the apologies and the recriminations, they laughed softly, chuckling and smiling at their shared nudity.

"There's nothing as ridiculous as the male figure."

"At rest," admitted Irv.

"If you think that's funny, you should see yourself——"

"Hush, allow me the male privilege of total self-illusion." Romance didn't hide the facts of life from them. This was better than that, for he was a doctor and she was another man's wife trying to forget that and failing, not stopping.

Alone, they knew their need and that their quick surrender to passion that one night was more excusable than this: the calculated deceivings of an affair that had turned into a descent. This had become hunger instead of need. They made love for their own satisfaction as much as for the other's; this was taking as much as giving, and once it started, they could not stop. The sure knowledge of sin, the inevitable guilt each began to feel, seemed only to stimulate their appetites when they were together.

They both knew how unimportant the body was, how silly its trying to walk upright, how uncivilized the residual patches of animal hair, how interconnected the organs of love and the organs of excretion. This was the knowledge that made the wonder more wonderful as he traced a finger on her breast, or as each would kiss a shoulder, butterfly-kiss an abdomen, kiss with lips cool and familiar, soft or hard. Irv rose and delivered lengthy sermons on a theory of love, trying to say what she knew, he laughing at himself and seeing the spectacle he made pacing the bedroom, yet willing to let her see him ridiculous—the ultimate revelation—and she lay back, satisfied because she had satisfied him, more than that, given him something he needed. Bets knew she was no permanent solution, but she could halt his doubts, populate his loneliness; most important, she could, with this liaison, which the world would call shameful, give Irv his self-respect. "You, Dr. Frank, are a marvelous lover."

He looked down at her and she understood the question in his eyes, the question that he had the pride not to ask but that was fundamental to the natural competitiveness of man. She smiled and kissed him, knowing she would not, from loyalty, from love, perhaps even from propriety, compare her husband with her lover. She changed the mood by suggesting, "Will you take a shower with me?"

"My pleasure." He stood up, bowed Japanese style, and they washed, scrubbing each other, appreciating the sliding lubrication of the soap, this new intimacy, this moment that became memory as it was lived, a feeling stored up and hoarded against the famine that must come.

She left the apartment first and was in the office when he walked through, not speaking, just sharply rapping the corner of her desk twice, their secret signal. Bets could not shamelessly mesh her two lives, for they were in conflict and therefore she had to keep them in separate compartments. She rose early, showering and caring for her children and getting them off to school before she faced her mother over the second cup of coffee. This was a time hard for them because her mother obviously wanted a "talk" and Bets would not let her invade the other compartment of her life.

Her mother was never direct. She would simply say, "How is that doctor?" And Bets, poised in her office dress, sophisticated and composed, would answer, "He looks all right when I see him." And her mother would ask, "And your husband?" Not Brad, but "Your husband, he's happy?"

"Oh, Mother, you know he's never going to be happy."

"Of course not. When's he coming home?"

"Never, he says," Bets would say with a shrug.

"And you go to see him, you're not missing that."

"No, I'm faithful, in my fashion." She would go on before her mother could speak. "He doesn't want me to, but I visit him regularly, every other day, the only wife who goes to the ward now, the only one."

Her mother would nod her knowing nod, "But because people do or don't do things doesn't make it right, my girl. Murder, boozooling, speeding the cars, monkeyshines, aren't right, remember." And realizing that they had had their little talk, Bets would rise, offer to do the dishes, and her mother would insist on doing them, and Bets would drive to the office.

She was proud of Irv's need for her and she detested their deceit, their secret plans and careful stories. Yet she could not, once she had given herself to Irv, say the single word "no." When she was alone with Irv, time, responsibility, right, seemed to dance and twirl as aimlessly and happily as the winged seedlings from the maple tree or autumn leaves wearing brave colors to their death, abandoned, lost and yet enjoying it, a last mad sweeping and scampering through the forest, darting, floating, soaring, and turning, rising and falling and dying crisp brown. And yet Bets felt the need to justify their affair. "Sex is so little of what we have, Irv."

"It is?" he asked in mock surprise, twisting the car along the dark road.

"I mean, it's wonderful, oh, I don't know, important, but that's only a few minutes, really, out of days." He started to interrupt. "No, Irv, I'm serious. Let me try to say what I mean. We are all confused about sex and make it all-important in advertisements and things like that, but we don't recognize its importance as a symbol."

"You're not making a great deal of sense," and he added the not-yet-casual "darling."

"Well, I mean, sex is just a symbol of how we feel, what we need, what we have to give each other."

Irv laughed. "You mean, you make everything sexy."

"Oh, you, not willing to be serious about anything."

"Oh, I'm serious," he said, his voice lowered. "I was joking, but I realize I'm serious. This forbidden thing we're sharing, this intimate discovery of each other, impregnates all life. Why, eating a hamburger with you is a sexual experience."

"You're sick, Irv," Bets said with a laugh. "Insane. Crazy. Nuts."

"Yes, I am," he answered proudly. "We ordered cheeseburgers back there and coffee milk shakes at the drive-in and we ate them."

"Sexually," she said with a twist to her tone.

"Right. I did anyway. I was aware of the warmth of the bun I picked up. The soft skin of the crust and its ripe curve. I felt my teeth cut through it. I mean I eat food all the time, but I can't remember when I felt myself take a bite. I enjoyed the pressure of my jaw, the texture of the bread, I felt a spurt of hot meat juice in my mouth, the taste of meat and cheese and bread, pickle and ketchup. But not just the taste but the texture of hamburger, crisp brown outside, warm red inside, chewy cheese, sharp pickle."

"You've gone over the hill."

"And the milk shake. Now that was sexy. Cold, thick, too sweet almost, a sucked-up jet of rich, creamy fluid I felt all the way down into my stomach. It was a real sexual experience."

"I suppose catching fish with me is also a sexual experience."

"Right. It is. Back there on the beach, casting the line out into the surf, I was aware of so many things. Your sharing this, your joy at hooking a fish, the lithe bending of your body whipping out the line and the leaning back, pulling it in. The sand under my feet felt different than it ever had, the purple light at the ocean rim, the hushed sound of the sea—it was all different, unusual, even significant, somehow, with you."

"I know what you mean."

"You do?"

"Of course, that's why I'm here."

"Smug, goddamn woman, I suppose you were born knowing it."

"Naturally." They smiled and she touched his leg with her hand and left it there, casually, familiarly, knowing too how much this man she once thought cold needed another person to touch him and how surprised that his gross, dark features, which she once would have thought repulsive, had become dear to her. Bets felt an unexpected tenderness toward this man, a warming familiarity with the way his smile came first to his eyes, the hunch of his shoulders when he leaned into a subject he was talking about, his gentleness with those who really hurt or who were the innocents—the children and the aged—the standards he set for others, made sufferable because they were so much less than those he set for himself. Irv was a good man. He could not cover with humor or protect with sophistication the fact that his work was important and that he took it seriously. He cared too much and it was a magnificent fault.

Irv needed her and he displayed all his weaknesses for her, letting her see behind his professional face, his arrogance and confidence, appealing to her through revelations of his interior life, which she had always wanted from Brad and never had. Even now, Brad refused to allow her to share his world. He suffered her visits, tolerating her when she interrupted his affairs in the ward, where he ruled with a tough confidence.

"Brad," she told him just once, "if you can run this ward from your bed, you could run a business from home."

"No," he answered quickly, shutting her out of any discussion. "I've thought about that. I'd be a freak, selling magazines by phone or something, making sales by sympathy. I won't do it. I belong here, I'll stay here."

There was nothing she could say now; she almost admired his fierce independence. He was tougher, sharper, more a man than he had ever been, but she could not tell him this or much of anything. With him she was always outside, a visitor. He would not share his world or come to hers; he would not accept what she had to offer, sympathy, help, love—and unfaithfulness, she thought bitterly.

Hurt, and angry because she was hurt, and guilty because she was angry at her damned proud husband, she would go to Irv, right from the hospital, both of them trying to ignore where she had been, whom she had just seen.

Bets looked at Irv across the dark wood table, his face softened by the sputtering candlelight, her heart pleased by the pleasure in his face, and thought how strange this was. He was a good man and she was a good woman, people who did not ordinarily shirk their responsibilities, people who did not let appetites control them; yet she sitting here waiting for dessert, content with this man who was not her husband; she could not just imagine but could feel, in her legs, in her tense abdomen, in her warming loins, the pleasure that she would give him, that he would give her.

Bets could not explore the implication of these thoughts, could not yet see herself as she would have to see herself, not the person she thought she was, not even the person Brad thought she was, but someone else. This was not yet the time for that. For this handful of time that they had picked up impulsively and allowed to trickle through their fingers so fast, so very fast, there was no time yet to think of what this needing each other meant to the children, to Brad, to Irv's profession; no time yet to consider all the other people who are affected; just time—once that line was crossed, once the, yes, use the word, "adultery" was committed—to fall all the way, as far as the fallen can fall, to spin down, twisting, turning, falling, out of control.

They stood up together, the second cup of coffee gulped, trying not to rush, walking sedately out of the restaurant, people of good taste, nice people, properly dressed and properly acting, until they could be together and alone, discovering not only each other but also themselves, the stranger that had lived within each of them.

Irv wept that night, naked as he had never been, unclothed beside Bets; it was unmanly weeping, unexpected, unable to stop. It happened when he was weakened, spent. "I'm sorry," he said, and Bets answered without words, cradling his head, and he fought clear, still crying, and rolled to the side of the bed and sat up, and she followed him, kneeling behind him, and then, when he hunched his shoulders against her, she scrambled around on the floor, on her knees before him, touching his head, saying, "Cry, cry, it's all right." Bets crooned encouragement to him, and Irv, holding his head in his hands, wept silently, letting the tears come for he knew not what—Brad, the family that had died, for

Bets, but mostly, Irv knew, for himself, for all the loneliness and the caring. When he was done and they lay back, emptied, drained, pulled inside out, they did not talk but just held hands until at last he spoke.

"Brad's decided to have the operation, to have his pinch."

"I know."

"Monday."

"Yes."

"It means he's going to try to live, and I should be glad—or I suppose I should be angry, in case that ruins this. But, Bets, I don't feel anything."

"I don't either, just nothing, empty of hope for him. Afraid, I guess, he'll be the hero again with his pinch. Up and then down. He may need me now." She cried silently, great, awful tears. "He may need me and I don't need him, don't even want him, now."

Irv spoke at last, detached from her weeping: "We cry from self-pity. What deep-down terrible selfishness."

After a while, Bets answered, "Of course."

"Why of course?"

"We cry for ourselves, we pity ourselves," she said slowly, knowing the words were important, knowing too that they were ahead of her thoughts leading her, then, to a meaning. "Of course we pity ourselves, Irv." She hesitated. "Was it a Greek who said 'Know thyself'? He was right; it's the beginning of wisdom, and when we begin to know ourselves we have to weep with self-pity." She turned on an elbow and continued talking to him: "We talk about revealing ourselves to other people, and that's good, but the real revelation is to ourselves. It's easy for me to understand you, to know what you need, understand it and respect it, but can I respect myself, giving it to you? I, who am Brad's wife, who have his children, who thought herself better than all the others, the girls on the block who had to leave school early, their dreams turned to big bellies." She rolled back and stared at the shadow-patterned ceiling. "I weep too, Irv. I weep for you, and I weep for Brad, but I have to admit—and fight admitting it—that I weep most for myself."

"I'm sorry, Bets."

"Don't apologize, don't you ever dare apologize to me, Irving Frank. That would cheapen it." Bets challenged him, "I'm not sorry we've done this, are you?"

"No. No, I don't think so."

"I'm proud that I could reach out of the self that I thought I was, break through the shell and answer your need, your cry for help, and don't you apologize for that cry for help either, Irv. It gives purpose to me; it made me better than I ever was."

"Better? Doing this?"

"Yes, better, a woman who needs to give, and this was a greater giving. I'm proud, but I cry for Brad, for you, but most of all I cry, as we all do, for myself. I'm selfish, too, so awfully selfish."

"Because you're human."

"So very human."

Irv laughed. "My God, we're naked, no clothes and no illusions." His voice changed. "Is this the end of what we lived for, the gods we chose, the people we made ourselves? We destroyed those make-believe people and perhaps we've destroyed everything, come to the end."

They were silent for a long time, and then she said, wondering if he slept, "Irv."

"Yes, Bets."

"I don't know why, I can't argue it or defend it. I feel lost too, at the end; yet I somehow have a hunch, perhaps I'm just rationalizing us, trying to make an excuse, but I don't think so. I think if we've got the guts, if we can do the hardest thing of all, be honest with ourselves, find out what we are and accept it, then we may not be at an end but at a beginning."

He sat up, looking at his watch reluctantly. She laughed. "At least there's one thing we can be sure about."

"What's that?"

"We're different from what we were, you and I. We'll never be the same again, no matter what happens. Never in all our lives. Good or bad, we've changed almost as much as Brad."

25

In the special ward where you were prepped for surgery, Brad glared at the round dish with its puddle of applesauce, then hunched his shoulder forward, and his right arm swung in the sling. The fork strapped to his hand was on target. It hit the applesauce square in the middle and then, with the help of the counterbalance at the end of the sling, swung back and up to his mouth, where he sucked the few drops of applesauce from the tines of the fork. He stopped, glared at the applesauce, and attacked it again. The applesauce was good beyond reason, cool to his drug-dried mouth, sweet, full of the memories of a summer in childhood when he had had great crockery-thick bowls of applesauce, sprinkled with cinnamon, served by his grandmother. He lifted a few drips of applesauce at a time—again and again and again until he just stopped, unable even to hurl his fork to the table. What he needed was a spoon—and there it was, sitting beside the knife, insolvent, a few inches from his hand. But he could not put down his fork and pick up his spoon. He would have to holler and wait, holler and wait, holler and wait until some irritated female would walk the length of the corridor, unstrap his fork, and attach the spoon. And then he would need a fork again. What he needed was a pinch. Brad stared at his slack fingers in a fury at their uselessness. Well, he would get his glorious pinch and it would make him an inch less dependent on anyone.

Angrily he again swung the fork into the applesauce, thinking how his life was measured by self-respect and how each simple task could mark his independence. By feeding himself applesauce, he'd tell the world, do-gooder and do-badder alike, to leave him alone for a minute—screw them all. He quit the hopeless task of eating applesauce with a fork, but he couldn't fall back against the pillows; he had to sit the way he had been propped, staring at the brown pool of tasty applesauce, thinking how much he wanted that pinch, which he would achieve tomorrow if the operation were successful. He wanted it so badly and he resented wanting such a pitiful thing.

Brad remembered how once everything had been possible for him; what was unachievable for another man was within his reach. He'd never been hungry, not even in the army, except when he'd played at a struggle for survival on summer camping trips. He'd had warm clothes and an allowance earned by unimportant chores. He'd had a room of his own, friends who knew his father and who therefore made a place for him. He had had a good school, girls to kiss, a commission in the army, a job to accept—not a job to seek, but a job to accept. Health, happiness, Bets, the children, a friendly, comfortable God to go with his friendly, comfortable home. And thinking of all his past blessings, he looked at the unattainable applesauce. And he sat staring at it until he could wait no longer, and hating his weakness in giving them the satisfaction of asking, he yelled for them to come and take his tray away and unstrap his fork. He would not beg them to attach the spoon.

Brad thought all afternoon of the pinch—the ability to press two fingers and a thumb together at will, that was the trick—and he dreamed of the pinch that night, and waiting in the special room outside surgery the next morning, Brad tried to forget how much he wanted that goddamn nothing of a pinch that was everything. His mind kept betraying him, dwelling on what it would mean to him to be able to play cards with Jackson, turn the page of his own book, put down that fork and pick up a spoon, pull his sheet up to his chin. Each time he made himself think of the ward—the world—he came back to the pinch. He tried not to think, but he couldn't; he shut his eyes to sleep and he lay awake, waiting.

He'd flirted with Hope before and wanted none of her come-on yet. He'd think of Hank on Ward F, but find that his mind had leaped the track and he was practicing, in his mind's eye, the gadgetry that would be possible with the pinch. He would use the long tongs to extend his arm a yard, run the electric typewriter, use a speaker phone. With the pinch he might sell again, stocks or insurance. You could sell over the phone. With the pinch he could operate an answering service, pay his own way. With the pinch and the gadget Humphrey on Ward P had, you could blow your own nose. With the pinch . . .

Brad cursed the pinch and cursed his hunger for it. A man ought to want to be the strongest man in the world, seek fame or riches, success—not just the ability to press his right thumb against his two first fingers.

He tried to dream, to think of other things, to think of nothing, but he failed. It was all there in that pinch—his whole future, his life, and the operation might, just might, not work. To change the subject of his thoughts, Brad spoke angrily to a man who he knew was waiting but whom he couldn't see. "My name's Hastings."

"I'm Morse, Andy Morse."

"You waiting for the knife, too?" Brad asked, not really caring.

"Yep, and should be used to it, but I'm not. I hate waiting."

"How long have you been here, Andy?"

"Three years. Three whole years and eight operations, nine, counting this one, and I sure hope it'll be the last." Then he laughed grimly and said, "I mean, I hope it will be the last in the series."

"What do they say?"

"Nothing. You know how it is; you're not supposed to bother them." Morse rambled on, obviously eager to talk, to make the time pass. "You know we get used to it, being treated like a number. That's what gets me. A week or two here is all it seems to take. They take away your name, face, who you are, almost as easily as they take away your clothes. We all think we're something, somebody, and then—pfuff—nothing. A carpenter, that's what I was, first man on the job and I was known by it. Funny, the things we're known by. I've got three boys—they know me as a father; no one else sees me just like they do. I'm real to them. To my wife I'm her husband, I suppose a kid still to my mother; to most of the neighbors, a nut who grows grapes. The boss? He knows me as a man who will work up high. Who else knows me? Not many more, and I suppose none of them know much of me, but it's enough. Here I'm a gut with a growth. And I take it from them, let them treat me as a thing. I even feel grateful when they talk over my head as if I were a piece of haddock, even when everyone treats me as if I were invisible." He snorted. "Coming to County is like being erased off a slate—one swipe and you're gone."

"Here's the last on the list." Brad saw a huge, fat man, flat-footed, in hospital greens.

"Yeah, and it's a long one."

"It's a man," Brad shouted, as surprised at his yell as they were. They stopped, their stupid faces staring at him. "It's not an it, god damn it, it's a man. His name is Andy Morse. Mister Morse to you. A man, you ignorant, unfeeling slobs; a human being, a father, a husband, a carpenter. He's not an it."

The two orderlies nodded knowingly at each other and then started pushing him out the door. Before it closed, Morse called back, "You tell 'em, you tell 'em."

The door whooshed shut and Brad laughed to himself in the empty room. "I'll tell them, but they won't listen."

"But it does you good to tell them, does you good."

Brad would have jumped in astonishment if he could have. Instead, he swallowed his anger that he was victim to such surprise. Bitterly he said, "I thought I was alone."

"I didn't know you were here either until you talked to the other one. I'm blind." There wasn't anything to say to that and so Brad waited until the unexpected roommate went on. "I've been here since last night, yesterday morning, in fact."

"Why?"

"I was left over," the voice said simply. It was an old voice and Brad couldn't be sure if it were male or female.

"The bastards," Brad sympathized.

"You're young."

"I guess."

"You know, I've been here thirty-three years. Came here to die. Sent by the family and outlived them all. I was seventy."

"You're a hundred and three?" Brad asked incredulously.

"Yep, the care can't be as bad as it seems." The voice cracked with chuckles. "Or I'm tough."

Trying to think of something to say, Brad said, "I can't see you but you sound in good health."

"Oh, I guess, I guess, have to repair a pipe—and you know,"

he added in wonder, "I'm lying here wanting to live, wanting it real bad."

Brad answered before he thought, starting and then stopping. "I thought, well, I mean when you're old, had your time . . ."

The old voice laughed. "I did too, couldn't understand my grandpop's grin when an old friend died. He was real happy, real happy. Now I'm the same."

"I wanted to die."

"Oh, I guess we all say we do at times. I don't know. I'd like to see, to run, to kiss a pretty girl, to eat a steak with my own teeth."

"Why'd they leave you here all night? Did they forget you?"

"Perhaps, but I got something to eat this morning." Then the two spooks came for Brad and he asked angrily, "Hey, what about him? He's been here since last night."

"Dunno," said the fat one. "All we got's orders for you."

"Hey, good luck to you, good luck," the old man called.

"Thanks, and you too. I'll see about you. I'll tell 'em," Brad promised.

"We're friends despite the fact we've never seen each other," Brad thought as he was pushed under a strange ceiling, "friends because we have the same enemies—the bastards on the outside." Brad resented the men who pushed him, resented the strange turnings of the unfamiliar corridor and wished he had never left Ward F. When the surgical faces looked over him, sexless, expressionless in their masks, he felt a fury rise in him.

"Good morning, Brad."

He glared up at Irv's eyes. "There's an old man in there, Irv, a hundred and three."

"That's a pretty fine age." Irv was making conversation, his mouth a shadow hidden by the gauze.

"Don't put me off. He was left over from yesterday, forgotten. He's blind. They just forgot him."

"He isn't left over," a nurse explained, "and he's been there a month. It's where he stays. He has to be pumped out every day. We have to have him here handy, and he gets time mixed up." Brad didn't speak anymore, just waited for them to put him to sleep. He thought of the old man's world, wondered why he wanted to live, and realized it was somehow more horrible that the old man was being treated than mistreated. If they were doing him wrong, you could blame them; but who could you blame if they were doing him right, if he wanted to be kept alive and they were doing just that? Who could you blame?

When Brad came to, he saw he was back on Ward F by that old familiar ceiling—the crack and the white fingerprints near the light fixture. Then he saw the faces looking down at him, Bets and Irv together. He looked up at them and felt the weary anger. Why was he a baby in a crib, so goddamned dependent? He wanted to ask them the question, but he wouldn't give them the satisfaction of knowing how much he wanted that puny ability to pinch, to pick up a piece of bread in his own hand instead of having a fork strapped to his useless hand, one utensil for each meal. He would not ask them how it went. He would not let them see how much he wanted it. He would not beg.

"How'd Morse do?"

"Who's he?" Irv answered, surprised.

"The guy who went in before me—a plumbing job."

"I don't know; you were my patient."

"He died," Brad said, sure now, disgusted that Irv didn't know him—or care.

"I'm not sure; one did die."

"One what?"

"One patient," Irv answered, puzzled.

Knowing he wasn't being fair, Brad still snarled at Irv, "He wasn't a patient, he was a man." He could see them look at each other, wondering, and he realized he hadn't seen them together in a long, long time. He spoke to Bets: "We get fed up at the men in white around here. They don't seem at all like gods to us."

"Brad, I'm surprised." Her voice was cross and puzzled, but she defended Irv. "You should be glad about this particular man in white, anyway. He just did a fine job."

It was all wrong and he knew it, yet he could not take back his angry resentment and it made him even more cross when Irv seemed to understand, answering Brad's rage with a quiet, "We hope we had luck, Brad. It seemed to go well. You know it will take a few weeks before we can be sure."

Brad tried to thank him. "I know I should be pleased, but it isn't very much, you know. A goddamned pinch."

"I know," Irv answered as if he were guilty, and Brad saw Bets look at him as if there were something Brad didn't know.

"Look. I can take it," Brad said. "If it was a foul-up, tell me." He felt frustrated, as if they were keeping a secret from him, and his anger came out with a cruel twist. "It isn't as if the operation meant I could walk."

"There's no secret, Brad," Irv said softly, looking at Bets.

"I simply do not understand you, Brad. I simply don't." Bets glared at him.

"No, don't," Irv said and touched her arm.

"I will. He doesn't need to be grateful, perhaps, but he shouldn't attack you." Bets turned back to him. "Brad, you know what the operation meant, and Irv did a fine job. He's a good surgeon and a good friend, too. It's not his fault you're here—it isn't anybody's fault."

Brad wanted to put the words together in the right order, with the right turn, but it didn't work out that way. "I can't help it. The two of you, standing there, hell, I guess I envy your health. This is a pretty sick place. Will you go?" They looked at each other and it somehow made him mad. "This is the last thing you can give me, a pinch. If I've got it, fine, I've come back as far as I can. Now go. I'm wrong, but it's the way I feel."

"You know, you ought to thank him." Bets' voice rose and she ignored Irv's hand. "He's been awfully good to you, to me, more than a doctor. He's kind and gentle and he cares."

"I'm thankful," Brad heard himself say, his voice cruelly flat. "So now go. I don't want to be mourned. I want to be as independent as I can. What I have to take I'll take from strangers, so I'll live my life here, where I belong, where there isn't any pity. You have your world and I have mine. Now go, and thanks." They stared at him, standing together at the crib sides of his bed. He saw them and he saw the sides of the bed, which he did not need, for he would not toss or turn or roll over. He was safe, he thought bitterly, and he shut his eyes. Brad heard them go and he didn't bother to open his eyes. The drugs took over, but when he woke again, Paxton asked the question that had been only in his nightmares and had been put away with shame.

"Hastings, I don't mean to say it," Paxton breathed, "but are they, well, involved?"

"Who?" Brad answered sleepily, but Paxton would not be put off.

"Your wife and the doctor. I mean, to me they seem like too-good friends. They wouldn't do that to you, here, would they? I mean, you like that. Now, they wouldn't do that to you. . . ."

"Drop dead," Brad snarled. "Shut up and drop dead." He was surprised at himself for not denying it. And lying there, he knew. He could smell it. Paxton was right; of all people, Paxton had to be the one. The way he touched her arm, the way she defended him. They hadn't been in together in months, not even by accident. He never, ever, mentioned Bets and she never talked of Irv. The look she gave him, the way she had acted on her visits, the reason Irv hadn't gotten mad at Brad, the way he would have if he hadn't been guilty. His wife. His doctor, his friend.

That afternoon and that night, awake and in his dreams, Brad knew, and when he woke in the morning, it was the first thing he knew.

26

Clocks had not stopped running; the pages on the calendar had continued to turn. Summer became fall and turned into winter, and the waiter, his manner ingratiating, his face hard, became too familiar to Bets. "I knew you'd like this quiet booth," he said with a smirk. "It's secluded, by itself." Bets looked at the waiter they'd got to know so well and didn't know at all. She saw the gravy stains on the right sleeve of his short red jacket and then realized that his bow tie was a fraud—he clipped it on—and in his eyes she saw his insolent knowledge of their relationship. When he left, she told Irv, "He knows who we are."

"I don't think so, darling." The word was easy on his lips now, almost as meaningless as a husband's good-bye kiss.

"He knows, he knows."

"Look, Bets, if he does and if he were going to start trouble, he'd have done it by now."

"Trouble?"

"You know—money, blackmail."

She gasped, realizing they had become so vulnerable, and answered quickly, "No, I don't mean that. I mean, he looks at us as if we were, well, characters in a dirty joke."

Their drinks came without their having ordered them. The waiter knew what they wanted, and for the first time Bets wasn't flattered by the service. "No, no, I want a daiquiri tonight." The waiter looked at her, swallowed his argument, and smiled as if he understood. "You see, Irv, he knows all about us. He knows our situation."

Irv shrugged, his face sad. "I suppose he does—we're not the first."

"Not your first?"

"I didn't say that," he answered wearily. "Yes, you're my first."

The daiquiri came and again they were quiet until the waiter left. Then Bets picked up the argument: "Your first adulteress?"

Irv closed his eyes as if he were praying and then answered, "Bets, Bets. It doesn't do any good."

"But I hate it, being known." Her voice was close to tears. "I don't like sneaking, feeling ashamed, lying. I want to be proud of you and of us, I guess."

He finished his drink. "And I, who wanted to be alone?" he snorted. "Hah. Now I want a wife. You. I want children, a little house, a power lawn mower." He shrugged. The argument was over as she touched his hand to comfort him, but in a day or a week or an hour it would come back when it was least expected. The sight of a family, the memory of Brad, an innocent remark of the children's, the perhaps knowing look of a friend.

"This love of ours is selfish," Bets said once, lying beside him in the motel while the trucks rocked by on the highway. "It's taking, not giving."

"It's giving too, Bets."

"Yes, but, well, I guess it isn't going anywhere, it isn't building anything. It's all an end in itself—a new kiss or position, new dexterity."

"You enjoy it. I know you do."

"Of course I do, but I'm ashamed."

"You said you'd never be ashamed."

"I've said a lot of things, Irv, a lot of things."

He didn't answer and they were quiet while they dressed and drove back to the city. On the way, the night grew blacker than any night she'd ever seen, and there was thunder and lightning and sheeting rain, which made things slow down, and a roaring, sliding trailer truck, its horn blasting, skidded by them out of the dark, into the dark, gone, and all Bets could think of was the stories in the newspaper if their bodies were found. And she knew the stories would be right. Everyone would read the story and understand, oh, how they'd understand, Irv's hunger and hers. No one could see, could see their love, their passion, their sharing as clean and wonderful, because it wasn't. The gossip always won. They weren't extraordinary. They were most ordinary. And in a week they were together again.

They were in another restaurant outside of town where the waiter did not know them. Irv said, "This cannot be, Bets. Perhaps other people could, but we can't. We have to live within our limitations."

"The same way Brad does."

"Exactly," Irv said and nodded. "As cold as that and as clear. Brad can't walk, ever. We can't love each other——"

"In that way," Bets interrupted.

"In that way, in any way, really. Love is sex and caring and meaning and respect. We're grown-up people. This isn't mother love or brotherly love or love of country. This is love of man and woman and it's forbidden for us. No grays." He nodded. "We thought there were grays, that rules were different for us, that we were free to do what others couldn't, shouldn't, do. We weren't. We were wrong."

"We were a dirty joke."

"A familiar story, anyway. A lot of people would say we were inevitable, a joke older than Chaucer." He paused before going on, realizing suddenly how much they talked now, seeking reasons and excuses, analyzing and probing, when they hadn't needed words at first. "We can't turn away from it, Bets. We may be nice people, intelligent, well washed and all that, but whether we worship Jehovah or Freud, we've run aground—and we've done a very ordinary thing. We've got to admit that. Yes, you and I, the wonder of us, has indeed become a dirty joke, the oldest plot in the world."

"Is it really like that, Irv?"

"Perhaps not yet, but it can become that, and I'm afraid that time is running out. You know I've wondered about those couples who never get married. Do you know Scottie who runs the lab we use?"

"Yes, a gentle man, sweet and gentle. He hates every bad report he has to give."

"Well, he's been living with a woman for twenty years."

"He has?" Bets laughed in astonishment.

"Yes, he keeps an apartment, but he's never there. He lives with Gladys, a telephone operator who's as nice as he is. Not as well educated, but good, a plump, middle-aged woman. A proper housewife."

"Why didn't they get married?"

"I don't know. For some reason they waited too long. Perhaps they were fearful, but they have always seemed more married to me than most people. Sedate. They do everything together. Now I realize they aren't married at all. They don't have children, a home, each other in the eyes of the world, and these things are important, very important."

"You want to get married and have children?"

"Yes, you know that." He took her hand across the table. "I want you, I want your children. I need you. Get a divorce. I'll brave it through with you. But if I can't have you that way . . ."

She looked right into his eyes, letting him see her tears.

"And we cannot talk of divorce," he continued. It was not a question but a statement.

They left the restaurant and went to his apartment as they had planned, and they committed another act of adultery, not because they wanted to but because each thought the other one wanted to and so they gave themselves. There was no passion, for they could not lose themselves in the act. "We're never alone now, are we?" Bets asked, smiling sadly.

They did lie together naked as they used to, talking and touching, being together. They dressed quickly, hiding not from each other but from themselves, and went to the living room to have a drink, aware of the calls that might come from the hospital, the obligations at home, the hour they both had to get to work. Irv smiled. "We all have trouble deciding which is heaven and which is hell, don't we?"

"We've changed."

"Yes, we have, Bets, grown up. I would have thought this was just what the doctor ordered"—he grinned wryly—"a built-in non-entanglement. Have sex, companionship, but no mortgage, no babies, no frightening demands."

"And now you want them?"

"I'm sorry, Bets, I do. We have to live in the world. You hated the suburbs, but you have to live there. You belong there and so does Brad."

"He'll come home?"

"I think so. I think he will, Bets."

She was quiet. Then she said, "I'll be there for him, Irv. You have to be a doctor, to go on doing what you have to be. I have to be a wife, if Brad will take me back."

"He'll take you back, Bets," Irv said, smiling grimly. "He has to." He shook his head sadly. "We live as if we had choices, but we don't, not when we feel the pinch." He grinned a sad apology for the poor joke. "I suppose this is what it's all about, the accident, everything. In a free country we aren't so free."

"We have choices, Irv. Not to quit, to go on."

"Yes"—he smiled at her—"to go on doing what we have to do. It's not much choice, really, when all our genes and our living and our society and everything we are and everything that is around us says there's really only one thing we can do and we do it. And yet it's the hardest thing sometimes—isn't it?—to do what we have to do."

"To live with a pinch," Bets said, trying to speak calmly. "We got cross at Brad, or I did, for his difficulty in seeing the inevitable, his inevitable. I guess that's our trouble. We can see the other one's inevitable but not our own."

Irv nodded, agreeing, and said, "Limitations. Where did we get the idea there were no limits? Is the hero the guy who breaks down the limits or the man who lives with them?" He stood up, his face suddenly hard, his words angry. "Words. Nothing but words and words and more words and I've had enough of words." He moved quickly to Bets and touched her.

"Not one last time, Bets? Not one dramatic good-bye?"

"No one last time, Irv darling. We have our memories and they are good. And no good-byes, because we'll be seeing each other. We're involved, with Brad."

He grinned wryly and said, "In a triangle. Tied to each other by a hundred obligations, love and hate and envy and guilt and God knows what. It's so different from the movies and so much the same." He laughed and his voice strained with the effort. "We've become pretty damn smug tonight. Pretty soon we'll be convinced we fell in love out of a sense of civic responsibility or cosmic inevitability."

"I like you, Irv Frank."

"And I like you, Bets, very much."

They stood at the door as if they were back at the beginning, not knowing whether to kiss, and realizing this, they laughed and shook hands. She laughed with him, but their grip was hard, painful—a last desperate communication—and then the door opened, shut, and they were apart.

27

It was the second winter of Brad's imprisonment within himself, and he found contentment in small things. When there was a break in the routine of bathings and massagings, when he was not exhausted by the effort of shaving or eating, he would run his electric wheelchair to the window at the end of the ward. There he could see the jagged branches of a bare linden close by and beyond it the black smokestack of the hospital power plant and still further away the New England winter sky. That was all, and Brad found it view enough this winter.

The graceless, sharp-elbowed patterns of the twigs and tree arms at first appeared to change from day to day, but after a month of watching, Brad decided that it was his vision of their design that changed, that his eyes rearranged the network of black, intercrossing lines. Even the black changed. Some days the tree was bright with rain or ice; other days it was dull from swallowing all the light it could find. It was never all black—it was blue, gray, purple, brown, and red-brown, shaded and spotted, reflecting the day.

Brad never tired of his tree, and people rarely bothered him when he was sitting looking out. They imagined, he supposed, that he was staring at a past or a future, suffering memories or hopes, when all he was doing was watching his view of the sky, dark gray or blue, the weather moving across his window, right to left, west to east. He didn't share his view or try to edit it. He accepted the chimney stack, black and ugly with its slanting guy wires and belch of smoke; took his view as he could get it—God-made and man-made—always the same in its always changing.

Bets found him there and he swung around, not even sharing it with her. "Still bandaged," he said, sharing that with her, his frustration and his hopes. "Will you give me a ride?" he asked, knowing it pleased her to push the wheelchair, which didn't need pushing, to do something. "I want you to see what Bragg can do. He was an architect. Was on a vacation trip with his wife when an oil truck hit them. He was burned pretty badly."

"His wife?"

"She was lucky," Brad said without self-pity—simply as fact. "She died."

She pushed him down through Ward F and the gauntlet of jokes and greetings, still not used to the lack of privacy, the lines of staring faces with nothing to do but watch, eyes that didn't care but were still curious from habit. They traveled between the rows of bed after bed, then out the corridor between the rows of wheelchairs filled with people staring at long benches of other people, more like things than people, men and women, gray hair razor-cropped almost the same, who stared back at one another, unseeing, uncaring. Bets was discomforted when she was followed by the beady eyes, but more disturbed by those who paid no attention to their whizzing past. She hurried down the corridor, turning to Brad's commands until they came to Ward Q. "In here, Bets," and down another row of beds filled with lumps of people until Brad said, "Here's Bragg."

She made herself look at Bragg, at his pink, newly grafted skin, the nose in the making, which looked as if it were put on by kindergarten fingers still damp from clay, the hole that was a mouth, the flaps for ears.

He sat propped up in the bed, his left arm bandaged and his right arm fitting into a contraption, half scissor, half claw, which was made of gleaming stainless steel. On the table in front of the architect were simple plastic tile building blocks, the same kind Eric used to play with before he was nine. She looked up at the eyes, which were sewn shut, as Brad introduced her: "Bragg, here's my wife. I'd sure like to have you show her what you can do."

Bets steadied her voice and said, "Glad to meet you, Bragg," and she tried to understand the sounds, the rumble and whistle, that Bragg pumped out of him in answer.

"That's right, she's the Bets I've been talking about," she heard Brad say. She listened more carefully—were the sounds really words?—and thought she may have heard "visit" but wasn't sure and made the social lie. "Brad talks all the time about what you do," she said, hoping that was the right thing. "He's certainly impressed." Sounds again came out of the unmoving hole; there were no lips to read. Brad said nothing and she waited to see what he could do, making herself remember that this was a man, a man who had found a way back to pride.

The thing on the bed, the human being named Bragg, made a sound that he may have meant to be a deprecating laugh and moved the stainless-steel thing, which was his arm, raised up and reached over to the blocks on the over-the-bed hospital table.

The silence, even in the ward, was terrible in its waiting while everyone watched this man, crippled and burned and blind, maneuver his stainless-steel tongs with their rubber tips among the frivolous plastic tiles. First the claw cleared a space and then it built a foundation. Bets watched in wonder and in suspense, hoping for success as he placed brick on brick, building a tower. Standing beside Brad, she didn't understand Bragg's problem—she felt it. Bragg couldn't feel the bricks, not through those metal fingers. He had to remember the sizes of the blocks, and Bets wondered how he knew them. Were they held to his other, useless, hand so that he could feel their size? Had he explored them with his tongue or had someone simply told him and had he accepted their word on faith? Bets watched the claw moving slowly over to pick up a brick. He poked it, she saw, and, hearing the dull clack, knew which side was up. He turned it if it was needed and put it in place; then went to get another, hoping he would not hear the clatter that would tell him his tower had come tumbling down. Bets was very aware that Bragg was working in the dark, totally deprived of the sight of what he was doing. He didn't know if his tower was going up. He had created a vision in his mind, a dream of a tower, and he was following that invisible plan, and on the table in front of him a tower was being built, brick by brick, around and around the square, until at last he finished and he gasped and grunted with success, and Bets, understanding the sounds now, laughed with him and she praised his trick, not too much, understanding that he knew how much and how little it was.

They chatted awhile and Bets recognized that somehow with that trick, Bragg, despite his ugliness, his incredible, inhuman ugliness, had made himself a man, and after a while Bets said to Bragg, "I'll be back to see you," knowing she would, and she pushed Brad back to Ward F. They didn't talk about Bragg, but when she left she said, "Thank you for introducing me to Bragg," and Brad nodded, understanding. The next day they were quieter together—they didn't have to chat—and the day after that, Brad showed her his view, and on Sunday, when she took him to an empty dayroom, filled with the cool sun of false spring, they talked. "It's one of those days, Bets, that you used to fear so much," Brad started, "when the sun's too bright, the sky too clear, the world too beautiful, when you feel a sort of premature nostalgia, being aware life has to pass." He laughed. "I used to think you were nuts, but now I know how you felt."

They were quiet a long time, and then she said, "You know a lot of things now."

"Too little and too much, far too much." His voice was bitter.

"It's over," she answered.

"What's over?" He suddenly swung his wheelchair around so that he faced her on the couch, pinning her there.

"You know," she said, her head down.

Knowing, nodding, he still commanded her, "Tell me."

She looked up and spoke clearly: "My affair with Irv."

His face twisted meanly and he almost stuttered when he said, "I guessed. I guess I knew, but you imagine a lot of things here, when you're like this. I had hoped I was wrong."

She didn't look away from him. "It's over."

He nodded. "But it happened?"

"Yes, it happened."

They sat in the strange cool warmth of the winter sun and after a long time Brad said, "I killed a man."

Bets almost laughed. "Who?"

"Carey."

"But he died of cancer."

"No, he killed himself."

"How could he, how could you . . ."

"Help him?" Brad smiled. "I saved the drug for him." And he described Carey's nightly trip to pluck the capsules from his teeth.

"Didn't they investigate?" she asked. Brad snorted for an answer. Bets pressed on: "He killed himself. You didn't kill him."

"Yes, but I helped. I was involved and I know all the reasons; yet there's guilt there. And you know, I didn't mourn him. When I knew he was dead, I felt free, happy. I was free of him and you and life. That's what I thought. I'm guilty—of helping him and of being happy he was dead."

"I'm guilty too—about the Chicago plane."

"What?"

"You didn't take the early plane because I was testing your love. I hated your belonging, your being the man who had everything and needed nothing. I've got that guilt worse than Irv, in a way."

"I never once had thought about changing my plane to go to Chicago." He shook his head in wonder. "Never once thought of that. If I'd gone with Irv and taken the early plane . . ." Again they sat silently together.

"Can you forgive me, Brad?"

"For the plane?"

She nodded.

"Of course." And he changed the subject. "You know, Bragg's doing other things. God, I don't know how he does it. He's going home, he says, and he'll make it, by God, he will. He talks of running a telephone-answering service, he has all sorts of plans, even selling. You know, I could sell on the phone myself. He's learning to talk better and he makes plans. He never once, not for a minute, wasn't a man. You know, Bets"—he raised his bandaged right hand—"I want this pinch more than I've ever wanted anything in my life. If he can use that claw, think what I can do with a pinch, and I'm scared because I want it so much."

"Brad, can you ever forgive me for Irv? Can you forgive Irv?"

"No."

"You can't?" Bets was surprised at the surprise in her voice.

"Christ, no, I can't." His face was ugly with rage. "I'm no saint. I don't like being a cripple. I've found no superior wisdom. I'm angry and bitter and full of self-pity—and frustration. Lord, how I'm full of frustration. I think of you and him, together, doing it, and I want to kill you both. I can't do it again—at least not as he can, not as a real man. I'm no saint because I'm here. Don't ever forget it." He breathed deeply and his whole body seemed to shudder. "If you want out, take off. If you expect forgiveness, forget it. I don't have it, and I won't. Understanding?" He laughed nastily. "Oh, I understand—all of it. The need, the hunger, the excuses, the good, solid, old-fashioned screwing, but I can't forget it and I can't forgive it. Part of me will always hate you and part of me will never trust you." She had nothing to say and at last he went on: "And part of me will always love you, I suppose. We have a marriage still, better or worse. I suspect you have to stay with me and I need you, but let's not talk about it now."

"All right, Brad."

"Take me back to the ward." She started to get up. "No, stay here for a while. Let me go back by myself. I want to be just with myself."

Brad found he could stoke his rage by looking at his view, visiting Bragg, rationing his hopes for the pinch, but still making plans for plans of the future—mail-order sales with Bets to help him, specialty foods; he knew the business. He skirted the edges of his plans for the future, trying not to count too much on the pinch, on Bets, on success. He played out his role as king of the ward, enjoying his status, proud of his ability to raise hell and get things done. Ward F was painted now and they had a radio and the bedpans were warm. He knew every man in the ward and a hundred or more, he guessed, outside it, but he found himself jealous of his privacy, seeking time to be alone as he had never wanted to be before.

When it was time to take off the bandages, Irv pushed him down the corridor to the examining room, not saying much because they didn't seem to have much to say these days. And then suddenly, even before the bandages were cut off, Brad had to stop Irv. "I know."

Irv stopped cutting and leaned back against the sink, his scissors awkwardly held in his hand. "Yes, I know, Brad."

"You want me to forgive you?"

Irv smiled bitterly. "It wouldn't make much difference. I've got to live with it. It can't be taken back."

"Or forgotten, Irv." In his anguish, Brad's hand, the bandage streaming from it, flapped up and down uselessly. "Let's clear the air, Irv Frank. There's no forgiving and there's no forgetting. If you'll be my doctor, I'll have you. I guess I've got to—you know the case; but I told Bets part of me will always hate her and mistrust her. The same goes for you." Irv nodded; he had nothing to say. "You're going to take over here as medical director."

"The hell I am."

"There's an opening and you can get it for the asking."

"Brad, I don't want—"

"Shut up, Irv Frank. I know you can do it. It's a part-time job. It'll cut into your practice and cut out your research, but we need you instead of the drunken political hacks we've had."

"What are you doing ordering me around?"

"You know what I'm doing."

"Blackmail?" Irv said in wonder.

"Exactly. You'll look like a saint, giving up that fat chunk of practice for the old crocks at County. We'll be quite a team, you and I, prize stoolie when I'm in here—and when I get out I'm going on tour. I'm going to make a spectacle of myself at every meeting that'll have me—church groups, luncheon clubs, political organizations, men's clubs and women's clubs—I'll put on a show for them all. I'm going to tell them about County and show them what can happen to them."

Brad saw Irv looking down at him and he knew. "So, I've wet my pants like a baby. And I didn't even know it. It shows I'm pretty excited, doesn't it? And not as tough as I sound. OK. I'm not so tough, but I'm mean, goddamn miserable mean. You take the job—decide you have a social obligation, guilt, whatever you want to tell people, but you get that job or I'll blow the whistle on you." He saw Irv looking at him in astonishment and in case he didn't get the message, he went on, his voice cold with rage: "And if I can let people see me like this—a thing, a quad who's peed in his pants, if I'm angry enough and bitter enough and mean enough to put myself on display, I'll be mean enough to let them know I'm a cuckold, to let them know my doctor screwed my wife while I was here, like this, unable to kill the bastard. You remember the Hippocratic Oath you took when you became a doctor—'into whatsoever houses I enter, I enter to help the sick, and I will abstain from all intentional wrongdoing and harm, especially from abusing the bodies of man or woman, bond or free.' I looked it up, Irv Frank. Did I memorize it accurately? Did I, you bastard? Can I have you disbarred or defrocked or whatever they do to doctors who use a cripple's wife? Can I? You're damn right I can. Now cut off the bandages and give me my pinch."

Irv, not talking, cut off the bandage and examined the hand and finally, in a strange professional tone, laid out the exercises. "It'll hurt, Brad, but you have to work it."

Brad looked Irv in the eye. "I think I can take a little hurt, Doctor." He laughed almost easily. "And isn't that a proud little pouter pigeon of a remark?"

Irv nodded, ignoring that. "You bastard. I've never been told off like that before," he said with a smile. "I'm proud, too, and I don't like it."

"But you'll take the job?"

"I have a choice?" He grinned.

"I expect we'll make a team."

"And be friends, in our fashion," Irv said. "Now you're a patient, remember that. Do just what I say. Don't try too much with that pinch; don't be too tough. Just take it a day at a time."

Brad nodded. "Don't worry. I want that pinch, that silly goddamn pinch. I want it."

His life became identified with the pinch. Brad could see the future now. First the pinch, that single, simple ability that could make him a man. He would learn to use every bit of skill there was in the pinch, day by day, and when he came to the end of that road, he would learn to use the gadgets: the long-reaching pincers; the comb and toothbrush, the spoons; the special fork, which was half knife; the rubber-tipped page turner; the dial on the radio; the new push-button telephone arranged by Pete; the tape recorder brought in by Ames. He would master them one by one until he didn't have to think about them any more than he'd once had to think about walking across a room, and then he'd use them to support his family and to raise hell.

"The bastards," he thought. Irv, Bets, himself before the accident, smug and unknowing. The very next county had one of the best rehabilitation programs in the country. Pete, the O.T., had told him about it, and Miss Harris. "Just seventeen miles away, doctors trained to help, therapists, equipment, experience and hope. All over the country they're doing the impossible—helping us do the impossible. But not here. Irv knows nothing. Nobody knows anything. But they will, they will.

"God damn them here, forgetting us." His hand jumped and Brad felt the pulsing anger, rising and going nowhere. Short circuited. "God damn them." He spat the curse out through his teeth. Then the anger ran out and unexpectedly he felt a tear, a single itching tear he couldn't wipe away. "I'll teach them," Brad promised, "send them to school, get the money from the conscience of the 'good' people. We'll learn and then we'll train others—right here in this vomit-colored building." Brad grinned and spoke out loud, "We'll even paint the walls."

It was a day a couple of weeks later when Bets walked into Ward F and saw Brad was still in bed. "He'll have raised merry Cain with them about that," she told herself and hurried to him, stopping first by the Smiler's bed. Brad hadn't heard the clacking of her high heels, hadn't heard or seen anything, in fact; for he was so utterly absorbed in what he was doing.

She watched his right hand, still raw, scarred from the operation but unbandaged. It was painful, with the skin puckered taut along the incisions, but still he worked his pinch every minute he could. She thought with wonder how he had come to live with discomfort, even pain; no wonder he was unstable. Look at him now, a grown man, a proud man, concentrating everything he had on one simple task. He was trying to arrange a hand of cards.

He hunched his shoulder so those muscles would throw his right arm in the direction of the card. It missed and his hand cruelly banged into the hospital table, but he didn't even swear —he hunched his shoulder back and tried again and once again and once more until his pinch landed right in front of the card and he scooped it up, his pinch snapping on it and carrying it to his other hand, which was lying face up where it had been placed. He tucked this card beside the others, which were stuck between the two fingers of his left hand that were crippled in a position which could hold cards.

Bets remembered Brad's quick fingers shuffling the cards in the past. Hardly looking at them, Brad would blend them with a crisp ruffle and then they would sail out from his fingers as he dealt the hands around the table. It always amazed her how efficiently, how gracefully, he arranged his own hand, and she could see his face in the past smiling at her, at everyone, as he waited patiently for the others to get their hands arranged.

Now Brad hunched his shoulder and swooped down on another card. This time he made it on the second attempt and he held the card all the way over to his other hand. Bets saw the sweat on his eyebrows, where he couldn't wipe it off, and she wanted to go to him and wipe it for him and she knew she couldn't. He had to live with it. She couldn't baby him even when it took all of a strong man's effort to think out the motions that would allow his muscles to pick up a single playing card and then perform the impossible task of placing thirteen cards in his left hand.

Bets stood by the Smiler's bed and found herself sociably nodding and grinning at the old man's vacuous smile and was horrified and turned back to see her husband pick up the last card and start over with it, when it dropped onto the bedclothes and he cursed silently, his lips snarling out obscenities. Aching to help him, and knowing she couldn't, Bets made herself stand still and study her husband's face.

It was hard, a face that would be sketched by an artist with bold, slashing lines. The eyes were narrowed by the concentration of the task. His beak of a nose, a mean, aggressive bone, was pointed right at the job he was doing and his cheekbones stood out above his clenching jaw muscles. His chin moved in an angry, biting motion and his mouth was just another line among the many lines of anger and frustration that lacerated his face, scars that came from inside him. It was a face she had never seen before—anywhere—at a party, on a train, or in a crowd. It was the face of a single individual man different from all the other men in the world.

Suddenly, Brad speared the card with his pinch and with a triumphant snarl stuck it in with the others. He looked up proudly, but, seeing Bets, his eyes grew wary. He examined her and she felt afraid of this angry, bitter man. He studied her for a long time, openly speculating if he could trust her, trying to figure out if she would give him too much or too little praise for his card trick—he knew how little and how much he could do—if she would give him pity.

"Want to play?" Bets asked, her voice sounding as if it didn't make any difference at all. Brad kept looking at her steadily. She still felt fear, but also an admiration, a deep-down respect for this human animal who was tough, mean, good, hard—a man. Finally, making believe they had a choice, Brad said, "Your deal," and smiled, sharing what he could—the small, bitter joke—with her.